EMPIRE STATE

"Adam Christopher's debut novel is a noir, Philip K Dickish science fiction superhero story. It's often fascinating, as captivating as a kaleidoscope... Just feel it in all its weird glory."

CORY DOCTOROW, *New York Times-bestselling author of* Makers *and* Little Brother

"Adam Christopher maintains a punchy, bestseller prose style that keeps the action rocketing along... *Empire State* is an excellent, involving read, and it f... to be the start of a new universe."

PAUL CORNELL, Doctor ... of Stormwatch *and* Demon...

"A daring, dreamlike, alm... thriller, one that plays with the conv... of pulp fiction and superheroes like a cat with a ball of yarn."

KURT BUSIEK, *Eisner Award-winning writer of* Astro City *and* Marvels

"Down these steam driven streets a man must go... straight into a pocket universe of trouble. Brutal, knowing and deft, Adam Christopher delivers."

JON COURTENAY GRIMWOOD, *author of* The Fallen Blade

"Stylish, sinister, and wickedly fun, *Empire State* is not your average sexy retro parallel universe superhero noir."

LAUREN BEUKES, *Arthur C Clarke Award-winning author of* Zoo City

"Destined to be a science fiction classic, *Empire State* is a breathtakingly original noir tale of intrigue, mystery, and quantum physics, deftly played out in storytelling so brilliant I'm finding it hard not to hate the author."

DIANA ROWLAND, *author of* My Life as a White Trash Zombie

"Adam Christopher's *Empire State* is a fascinating debut novel that meshes noir sensibilities and science fiction together and keeps the reader guessing throughout."

MICHAEL STACKPOLE, *New York Times-bestselling author of* I, Jedi

"From first to last page, Adam Christopher's *Empire State* careens along at a furious pace. Along the way, he beautifully meshes the best noir tropes with science fiction and wraps it up in a world (or two) that rivals some of the classics of speculative fiction."

JOHN HORNOR JACOBS, *author of* Southern Gods

"*Empire State* doesn't screw around. Murders, mysteries and multiple realities are just the icing atop this pulp noir cake: the action starts on the opening page but it isn't long before you fall in love with the characters and the unique world Adam Christopher has built for them. Trust me when I say: you want to visit *Empire State*."

CHUCK WENDIG, *author of* Double Dead

"A double shot of jet-noir steampunk nitroglycerine – a startling, throat-grabbing novel that echoes Chandler, Auster and Mieville while blazing its own mind-bending trail and searing itself onto your memory."

WILL HILL, *author of* Department 19

"From the first explosive rat-a-tat-tat of bullets to the very last twist and turn, *Empire State* surely cannot be a début novel. Adam Christopher must be playing with us, as this bears all the skill and patience of an experienced master craftsman at work. The fantastical dreams of Verne and Wells mixed with the noir reality of Spillane or Chandler, this is a book that doesn't play by the rules – and is all the better for it."

TONY LEE, *New York Times-bestselling author and* Doctor Who *comic writer*

ADAM CHRISTOPHER

EMPIRE STATE

ANGRY
ROBOT

ANGRY ROBOT

A member of the Osprey Group

Lace Market House,
54-56 High Pavement,
Nottingham
NG1 1HW, UK

www.angryrobotbooks.com
There's more than one of everything

An Angry Robot paperback original 2012

ISBN 978-0-85766-193-7
EBook ISBN 978-0-85766-194-4

Printed in the United States of America

9 8 7 6 5 4 3 2 1

For Sandra, without whom
there is nothing.

AUTHOR'S NOTE

New York City is an amazing and fantastical place, and it doesn't need an author like me to make it any more so. However, the Empire State is Manhattan reflected through a clouded lens, and I have exercised artistic licence where the story demanded. I hope the reader will forgive any liberties taken, be they geographical, topographical, or temporal.

PART ONE
THE MEAN STREETS

"Judge Crater, call your office," said the man with the microphone.

Everybody laughed.

ONE

JEROME GUNNED THE ACCELERATOR, and turned sharp left. Rex slid on the bench seat, but grabbed the leather strap dangling over his door fast enough to stop him landing in the driver's lap. Jerome whistled, knuckles white as they gripped the wheel. Rex looked over his shoulder. He sure as hell hoped Jerome knew where he was going.

"For cryin' out loud!" Rex winced as his head met the roof of the car, the thin felt of his hat providing little protection as Jerome pushed two wheels over the curb to dodge oncoming traffic.

"Complain later, boss. Keep yer head down and hold on." Jerome's eyes didn't leave the road. Rex frowned and hunkered down in the seat, gripping the top edge with both hands as he turned to look out the back. Two crates of green bottles rattled in the back seat under Rex's nose as Jerome navigated the wet streets as fast as he dared.

Rex squinted, trying to see through the smattering of rain on the car's tiny rear window, but the droplets of water seemed to pull the light of the city in, refracting it into a thousand glowing, multicoloured points. The car shuddered against the gutter as Jerome swerved around another obstacle, throwing up a huge steam-like spray of runoff, obscuring the view even more.

"What's the deal?" Jerome asked.

Rex relaxed his grip and turned back around. Jerome was leaning over the wheel, his keen, experienced eyes picking out the path ahead in the downtown traffic. It was late, but New Yorkers had a well-known disregard for the time of day. Jerome was doing a fine job threading the boat-sized Studebaker through the maze of cars, but surely their luck was going to run out. Somehow they'd managed to avoid the police, but they'd be spotted sooner rather than later. Evading one pursuer was possible; add two, three, four cop cars and the odds shortened, and not in their favour.

"Looks clear," said Rex. "Think we lost 'em. Nice driving."

Jerome allowed one thin hand to unwrap from the steering wheel to tip an invisible hat. His face cracked into a grin so wide all Rex could see was a row of teeth stretching up from the driver's chin to his ear.

"How about that, huh? People movin' in, causin' trouble. How's an honest man supposed to make a living in this town, huh, Rex?"

Rex sighed. "Tell me about it."

Jerome laughed and slapped the wheel. He began talking, but Rex tuned it out. His night was not going as planned and his partner's jabber was the last thing he needed. Rex closed his eyes and rubbed their lids, watching the purple-orange shapes float for a while. Then something flared red across his vision.

"Jerome!"

Rex grabbed the wheel and pulled it hard right. The driver returned his attention to the road just in time to see the side of another car slide past, right across their path. Jerome spun the wheel in the opposite direction as Rex let go, negotiating the Studebaker around the rear of the vehicle mostly by good luck. Rex grabbed for the leather strap again as the car slid on its rear wheels.

There was a *rat-a-tat-tat* like a jazz drummer practicing a solo on a tin roof, and the rear windshield exploded, filling the car with the hot smell of cordite. Rex ducked instinctively behind the seat, and when he poked his head up to check the rear view again he saw the white car in hot pursuit, two men inside and one perched on the running board on the passenger side. The man raised his tommy gun just for a moment as the car bumped over a pothole, then brought it down again. Rex ducked as a second volley of slugs peppered the car, splitting the Studebaker's front windshield right in front of him, turning the pane of glass into an opaque spider's web. The car lurched as Jerome pumped the accelerator and brake in quick succession in the confusion. It was like suddenly driving into a blizzard.

"Rex!"

Rex twisted awkwardly in the seat. "Yeah, I got it." He lay almost flat on his back, and raised his right leg up over the dash. A few kicks and the crumbling windshield popped out, sliding over the hood with the sound of a tortured blackboard.

"Shit," muttered Jerome as he bobbed his head down, squinting against the stiff, wet wind. They were in a four-lane street now, which was completely clear ahead in both directions. The white car took the opportunity and revved behind them, headlights sweeping through the cab of the Studebaker as they pulled out and around.

Rex jerked his head right, in time to see the prow of the other car begin to pull up alongside. The gunner, fortunately, was on the other side, but Rex could see his head and the tommy gun being held aloft as he shifted to get an aim over the white car's roof.

"Lose 'em, Jerome!"

Jerome glanced right, then left, grin transformed into a grimace of concentration.

"I see it. Hold on."

Jerome twisted the wheel and the car bucked left, the rear end swinging out and the left-side wheels lifting as the vehicle attempted a hairpin at high speed. The white car saw and pulled away, but too late, the rear of the Studebaker connecting with the driver's door just as it jerked away. There was a crunch and the Studebaker bounced roughly but, as the airborne wheels made contact with the road again, traction was regained and Jerome floored it, sending them down the narrower side street with perfect aim.

"Ah, shit!" said Jerome again, this time raising an arm to protect his eyes. The car was flooded with blue and white light. Rex blinked away purple spots just in time to see the police cordon ahead, but it was too late. He reached for the wheel and pulled again, ignoring Jerome's protest, but there was nowhere to go. There were police cars on either side of the street, and a temporary wooden barrier ahead. Rex's rash action caused the automobile to skid around, turning it sideways but maintaining forward motion as Jerome slammed the brakes on. All around them, police and pedestrians alike scattered. There was shouting, a lot of it, then a *crack* as the wooden boom of the roadblock snapped against the passenger side. The impact was surprisingly solid, throwing Rex across the bench seat and finally tearing Jerome off the steering wheel.

The Studebaker was large and heavy, and the road was slick. The police barrier hadn't stolen enough of their momentum. The last thing Rex saw before the car stuck on something and tumbled sideways onto its roof was fireworks over the squat, blunt shape of the half-completed Empire State Building a block ahead of them. He wondered what the occasion was as red, green and blue explosions lit the sky, silhouetting the construction cranes balanced high over the city. He wondered what the building would look like and how tall it would be when it was finished.

Two more thoughts crossed Rex's mind before the car stopped and unconsciousness claimed him. Firstly, that he really needed a drink, and secondly, that his night had been going so well before McCabe showed up.

Rex tipped his hat, straightened his tie, and rubbed a thumb over the lapel of his double-breasted jacket. It was his way of showing that he was relaxed and comfortable, that Martin Jeremy's last statement had made perfect sense and hadn't thrown him in the slightest. Behind him he heard Jerome crack a knuckle. His junior partner was slightly less careful with hiding his thoughts.

This was how it worked. Rex was the businessman. Jerome was the muscle. Rex did the deals and listened to his customers. Jerome made the customers change their minds and accept Rex's terms. Times were tough. The Depression wasn't just biting into the pockets of ordinary New Yorkers, it was *killing* people. But in such trying times, Rex was doing just swell. Because in such trying times those ordinary New Yorkers drank, and drank, and drank. Hell, even the government was on Rex's side, with Prohibition just a way of charging more and more for his product. The bootlegging business was booming and Rex was reaping the rewards. Jerome too. He bought the kid a flash new car, a Studebaker the size of a bus. That kept Jerome happy, but also made sense as a business investment. Not only could they haul liquor in the car's capacious interior without tipping the police off, it was one of the fastest automobiles money could buy. Rex didn't drive, but with Jerome at the wheel getaways were easy.

"Martin, Martin," said Rex with a smile, placing a hand on the barkeep's shoulder with just enough pressure to show the conversation had taken a very serious turn. "You gotta understand, buddy. Me and Jerome here are just trying to make a living. Understand?"

Martin Jeremy was thin and bald. Standing in the dead backstreet behind his speakeasy the streetlight shone off his pate, damp with a light evening drizzle and a healthy dash of cold sweat.

Rex licked his lips and watched the barkeep. Something was up, something more than he had let on. He squeezed the man's shoulder a little harder. Martin flinched, but said nothing.

Huh. The usual form of quiet intimidation wasn't working. And Rex hated the next part. Beating on an old man was not something he enjoyed at all. Which was why he got Jerome to do it.

"Rex, my friend, we have done some good business in the past," said Martin at last. His voice wavered but with age, not fear. He proudly held his head up, thin jowls swinging under his chin as he spoke. Rex raised an eyebrow.

"I think you misunderstand, Mr Jeremy. Changing suppliers is not an option. My business supplies the whole of Midtown. Ain't nobody else in this neighbourhood gonna sell you the goods. So, what'd'ya say we just shake on it and you pay me an extra hundred dollars now for, ah, renegotiation of terms, and we won't mention it again." Rex turned to his partner. "Jerome, unload the car."

The teen nodded and headed off towards the side street where the Studebaker was parked.

When Rex turned back to the barkeep, he just caught the end of a smile on the man's face that he didn't much like at all. He frowned as the barkeep took a step backwards, and he made to take a step closer himself, maintaining the distance of intimidation and control, as he liked to think of it, but stopped short as three men peeled out from around the speakeasy's loading door.

"Well now, that ain't very nice," said the first man. "These two giving you trouble, Mr Jeremy?" He was tall and wide, not fat but built, like a football quarterback. His companions were a small, wiry teenager and another man who towered over both of them. The man who spoke raised an arm up to adjust a cufflink; a diamond the size of a pea glinted in the streetlight. "After all, ya can't trust a *nigger*."

"McCabe, you sonovabitch," whispered Rex. It was suddenly too hot and the air too thin. Rex gulped, but stayed still, hoping the poor light hid his fear.

McCabe. The sonovabitch. Head of a family business running liquor and a dozen other rackets. One of the most powerful of New York's underworld. Richest too. Rex had done a few jobs for him, years ago, before branching out on his own. While McCabe had seemed happy to let him go, Rex knew that one day it would come back to bite him. You didn't make friends in this business, only enemies.

McCabe sat at the centre of a web that spread far and wide over the five boroughs, but Rex had thought he was safe. Midtown and downtown Manhattan hadn't interested McCabe much in the past, the gangster apparently happy to let other mobs control the city. Rex had always thought that was odd, given the concentration of speakeasies in the area and the rich pickings they represented. It had only to be a matter of time, he was sure, before McCabe made his move, but in the meantime there was moonshine to sell and barkeeps to squeeze. He'd forgotten about McCabe, but clearly McCabe hadn't forgotten about Rex. The time had come to add Midtown to his empire, and two black guys pushing liquor was the obvious place to start.

"Oh, language please, Rex. Didn't they teach you to speak nice down on the plantation?" McCabe laughed and his heavy sniggered; the teenager – the driver, thought Rex – was expressionless. He probably had no clue what McCabe was talking about, and he sure didn't want to show it.

Rex held his hands up.

"McCabe, I apologise, I really do. So how about we have a drink and talk things over? I'm sure we can come to an arrangement."

McCabe smiled. Rex dropped his hands.

"I'm sure we can, Rex, I'm sure we can. And it starts with the disappearance of two amateurs causing trouble. How about that, huh?"

Rex ran his tongue along his bottom teeth. He tensed his calves, ready to make his move. Jerome hadn't returned from the car, which either meant McCabe had more men around the side of the building or that he'd seen or sensed trouble and was waiting at the wheel. He hoped it was the latter.

"Not your style, McCabe. How about you just buy me out and I retire to somewhere nice in New Jersey, huh?"

McCabe laughed and the heavy sniggered again. Rex thought that perhaps the heavy understood as little as the driver and was just matching his employer's mood because he was paid to. Behind the trio, Martin Jeremy slipped through the loading door and back into his speakeasy. Wise man, thought Rex. Trouble was brewing.

"Billy, fetch the car," McCabe called over his shoulder. The teen nodded and turned, heading down the back street. McCabe smiled at Rex again, then looked up at his muscular companion.

"You wanna grab some dinner after, George?"

The heavy nodded and balled his fists. "Sounds nice, Mr McCabe. I feel like steak."

McCabe clicked his fingers. "Oh, yeah, me too. We should head down to that grill on Fourth."

"Sounds great."

The pair took a step forward.

"Aw, you guys are sweet," said Rex, taking a step backwards. "When's the big day?"

White light swept into the alley as a car turned in, engine purring as it coasted towards them in low gear.

"We're taking a little ride, you and me, Rex," said Mc-Cabe. He put his hands into the pockets of his jacket and nodded at George. "You can either get into the car, or George here can fold you up and put you in the trunk. That's up to you."

The car was nothing but two spotlights in the dark. As it slowed, McCabe moved to one side to allow more room, then reached out for the door.

The door swung out and back in one swift movement, connecting with the gangster with enough force to knock him off his feet. He hit the tarmac on his backside, but George was at his side in a second, helping him up.

"Rex!"

He didn't need the invitation. Rex was halfway to the car when Jerome called, the driver leaning over to open the passenger door. Rex dived in head-first, head landing practically on Jerome's lap. Jerome put the car into gear and pushed the accelerator to the floor, Rex's legs flapping out of the open door as they powered out of the street.

TWO

REX WOKE UP IN THE DARK and rolled over into a large puddle. He jerked at the shock and knocked his forehead into the curb.

"Ah, *Jesus*..." Rex grabbed for his forehead with one hand and the curb with his other. He pulled himself up and held the free hand in front of him until it rested on a wet wall, his forehead following close behind. His head hurt, and he was dizzy. For a moment he didn't know his name.

Shit. The car. He spun around, finally focussing on the commotion around him. Or rather, near him. He was in the lip of an alley, in the dark. The main street ahead was a flurry of activity. People were gathered, lots and *lots* of people. Tourists and locals sandwiched together behind a flimsy police barricade, the boys in blue desperately trying to hold a line. The car – the huge, expensive, fast Studebaker – was upside down in the middle of the street, smoke curling from the undercarriage. Jerome was lying awkwardly over the lip of the missing windshield, and wasn't moving.

Rex's mouth dropped open in surprise, and he patted himself down. But aside from a bump on the forehead, he felt fine. The car was angled slightly towards him, the one intact and functioning headlight spotting the wall next to him.

"Holy Mother of God..."

Rex kicked at something soft that tangled his feet. It was a stack of wet newspapers. He'd been thrown clear in the crash, through the missing windshield, into the mush of rotting paper. It was remarkable, miraculous. Rex didn't believe in God, but he muttered a thank-you just in case.

Then he noticed something. The police and the crowd weren't looking at the car, or the dead body of the nineteen-year-old under it. The wreck was a sideshow, a distraction even, from the main event that shone across the street in brilliant flashes of red and blue.

Over the half-finished shell of the Empire State Building, two superheroes were punching seven shades of shit out of each other, their tiny, doll-like bodies silhouetted against the maelstrom of energy that erupted around them with each connecting blow.

Rex staggered to the corner to get a look. It was mesmerising. Exactly what he needed. Dragging his eyes away, he checked the crowd over. Everyone, police included, were looking away. He snuck out, hugged the corner and quietly ducked under the police barrier, the replacement for the broken boom which had been pushed into the gutter opposite. Safe in the crowd, confident that McCabe had probably taken off as soon he saw the Studebaker flip right in front of the police, Rex looked back toward the Empire State Building.

There was a flash of green so bright the crowd gasped as one, followed a second later by a colossal sonic boom, so loud the crowd ducked. This was a heck of a fight between New York's two superheroes. In Rex's dazed state it pushed McCabe and Jerome and his shattered business clean out of his mind for a moment.

Two superheroes? Scratch that. One superhero, one supervillain. It was a great story, one that Rex – and everyone else in the city, if not the country – knew, a tale of friendship and betrayal so perfect the movie was just waiting to be made.

The Skyguard and the Science Pirate had been partners, friends since childhood. Brought up in the wrong part of town, they'd formed a dynamic duo even at school, watching each other's backs as they fought their way through their teenage years. As adults, they became rocket-powered heroes, the protectors of New York. They fought crime, corruption, enemy agents and infiltrators. They fought fascists and lefties, the mob, petty criminals. Bootleggers and Prohibition breakers. They defended the Constitution of the United States of America with fairness and impartiality. The ultimate patriots, given the freedom of the city and state, publicly awarded by Coolidge just a couple of years before.

So the story went, anyway.

Rex had been lucky. By the time he'd left McCabe's employ, the golden age of heroism had passed. The Skyguard and the Science Pirate stopped fighting crime and started fighting each other, effectively handing the city back to the overworked, underpaid, and highly corruptible NYPD.

Nobody knew what went wrong exactly, or when, or how, or why. The Science Pirate turned against his partner, and the two became bitterest of rivals. Gone was the crime-fighting, the crusade against the mobs and gangs: the dealers, smugglers, predators. Instead the Skyguard and the Science Pirate declared open war on each other, each dedicating all their efforts and resources to this new monomania. And while the Skyguard and the Science Pirate fought, the city suffered. The mob made inroads again, and corruption – both local and Federal – began to eat at the core of the Big Apple. The police were stretched to the limit. The FBI was called in as McCabe and McCabe's ilk returned to the city and crime became organised once more, the city's sworn protectors having abandoned their cause. Which was all good for Rex, of course. He kept his own little business empire *just so*, large enough to make a tasty profit, small enough to stay out of

McCabe's way. Until tonight, that is. Rex rubbed his head, wondering where his hat was and whether he could afford another car. Or, for that matter, another driver.

Nobody really knew exactly who was the hero and who the villain. Certainly the crowd in the street was almost evenly split as they *oohed* and *aahed* and cheered the terrible battle in the sky. This was spectacle, entertainment. Hell, people needed it these days, Rex knew that. Two superpowered, costumed crime fighters who could fly and shoot rays, slugging it out in the open air. It was quite a sight.

The Skyguard and the Science Pirate looked similar; even without knowing their history, you could tell they were, or had once been, a team. Visored helmets and long cloaks, each wearing the remarkable inventions of the Science Pirate which had enabled them to protect Manhattan from the air. He was the brains – as his chosen moniker reflected – and the Skyguard was the brawn, although in truth they were pretty evenly matched. But each acting alone, people weren't sure. How could the Skyguard maintain his arsenal of amazing equipment that had been designed and built by the Science Pirate? And how could the Science Pirate counter his opponent's battle plans and tactics?

The crowd chattered and a single thought entered Rex's head. This was it, the final showdown, the ultimate battle which would finally decide who had the right to protect the citizens of New York, and who would be denounced as a traitor and a criminal, locked up forever and a day.

Rex silently cursed the tall man in front of him who had just shuffled into his line of vision, dragging his lady friend with him for a better look. Rex tried standing on tip-toe to get a better view, but it was no good. There was another flash and another bang and the couple moved. The man laughed, and smiled down at his lady friend. Rex scowled but the man wasn't looking, which was probably a good thing.

Rex had a theory about the city's two protectors. He knew, *knew*, the Skyguard was the patriot, and had been protecting the Science Pirate all the time they were together. He'd heard rumours, heard the talk about where the Science Pirate had come from, that in his past life the Feds had taken an interest and he'd been hauled in front of a Senate subcommittee for some reason or another. The Skyguard had taken him in as his ward, swearing to rehabilitate his misguided friend. In the Skyguard's custody, the Science Pirate was untouchable.

But it hadn't worked out. The Science Pirate had shown his true colours. What kind of hero calls himself a pirate, anyway? And why was he so happy to let the Skyguard take all the glory and make all the speeches and just stay in the background?

Rex needed a drink. His mouth was dry. Later. He'd watch the fight and wait until the crowd was clear. He felt OK, surrounded as he was, but who knew who was lurking on the side streets? If not McCabe, then maybe McCabe's boyfriend. Rex sniggered, then ducked as another explosion, much louder this time, echoed around the city blocks.

Looking up, he saw the two crime fighters were heading towards the crowd, and at some speed. The crowd buckled and there were some shouts. A police officer, or perhaps a couple, tried to use loudhailers to calm people down, but nobody was listening. The Skyguard and the Science Pirate were only a hundred yards away now and just fifty in the air. Maybe one had thrown the other off the building. Whatever, they were here, and it was close. The crowd backed away, but only a little. Nobody wanted to miss this.

The Skyguard let loose a quick one-two, forcing his opponent back in the air several feet. He shot forward on his rocket boots and finished with a savage uppercut, sending the Science Pirate tumbling head over heels into the sky.

The crowd cheered and the Skyguard paused, watching the trajectory of his opponent.

When the Science Pirate reached the apex of his climb, he recovered and turned himself back upright. Spinning around his centre of gravity, he stretched into a long shape, fists pointed down towards the Skyguard, and with cloak streaming behind, accelerated towards his target. The Skyguard drifted out of the way by a little, but was caught in the twin energy rays projected from the Pirate's eyes. He screamed, his cry a weird, machine-like screeching from inside his helmet, as he convulsed in mid-air above the heads of the crowd. The Science Pirate collided with him, bending the Skyguard almost in two over his outstretched fists. The Science Pirate didn't stop, and with the Skyguard wrapped over his arms, ploughed straight into the cleared street ahead of the police barriers. The explosion was frighteningly loud and sent hot tarmac, concrete and dirt raining down on the crowd. Some cheered and some screamed, and the gathered mass of bodies recoiled slightly again. The police line at the front tripped and collapsed in a couple of places as the crowd it was attempting to hold back suddenly retreated.

For a second there was silence. The initial pall of smoke cleared, revealing a huge crater carved deep into the Earth. The crowd regained its composure and edged forward a little, Rex carried with them, the group hushed with collective anticipation. Had the Science Pirate succeeded? Had both been pulverised by the impact? Both were protected by their armour, but they were only human. Weren't they?

Taking the opportunity, the police line reorganised and began herding people away. Gaps appeared in the crowd as people were pushed and pulled around, and seeing his chance, Rex ducked under the linked arms of yet another couple, then pushed past two young boys up way past their bedtime. He tripped over another person walking backwards, and righting himself Rex found he was at the front line, chest being pushed by a policeman. The policeman looked him in the eye and shook his head, and Rex just nodded. The officer relaxed, happy Rex wasn't going to try to get any closer.

The crater in the street was massive, like something from the moon. Smoke billowed from it in a great grey cloud, but there was no sign of the two combatants. Several police peered nervously into it, hands ready on their holstered guns.

Rex frowned. Was that it? The two forces had cancelled each other out, leaving... nothing?

Something moved in the smoke, and a half-dozen police guns were pulled out as one. Someone snapped on a flashlight and played the beam over the smoke, picking out a black form, elongating it into a wispy shadow. A cloaked figure, with tall, winged helmet.

The Skyguard! Rex felt his heart race. The Skyguard had triumphed. Ah, shit. If the Skyguard was the good guy, then his night had just got a whole lot worse. Rex wondered if this was a sign to leave New York altogether. Perhaps he hadn't been joking about New Jersey.

The figure stepped out of the smoke, and held an arm up against the flashlight that now focussed on his face. Dirty and battered, he was an impressive figure on the ground. Tall and proud, the victor.

The figure's arm dropped away, along with Rex's thoughts of relocation. Out of the curtain of smoke, the long shadows of the Skyguard's helmet and flanged gauntlets collapsed into the more austere, compact profile of the Science Pirate. The figure stopped in front of the crowd. Some clapped, and some cheered. Rex was suddenly unsure whether he'd got the good or the bad guys around the right way. The Science Pirate had won. Rex spat at the ground and the policeman in front of him raised an eyebrow.

Then people started shouting. There were cheers and jeers, and soon the cheers were outnumbered. Rex kept his mouth shut and his eyes open. The crowd seemed to think New York City was doomed. The Skyguard was down and now the Science Pirate had free rein. As the intensity of the crowd's reaction increased, Rex realised that perhaps more people subscribed to his traitor theory than he had thought.

The Science Pirate stood and watched the crowd. He had supporters, but they were vastly outnumbered by those crowing for a retrial, that the fight had been staged, that the Pirate had cheated, that justice needed to be served. The Science Pirate raised a hand, not to silence anyone, but to acknowledge his supporters; but this only increased the ferocity of his detractors. A policeman, someone important with scrambled eggs on his hat and braiding on his shoulder, walked towards him with one hand out, shaking his head, the other resting on his gun.

Go on. Rex spat again. Finish it. It would be easier, after all. Either the Science Pirate was the hero, in which case things were going to get mighty tight in the city again, or he was the villain, which either meant pledging allegiance – and a percentage of the profits – or being run out of town. Or, depending on McCabe's position in the new hierarchy, worse. McCabe would be furious that Rex was still alive, and if he had the ear of the new boss in town, well...

Rex smirked as the Science Pirate took a step backwards. The policeman stopped and said something, but Rex was too far away to hear. And then the Science Pirate did something remarkable.

She took her helmet off.

It was like a movie theatre. The crowd fell silent with a collective *whoosh* of inhaled air. A few seconds later came a couple of wolf whistles, and someone shouting something that everybody could hear, but nobody could make out.

Then a rumble, low and quiet as, having recovered from the shock, people started talking to each other. The police kept the line, but most craned their necks around to see what was going on.

The Science Pirate was a woman. Her long brown hair unpiled from inside the helmet, and fell halfway down her back. Her face was flushed and slick with sweat, but at this distance Rex could see she was quite a looker.

A... girl? The Science Pirate was a girl. Well, thirty-something. Brunette. Attractive. Rex's throat was tight. He still needed that drink, and his lips were still dry. He ran his tongue along them, but that was dry too.

The policeman was saying something and the woman in the costume said something back. The crowd's baying obscured their conversation, but Rex wasn't really trying to listen anyway. He ignored all as he stared at the unmasked rocketeer.

What was this? Did she have some kind of point to make, unmasking herself? Rex's head was filled with a hundred questions. Were we supposed to know who she was? Were we supposed to feel sorry for her? Proud of her? Frightened of her? What, exactly? His face went hot with embarrassment that he'd been frightened of a goddamn *woman*, although he didn't admit it, even to himself. He rubbed his aching head and the world spun a little. Keep it calm, keep it together. Concussion, was all. He'd had it before, several times, working with McCabe. Rex took a breath.

The policeman was shouting now and the Science Pirate was shouting back, but Rex wasn't listening. He watched as the Science Pirate stamped and shouted and pointed at the crater, shaking off the cop's hand as he made a grab for her arm. She stepped back, then took off vertically, the policeman staggering backwards to avoid the flame of her rocket boots. Holding her helmet under one arm, the Science Pirate disappeared over the city on a trail of glowing orange smoke.

Rex felt angry for a moment, then inspiration struck. The Science Pirate was a woman. Women were not an obstacle, never had been. Now he knew her weakness – her *sex* – then maybe he could take the upper hand. Maybe he could even usurp McCabe and his cronies, not only saving his own neck, but taking over the city completely. More importantly, there was an opening here to put a lean on City Hall. If he could capture the Science Pirate – no, *remove* her, dumping her body on the mayor's desk, he'd be untouchable, top of the totem pole. Even McCabe would come crawling. He'd be the man who saved New York and put everyone – McCabe included – back in business.

It made perfect sense. The night was looking up.

Rex stood for a while as the crowd thinned and the police gathered around the crater in the middle of the street. He ran the idea over and over and over. It would work. It would be easy. He just needed to figure her out, watch her, trail her. The suit was a powerful weapon, but without it she looked like she'd be a tiny little girl. Easy.

The tall man and his lady walked by again but Rex ignored them. He was looking at the crater, with smoke rising and a ring of police gingerly keeping their distance.

He needed a drink. He needed several drinks, and then he'd see about the Science Pirate. Who would protect her now the Skyguard was gone? Nobody, was who.

Payday was a-comin'.

THREE

IT WAS HER. It was damn well *her*. Rex ducked into a shop doorway, his fingertips pressing the ice-cold glass behind him as he leaned against the window. He couldn't believe his luck.

With the fight over, a few of the crowd had loitered around the overturned Studebaker, and the police had finally turned their attention to moving it and Jerome out of the way. Rex skirted the scene carefully, checking the faces around him in case McCabe had sent some of his thugs in.

So far, so good. First step was a drink. Rex turned away as Jerome's body was pulled from under the front of the car, and jogged down the alley into which he'd been thrown in the crash. In the gutter ahead he saw his hat, damp but intact. He bent down and flipped it onto his head, and when he looked up, Rex saw her.

There, at the end, just turning a corner, was a woman with long brown hair. Rex came to a halt behind the pile of wet newspapers that had saved him, watching. Could it have been her? Surely not. Just a broad, taking a shortcut. Looking at her outfit, a working girl too.

Then she turned to look back down the alley, towards Rex. It *was* her. Cheeky bitch. She'd taken off, ditched the suit, and come back to watch the cleanup. She saw Rex, she must have, he was as large as life in the middle of the alley, but she just turned and disappeared around the corner. Rex flexed his fingers. This was a gift. No suit. Quiet back streets. Perfect.

He trailed her for a while, keeping his head down. He wasn't good at following discreetly – there wasn't much call for it in his particular line of work – and after an hour of hustling across downtown, it was obvious that the girl knew she was being followed and was trying to shake him off. A series of double-backs and dead-ends had led him a merry chase indeed. It was hard to get genuinely lost in Manhattan, or to get stuck in a cul-de-sac as there was almost always an alley or a passageway out.

But Rex's luck held. The bitch had taken a wrong turn down a dead alley. Rex smiled and stuck to the damp wall. Perfect.

Although... Rex's smirk vanished. Shit. What if she had been looking for a quiet, empty spot to fight? No. She wasn't wearing the suit. Rex flexed his biceps under his trench coat. They were tight and he wasn't a small man. And without her fancy rockets and suit of armour she was a tiny broad. A tiny broad in high heels and a red dress.

His smirk returned. Odd clothes to wear under the rocket armour. Rex laughed. Who knew what she got up to when off-duty. Perhaps they *were* a set of working clothes. That wouldn't surprise him.

Maybe she'd taken a knock to the head in the big fight and had concussion or some such, because coming back to the scene of the battle was a dumb move, lady, very dumb, especially after taking her helmet off in front of everyone. Now she was tottering around on those big heels, and she looked cold too, and frightened. But it was her. He'd taken a good, long look, imprinting her face in his memory. She was his meal ticket. He wasn't going to lose her now.

Rex laughed. His head felt light. He peered down the alley, and saw she was still walking away, slower now. She seemed to be looking around, looking for a way out. This was it. He was about to "save" New York City, and after handing over the city's most wanted he'd have the mayor and police chief right in his pocket. McCabe would come *begging* and his illicit empire would be able to expand, unimpeded. With freedom to eliminate the competition, within a few months he'd be in control of the whole goddamn city. He could buy a new car and a new driver.

He pinched the collar of his coat up, and pulled his hat back a little so the rim didn't obscure his vision. She was trapped like a rat.

As he walked forward the clouds opened again, Mother Nature dumping her load on the already saturated city. He wondered how difficult it was going to be to kill a person with his bare hands. He'd shot people, of course, and in his younger days with McCabe he'd dealt out a variety of punishments with a selection of handheld weapons. But he was unarmed now. Jerome had insisted on being the triggerman and Rex had indulged him. He'd killed chickens and rabbits with nothing but his hands before, back on his uncle's farm upstate. He'd been a teenager and it was easy, and now he was twice the size and the bitch was tiny – a thin, fragile girl. He balled his wet fists, feeling the solidity of his knuckles under his tight skin. This was going to be a piece of cake.

When the girl eventually stopped casing the alley and turned at the sound of Rex's footsteps, she actually looked relieved. Her shoulders slumped, and her chest heaved as if she exhaled a heavy sigh, which Rex couldn't hear past the steady patter of the rain. She took a few steps forwards and opened her arms out, like she was going to say something real important, and then stopped as she saw that Rex hadn't slowed. She stood for a second, her arms still sticking out sideways, and then took a step backwards. Her mouth pulled down at the corners and her lower lip quivered as she spoke.

"Do you know the way back to Fifth and Soma? I'm not sure which way I've come. I just need to get home."

Rex stopped, and held his arms straight against his sides. He tightened his fists, feeling the uneven trim of his nails dig into the fleshy pads at the base of each thumb. The rain skittered around the brim of his hat, and he could feel the liquid roll backwards as he tilted his head.

He hadn't expected her to talk. He hadn't planned on her making any noise at all, as a matter of fact. Her face was small and while her mouth was wide, the palm of one of his large hands would practically cover her entire face.

The girl took a half-step back again, getting both feet solidly underneath her. Her dress sure was damn short, and the heels were way too high. While it made her look taller and exaggerated the stretch of her legs, clutched together her knees were pushed forward like two ugly wrinkled grapefruit.

"Please, I just need to get home," said the girl. She pushed her hair off her forehead with the heel of one hand, pulling the skin on her face tight as she did so. "Please, I have a headache, I just need to get home."

Rex moved his head and the water in the brim of his hat finally reached bursting point and trickled over the edge and down in front of his face. He was taking too long. He had to quit thinking about it, and quit letting her gas on, and just do it, now, or it would be too late. It was like anything important. There was a moment, a brief alignment of the stars when the time was right; when that happened, if you were in the right place at the right time with the right idea, you could do anything. That's what his uncle had always told him, up at the farm. Anybody can do anything. Don't think, do. Rex hissed a breath out between clenched teeth and took a step forward.

The girl seemed to stagger backwards, now with both hands rubbing her forehead. When she looked up, her eyes seemed to spin a little. She looked like she was going to faint.

"Please, Fifth and Soma, which way is it?"

Rex clicked his tongue. "Don't know what you're talking about, lady. Ain't never heard of no Soma Street. You really are lost."

Dammit! This was part of it, now he was sure. She was a goddamn supervillain, and even without the stupid rocket suit, she was dangerous. She was playing him. The confusion, the conversation, it was all an act.

Don't think, *do*.

Rex pushed off from the ground with the toes of his right foot, moving at something between a jog and a fast walk. He raised his fists, and swung back, and the girl dropped her hands. Before he could get a hand over her mouth like he wanted, she screamed.

PART TWO
THE CITY THAT SLEEPS

"Albeit, much about this time it did fall out that the thrice renowned and delectable city of Gotham did suffer great discomfiture, and was reduced to perilous extremity..."
Washington Irving, SALMAGUNDI, 11 November 1807

"Six months ago prohibition was about as much of an issue as Mormonism, pragmatism or the fourth dimension."
THE NEW YORK WORLD, 1914

FOUR

"WHAT KIND OF A NAME," asked the man in the gas mask, "is 'Rad', anyway?"

Rad shuffled on the alley floor a little, trying to get more comfortable, when more comfortable meant a rectangular brick digging into his back instead of a triangular one. It was wet, and Rad was sitting in a puddle. He half-wondered how much the cleaning bill would be for his one and only good suit.

"'Rad' is my kind of name, is what," said Rad. He didn't bother looking up at his assailants. The masks and hats were a great disguise. Kooky. Instead he stared ahead and dabbed at his bottom lip with a bloody handkerchief.

The first goon's shoes moved into Rad's field of vision, black wingtips shining wetly in the cast-off from the streetlamp just around the lip of the alley. The rain had collected in the punch pattern on the shoes and each step threw a fine spray, some of which collected in the man's pinstripe turn-ups. Rad figured it was all part of the disguise, the unfashionable shoes, the unfashionable suits, the unfashionable gas masks. The name of some annual affair near the end of the year that was all about ghosts and candy and weird costumes itched at the back of Rad's mind, but he couldn't remember what it was and the thought slipped away as he tried to grasp it.

The goon bent down and the gas mask came into view. Two circular goggles in a rubber face, single soup-can canister bobbing over where the mouth would be. The goon's voice was clear as a whistle despite the business that sat between his lips and Rad's ears, but echoed in the soup can like it was coming out of a radio set.

"What do you know about nineteen fifty?"

Rad pulled the handkerchief away and looked at it, then moved his jaw like he was chewing toffee. His teeth were all there, so he was happy. A fat lip he could live with. What he really wanted was a drink, something strong that you couldn't buy, not legally anyway. He tongued the inside of his lip and the pepper-copper taste of blood filled his mouth again. That wasn't what he had in mind.

"That's the second time you've asked me that, pal," said Rad. "And for the second time I'm gonna say I don't know about nineteen fifty. If you're looking for street directions, then there are nicer ways of going about it."

The gas mask disappeared upwards and Rad shook his head. He felt his own fedora shift against the brick wall behind him. At least he'd kept that on during the fight.

Not that it had been much of a fight. One minute he was walking down Fifth, next an arm pulled him out of the light and into the alley, and after just one question a one-two landed with some success on his face, and he was sitting on the floor with a bruised tailbone and a wet backside and a cheekbone that alternated between needle-pain and numbness.

They weren't after money. Once on the ground, the first goon – a tall wide no-neck, who seemed to be doing everything for the entertainment of his thin friend who just stood and watched in silence behind his black goggles – grabbed his wallet, and together the four glass eyes stared at his ID for a while before the card and wallet were returned to Rad's inside coat pocket. This was no mugging. It was planned, calculated. They were professionals. The fist responsible for Rad's aching face was on the end of a trained arm, and the crazy get-up wasn't something you could pick up downtown. They'd collared Rad for nineteen hundred and fifty somethings. Nineteen fifty what? His office was 434 West Fourteenth Street, 5-A. His home was 5-B. Rad ran through addresses, locations, places that people in unfashionable suits and strange masks might have an interest in. No dice.

A hand under the armpit and Rad was on his feet again. The thin goon had his hands in his pockets and still hadn't moved. No-neck let go of Rad and pushed him against the wall, stepped back, and pulled a gun out of the holster underneath his trench coat. The alley was dark, but the streetlight was enough to glint off a buckle and a shiny leather strap before the trench coat was closed again. Body holster. Rad had always wanted one because it was professional, but professional was expensive and it would have meant attention from the city, and he tried to avoid that most times.

The goon cocked the gun and then cocked his head to the side, like he was expecting something. Rad's eyes flicked from the rubber face to the gun and back, and he thought he got the point. The gun was a revolver, but the barrel was wide, as wide as the soup-can respirator but a little longer, like a gun for flares or something. Whatever it shot, Rad thought it would probably do the job given the hot end was being held six inches in front of his face.

"Rad Bradley." There was a click from behind the gas mask and then a pause, like the goon was thinking something over. His friend still hadn't moved. Rad wondered if he was awake in there.

Rad licked his split lip again. "You seem to have a real problem with my name."

The gun's barrel crept forward an eighth of an inch. Rad kept his eyes on the glass portholes in the mask.

"You must be from the other side of town," Rad continued. "You want directions to nineteen fifty-something avenue, why not ask a cop? There are plenty down on Fifth." He flicked his head towards the glowing opening of the alley. People walked by in the rain, the bright light of the main thoroughfare rendering the alley and the goons and the gun being pointed at the private detective completely invisible.

Something blue and vaporous began curling out of the barrel. It made Rad's nose itch and he wondered what it was, given that the gun hadn't been fired yet. Over the goon's shoulder he saw the thin, silent partner suddenly fidget and turn to the right, looking deeper into the alley while his hands stayed in his pockets.

The soup can in front of Rad's face wobbled as the goon with the gun titled his own head slightly in the same direction. His voice was hollow, flat, metallic.

"What's wrong?"

The alley was quiet, and Rad could hear the other goon's sharp intake of breath amplified by the echo chamber of his gas mask. Something else followed the gasp, the start of a shout, or maybe a warning, but it was cut off in mid-flow. A moment later the thin goon was on the alley floor, not far from where Rad had originally fallen, enveloped in something large and black and smooth.

No-neck spun the strange gun around a clean arc, bringing it to bear on his fallen comrade and whatever was on him.

"Grieves? Can you hear me?" was all he managed to say – before a gloved hand rocketed up, from the black mass on the alley floor, and caught the goon with the gun just under the chin. There was a gurgle but the gas mask held firm, although its wearer was lifted a clear foot into the air and held there by one hell of a strong arm.

Rad backed himself along the rough brick of the wall, trying to keep his not insubstantial frame away from the new, violent arrival. The floored goon stayed floored, mask at a slight angle. Unconscious. The second recovered from his shock at being held up in the air with his legs swinging and lifted the fat-barrelled gun towards the face of his attacker. The trigger tightened and more of the blue smoke escaped the barrel, but it was knocked up and back by the free hand of the newcomer. There was a crack and the large gun arced towards Rad, bouncing off the wall. More sounds came from behind the soup can, a cry of surprise or pain, and then maybe something that was either an insult or a plea for help – Rad couldn't quite tell which, the goon was being strangled, after all – and then the attacker let go.

The goon dropped to his feet, then his knees buckled and he toppled sideways. He lay there, clutching his nonexistent neck with both hands, head bobbing and wobbling the respirator as he desperately sucked city air past the filter.

Rad tasted something sour and touched his lip. In his quickstep he'd knocked or bitten his wound again, and the back of his hand came away dark and slick from his chin. And then he realised he'd been saved from something like death by a big man in a cape.

The man stood in the alley, unconscious goon flat out on one side, choked but recovering goon rolling on the other. The man was wearing black, but Rad could see lines and shapes differentiating parts of the uniform. The black cape – Rad was fairly sure it was black, so absolute was the void it created – hung from the vast shoulders like the side of a circus tent, covering nearly his entire body, open only in a triangle at the neck which swept down to a scalloped edge that trailed in the puddles left by that evening's heavy downpour.

As the man moved his head to look first at his two defeated opponents, and then at Rad, the weak light reflected off an angled helmet, a sharp-fronted slatted visor covering the entire face and continuing back and up past the ears. The edges stood nearly a foot away from the top of the man's head, and were fluted into sharp points, like the flight feathers of a bird's wing. Two eyes glowed white in the dark, as though lit from within the weird helmet.

The uniform was outrageous, far odder than the two masked villains that lay insensible at his feet. Rad relaxed a little, recognising his saviour, but still keeping his back to the wall. He knew he was safe – assumed he was safe, anyway – but he'd... heard things. Not all of them good.

The Skyguard. A legend, a bedtime story for good little boys. A story that the Empire State would rather not be told. A hero, a helper, and according to the city, a vigilante, criminal, and terrorist. Someone who couldn't be there, not tonight.

"Ah..." Rad said at first and then closed his mouth a little too tightly. His lip stung and he winced. Rescued by the Skyguard. Well, OK. Rad was pretty sure he should have been somewhat surprised. And he was. He just didn't know how to show it.

The Skyguard stepped towards him.

"Are you hurt?"

"Ah..." Rad said again. His head hurt and his face was going to be bruised in the morning, and his ass was wet. But other than that...

"No, no, I'm good." Rad pocketed his bloody hanky. "Thanks, by the way." He glanced down at the goons. No-neck seemed to have recovered and was sitting tensely, watching his attacker. If the Skyguard noticed he didn't show it.

"You know these guys?" Rad continued.

"Do you?"

Rad's mouth opened and then shut again, and he thought before he answered. "No, but they seem to know me. Or at least, they thought they did."

The Skyguard's visor shifted but he didn't say anything.

"I mean, they grabbed me from the street, but they didn't seem to get my name. Seemed a surprise."

"That a fact?"

"Ask them."

No-neck got to his feet, and began brushing down his trench coat. The Skyguard didn't turn around.

"They've been following you." The Skyguard's uniform creaked and there was another sound, like ceramics rubbing. "So have I. You need to be careful, Mr Bradley. They'll come for you again."

"Well, I'm glad I've got you on my side, but you wanna fill me in on this one? Because I got nothing. I haven't had a case in weeks and there ain't no loose ends left hanging. Can't think of who would have a grudge. I'm small fry."

The sound from behind the Skyguard's visor might have been a chuckle, but it was late and he was sore and Rad wasn't much in the mood for guessing games. He stepped away from the wall and pointed at where No-neck was standing.

Had been standing. The goons were gone, both of them. The alley was empty, save for a private dick with a sore chin and a big guy in a cape.

"Oh, come on!" Rad felt more comfortable now his attackers had gone, but there was no way they could have left the alley without being seen. The night was getting stranger.

"They're gone."

Rad raised his arms and slapped them against his sides in frustration. "No shit! Where did they go, how did you let them go? Didn't you see them? I didn't."

The Skyguard turned slowly and surveyed the alley.

"They've left."

The observation wasn't helpful.

"Left? Left how? Gone where?"

The Skyguard turned back to Rad. "They've left the city. They'll be back. Be vigilant."

Rad had just enough energy to start another objection, but as he drew breath to speak the Skyguard shot directly upwards on a column of blue flame. In seconds he was out of sight, the glow of his rocket boots fading slowly into the low clouds.

Rad adjusted his hat and sighed. He still needed that drink to wash the cold metal taste out of his mouth. He glanced around, just in case he'd missed the goons hiding in the shadows, crouching in their gas masks and trench coats behind a dumpster or stack of wet newspaper. But he was alone.

He turned and walked out, running the Skyguard's words around his head. Left the city? What did that mean? He shook his head, unable to process the statement.

Because you couldn't leave the city. The city was the Empire State, and it was... well, it was impossible to leave. No, not impossible. Inconceivable. The concept, alien in nature, rattled around Rad's head. You couldn't leave the city, because the city was the Empire State, and there wasn't anywhere else.

Rad gingerly fingered his lip and hobbled out into the street.

FIVE

RAD SAT THE CUP AND SAUCER DOWN FIRST, then pulled the chair out and dropped himself into it. His hat was still damp (although no more nor less so than the rest of him) so Rad shucked it off and dropped it onto the table between him and Kane Fortuna. Kane winked, then frowned as he looked at Rad's swollen lip.

"You're late," Kane said. He held his own dainty teacup between an elegant thumb and forefinger, midway between the table and his mouth. He waited for a response, got none, so took a sip.

Rad pushed his cup around the tabletop for just a moment, then quickly checked his watch. "No, actually you're early." He moved the cup again, then rechecked his watch. "Yes, actually I am late. I think my watch is busted." He gave the dial a flick and the second hand began to move again.

"Like your lip."

Rad took a sip and immediately yanked the cup away from his mouth like it was a hot iron. Kane tried not to laugh.

"Rough night? I thought you weren't working at the moment?"

Rad raised a single eyebrow at his friend, and sipped more carefully a second time. "I'm not. But the city is full of some interesting folk."

Kane laughed this time, causing Rad to smile too broadly, pulling the split in his lip. Kane's laugh grew and he gestured around the dark room with his cup.

"You say this city has some interesting folk as you sit in this place! Nice to see a few weeks out of work haven't dulled those amazing detecting skills of yours."

Rad held his breath and with another sip allowed the clear strong liquor to bathe his injured mouth, enjoying the sensation as the initial sharp sting dulled to near numbness after just a few seconds. He wasn't sure he'd be able to speak or eat in the morning, so for now keeping his jaw exercised so it didn't seize up seemed like a good idea. And Kane liked to listen.

"You look like you were hit by a brick wall," Kane continued, sitting up in his chair a little to look Rad up and down. "You're wet."

"Speaking of amazing powers of detection."

Kane waved his hand, all the while the smile never leaving his face. Rad felt the warmth of the alcohol spread over his body, and smiled in return. You just couldn't help it in Kane's presence. Young, good looking, wide eyes and slick black hair that fell over his forehead in a way that Rad imagined drove the girls wild. Rad liked to pretend he'd been like that once, when he was Kane's age. It was too long ago to remember properly, but he knew it was a lie. A comfortable one.

"So...?"

Rad drained his teacup and set it rattling in its saucer, and quickly caught the attention of Jerry, the barkeep, to order a second.

"So," Rad began. He relaxed his shoulders. The drink was starting to have exactly the effect he'd been looking for

"So I was walking down Fifth, no problem, heading back to the office. And there's people around, y'know, the theatre crowd. And cops, of course. Plenty of cops.

"And then I'm somewhere north of... well, somewhere, and I've got an arm around my neck and I'm scuffing my heels in an alley."

Kane's smile vanished, replaced by an open oval of surprise. "You got *mugged*?"

"I'm not sure." Rad shook his head and looked around for his next drink, which hadn't arrived. "I don't think so, anyway. Two goons in *masks* – like gas masks, big things with respirators, and they had these fedoras pulled down low – these two goons and me in an alley in the dark, and I'm thinking this isn't my night, but the first one asks me a question and then he doesn't like my answer, so he lays it on."

Kane drained his cup. Jerry appeared and switched Rad's empty cup for a full one. Kane flicked a finger discreetly to indicate another for himself, and waited until Jerry had moved away. He leaned in and lowered his voice.

"What did they ask?"

Rad's eyebrow went up again. The drink was loosening him up. He picked up his new cup and had a sour mouthful.

"They wanted to know about nineteen fifty."

"Nineteen fifty what?"

Rad shrugged, jogging the rim of the cup against his teeth, absently making sure they really were all still there.

"Exactly. Figured it might have been an address. Can't think what else."

Kane mouthed the number silently to himself, then shook his head and shrugged. Rad began to fill him in on the rest, but before he reached the end Kane held a hand up.

"Smoke?"

Rad nodded. "Blue. Thin. Gas, maybe, not smoke. No clue. He never actually fired the gun."

"You were right about the city being full of interesting folk. G-men maybe?"

"Suppose. You don't get gear like that just anywhere. But why the fancy dress? There are easier ways to disguise yourself. Those masks sure as hell couldn't have been comfortable." Rad paused and wondered idly whether he needed a third drink. He didn't have any plans for the following day, except to have a sore face and a sore head and to keep himself to himself. He got Jerry's attention again.

"There was something about them," he said. His eyes weren't quite focussed on Kane, who hadn't touched his second drink yet. Rad wondered whether he actually liked the stuff, or whether he just came to Jerry's speakeasy because it made Rad happy. No, he had to like it. You don't break the Prohibition just to win friends and influence people. Or perhaps you did.

"You mean apart from the masks and the hats and the smoke gun and the math questions?"

Rad laughed. "No, I mean *something*. But I didn't get much of a chance to grill them myself, not when the Skyguard arrived."

Kane froze. He was about to lift the teacup he hadn't touched, and for a moment looked into it – like he was reading the tea leaves that should have been there, but weren't. He downed the alcohol in one mouthful and exhaled hotly. The smile was gone and he pushed his hair off his forehead.

"I think your friend in the gas mask hit you too hard."

Rad snorted and looked at his cup. "That so?"

"You sit there an' talk about an audience with the Skyguard like it was tea with Grandma."

Rad shrugged. Maybe Kane was right and the punch had been harder than he thought.

Kane reached down beside his chair and pulled up a slim, brown leather satchel. It was unbuckled already, and from within he pulled a stack of loose papers. They were bent, and crinkled, and rough; pages torn from a notepad and covered with small writing in black ink.

Rad recognised them. Kane had shown them to him many times over the last couple of months. His notes from the prison.

And then it clicked. Kane's week-long feature on the Sky-guard for the *Sentinel* was due to end with the next morning's edition, and already Kane's star was rising on the back of the impressive piece of serial journalism. Rad felt tight in the chest and his head spun, just a little. He'd had too much to drink. That had to be it.

Kane piled the notes out onto the table, but continued to flick through the bag until he pulled out a folded newspaper. The paper was crisp, virgin white, literally hot off the press. Kane saw Rad's look and held the newspaper, headline up, towards him. He twisted his wrist as he held it and checked his watch. "Should be on sale in an hour."

Rad leaned forward, taking the newspaper with slow hands. The main headline was huge, stretching right across the upper half of the paper, dwarfing the masthead.

EXECUTED!
JUSTICE SERVED AS VIGILANTE PUT TO DEATH

Rad slumped back into his chair, paper in his lap. Below the headline was a mugshot, so badly reproduced he could barely make out the facial features. He didn't need to. He knew who it was. The whole city knew who it was.

The unmasked face of the Skyguard. Deceased.

He glanced down the column, past Kane's byline. The Skyguard had been executed at twenty-hundred hours, three or four hours at least before he'd rescued Rad from the masked goons. Not that that detail was particularly relevant. The Skyguard had been in prison for nineteen years anyway.

"Huh."

Kane reached over and took the paper away. "I was there tonight, Rad. The Skyguard is dead."

Rad's fingers groped for his teacup. He knocked it at first, the hard porcelain of cup and saucer clattering together unpleasantly. "Someone needs to tell him that. He flies well for a dead guy."

Kane grabbed his notes by the handful and began shoving them back into his bag. He kept his eyes off Rad and on the table.

"So when are you going to get back on a case, Rad? The Empire State is a big city. There must be plenty that needs investigating."

Rad eyed his reporter friend over the rim of his cup. "What? You saying I ran into a brick wall to give me a lip just so I'd have a nice story to tell? Is this what they call investigative journalism? Because you don't seem too interested for a reporter. Two guys in masks ask me for directions and the Skyguard – deceased – says he's following me. You saying it's all in my mind?" He tapped his temple.

Kane sat still, trying to read Rad's face. His lip was continuing to swell, and Rad kept a hand close to his jaw and cheek, as if trying to protect them from further blows. Sweat stood out on his big bald head and glistened in his goatee.

"You've had enough, Rad. Come on, let me get you home. You're gonna need to look after that pretty face of yours for a few days."

Kane stood and swung the strap of his satchel over a

shoulder before moving around the table and gently taking Rad's arm. Rad pushed him off and mumbled something, but Kane tried again, this time with a firmer grip. Rad slumped, defeated, and then pulled himself to his feet.

"Must be someone else then." Rad's speech was slurring now, and Kane had to lean in to hear. He nodded and patted his friend's broad back.

"Come on, big fella. Home time." He turned to the bar. "Thanks, Jerry."

The red-jacketed barman nodded in return.

"It's someone else, Kane. Someone else. Has to be," said Rad. Kane gently guided him to the steps that led from the office basement commandeered by the bootleggers to street level. Rad managed the first few no problem, but the sudden physical exertion after a few strong drinks now took its toll. But the stairway was narrow, fortunately, and Kane let Rad knock against the side. Kane slipped his head under his friend's arm and half-dragged him up the remaining steps. Just another night at Jerry's speakeasy.

Luckily it wasn't far to Rad's office. Kane hadn't been able to believe Rad's luck when the illegal bar opened on a quiet backstreet so close to his building. Discreetly hidden in a area of the city that wasn't so much downtrodden as merely worn at the edges – dirty, just a little, but not enough to grab the attention of the police – the only real danger of detection was perhaps from a police surveillance blimp passing overhead, but that had been considered. The top of the stairs ended at a plain door which opened immediately into a sunken porch, separated from the street itself by railings and a concrete staircase set at ninety degrees. Jerry had installed an angled mirror in the overhang of the building above the concealed exit, so looking up, you could check both the street and the sky, safe in the knowledge that your departure would go undetected.

Kane opened the door, stopped, and checked the mirror. A sea of dark buildings lit in the faded orange of the street-lights was reflected back at him. Looking past the mirror, Kane saw a cloudy glowing sky. It had stopped raining. There were no blimps tonight.

Rad sucked in the cold outside air with a wet slurp, and pushed against Kane, not aggressively but instinctively, and straightened up.

"You OK, buddy?" Kane slipped out from under Rad's arm and placed one hand on his friend's chest, one hand on his back. Rad was swaying and it was a steep drop back down into Jerry's den.

Rad puffed again and nodded. Kane could see that while the cold air didn't really clear his head, like a shot of coffee it woke him up. Rad seemed to know it himself and nodded again at Kane. An awake drunk was at least easier to move than a comatose one.

"Yeah, I'm good, I'm good. Nice night."

Kane's smile reappeared. "You betcha. Come on. Home time."

Rad huffed the wet air and attempted the second set of stairs. Kane kept his arm across Rad's back.

Rad stopped. "Listen." He looked up into the sky. Kane shuffled his feet.

"What? I don't hear anything. It's late."

"Wait, wait... there." Rad craned his head around to Kane. "The docks?"

Kane paused, squinting as he concentrated. It was late, very late, late enough for the city – this part at least – to be quiet, near silent. The harbour wasn't far away at all, just a few blocks, but at this time of night even the dockyards were dead.

The sound was faint, caught on a wind blowing in the wrong direction. A heartbeat, a ticking and chuffing and puffing. Faint, but unmistakeable.

"Well now," said Kane.

"An ironclad?"

Kane nodded. "Sounds it." He looked at Rad's swollen face just inches away from his own. At this range, his breath was strong enough to sterilise an operating theatre.

"Come on. Home."

Rad waved both hands impatiently and rocked on his heels.

"I want to see this. No, I'll be fine. The exercise and fresh air will do me good. Really. Let's go. Home, but docks first. It's not far."

Rad spun and tottered up the stairs and across the street. Kane almost called out, but thought better of it. Behind him the door to Jerry's speakeasy was closed and dark, no hint of the illicit nightlife within. There were no blimps, no pedestrians, no traffic. But it paid to be careful. Agents of the State could be, would be, anywhere.

Kane skipped up the stairs two at a time and ran after his friend.

SIX

THE DOCKLANDS OF THE Empire State were vast, a spread of wharfs, cranes, piers, warehouses and cargo yards stretching down one side of the island on which the city sat. They might have once been the commercial hub of the State, but Wartime had changed things. Surrounded by the Enemy, there was no longer any need for a trading port. But the city had a use for them still, and soon the whole zone had been turned into a great war machine, the naval foundries working day and night to produce the ironclads, the great fleet of warships that protected the city, taking the fight to the Enemy. Ironclads, like the one that was now anchored far out in the misty dark.

Rad savoured the cold night air. He was feeling better, sobering up almost with each step from Jerry's. It was times like this he wished he was in better shape – while naturally a large man, the lack of work in the last few months had taken a toll on his fitness.

They'd walked much further than he'd expected, as far south as you could go, in fact, close to the Battery, right into the heart of the naval zone. But Rad had been determined to get a good look and Kane hadn't really protested that much. But Rad knew that being out this late, in this area, was bound to arouse suspicion. There were lights on in the squat, functional naval buildings that surrounded them. They were being watched, no doubt about it.

Rad looked out at the anchored ironclad. Its lights were on, and even though their glare made it hard to focus on the boat itself, its indistinct silhouette was a huge, brooding presence. He thought it would be very hard to keep the ironclad's return a secret. So far, lights blazing, it looked like they weren't bothering to try.

Something uncomfortable wormed at the back of Rad's mind. The fact was that of the hundreds of metal warships that headed out to the war once or twice a year, not a single one had ever come back. Ever. The ships were constructed at a prodigious rate, and when enough were ready a fleet was assembled and a ticker-tape parade organised and they steamed off into the fog, out of sight, and out of mind. And then six months later the cheering crowds gathered again. And again. And again. But the ironclads never returned, and nobody ever talked about it, and the State pretended that the war was going well. And you didn't argue with the State.

"Well now," said Rad. He felt sober, although he wasn't entirely sure where his feet were, so he leaned on the railing, just in case. "Don't tell me we're winning the war after all?"

Kane touched the railing, then seemed to think better of it and took his hand away. The browned metal was cold, icy, but Rad enjoyed the sensation.

"I kinda get the feeling that if this ship was supposed to come back, we would have heard about it," Kane said. "The Chairman of the City Commissioners would be on the steps of city hall gassing to the press. And nobody at the paper has mentioned this at all, and believe me, we'd be the first to know."

Rad clicked his tongue. "Which means nobody knew it was coming back. Not even the Commissioners." He laughed.

"Now there's a nice surprise."

"So what's it doing back?"

"And what are they going to do with it now?"

Kane stood straight and stretched his back. He glanced at the shadows moving passed the windows behind them. Rad followed his look; they shouldn't linger too long.

Kane smiled. "Perhaps you can get your friend the Skyguard to take a look?"

Rad huffed, low. "Very funny."

"Sorry," said Kane. "The *new* Skyguard."

Rad pointed to the ship with a fat finger and wagged it. His face split into a too-wide grin and he winced a little.

"Quarantine!"

Kane frowned. "Quarantine?"

"Yep, quarantine. Look." He pointed again. "The ship is out near the harbour entrance, but it's anchored and it's lit. So it's got power still, it's not damaged or wrecked or out of control. It's stopped, and anchored, far enough out that nobody can get to it very easily.

"But that's not all. Those big blue eyes of yours don't work in the dark? Hell, I've a belly full of moonshine, but even I can see it. There's other boats out there. *Unlit* boats, all around it. A perimeter, just enough to establish a line. See?"

Kane frowned and squinted. The waterfront was brightly lit by the streetlights, which reflected off the promenade and into the water. The ironclad's lights, a bright chain of globes that cast odd shadows against the angled metal hull of the warship, reflected back into the water around it. Between the two belts of light, there was a black void. The night was cloudy and the water's dull and calm surface spoiled only when a sharp wave crested, which wasn't often.

Kane raised his hand to his brow, blotting out the glare of the streetlights. Rad pointed again. There, gently moving against the absolute black of the water: shapes. Rectangles and triangles and squares, indistinct but solid. Several boats, stand-ing off the ironclad, between it and the city. A defensive line.

Quarantine.

"You're pretty smart for a drunk guy."

"Hey hey," said Rad, standing up again and swaying a little. "Drunk private detective, thank you *very* much."

There was a noise from the building behind them. Kane looked over his shoulder, then took Rad's arm and pulled him slightly away, nodding towards the building. Rad turned with no subtlety at all, searching for the alarm and then saw more shapes moving in the windows. Someone was about to come and take a closer look. Rad nodded and let Kane guide him away, tripping slightly over his shoes.

"Home time, Mr Fortuna. I think I need a drink."

"You know there's a word for people like you, Rad. It's called 'functional alcoholic'."

Rad laughed. "That's two words. Don't they teach you anything at fancy journalism school? And I meant tea, dear boy, *tea*." Rad stumbled a little. "And bed. Maybe in reverse order. Maybe tomorrow. I ain't got no plans. You?"

Kane pursed his lips and Rad grinned. As they walked off, Rad watched reflections move on the wet street as they headed back up town. Kane's mouth moved without sound, and Rad recognised the way he was looking vaguely into the middle distance ahead of them.

"I know that look," said Rad. Kane winked.

"'Quarantine'," he said. "Yeah, I think I've got an idea for my next story."

By the time Kane led Rad to his building, it had stopped being late and had started being early. Rad waved Kane off and watched as his friend paused, then turned on his heel and headed home with a wave over his shoulder. Rad nod-ded, then disappeared through the front door.

● ● ● ●

Across the street, two men in gas masks and fedoras and trench coats watched Kane walk away. They stood in the shadow of a building for a few minutes, and then left the Empire State.

SEVEN

THE RINGING IN RAD'S HEAD was loud enough to wake him, and once he was awake it didn't stop. He rolled over, noticing that the room was bright and the insides of his eyelids were red. It was day. He had no idea when he'd got to bed, and no idea how long he'd slept for. The ringing continued.

Rad jerked upright. It was the telephone in the office. He sighed, and rubbed his face, then winced as the left side smarted like all hell. His fat lip had bled in the night and gummed his bottom teeth up. He touched the side of his face again. It stung when he touched it, and was comfortably numb when he didn't. That would do.

The phone kept ringing and Rad got out of bed. He was still dressed, although without his coat and jacket and shoes. He rubbed his bald scalp as he glanced around the room, and wondered where his hat was.

The phone kept ringing and Rad stood up. He felt OK. It wasn't like drinking was a new experience. He was a regular at Jerry's. Jerry was a pal. But right now he needed coffee, black and strong and hot, by the pot. Rad shuffled in his socks over the floorboards towards the hotplate on the dresser. His kitchen was in his bedroom, as was his living room. Apartments in the Empire State didn't come cheap, which is why he didn't have one. The back room of his office did the trick. It was only him, after all, and he was lucky that his building had been a hotel once upon a time, as it meant he even had a basic washroom with a working shower.

The phone kept ringing and Rad thought about answering it, but it was too early for a phone call, that was just rude. Unless it was four in the afternoon, in which case the phone call was polite and not answering it was rude. He found the coffee, but it was Wartime and it was rationed and there wasn't enough for the magic pot. If he eked it out, this week's ration would last a few more days. But this week was being interesting, so Rad threw caution to the wind and decided to use all the coffee right now. He knew he'd regret it later, but right at the moment he knew his head would thank him for it.

Rad put a kettle on the hotplate and the phone stopped ringing. Rad started cleaning dried blood off his bottom teeth carefully with his tongue, and checked the grandfather clock sagging like an old man the corner. It was four in the afternoon and he'd been rude. Maybe it was a job? Maybe it was Kane? Maybe Kane had found out what was going on down at the docks with the quarantined ironclad. Dammit, he'd missed the phone call.

The coffee was good. Making it stronger than usual seemed to improve it, as it was hardly the best money could buy, considering it wasn't bought with money but with coupons. He had it black, even though he normally took it with canned milk. But the milk ration was even smaller than the coffee ration, so he decided to save it.

Rad still couldn't see his hat, but the coffee warmed him and began to clear his head as well as the bloody debris in his mouth. He thought about the phone call he'd missed and about the ironclad, and about where he'd left his hat. His shirt and pants had dried out as he slept, but the shirt was creased badly and the pants were still filthy from sitting in a puddle in an alleyway. He thought about the goons with gas masks and fedoras, and he wondered where he'd left *his* fedora.

The office of Rad Bradley, Private Detective, was separated from the back room-*cum*-apartment by the same kind of door that led into the office itself from the main building corridor. Half wood, half bubbled glass, thin and cheap, suitable for low-rent office space but not something you'd want in your home. His name wasn't stencilled on the inner door because it was just supposed to separate the big office from the small office.

The bubbled glass offered enough privacy, but was clear enough for Rad to now see someone walking around his office. He checked the clock again. Four-ten. Technically office hours, although he didn't like the fact that his front door was unlocked. But he didn't remember locking it the previous night, so he only had himself to blame. Himself and Jerry and Jerry's magical moonshine.

The hard soles of the person in the office hammered sharply on the wooden floor as they paced around. Maybe they'd been sitting in the chair in front of Rad's desk all this time, and now having seen Rad's shadow moving around decided to get his attention. Maybe they'd had just come in. Maybe it was a client? Maybe it was a burglar. Maybe it was a goon in a gas mask and a fedora, and Rad frowned as he still couldn't see where his hat was.

There was no time to change. Maybe it was a client, a job, the first in a few months. Wartime was hard on a PI and he was now out of coffee rations.

He opened the connecting door six inches. The shadow stopped walking around and resolved itself into a woman in a red dress and black hat, holding a black clutch. She was made up, the skin of her face uniformly powdered to a perfect matte finish, which only popped the glossy red of her lips out even more. She was wearing red heels, immaculate and loud against the wooden floor. Rad's socks were much quieter as he stepped into the main office and closed the inner door behind him with one hand, the half cup of coffee in the other. He smiled, nicely he thought, but the woman flinched and backed away. She raised the clutch bag in front of her in an instinctively defensive pose, and shook her head.

"I'm sorry, I shouldn't have disturbed you. I'm fine, thanks," she said as she took two steps backwards, *bang bang*, then turned and took another two, *bang bang*, towards the closed but unlocked main door.

Rad slid over to his desk, and the woman turned. Her eyes were grey, part of the monochrome of her powdered face. She looked expectantly at Rad, clearly afraid and wanting him to make the first move, to take charge. It was obvious she was out of her depth, in unknown territory. But Rad was one of the good guys, he liked to think, licensed and everything. Then he realised it was nearly five in the afternoon and he was standing in his socks, and a creased shirt, and dirty pants, holding a half mug of coffee. He smiled broadly, then shrank it a little as he remembered his blood-blackened lower teeth. His desk was near the inner door, so he slowly reached over and put the mug down.

"Well, ma'am, I wasn't expecting you but that doesn't mean you're not welcome," Rad began, turning at the corner of his desk. His prospective new client was pretty and . nervous. He smiled again, keeping his lips tight. He needed to get paid and, looking at her attire, her makeup, and hat, she looked like she could provide handsomely.

"I, that is, well, I..." The woman didn't move any closer, but instead waved the clutch purse around with each syllable spoken. Her eyes were on Rad most of the time, but spent a good while flicking to the corners of the room, checking the office out, making sure she'd made the right decision and come to the right place.

"Ma'am, take a seat." Rad gestured to the chair in front of the desk, and the woman hesitated only a moment before taking two steps and sitting down. She perched on the edge, as you did in that kind of dress in this kind of office in that part of town, sitting across from a dirty man in old white socks. The clutch was now pressed firmly to her chest.

Rad took a slow sip of his coffee, letting his eyes drift from the woman to show her he was relaxed. "My name is Rad Bradley, but I'm guessing you know that thanks to the fancy sign outside, and I'm a private detective, licensed by the Empire State. But I'm guessing you know that as well, because that's why you're here. How you got my name, address and occupation is none of my business. What *is* my business is your problem, because clearly you have a problem." Rad spread his hands out, palms out. "You're free to tell me about it, and I can let you know if it's the kind of difficulty I can assist with, and it won't cost a dime." And then he shut up, and wondered whether he'd blabbed at her for too long and put her off.

The woman didn't move on the edge of the chair, but as Rad swigged from the mug again he saw her shoulders drop an inch. Whoever she was, she'd be lousy at poker.

She ran the fingers of one hand along the top of her purse, and when they stopped at the edge she pinched the black leather hard enough to push the blood out of her fingertips. Her lip gloss was as thick as house paint, and when she opened her mouth to speak Rad saw a set of perfect white teeth. She wasn't from this end of the city, that was for sure. Not that this end of the city was bad. Rad knew there were a hundred worse places, dangerous places even, you could find yourself in on the island of the Empire State.

But for a woman like her, Rad's office was practically in the middle of a warzone.

"You are correct, Mr Bradley," the woman said slowly and clearly, taking care with each word and speaking them with a voice that only came from an expensive education in an old family pile on the Upper East Side.

"You have a problem?" Rad's voice echoed in his coffee mug.

"I have a problem." Her voice was tight. She was trying to hold it in, to stay calm and poised, but as she spoke her words-per-minute started tracking upwards. Rad was used to nervous clients and people in trouble, so he sat back and said nothing, and let her spill it out.

"I really don't know quite who to turn to, Mr Bradley. The police don't want to know. Worse than that, in fact. They've told me not to call them again. They're not interested in the slightest. I guess what with it being difficult for everyone, being Wartime."

Rad nodded. "Being Wartime," he agreed, but he wasn't really sure and didn't say any more.

"I want to employ you, or hire you, whatever the right word is for a private detective, to find my partner. Sam has been missing for three days now."

The woman's grip on her small bag increased. She tried to moisten her lips before she continued, but the scarlet gloss proved an impenetrable, waterproof barrier. Rad coughed and cut in quietly.

"Your partner, he's missing? Are you married, or is it something else?"

The woman shook her head. "My partner. We're not married... it's something else. I have a photo." She looked down to unclip her bag, and her face vanished behind the broad rim of her black hat. When it reappeared there were trails under her eyes where tears cut through the powder foundation, and when she handed Rad the half-letter card photograph her hand was shaking.

The photo was blank-side-up, so Rad took it and flipped it over. The photo was of another woman, impeccable and porcelain and just as monochromatic as her partner.

Rad raised his eyebrows. He couldn't help it. It was unusual, to say the least, but that was all that crossed his mind. It was perhaps no wonder that the police didn't care.

"Sam?"

"Samantha." The woman nodded. "Samantha Saturn."

"And you are?"

"Katherine Kopek." Ms Kopek lowered her head again, hiding her face.

"And Ms Saturn is missing, and the police don't care, so you came to me?"

The hat moved. "We live in the nature of a marriage, if that's what you're wanting to ask," came a small voice from under the brim.

Rad leaned forward, tossing the photo onto his desk and putting his shirtsleeved arms on his dirty but unused blotter.

"Ms Kopek, it's none of my business. What is my business is that you've got a missing person. Someone important, and you've got nobody else to ask. Let's be clear. What would you like me to do?"

Ms Kopek raised her head sharply, causing the hat brim to bob when it stopped moving. She looked surprised again, frightened. Rad frowned, realising that the police had probably asked the very same question, maybe not so politely.

"Find her!" said Rad's new client, too loud and too quickly. She glanced down with embarrassment, but another tear streaked through her makeup. "I'd like you to find her, Mr Bradley."

Rad smiled, but Ms Kopek wasn't looking.

"I can certainly try, ma'am. So let's go back to the beginning. If I'm going to make a job of this I need data, information. Times and dates, people and places, that kind of thing." He stopped as Ms Kopek raised her head at last. Their eyes met, Ms Kopek blinked, and then she smiled. Just a little, just an upturn at the corners of her mouth.

Rad tapped his fingers on the blotter. "I'd offer you a drink, but I'm out of coffee. Unless you'd like a shot glass of canned milk?"

Ms Kopek's smile widened and she laughed. "I could use something stronger."

Rad shook his head, smiling. "No can do. Prohibition, remember?"

"I could use a smoke."

Rad leaned back and put his hands behind his neck. He gazed up at the ceiling of his office.

"Oh, I remember cigarettes. Sweet, sweet elixir."

Ms Kopek laughed again. Her mood lifted, and then she whispered: "Wartime."

Rad nodded. "Wartime."

It was dark when Ms Kopek finally left, but then the dark came early in the Empire State at this time of year and Rad had only been up since four, anyway.

He sat behind his desk, regretting he'd used up his coffee ration earlier. He'd have to swing by Jerry's and see if he could wheedle anything out of the old bootlegger. He'd heard he dealt a little in ration book fraud. Rad frowned. Maybe not. It was only coffee, and ration book fraud was a capital offence in Wartime.

There was a large window behind Rad's desk. It was not quite square, wider slightly than tall, but still took up most of the wall. It was one of the reasons – scratch that, the *only* reason – Rad had taken the office in the first place. Uptown you'd kill for a window like that in an office half the size. Here, nobody was interested much in views. But Rad was. He liked light, and views, and the window gave the small office a much needed sense of space.

Not that Rad had spent that much time in the office of late. The blinds were closed and they were dusty. Reaching forward from his creaky chair, he twirled the wooden rod that hung by the window and the slats twisted open. Rad spent a few minutes looking at his own reflection in the dark glass. As he shifted in his chair, the office stretched behind him, wobbling slightly thanks to the old runny glass. It was too late for any views, too dark. Rad promised himself he'd open the blinds tomorrow.

He leaned forward to close the blinds but stopped, arm outstretched towards the rod. He'd been looking at his own reflection, checking on the fat lip, thinking that he needed to shave and wash and get into some clean clothes. Behind him the office was reflected clearly, the dim yellow bulb hanging on a bare wire from the ceiling providing ample illumination.

Except at the back, something moved. In a corner, in a shadow, beside a wooden filing cabinet with a roller-front door. Just nothing, a shape, a flicker.

Rad shook his head, and felt his heart rate drop. It didn't pay to be jumpy in his business. His office was near the waterfront, and the waterfront had a fair share of gulls flying around. It was dark and although the window was acting like a mirror he could still see things outside.

He flicked the blinds shut and swivelled his chair around.

He had a case. An actual job. It felt good, not just to be back in business, but to be back in the black. Ms Kopek had left a sizeable advance. Rad wondered if perhaps he could risk some black market coffee coupons after all.

It also felt good to be back in the real world. He was a naturally lazy person – this wasn't some grim revelation, or hard-hitting truth, it was just a fact. He'd worked it out a long, long time ago. So with no work to be had, his part-time (and unlicensed) partner Kane got busy again at the paper, leaving Rad to spend a lot of time contemplating his navel and talking to Jerry. It was just the natural basic level of his life – he was unsociable and a loner, no problem, but prolonged periods of unemployment left him restless and, perhaps, depressed.

With this job, he felt like he was taking part again, like he'd been admitted back into society. He rubbed his chin to check the stubble length. Time to smarten up. Rad went to stand, then glanced at his desk and saw the book that Ms Kopek had left. He sat back down and rubbed his bald scalp to check the stubble length. It was smooth on top and had been for twenty years, but was a little rough around the edges. He looked at the book, but didn't move to open it.

The facts of the case were simple, and simple usually meant complicated. Ms Kopek and Ms Saturn were partners, lovers. There were laws against it, sure, but Rad couldn't have cared less. Ms Kopek wasn't the first client to come to him who wasn't exactly on the straight and narrow them-selves. In their case, the law might have been meaningless anyway if it wasn't for the fact that Sam Saturn had gone missing. Then things became difficult. The police didn't want to know – their partnership wasn't recognised by law, and Ms Kopek had to skirt around the issue with them anyway.

Katherine didn't work. Sam did, but Katherine didn't know at what. Maybe it wasn't so ridiculous – they had to keep a low profile, so really only knew the minimum amount of information about each other. They had separate bank accounts and neither of them knew what the other had in theirs. Ms Kopek was rich, that much was obvious, and owned the house in which they lived. But they split ex-penses and were careful to keep a separate paper trail for each of them. From an outsider's point of view, they were roommates that hardly knew each other. It was sad and ridiculous. But that was the Empire State.

Sam worked nights. That's all Ms Kopek knew. One night last week she'd left the house, and not returned. That was three nights ago. Ms Kopek had done her own search on foot around their neighbourhood, and had checked in on friends, but nobody had seen her. She'd called the police, but the police displayed their characteristic disinterest in the citizens of the Empire State. Not for the first time, Rad wondered exactly what the police were for. So Ms Kopek found Rad and came to his office.

And she'd left the book.

The more Rad looked at its cover, the more he knew that the police's inaction was likely nothing to do with Katherine and Sam's situation – they'd probably guessed they were in breach of the law. The carefully separated existence of each woman (on paper) made it impossible for the police to lay anything on them, though it gave them a perfect excuse to ignore their plight. Bastards.

But then there was the book, and Rad knew that this was the reason.

It was a hardcover, in battered red linen worn brown at the corners. The weave of the linen had been carefully cut to form a geometric pattern, which would have been hidden underneath the original paper dust jacket. A dust jacket in black and white, with the book's title in bold red. Rad had seen it before, dust jacket intact, and when Ms Kopek had squeezed it out of her purse, he knew exactly what it was and a sinking feeling crept up from his stomach and down from his heart at the same time, meeting somewhere in the middle and giving him indigestion.

Ms Kopek had found the book in Sam's things in the closet. It was in the inside pocket of a coat that Sam wore a few nights a week. It wasn't hidden, or secreted, mostly likely because Sam hadn't ever thought that Katherine would be looking through her things.

Ms Kopek didn't really know what it was, but she said she thought it was important. She'd heard things, here and there, but wasn't sure: maybe the private detective would know, maybe it would be useful or important or meaningful for the investigation.

The private detective did know. With one finger he caught the edge of the cover and flicked it open, then immediately sat back again and sighed.

The Seduction of the Innocent, by the Pastor of Lost Souls. The Empire State's most wanted.

Maybe Sam Saturn hadn't gone missing at all. Perhaps she wasn't dead. Although if she'd fallen in the Pastor's clutches, she might as well be. Had Sam Saturn joined his cult?

Maybe Katherine knew it or guessed it. Rad hadn't said anything. When she brought the book out he gulped and coughed and then controlled his breathing. She'd noticed, but hadn't said anything, so perhaps she knew. Rad took the book with a fake smile and then outlined his fees, and said he'd be in touch.

That was an hour ago. Rad had sat in the chair as the evening drew in since then, thinking. Thinking about a person vanishing in Wartime and that he could now pay the heating bill and, finally, his tab at Jerry's.

He checked the time. Late, but not quite late enough for Jerry's. Perhaps he'd give Kane a call, if he could get him away from the newspaper. Before moving through the connecting door to his illegal apartment, Rad pulled the top layer off his desk blotter to reveal a crisp, clean white sheet, and flipped his desk calendar over several days until he was up to date. September 30th, Nineteen. Rad whistled. Already? Soon enough it would be Twenty, a brand new decade. Had

he really been in this business that long? Had his business really been dead for that many weeks?

He closed the connecting door, needing to take a shower
and wanting to keep the heat in. Under the hot water and
behind the closed door and with a head full of ideas perco-
lating about the disappearance of Sam Saturn, Rad didn't
hear the phone ring again.

EIGHT

IT HADN'T TAKEN LONG to locate the church. Rad wasn't exactly sure if that was the right name for it, but what were you supposed to call an illegal, backstreet gathering of the faithful? "Church" would do.

He hadn't been able to reach Kane all day. Rad waited until Jerry's was open and then waited some more in the company of a drink, but his friend never showed. He imagined the newspaper would be pretty busy covering the mystery of the returned ironclad, and now that his Skyguard feature was done and he was the talk of the town, Kane Fortuna was probably leading the charge on the news story.

At Jerry's he found his hat, and at least that made him feel better, as did the shot or two of the clear, flavourless liquid Jerry liked to label as "liquor". Rad's belly radiated a deep, warm heat after that, which made the cold, wet night streets a little easier. Not much, but it helped.

He'd wanted to ask Kane about the Pastor and the book, as he was sure he remembered the paper covering them once. Perhaps Kane had a contact, or a suggestion, or just some advice. But Kane wasn't there and after his second drink Rad laughed, loud and hard, drawing the attention of nearly everyone in the little basement speakeasy. He waved his apologies and ordered another one.

"So I'm back in the game for less than a day, and already I'm looking for someone else to do the hard work for me. Right?"

Jerry smiled and nodded and dried a cup.

"But that's wrong, just the wrong way to do it. I mean, I'm a lazy sonovabitch, right, but if I'm going make some bread and save this girl – I told you there was a girl, right? – then I need to do some investigating. Because that's what I am. A private investigator. Am I right?"

Jerry smiled, nodding, and kept drying, his eyes grey and unfocussed. Rad saw the look of total disinterest, and blinked, and realised perhaps he hadn't needed that second drink after all.

"Thanks for keeping my hat warm, Jerry. Now if you'll excuse me, I have a priest to find."

Jerry put the glass down. "Anytime, Rad, anytime. Where's your friend anyway? Don't often see you in here on your lonesome."

Rad slapped a handful of bills on the counter and adjusted his hat.

"Busy with the boat, I'm guessing." Rad paused. "You heard anything about that?"

Jerry's chin creased as he pouted and shook his head. "Ain't heard nothing here, pal. Is it important?"

"Important?"

Jerry picked up another cup and began rubbing a tea cloth against the rim between his finger and thumb. He kept one eye on his handiwork as he talked.

"I mean if the ships are coming back, that means we're doing good, right? I mean, maybe Wartime is over?"

Rad considered the deadpan manner of the barkeep, then asked: "I know you're an excitable man, Jerry, but you don't seem too enamoured about Wartime being over."

Jerry laughed and shrugged. He didn't stop polishing the cup. "Wartime is good for business."

"For some."

"For some. So if Wartime is over you're looking to confess your sins, eh?"

"The what now?"

Jerry put the cup down. "You said you was lookin' for a priest."

Rad froze, then rolled his mind back through the conversation. "Oh. Well, not for me, for the case. You heard of the Pastor of Lost Souls?"

Jerry leaned over the counter, his eye alight with genuine interest for the first time that night. "Oh, who hasn't, Rad? The whole city is out to get him. He's bad news, Rad. Bad news."

"Yeah. They're gonna have to get in line. Know where I can find him?"

Jerry stood back up and exhaled. "No clue on that, although I heard there are meetings all over the city. I had a pair in here a few nights ago talking about it. Couple of guys, they met someone, and went off together."

"You spoke to them?"

"No, no," said Jerry with a shake of the head. "But it pays to keep an ear open. This place has a rather precarious position, as you'll understand. And these two guys were new, hadn't seen them, so I kept close."

"Who'd they meet?"

"A girl. Pretty thing, too."

"That so?"

Jerry nodded. "It is."

"And...?"

"And try down on Hanover and Exchange. Doesn't sound like they do much in the way of hiding. The police have more important things to worry about, I guess."

"Jerry, you're a doll. But I need to know."

"Know what?"

"How come you're telling me this? Careless talk, Jerry."

"You're one of my best customers, and you're a man of the law, so to speak. And it sounds like you got a girl to rescue."

Rad smiled and tipped his hat. "So you were listening?"

Jerry smiled back. "Always listening, Rad, always listening."

"OK," said Rad. "Better check it. You see Kane, you tell him to call."

"Surely will."

Jerry had been right. Rad walked through dark streets in the rain, but as soon as he hit the corner of Hanover he knew he was in the right place.

It was a built-up area of office blocks and tall buildings, devoid of much nightlife, except for this one old brown-stone. The doors were open and the curtains hadn't been drawn on any of the three floors. In the misty wet air, the place glowed like a beacon in the night. Rad stopped across the street and figured that this was exactly the intention.

He could see people inside – most on the ground floor in what looked to be a parlour. A few more on the second, hardly any on the top. The front door was flanked by two men who could almost have been bouncers, if Rad didn't know this was actually a church meeting.

The Pastor himself couldn't be here. The place was wide open and the police could take it down in minutes, if they tried. Even from the air, the congregation would be sitting ducks. The building had a wide, flat roof perfect for a police blimp, but looking into the sky Rad couldn't see any air traffic at all floating under the thick orange clouds.

Rad adjusted his hat and checked the buttons on his trench coat, then took a breath and crossed the street.

The front door of the house was up off the street. Rad skipped up four steps with confidence, then stopped. He looked up into the light streaming out of the door, and deliberately pulled his hat back so the two doormen could see his face. No point going in under an air of suspicion.

The doormen smiled. One gestured expansively to the door.

"Welcome. Please, come in and make yourself at home."

Rad knocked the brim of his hat with an index finger and hoped his own smile didn't look too forced. He jogged up the remaining stairs, careful to affect the same nonchalance as he did when he first approached, and entered the house.

It was warm and bright, and it looked like a normal house, albeit one that had now been divided into apartments or even offices from the original single dwelling. The hall was wide but bare, and had stairs on the left directly ahead. Before the stairs there was a door on the left, and two on the right. The hallway ran back from the street and ended in another door. All were open and the lights were on in every room. Everyone seemed to be in the room to his left, so Rad slipped his hat off, rubbed his scalp, and walked in.

The parlour was longer than it was wide. Behind him a large bay window gave a view to the street, although being dark outside and light in, it was nothing more than a mirror. Checking over his shoulder, Rad saw the room reflected and the back of fifty people's heads, and a man standing on some kind of makeshift stage – a table – at the front. He was standing still, and after a few seconds Rad saw some of the heads in the window turn to look around. Rad realised they were looking at him, and turned around himself.

The man on the table wore a brown suit, like any kind of suit Rad had ever seen. He stood on the table in his brown shoes and his tie was blue against a cream shirt. Everyday. The man raised both arms in front of him. In one hand he held a book. In the other a small axe, a hatchet. Rad bit his top lip but kept his cool. All part of the act, for both him and the guy on the table.

"Welcome, my brother, welcome. Please, make yourself comfortable."

The everyday man spoke through a hood. It was of white cloth, and sat over his head like a big napkin. It looked homemade and odd, but the way the two eyeholes and face were aligned properly and didn't slip as he moved made Rad think there was more to it underneath.

He was starting to get sick of people in funny masks. He looked around the room, expecting to see two guys in gas masks or maybe someone in the Skyguard's helmet, wondering whether his expectation was silly or serious.

Aware that the room, and the man in the hood, appeared to be waiting for him, he smiled and held his own hat up in a friendly greeting. Apparently satisfied, those that were looking at him turned back to the man in the hood, who began to speak again.

Rad looked around, but saw that all the chairs were taken, and that around a third of the room's occupants, himself included, were standing at the back. Rad found a spare patch of frame in the bay window and leaned against it as comfortably as he could. Even though there were people in front of him much taller than he was, he could see the man in the hood quite clearly from the elbows up as he stood on the table. Rad crinkled his nose as he noticed a strange smell, faint, like the echo of incense. He decided he didn't want to stay long enough to find out what it was.

The meeting was in full flow already, and Rad couldn't quite get caught up with what the man in the hood was saying. Something about the moral nature of society. Not for the first time that night, Rad regretted the second drink at Jerry's. He folded his arms and in the close warmth of the house on Hanover Street he found it increasingly difficult to keep his eyes open. The man's voice droned on, quietly and calmly, but constantly. Nobody else spoke. If the room

was full of gangsters and terrorists and criminals as he had
been led to believe – as everyone in the whole city had been
led to believe – they were a nice, polite bunch. Perhaps it
was the wrong house after all. Perhaps Jerry had been
wrong, perhaps this really was a church. The doors were
open, and the lights were on, and it was hardly a secret
meeting. Sure, the speaker wore a hood, but then the priests
of a regular church wore long robes and funny hats and nobody thought that was strange.

Rad flicked his eyes open as something hard nudged his
elbow. He blinked in the light and concentrated against the
effects of the drink. The person next to him prodded his
elbow again and Rad turned around with a jerk. Maybe he
had dropped off a little.

The man next to him smiled like the guys on the door
had smiled – actually it was one of the guys from the door.
He was poking Rad with a small book, a hardcover bound
in red linen, sans jacket. He tilted the book a little, indicating
that Rad should take it, and in the bright light of the room
the geometric pattern on the cover shone where the finger
marks of heavy use had held the book by the edges.

The Seduction of the Innocent. Rad's head cleared, and he
stood straight, taking the book.

He was in the right place.

Rad had arrived late, but not by much, and the meeting was
a long one. The man in the hood was the Pastor of Lost
Souls, the city's most wanted. As large as life in a house
with no curtains and lights a-blazing. Rad sighed. Well now.

The Pastor was discussing a chapter of *The Seduction of the
Innocent* at some length: Rad followed for a time, trying to
understand, trying to get what the congregation, the cult
was about. But after thirty minutes his brain felt fuzzy and
he decided he'd get more out of this visit by observing the

people in the room. He kept the book open, balanced on the palm of one hand, as he looked around the room. He wasn't conspicuous – half of the fifty or so people had their heads down, following the text. The other half gazed at their leader as he kept the monologue up. He was calm and measured, but driven. There was an edge behind it which Rad didn't like, no matter how nicely spoken the words were. He wasn't sure from this far back, but the man's eyes didn't blink enough, or at least it didn't look like they did with the cloth over the rest of his face. The bottom of the mask flapped around as his jaw moved. And he didn't stop speaking. He didn't read from the book, although it was clear he could quote passages from it, whole pages, from memory.

The crowd was a real mix. Young and old, men and women. No elderly, no children. Tidy and respectable, normal hair, normal clothes, normal shoes. Nothing outlandish, no punks or gangsters or goons in gas masks. If anything, Rad was the odd one out, in his belted trench coat and clutching a half-folded fedora in one hand.

Rad frowned, and the man in the hood kept speaking, and Rad was getting nowhere fast.

Sure, he was in the right place. He'd infiltrated a cult, if infiltrated meant walking in the front door of a brightly lit house to be welcomed with open arms. He was in the middle of a room full, by legal definition, of insane terrorists and murderers. Rad tried to reconcile the assembly of nobodies with the official picture, but it didn't work. He was surrounded by people with respectable haircuts and normal clothes who maybe thought girls' skirts were too short nowadays. People you'd find anywhere.

True, they were listening to a guy in a hood talk, and technically, the meeting was illegal by definition – no gatherings of more than six people were permitted in Wartime.

Which made it all the stranger that the group was holding a meeting in, if not quite a public, then a conspicuous way. Rad knew the police weren't interested in much these days – Katherine Kopek's dilemma a case in point – unless it suited them. But this was ridiculous. They could take the Pastor out in a second.

Unless there was something else going down. Like, maybe this meeting was unusual, called while the authorities were busy elsewhere? The mysterious return of an ironclad, perhaps? Although that suggested someone on the inside, keeping tabs on what the police were doing.

Rad frowned and wished he hadn't slept most of the day. He checked his watch, and saw it was well after midnight and heading around to the very, very small hours. He yawned, and when he closed his mouth, he noticed the sermon was over. The man in the hood had gone, and people were now milling around. Some remained sitting, some stood; most turned to their neighbour to discuss the lessons received. A nicer bunch of evil cultists Rad couldn't imagine.

"I haven't seen you here before," said the man immediately on Rad's right. It was the doorman again, the guy who had given him the spare copy of *Seduction*. Rad smiled and offered the book back, tugging open the corner of his trench coat to reveal Sam Saturn's copy of the same book nestled in an inside pocket. The man nodded and smiled, his eyes alight, pupils tiny.

"Oh, you have been here before? My name is Frederic." Frederic held a hand out and Rad took it. His handshake was firm and matched the solid muscle of Frederic's frame. Rad couldn't hold back a wince. Looked like he really was a bouncer.

Rad retracted his hand and rubbed it absently. "Actually, no, this is my first time. Someone gave me the book; actually I thought they might be here. You know a Sam?"

Frederic's smile stayed on his face but it looked fixed. Rad realised his mistake, but decided to play innocent. Open public meeting this might be, but maybe the reason why it hadn't been shut down was because it was being watched. Maybe some of the fifty in the parlour were agents, and more importantly, maybe the guy in the hood and his gang knew that too. Maybe Frederic thought Rad was one of them.

The only way out of it was to keep talking and keep it light. Rad tried to look nice. Something must have worked because Frederic seemed to relax a little. Rad was rusty, and swore he'd teach himself a lesson or two as soon as possible, preferably over some liquid refreshment back at Jerry's.

"Can't say I know a Sam," said Frederic. "You a friend of his?"

Rad shook his head and reached into his coat to the inside pocket opposite the book. He took out the photo that Katherine had given him and held it in front of Frederic, the right way around.

"Samantha Saturn. Thought she might be here."

Frederic took the edge of the picture with one hand and studied the image.

"You carry a picture of all your friends around?"

Rad pulled the photo back a little. Time to get professional.

"Truth is, Frederic, she's gone missing, and I'm looking for her. She's in no trouble, but some people are worried about her. She's a member of this church, that much I know, but if you haven't seen her..."

Frederic held a hand up. "Hold up. I said I didn't know a Sam. A Saturn, on the other hand... wait." Frederic turned and walked sharply away, leaving Rad leaning against the window frame in the bay window.

Rad waited quietly, noticing that a few people had

started to give him sideways looks. People were nervous. They'd probably heard him and seen him holding the photo, and then put the hat and trench coat and the fact that Rad was a total stranger together and come up with something that wasn't good for any of them. Rad sighed again. If there were any agents at the meeting, or if the meeting was being watched in some other way, he'd just put himself on the list. His mind wandered back to the gas masks in the alley and he idly wondered whether he was already on it.

He was rubbing the side of his face that was still sore when Frederic returned. The bulky man stood aside, and from behind him, the man in the brown suit and the white mask stretched out a hand. Rad took it, unable to take his eyes off the man's cloth-covered face.

"Welcome, brother, to the church. I am the Pastor of Lost Souls."

The Pastor's office was on the third floor of the brown-stone, but like the rest of the house, it was anything but private. The door to the room, which had probably been some kind of servants' quarters back when the house had been built in the heyday of... whenever it was, was open, and the windows were curtained but the curtains were drawn back. The night outside was pitchy black through the open window.

Rad sat in an armchair in front of the Pastor's desk. It was comfortable but not flashy, with high rounded arms and up-holstery that was pleasantly rough on Rad's fingertips. The room was dominated by the large dark desk, but was devoid of anything else except for the three items of furniture. The walls were painted entirely in white that practically glowed in the bright electric light. The desk had some notepads, an ink and pen set, and an old black typewriter. The Pastor sat

with his elbows on the centre of the desk and his hands
steepled in front of his covered mouth. Next to one elbow
was a stack, three high, of *The Seduction of the Innocent*, clean
and unused and still in their distinctive black and white dust
jackets. By the other elbow was a black telephone. The
handset had rocked ever so slightly when the Pastor had
sat down.

In front of him was Sam Saturn's photo. Rad had put it
there without asking, and for a moment the Pastor and the
detective eyed each other and the photo between them. The
quiet murmur of conversation drifted from two floors
below, through the open door.

The Pastor's group – church, cult, call it whatever – didn't
seem too bad, but Rad had to draw the line at the mask. The
mask was strange and sinister and it meant that the Pastor
had something to hide. Rad didn't like it but he didn't show
it. He was looking for Sam, not trying to take down the cult
single-handed. For all he knew, such matters were already
being taken care of.

The Pastor nudged the photograph with his fingers. In the
bright office light the cufflinks on his shirt sparkled. Then
the cloth mask moved.

"I'm a little concerned, detective, that you did not come
to us to repent and join our moral code."

The Pastor's tone was friendly, but Rad didn't like the
words. He presumed, rightly or wrongly, that any cult leader
was most likely insane. Nice and happy and *tra-la-la* the
meeting might have been, but he was in the top floor of
their building, with their leader in front of him and his
happy army downstairs. Rad needed information, and he
needed it fast, and then he needed to leave. It occurred to
him that maybe Sam *had* been here, and maybe the Pastor
was responsible for her disappearance. Rad felt very isolated
and very much in danger.

Rad opened his mouth to speak but the Pastor changed tack suddenly. The cloth mask hung away from his face and he looked down to the photograph again.

"Novice Saturn is a member of this glorious congregation. So yes, you are correct, she has been here."

Rad began to speak again; the Pastor looked up sharply. The bottom edge of the mask reached the top of his sternum and it swung to and fro, and then jogged up and down as he spoke.

"But not," he said, raising one hand, "for some days. As an initiate she is expected to attend each and every night. A single absence is not tolerated, but an absence of three nights speaks of something untoward." He picked the photo up and offered it back to Rad. Rad took it, and replaced it in his coat pocket, sliding it against Sam's copy of *Seduction*.

"So you haven't seen her since, what, Thursday last?"

The Pastor nodded. "This is so."

"And you wouldn't have any idea where she might be?"

The Pastor shook his head, mask swaying. "No. As I said, she is expected here. We're as interested in finding her as you are."

Rad paused, then said: "Yes" slowly. The Pastor said nothing, his expression unreadable behind the cloth. Only his eyes showed, brown and squinting. Rad wasn't sure if he was squinting in the bright office light or for some other reason.

"Mr... ah, Pastor..."

"Yes?"

Rad wanted to ask about the get-up, the mask, and the weird house and all the lights and the open doors, but thought better of it. He stood to leave.

"Thank-you for your time."

"Not at all." The Pastor stood and gestured towards the office door. "Please, after you."

Rad unfolded his hat and squeezed it onto his head. He reached the doorway, and hesitated. Behind him he heard the Pastor stop in his tracks, and Rad turned to face him.

"What's it about?"

The Pastor didn't answer immediately. "What is what about?"

Rad couldn't hold back his curiosity any longer, and after all, there was still some connection between the weird house and Sam's disappearance. Certainly the Pastor had something to hide.

"This." Rad looked up at the white ceiling, and waved his hands around. "All this – the house, the people, the meeting." He pointed to the stack of books on the desk. "*The Seduction of the Innocent*. What's it all about, what's it all for, and why do people come here? What are you telling them?"

The Pastor might have chuckled, but if he did it was muffled behind the white cloth. Rad didn't hear it, but watched the mask wobble as the Pastor worked his jaw for a few seconds.

"The Empire State is not a happy place, detective. You know that, I know that. We're in a state of war with an enemy vast, powerful, unknowable. Life is difficult for all of us, and to survive and to prosper and to rebuild when Wartime is over, we need self-control, dignity and pride. We need to be in control of our actions and of our thoughts. People must live by a moral code or we descend to the level of animals."

Rad sniffed. "Moral code? You must love the Prohibition."

This time the Pastor did laugh, and with some volume. "You have us there, detective. We may not support the corrupt government of the Empire State, but the Prohibition is their best policy. This is Wartime. No citizen can afford to lose control, not even for a moment."

"Thank-you, sir." Rad tipped his hat and trotted down the stairs. He went out the door and made sure he patted

Frederic the doorman on the shoulder as he passed, and walked across the street in the drizzle and mist. All this talk of Prohibition and moral codes made him thirsty.

He needed a drink.

NINE

RAD COULD HEAR THE TELEPHONE RINGING from down the hall. He'd decided to take the stairs, because if he was back in business he needed to get back into shape. He was bulky, not fat exactly, but he'd let his condition run down. He started the stairs at a quickstep and finished them with a slow waltz.

His office was close to the corner of the building and close to the stairs, and he knew the sound of his telephone. Most of the offices and rooms in his part of the building were empty anyway. Or at least he'd never heard or seen anyone else.

Rad took a breath that was harder than it should have been, and tried a brisk walk to his office. This time he had locked it as he should have, and fumbling with the keys robbed him of his urgency. He swore as he hit the wrong pocket first, then swore again as his hot, thick fingers tangled the mess of keys on the ring worse. He wasn't even sure what most of the keys were for. The phone was ringing still.

The door opened. He walked in, and the phone stopped ringing. Rad swore for a third time and kicked the door closed behind him. He let his trench coat slide off his shoulders and left it lying in a pool of beige on the floor. He needed to freshen up after the pit stop at Jerry's, but then he remembered he was low on coffee. Milk. He'd have to break into his precious stock of saved cans.

In the apartment, Rad picked a mug from the dresser just as the telephone sprang into life again. Rad dumped the mug back down and dived back into the office. He grabbed the stem of the phone in one hand, lifting it up to his mouth as he expertly swept the earpiece off the cradle with the other.

"Rad Bradley, private de…"

"Rad, get down here."

"Kane?"

"In no particular order, I got news and I got developments."

Rad thought for a moment. Did he know about Sam Saturn? He hadn't talked to Kane about his case yet.

"Kane, have you been calling?" Rad could hear Kane's breath on the mouthpiece at the other end of the line. He presumed, given the hour, that Kane was calling from Jerry's, even though he hadn't been there a quarter-hour ago.

"What? No, not today. Not all week." The pitch of Kane's voice picked up as he got back onto his original topic. "Rad, I need your expertise down here. You'll be interested, trust me."

"Huh. Interested in what, exactly?"

"Dammit, Rad, shake a tail feather. I've found a body."

Rad left the telephone rocking on his desk as he cut Kane off, swept his trench coat off the floor, and banged the office door shut behind him.

Kane had indeed been calling from Jerry's, and the alleyway in which the body lay wasn't too much of a stretch from the door of the speakeasy. Rad didn't speak for a while, focussing instead on catching his breath. The brick of the alley wall was wet to the touch and Rad recoiled at its chill. As he took deep, controlled breaths, he checked around to make sure there weren't any goons in gas masks waiting in the shadows.

Kane had been standing across the street from Jerry's as Rad came belting around the corner. It didn't pay to run in the Empire State. It was suspicious. But this part of town was dead at night and Rad thought a corpse was reason enough to risk it.

Likewise, calling attention to Jerry's was a bad idea as well. Rad liked drinking there and suspected Kane did too, and neither of them wanted to raise the ire of the barkeep. Considering the price on Jerry's head for selling the bootleg liquor, they had to play it cool. So Kane leaned on a lamp-post across the street, casually in plain sight in the yellow sodium streetlight.

Together, the pair turned and began a slow walk, down the block, around a corner and into an alley like any other. Narrow, framed by old red brick one side and smooth, newer stone on the other. It was wet from the rain and the street was rough and potholed. Fire escapes crowded on both sides at intervals down the passage. A few featureless doors opened out onto it, some with trash bags piled up outside. There was a yellow dumpster at the end of the alley, rusted and bent and packed full. As Kane led Rad further in, the smell of rotting vegetables became stronger and stronger.

Rad pulled one coat cuff over the whole of his hand, and held that hand up across his nose. He carefully sidestepped the trash, and noticed a third man waiting at the end of the alley. He stopped, and Kane turned around.

"Don't worry. This is Nelson. Photographer down at the paper. You've met before."

The silhouette of the photographer shuffled. Rad forced a smile, assuming he could be seen in the weak streetlight even if he couldn't see Nelson. Rad replaced the cuff of his coat across his face.

"I do have to ask, Kane, even though I know you're a hotshot newspaper reporter and you've got your sources and methods and what-have-you-Jack, but how did you and your friend find a body back here? I don't see anything in this trash."

Kane nodded to Nelson, and together they moved to the rusted dumpster. Knees bent, they each gripped an opposite end of the long, low rectangular metal bin, and heaved it from the wall with the harsh sound of metal gouging pavement. Rad felt his shoulders tense and rise up at the scraping, and waited until Kane invited him over with a wave to move forward. Rotting vegetables and rotting newspaper, and the smell of something else. Something sharp, nastily organic still but familiar somehow.

Kane pointed behind the dumpster. Rad took a long step forward so he could lean around. There – once wedged between the bin and the end wall, but now flopped and folded over on the wet ground – was a tangle of arms and legs. A body: dirty, wet, blood-covered and smashed up. Rad balanced on his toes, then rocked backwards, putting the dumpster between him and the body. He'd seen enough.

Nelson remained silent, his eyes glinting in the shadows. Kane looked expectantly at Rad. Rad stifled a cough that was almost a retch, then poked a finger at Kane.

"Now look, Kane, how the hell did you find a body here? Seems pretty well hidden from everywhere, unless you knew where to look. Now you ain't a killer, but I don't know about your friend here. This is way beyond crazy."

Kane slapped Rad's shoulder. Rad relaxed a little.

"Easy now, big fella," said Kane. "Yeah, the body sure is hidden pretty well. But you're right, we didn't hide it, but the fact is we didn't find it either. The police did."

Rad's mouth worked a little, but the conversation was starting to get beyond him.

"What do you mean, the police found it? Where are they?"

Kane stuffed his hands into the pockets of his suit, and stepped backwards as if to regard the human remains hidden, thankfully, from Rad's line of sight. Kane didn't seem too perturbed, but his usual cheerful demeanour had evaporated.

"The police aren't here."

"And I thought I was the private detective."

"Cut it, Rad." Kane turned to face his friend, his tone surprisingly sharp. Rad shrank back a little, then spoke.

"OK, OK. So spill. Tell me why I'm here."

Kane turned back to the body. "Someone got a call at the paper. Wasn't me, in fact I'm not sure who got it, but word was the police had found a body. Except instead of setting up a crime scene, they poked around for a little while, then packed up and went home."

Rad shook his head. "Even those bastards can't ignore a murder. I don't buy it."

Kane shrugged, his mouth downturned in a dramatic expression that said what-the-hell-do-I-know.

"I didn't buy it myself, but nobody was interested. We get all kinds of cranks and punks calling all day and all night. But I wanted to take a look, and the locale wasn't far. And here we are."

Rad took a breath through his mouth so he wouldn't have to smell the stench of the alley and its unfortunate contents, and stepped over a pile of soaked newspapers to stand next to Kane and take another look. It was female, and not so badly mangled that you couldn't tell. The body was on its side, the face half visible beneath long brown hair, matted with the rain and covered in junk from behind the dumpster.

Rad stared for a while. Something similar to heartburn began to bubble in his chest.

"I have a bad feeling about this."

"How so?"

Rad tore his eyes away from the crushed form behind the dumpster. He took Kane by the arm and led him away, just a little, but enough to indicate to Nelson that this was a private conversation. The silent photographer seemed to take the hint and his silhouette turned around.

Kane frowned. "Rad?"

"Why did you bring me here? To show me the body? Because you're a reporter, I'm the private investigator."

"I haven't got to that part yet."

Rad let go of Kane's arm and fumbled around inside his trench coat. After a moment he extracted the photo Ms Kopek had left him.

"Well, let me get to my part then. You don't know it yet but I've got a case, the sort that pays money." He held the photo up to Kane's face. Kane squinted in the dark and took the photo from Rad's hand. He turned it the right way up and tilted it to catch the light better.

"Little Miss Samantha Saturn is missing," Rad continued, "and I've been hired to find her, except it looks like you got there before me."

Kane looked confused. He continued to squint at the photo, holding it close to his eyes, as if that would make any difference in the low light.

"Ah... what?"

Rad almost snatched the photo back, and then jammed a finger in the direction of the body.

"There. Samantha Saturn, missing, confirmed deceased behind a dumpster. So how did you know?"

"How did I know what?"

"How did you know I was looking for Miss Saturn, and how did you know that was her when you hadn't seen her picture? Hell, how did you even know I had the case?"

Kane held both hands up. Given that Rad was standing

only six inches from him, his palms practically rested on his friend's lapels.

"Whoa, hold it now. That's not why I called you. I didn't know you had a case on." Kane smiled and patted Rad's chest. "Good work, detective."

Rad brushed him off, then paused. He hung his mouth open for a while, then closed it and tongued the inside of his fat lip. It was almost back to normal, but still hurt a little if he pushed it.

"What did you call me out for then?" he said eventually, calmly. "What's this body got to do with me, and what's it got to do with you, aside from idle curiosity?"

Kane smiled in the dark alley, which Rad didn't like. It was late, it was dark, someone had died and apparently the Empire State didn't care, yet Kane didn't seem too worried about any of it.

"Come on, Kane," Rad said. "Quit it. Someone's dead. What's the beef?"

Kane moved back and almost leaned against the rear wall of the alley. He took his hands from his pockets and dropped to a crouch, and pointed down at the ground.

Rad pushed wet newspaper out of his path with a shoe and joined Kane. The pair sat on their haunches and studied the ground.

Kane looked at Rad. "Odd place to find a body, right?"

Rad shrugged, but his professional interest was piqued. "The body was hidden."

"Yes, but not with any kind of care. And it takes two guys to shift this bin. It's completely full, probably has been for weeks."

"OK..."

Kane pointed back to the alley floor. The pale flagstones had been badly repaired with weak black tarmac. The tarmac was soft and crumbly like a wet sponge.

Rad looked at the tarmac closely, exchanged a look with Kane, then returned his attention to the tarmac. It was impressed with two triangular shapes, over a foot long each. They were pressed deeply into the ground, with precise, clean edges. Footprints of a very special kind.

Rad stood up. He wasn't sure. It was peculiar, to say the least. But he needed something else, something more than just a pair of screwy prints.

The reporter stood and seeing Rad's worried expression, smiled again and flicked his hair out of his eyes, which had lit up with excitement.

"There's more... *here*... and *here*."

Kane pointed first to the brick wall, and then to a point on the closest edge of the dumpster at more or less the same level. The dumpster's edge was buckled and the flaking yellow paint sheared off, along with a healthy dose of rust, to reveal unsullied virgin metal, shining silver in the dark. On the alley wall, the brickwork was scored. The scratches were deep, two lines in parallel.

Rad exhaled loudly and looked back at the body behind the dumpster.

"That's a mighty fine piece of investigation, Mr Fortuna. You ever considered writing for a newspaper?"

Kane laughed, but it didn't make Rad feel any better. The disappearance of Sam Saturn had just got a whole load more complicated.

Rad recognised the footprints, and the marks on the dumpster and the brick were the icing on the cake. Kane had done well to spot the evidence. Rad pulled his fedora off and rubbed his bald scalp. Kane stood with his arms folded. He nodded to Nelson, who came out into the light.

Nelson was holding a portable camera, something like a miniature accordion with a large half-sphere flash on top. He adjusted the concertina lens and, after a quick nod to both Kane and Rad, moved past them to get a better position. The camera flashes were blinding, and Rad turned his back.

Kane lowered his voice to a whisper, as if suddenly afraid of eavesdroppers. The alley was as dead as the girl, although there was the odd bit of traffic out on the main street. Not enough to be worried, certainly not enough that anyone might see or hear them.

"The footprints."

"A robot," said Rad.

"A robot."

Rad nodded, replacing his hat. "You're right."

"Which means..."

"Which means that ironclad didn't come back empty."

"Which means that quarantine was either too late or is too loose. It's in the city."

Rad tapped a finger against his lip. The ache of each contact was somehow warm and friendly, and helped him focus his thoughts. He stopped tapping and angled the finger towards his friend.

"A robot ever go rogue before?"

Kane frowned and shook his head. "I don't know. Not that I can remember. I can check it at the paper. If it's happened before we'll have a report, whether it was printed or not."

"That's a start," said Rad, and then he paused. "I can't tell Kopek yet. That's my client, the one looking for Ms Saturn here. I need more to go on. And then I might need some more money. I don't like it when a case goes like this. Explains why the police don't give half a damn."

"If it was a robot?"

Rad nodded. "They either knew in the first place, or they found the same signs. Or..."

"Or?"

"Or they were told to stand down by a higher authority?"

Kane looked over his shoulder as Nelson's camera continued to flash.

"What do we do with the body?"

Rad stared blankly at the alley wall, deep in thought. "Jerry. He'll know someone. We can't leave it here, we need to get it on ice, or maybe move it and get the police back. They might be happy to collect it from somewhere else if they can pretend it's nothing to do with a robot."

Kane pulled on Rad's shoulder. "We need to get to the ship."

"The what now?" Rad almost shouted, then seeing Nelson jerk his head up, lowered his voice and leaned in to Kane. "Do you have a death wish or something? That ain't going to happen."

Kane huffed. "We need to figure this out, don't we? For your client. The more coincidences we come across, the more likely they aren't coincidences at all. That ironclad comes back, the first one ever, and nobody seems to give a damn. That's odd in itself. But it looks like it brought back a robot, and that robot is in the city, and he killed your missing person. Don't tell me you think this is just another interesting night in the Empire State?"

Rad considered. Kane was right but it made him nervous. Nervous of getting involved with something that went way beyond the purview of a private detective. Missing persons was one thing, even murder and death wasn't that unusual for him. But the involvement of the robot, the return of the ironclad? This was getting deep into the business of the Empire State itself. And the Empire State didn't appreciate nosy citizens, private detective or not.

"I know someone. Two people, actually," said Kane, pushing the point, pulling his face close to Rad's. "We can get to the boat and nobody will know. You need to collect evidence for your client. I have a feeling I'm onto the hottest news story this city has seen since Wartime began. You follow?"

Rad's shoulders sank, and he nodded. It was too late to pull out now. He had an obligation to his client and bills to pay.

There was a roar overhead, and the alley was lit in shocking red and blue. Nelson stopped photographing the body and looked up, along with Kane and Rad.

A police blimp passed overhead, almost low enough to touch the roofs of the two buildings that formed the alley's walls. It slowed, and spun on its axis, and two white search lights stabbed downwards on Rad, Kane and Nelson, before playing over the rest of the alley. The trio quickly shrank back into the shadows in the corner, next to the body behind the dumpster. Rad tried not to look. He pulled his white hat off in case it acted like a beacon.

The blimp drifted on, but after a few seconds they could still hear its engines thrumming a small distance away.

Rad pulled his hat back on. "Come on," he said and, holding his breath and praying to whoever would listen, he helped the other two slide the dumpster back against the wall. The remains of Sam Saturn were hidden once more. As much as it rubbed him the wrong way, Rad knew they had no choice. The poor girl had to stay right where she was, for now.

"Time to leave," he said quietly. "Maybe they're coming back to clean up."

Kane and Nelson hurried out of the alley at a jog. Rad watched until they disappeared around the corner, then followed.

TEN

IF KANE FORTUNA SAID HE KNEW SOMEONE, usually with a nudge and a wink and a whisper, then in all likelihood he was telling the truth. The star reporter was a walking telephone directory, a gold mine of contacts and addresses and numbers. He knew people above the law, he knew people under the wire. He knew normal, everyday people, and he knew the interesting folk of the city.

Rad wondered if he knew two goons in fedoras and gas masks, but he didn't ask.

Sam Saturn's death was caused by a robot, and the robot had arrived on the ironclad anchored in the harbour. That much was clear. Now Kane wanted to go take a look at the ship, and on this point Rad wasn't so sure, because if the robot was on land, and if it was malfunctioning (and it had to be, otherwise why would it kill a random member of the public and dump the body behind a bin in a wet alley?) then it needed to be found and put out of action. A single robotic sailor with a squeaky set of cogs in a city like the Empire State...

Rad stopped walking, and pulled off his hat to rub his head. With a robot on the loose, by this time tomorrow they could all be dead. Him. Kane and Nelson and the staff of the newspaper. Jerry. The two guys in gas masks. Everyone in the city.

So OK, maybe there would be some clue on the ironclad, but maybe Kane was getting too far ahead. Interfering with such matters could get them both killed, if the malfunctioning robot didn't get them first anyway.

Kane said, "You look a little peaky."

Kane strolled back to Rad, and Rad put his hat back on. The rain had broken at last, but the air felt thick and clammy. For the nth time, Rad had lost a day. How Kane could put up with working all day and all night, he never knew. Maybe that's what made him good at what he did, and good he was. The best.

"I need some sleep and I need some goddamn daylight. How do you do it?"

Kane shrugged. "Lots of coffee?"

"Huh," said Rad. "Don't remind me. I used a month's ration in two days."

Kane whistled. "That's gotta be tough. Two weeks until the next ration book."

"Yeah, yeah." Rad waved Kane on. "Come on, we there yet?"

The Upper East Side was not an area Rad was used to visiting. The people who could afford to live in these digs could afford a better class of detective for their sordid private affairs. At least he assumed their affairs were sordid. What else was there for these people to do?

Tall, wide apartment buildings were dotted around private green yards bigger than most municipal parks in the rest of the city. Each gated and locked. Expensive and classy, but it didn't feel very friendly and Rad didn't feel comfortable.

They'd parked Kane's yacht of a car several blocks away. The Upper East Side was watched carefully, not just by the police blimps which cruised over this part of the island in notable numbers, but by a private army of security guards. Authorised by the City Commissioners and empowered to use just as much force as the regular law, they were not people you wanted to attract the attention of. Two well-dressed guys on a stroll, said Kane, were much less conspicuous than a slowly crawling car.

On the drive over from Kane's building, the reporter had given Rad a little information on who they were visiting, but nowhere near enough to satisfy his curiosity or, Rad hated to admit, his suspicions. When they'd pulled up, Rad had leaned over to the driver's side and gripped the steering wheel with one hand just as Kane moved to get out.

"Now hold on," said Rad. "Remind me about this guy."

Kane slumped back into the driver's seat and slid his backside around on the soft leather to better hold a conversation. They'd parked with other cars on an average street a few blocks away from their destination, but Kane had drifted the bulk of the vehicle away from the nearest streetlight. The pair were deep in shadow, the windshield nothing but a black oblong when seen from outside. If anyone was watching.

"Captain Carson isn't just a 'guy'," said Kane, exasperation but also a hint of excitement in his voice. Whoever this "Captain" was, Kane seemed to take some pride in having his acquaintance.

"He lives here with a friend. Both confirmed bachelors, both with unique experience and, more importantly, the skills and equipment we need to get in under the cordon and get onto that ship." Kane paused, fixing Rad's small brown eyes with his own large blue ones. "Do you want to solve the murder of Sam Saturn or not?"

Rad *hrmmed*. "You gonna tell him about the body?"

Kane shook his head. "No need, for now. I called in a favour at a precinct uptown. Friend of mine has it on ice and can keep people away."

"I thought the police weren't interested?"

"Not officially, but I have friends."

Rad smiled. "Handy," he said, then he pulled at his lip. "I don't know if you thought about it too much, but there might be a real, genuine reason for the ironclad to be in quarantine. Not just because it's an embarrassing secret for the Empire State. What if it's brought back some disease, or some germ weapon from the Enemy? Maybe it's out there in the harbour in the dark for a reason?"

Kane's face cracked into a huge grin. He bumped a clenched fist gently into the steering wheel, twice.

"Exactly, detective! That's why Captain Carson is just the man for this. Come on. When have I let you down?"

Rad coughed and shifted himself back over towards the passenger-side door. "Well, there was that one time..."

Kane slapped his friend on the shoulder. "Get outta town!"

Both exited the vehicle, snicking the doors closed as quietly as possible. Sticking to the night shadows cast by the wet, dripping trees on the curb, they slipped off towards the pricey end of town.

"Can I tempt you to a shortbread, detective?"

The plate was offered. Rad regarded the silver tongs held delicately between the thumb and ring finger of the left hand of the elderly gentleman in whose plush house he now sat, and eventually nodded. The old man smiled broadly and let out a satisfied sigh, dropping a yellow-brown confection onto the saucer of Rad's teacup. Seated next to Rad on the red leather, Kane closed his eyes, his smile threatening to evolve into a full laugh.

Captain Carson had welcomed Kane into the house like he was a long-lost friend. Rad stood out of the way of the hugs and handshakes and the talking over each other for a full minute; but after a brief introduction from Kane, Rad found himself on the end of this affection as well.

The Captain, as he insisted on being called, had led them from the gigantic front door, itself at least a storey and a half high, down a corridor laid with carpet so thick it was like walking on marshmallow, and into a parlour not entirely dissimilar to a miniature version of a tearoom, which Rad had once seen in one of the city's larger, more expensive hotels. Rad and Kane were invited to sit together on the settee, while their host slumped into a matching armchair so deep he practically vanished between the curved wing-like arms.

For an old man, Carson – the *Captain* – was what you might call sprightly. Once a tall, broad and muscular man, the Captain had managed to retain his solidity along with a full head of hair, now snowy white, which matched his finely trimmed, full moustache. Although evidently relaxing in his own home, he wore a two-piece suit in khaki drab, with the trouser legs tucked into almost knee-high brown boots. The jacket was belted at the waist and had silver buttons; Rad counted six down the front, along with one each on the four square pockets that sat two on the hips, two on the breast. Above the right breast pocket was a row of coloured insignia. Rad didn't know exactly what they meant, but he knew military decorations when he saw them. One bar, in bright red and yellow stripe, matched the colours of his tie, knotted expertly over a white shirt. The sagging skin of the Captain's neck hung over the collar, twisting left and right as he turned his head. The old man obviously took pride in his appearance.

As Kane had said, the Captain didn't live alone, but Rad had only met his companion when he brought the tea and cookies out. Tall and wide, and clad in a dark blue suit, the man was introduced as Byron. Rad stood and shook hands politely, hoping that his smile looked genuine enough to be accepted. Rad watched his reflection gulp in Byron's polished faceplate, and he quickly sat down.

Byron's helmet was nearly entirely spherical and looked like it was made of copper, with brass hatches inlaid apparently at random places all over its surface. In addition, there were taps and bolted ports, also in brass. The front of the helmet was a big black glass window. Byron's face was completely hidden, and when he later spoke his voice came out from somewhere in his chest, from under the suit.

Rad gulped again, sipped his tea, and took a bite of the delicious-looking biscuit. It tasted like nothing on Earth. Rad began to cough, his eyes wide as he looked first at Kane and then at Captain Carson, sitting in his chair, with Byron standing by his side.

"I apologise, detective, I should have warned you!" Carson threw his hands up dramatically, then, if Rad wasn't mistaken, winked at Kane. "Wartime, I'm afraid. There aren't enough ration coupons in the world for the sugar and butter needed for a fine shortbread, so I'm afraid Byron had to make do with... what did you use this time, Byron?"

The Captain craned around his chair to look up at his servant. Byron inclined his round head a little.

"Sawdust, sir."

"Ah!" said the Captain, as if that explained precisely everything. "Sawdust shortbread again. Well, they look very nice. My compliments, Byron."

Byron nodded. "Sir."

Rad's mouth had seized up. Captain Carson gestured with his own teacup. "Best washed down with a cup of the old char. You needn't skimp, plenty of that. Nobody drinks it these days so I happily swap ration coupons with the neighbours so they can have their coffee. Ghastly stuff."

Rad gulped the hot brew with thanks. Even after draining the cup, he felt a gritty residue stick to the sides of his throat. Byron swept forward on the thick carpet and took the cup and saucer.

"Allow me," he said, and left the room.

"Thank you, Byron," said Kane. He adjusted himself on the settee and addressed their host.

"Captain, I'm grateful that you could see us. I'm afraid, as pleasant as this is, this isn't a social call."

The Captain said something into his cup, but when his face re-emerged he was smiling. "Of course, my dear lad. It must be said, you only ever come here looking for help. However, I will not begrudge you this, for the pleasure of your company is so great." He nodded at Rad. "And of course I am delighted to finally make your acquaintance, detective. I have heard much!"

Kane grinned and glanced sideways at his friend. Rad smiled tightly and shifted in his seat. Byron returned with Rad's cup refreshed. Rad muttered his thanks and took a gulp of the searing liquid before speaking.

"Well now," he said, a puff of steam punctuating each syllable. "It's a very great pleasure to meet you, Captain, but you'll have to forgive me if I'm on the back foot, so to speak."

Rad turned pointedly to Kane, although he continued to speak to the Captain. "Thing is, I don't know much about what's going on, and what's more, I've had what you might call one of those weeks." His eyes met Kane's. Kane blinked slowly and Rad continued. "I've been a private detective for years, and I ain't never had problems like this."

"For how long?" The Captain's smile was suddenly tight. He paused, holding his cup, waiting for the answer.

"Excuse me?"

"How long have you been a private detective for?"

"Years. Like I just said."

The Captain sipped his tea. "Ah yes," he said, smacking his lips. "But for how many years, exactly?"

Rad set his cup down on the saucer with a loud *clack*. It was late, again. He didn't have time for this.

"For as long as I can remember. I'm a PI through and through."

"Yes," said the Captain, apparently satisfied. He nodded at Kane, as if to indicate understanding. Kane turned his face away from Rad a little.

Rad deposited his spent cup on the small table in front of the sofa. "Oh, now hold on a minute. What gives, Kane?" He jerked an elbow towards the Captain. "What have you been telling this guy? And what is it with guys in helmets and masks and stuff?" He looked up at the servant's face hidden behind the black curve of his odd helmet. "The last few days I've been tapped by guys in gas masks, been rescued by a rocket-powered crime fighter, criminal, take your pick, who should be dead – who *is* dead – and then I get my first case in months, a simple missing person job, only for the superstar reporter here to turn the body up in less than twenty-four hours. Meanwhile, an ironclad returns, a robot from which, says Kane, killed my missing person. And now I'm sitting in a mansion eating sawdust and talking to an old man and his... friend."

Kane set his own cup down on the table. His big eyes blinked, but he didn't smile. "Rad, please."

Rad stood up quickly. "Please what? I'm sick of this pussyfooting around. Someone needs to tell me what in the goddamned hell is going on."

"Detective."

Rad turned and looked at Captain Carson. The old man seemed tiny, enveloped in his enormous armchair. Rad was tall as well as broad, and even though the parlour was as spacious as a fancy restaurant, he seemed to tower over his host. Byron stood, gloved hands clasped in the front. Rad saw nothing but his own reflection in Byron's black glass faceplate.

"Detective," the Captain continued, "I can see that your

friend Mr Fortuna has done you something of an injustice, and that you are owed an apology and also an explanation." He drained the last of his cup, placed it on the table along with the two others, and then stood from his chair. Rad took a step back to give him a polite amount of personal space. The Captain straightened his tunic, and brushed his moustache with the thick fingers of his right hand.

"Please be assured, we are all friends here. I have known Mr Fortuna for some time now, and he has had reason to come to me for advice and assistance over the years. I have, shall we say, contacts, dear boy!"

The Captain patted Rad on the shoulder. "Come with me. I'll explain," he whispered with a wink, before nodding to Byron. Byron bowed, turned, and walked away out of the room. Carson gestured for Rad to follow. "Please. I think you'll find this very interesting."

Rad shoved his hands into the pockets of his coat, and fingered the rabbity felt of his rolled-up fedora. Kane and Carson were both smiling at him, and Rad realised that this house was as strange as the Pastor's church meeting. He sighed, and shook his head at no one in particular, and followed Byron through the door.

Captain Carson's house was huge. After walking down hallway after hallway, Rad realised that what he had thought were other houses or apartment buildings on the hill on which Carson's own house sat were actually extensions of his own residence. To afford all this real estate Carson had to be one of the richest men in the Empire State. This was old money, well-heeled and well-established.

Byron led the group into a large hall, something like a long dining room; the surprising width of the room and the dizzying height of the ceiling dwarfing the narrow table at the centre of the chamber, laid for a meal with elegant settings. Byron turned immediately on entering and stood with his back to the wall in a corner, while the Captain clapped his hands and strode briskly to a vast glass-fronted cabinet that stood along the centre of the left-hand wall, sandwiched between dozens of portraits and photographs in a mix of monochrome and sepia tones.

"Welcome to my collection." The Captain beamed at the detective, and cast his hand along the wall, indicating the items on display. "Somewhat vain, true, but then it seems silly to hide it all away, especially when there are precious few opportunities for exploration now, what with 'Wartime'." The Captain pronounced the word oddly, as if it wasn't quite the right descriptor. Rad picked up on the tone, but didn't think much of it. He was too engrossed by the pictures before him. He ignored the portraits – most of which were clearly of the Captain from his glory days as a young man with wide strongman's neck and shiny black hair. In nearly every picture, a slightly younger man with blond hair stood at Carson's shoulder. Rad rolled his tongue around behind his teeth for a spell, then his eyes fell on a landscape photograph. There was water, and towering cliffs captured in brown and cream. Rad whistled.

"Mighty fine paintings, Captain."

The Captain tutted. "Look again. Those are photographs from my last expedition, my lad."

Rad peered closer, his eyes an inch away from the frame. The picture had a grain and fine detail that was instantly recognisable, but Rad just frowned and stroked his goatee.

"Huh," he said after a moment. "Whatever you say, Captain."

Carson laughed, and Rad looked around to see Kane smiling broadly as well. He didn't like being made a fool of, especially late at night and especially after eating a cookie made of sawdust.

"What do you mean, expedition?"

The Captain drew in close, pointing first to a large landscape of white hills, and then to other, smaller pictures dotted over the wall. In a few of them, figures in furs and hoods stood out blackly against the white wilderness. The Captain, the blond man, others. In two of them, an airship, similar to the police blimps but larger and more rotund, the gas bag encased in a complex frame of metal plates like armour, hovered over either the sea or the strange low hills and uniform plains. Underneath the armoured bag the ship appeared to have a large cabin and hold stretching its entire length; immediately under the front of the bag there was a small row of windows, and under that a projecting conical nose with a blunt end. The strange craft was anchored down by a multitude of cables.

Rad rubbed his eyes. They weren't photographs, they were pictures, paintings, whatever the hell Carson wanted to call them. It was late; Rad was tired. Perhaps he was even asleep and dreaming.

The Captain tapped the gold frame of the big landscape. "I was an explorer, in the old days, before Wartime. The north was my field of expertise, polar exploration my forte. Ah, the space, the enormity of it all. It truly boggles the mind."

Rad felt dizzy, and turned away, looking instead into the glass-fronted cabinet. Inside was a mannequin dressed in the furs seen in the pictures, and arranged on several shelves were books, tools, artefacts. The personal effects of a trip to nowhere. Rad looked at the Captain.

"Nice imagination you've got up there, and nice game you're playing down here." Rad jerked a thumb at the collection. "But if you'll excuse me, I've got a murder to solve. It was a pleasure." Rad stuck his hand out to shake Carson's, ready to get the hell out. The Captain stood still, hands tucked into the large square pockets of his tunic.

"Mr Fortuna," said the Captain at length. Rad stood on the spot, and then retracted his hand. He had to leave. The mind games of an old man were a waste of time, and whatever obscure point Kane was trying to prove, he'd had enough. Sam Saturn's murderer was in the city. The iron-clad was none of his business.

Kane had hung back behind Rad for most of the tour. He now stepped forward. "Carson?"

"How much have you told him?"

"Actually," said Kane, looking back at his friend. "Nothing at all."

"I see. Byron?"

The helmeted servant stepped forward. "Sir."

"Open the hangar. We will join you presently."

"Sir." Byron turned and left. His steps were loud on the wooden floor of the hall. Glancing down, Rad noticed he was wearing large boots made of copper and brass like his helmet.

The Captain turned to the detective. "I do offer an apology. I had thought perhaps Mr Fortuna had briefed you beforehand, but I can see that is not the case. Therefore please do not worry yourself about the details of my collection. I would be happy to show you more at a more convenient moment, but given the lateness of the hour, I feel we should move directly to business. Mr Fortuna?"

Kane nodded, and he and the Captain pulled two dining chairs out from the table and sat down next to each other. Carson looked back over his shoulder. "You are welcome to join us if you so wish." The Captain immediately turned back around, and began discussing something with Kane.

Rad stood where he was, in the great hall, next to the impossible pictures, as his friend and the mad old man whispered nonsense. His scalp itched and he rubbed it. He had a sliver of wood chip from his shortbread stuck between two molars, and tongued it. It wouldn't shift, and it annoyed him.

He took a step forward, pulled a chair out, and sat down. Kane and Carson stopped talking, and Kane turned to Rad. The smile below his big blue eyes was warm and genuine, characteristic of the Kane that Rad knew well.

"Trust me, Rad. Forget all this." He waved over at the collection. "The Captain and Byron can get us to the ironclad, under the quarantine. You in?"

Rad drummed his fingers on the table, regarding the fine china and silver settings. You could sit at least twenty around the table with elbow room to spare. It was quite a sight. Rad sighed.

"Two things. One, I need a drink. Something stronger than tea, I'm sorry, Captain. Two, I'm in. If I live to regret this, I'll make sure the pair of you do too. But I've got a murder to solve and I'm open to ideas. Shoot."

"Capital!" The Captain clapped his hands again, the corners of his moustache poking upwards as he smiled at Rad. "Now then. I have enough suits. Mr Bradley, you are a man of some considerable build, so I will get Byron to adjust yours. Mr Fortuna, I think you will fit my spare."

Rad raised his eyebrows.

"Suits?"

"Yes indeed."

"Suits?" This time to Kane.

Kane nodded. "The Captain's collection isn't just for show. I told you he'd be the one to help."

"Ah – yeah, OK, but what suits?"

The Captain laughed. "Oh, excuse me, detective. You wish to get aboard the ironclad anchored in the harbour. I suggest *under* the cordon, so I propose we walk."

"OK, walk?" Rad tried very hard to keep up, but he was getting more confused by the second. The old man was frustratingly obtuse.

"Yes, my friend, walk. Under the harbour, under the

quarantine and the patrol boats, then up onto the ironclad. They'll never know we're there."

"Underwater?"

"Yes." Both Carson and Kane nodded as they answered in unison. Kane looked expectantly at his friend, his wide eyes and arched eyebrows urging Rad to agree, to trust him.

"OK," said Rad. "Underwater. Fine. What the hell. But I think I need that drink now, if you don't mind. Like I said, this has been a long week and it sounds like it's going to be getting longer."

The Captain stood and swung his chair away from the table. "A nightcap is an excellent suggestion. Gentlemen, follow me. We shall take brandies in the hangar, the contents of which you needn't concern yourself with, detective, but I have a few things to discuss with your friend."

Brandy. Actual, real alcohol, the kind you could drink. And then Rad wondered why he should be so surprised that old money would have a stockpile of the good stuff buried on the hill in the Upper East Side.

"Lead on," said Rad, rubbing his scalp and working at the wood chip in his teeth.

The hangar was underground, and despite the name wasn't quite as large as Rad had expected. Seeing the scale of Captain Carson's house, Rad had pictured a big empty building with vast arched roof, like the kind the police department kept their blimps in. He'd been in one a few times, on a couple of cases when he'd liaised with the force. He remembered flying in a blimp, seeing the Empire State from the air in its entirety, the skyscrapers cutting through the perpetual raincloud and mist majestically, the lights of the city glittering jewels against the black of night.

Rad shook his head, and looked up, and discovered what Carson was a captain of. It was the strange, armoured airship,

the same craft seen in the pictures upstairs in the collection.
It filled the entire space, and Rad realised that the hangar really was as big as he imagined it would be, it was just the
thing took up nearly all of it. Rad let out a low whistle.

"You ever take this thing for a spin, Captain? I ain't seen
it in the sky."

The Captain's footsteps echoed in the hangar as Rad walked
a little along the length of the craft, resisting the urge to touch
its silvered surface. The airship's cabin and hold rested on the
hangar floor on a set of wheels that looked far too small to
support such a structure. Two of the actual wheels themselves
were missing, the legs up on a frame of jacks. There was an
open toolbox nearby. Looking up, Rad could see the craft was
in some state of disrepair, a far cry from the magnificent machine shown in the Captain's weird pictures.

"Alas no, my dear boy," said the Captain, craning his neck
upwards and sighing with some drama. "We're grounded, I
have to say. You know how it is. Wartime." He said it again
with an odd tone.

"Ah," said Rad, and didn't press further. A brandy balloon
appeared in front of him, and Rad turned to find Byron at his
side. Byron inclined his helmet as Rad accepted the drink.
Rad drank nearly all of the fiery liquid in one gulp. It was, as
he was fond of reminding everyone, one of those weeks.

ELEVEN

RAD PACED THE SQUARE WHITE ROOM, looking around the walls, wondering if a window would magically appear. He peered into the corners where the walls met the ceiling. He squinted at the strip light. He looked at the door. No luck. So he pulled a chair out from under the table and sat down.

For once it wasn't late, it was early, but after an evening of brandy with the Captain and Kane, Rad really wished he was still in bed. His nocturnal lifestyle had fallen into a habit in the last week, and craving daylight like nothing else, he would have done anything to get out of the white room. There weren't any windows and the light was the harsh white of a tube that flickered just at the edge of his vision every time he blinked.

He'd had some sleep, just a handful of hours, but it hadn't helped. Every time he was an inch away from dropping off, the thoughts spinning in his head would jerk him back to consciousness. Images of huge white landscapes, men in furs. The Captain and his airship.

The door opened with a mechanical crunch as the heavy handle was yanked from the outside. Rad snapped out of his thoughts, realising that he was dropping off. He stood and turned around.

"Rad."

Rad nodded at the newcomer. "Claudia."

The woman walked into the room on heels slightly too high to be classy at this time of day. Behind her, a uniformed policeman slipped into the room, closed the door, and stood to one side of it. His hat was pulled low over his eyes and his vacant expression told Rad that he was there just as a formality, not to listen in. Rad wanted to believe that, but you couldn't believe anything in the Empire State.

Claudia sat opposite Rad at the small table, pulled the hem of her green dress up enough to allow her to cross her legs comfortably. She wore a fox around her neck, and the outfit was topped off by a green hat with black veil. Rad sighed, and knew where all his money was going. Claudia didn't say anything as she looked at Rad, and eventually Rad remembered he was wearing his own hat and took it off. He placed it in front of him on the table and worried the rim with his fingers.

Claudia watched the hat rotate on the table.

"You don't look well, Rad."

Rad sniggered. "You wouldn't believe the week I've had."

"I'm sure."

Rad closed his mouth. Oh yeah. He remembered now. He sighed again.

"You've got work then?" Claudia asked.

"Yes, I've got a client. Came to see me a few days ago. Quite a case, too."

"I'm sure."

There she went again. He wondered why he bothered, and then realised he didn't really, he was just going through the motions of politeness. Which was more effort than Claudia was making.

He said, "Nice fur."

"Thanks. It was a birthday gift from Declan."

"Declan?"

"Yes, Declan. My birthday was last week. Did you forget accidentally or deliberately?"

"I can't afford dead animals."

"Exactly." Claudia brought her hands to the table from her lap, and fiddled with something on her left hand. The motion was calculated to make Rad look. Rad looked, and saw the ring.

"Declan gave me something else for my birthday," she said.

"I'm sure."

Claudia shot Rad a sharp look, then held her hand up to his face. It wasn't the ladylike gesture of showing off a ring, it was aggressive, challenging. Rad sat and looked at the ring and tried not to move. He felt his shoulders tense up as he breathed slowly and counted in his head. He didn't want to show any reaction to Claudia. She wanted him to react, but he wasn't playing her game.

"Rad, I want a divorce."

He knew it had been coming. He'd known for a month, ever since he got the police summons to attend the precinct to receive a message from his estranged wife. Since she'd left, he'd maintained the legally required amount of communication, and since the judgement went against him, she'd been siphoning off his income, leaving him with one good suit and a coat and a hat and living in the back of his office.

A divorce, an actual, real, legal divorce, would stop all that. He'd be free of her forever, and she could marry Declan and not ever think of him again. From all angles it was the right decision, one that would benefit them both.

But it was her idea, and Rad didn't like that. It would mean she would win, and as ridiculous as it was, Rad didn't like that either. She always won and he always lost, but now he was his own person, leading his own life, and he'd deal with his business on his terms.

And then he thought of having her out of his hair, and how he could get on with life and his agency without her, and how this was really a good thing. The more he thought, the more sense it made. Didn't make it any easier though.

He sighed for a third time and kept playing with his hat. He felt the heat rise in his chest, and then in the silence that followed her statement, he shook his head.

"OK," he said. Life was too short to fight.

Claudia almost stood, but resisted, and instead pressed her fingers into the tabletop until their tips turned to chalk.

"OK?" she repeated. "Is that all you've got? After all we've...?"

Rad stood when Claudia couldn't, leaving the fedora spinning on the table.

"After all we've what, exactly? All we do is fight. All we ever did was fight. You asked me here to request for a divorce under Empire State supervision..." Rad strolled over to the policeman, who still wasn't looking or listening from under his tight-fitting hat. "... So that's what you're getting."

Claudia and Rad sighed at the same time.

"Rad."

Rad felt a muscle in his neck go rigid as he turned back to Claudia. In one movement he leaned across the table, supported on clenched fists, until his face was six inches from hers.

"What?!" he shouted. The small square room made his voice sound louder than it truly was and he felt heat wash over his face. Claudia drew the spittle off her cheek with an index finger and kept her eyes locked on her soon-to-be ex-husband. Rad felt the rage subside, and felt the dampness of sweat under his collar. It was too hot in the small room, and he'd kept his trench coat on. The policeman hadn't moved, and Rad's flush of anger was replaced by one of embarrassment. How had it come to this?

"How did it come to this, Rad?"

Rad flinched and stood up. Claudia knew him so well, knew exactly what he was thinking. Maybe that was the problem.

But there was another problem. He coughed, and ran a finger under his collar, and then rested the back of his fingers on his hot neck and counted his pulse. It twitched in a too-fast rhythm.

"I don't remember, Claudia. I'm sorry."

Claudia's painted nails tapped at the table, and when he next looked at her, Rad saw her smile. It was a small smile, totally devoid of happiness. It was a default, mechanical expression that appeared on your face when you couldn't think of what the right one should be.

Rad closed his eyes. He knew what was coming. He blamed Wartime, and the Empire State, and the day-to-day stresses of life. Keep calm and carry on, he thought to himself. Don't think too hard about it.

"It's OK, Rad," Claudia said eventually. "I don't either."

"That a fact?"

Her voice rose, in danger of rekindling the fight. "Yes, it is, and you damn well know it. It... it is what it is."

"I suppose we had good times. We must have. The Empire State says we did." The official file was on the table, next to Rad's hat. Neither of them wanted or needed to open it. They'd been through the paperwork a thousand times.

"Of course. We're married, aren't we?"

Rad laughed. "Not for much longer. Does it bother you?"

"If it bothered me I wouldn't be asking."

"No, not that." Rad shook his head.

Claudia's lips made a faint click as she parted them. "Oh, I don't know. Everyone's the same. Nobody remembers anything. Fact of life. They say..."

"Yeah, yeah. Wartime."

"Wartime."

Rad pulled his chair out and winced at the noise the wooden legs made on the tiled floor.

"So where do I sign?"

TWELVE

"DOES IT EVER BOTHER YOU? Not remembering?" Rad asked.

Kane sipped from his cup. Rad had emptied his, already. Rad knew he needed to stop. In fact they both did if their plan was going to work out.

He saw Kane's look and tapped the edge of his cup. "Yeah, yeah. A little Dutch courage is all. How's time?"

"Time's good. What does that even mean?" asked Kane.

"What does what mean?"

"'Dutch courage'."

"Huh." Rad frowned and sipped his drink. Tonight it was just him and Kane and Jerry, and Jerry was at the other end of the bar, cleaning cups as usual. There was no music or background noise, but Rad and Kane didn't need to worry about eavesdroppers in Jerry's basement.

"Something to do with the city founders?" Rad shrugged over his drink.

"Yeah, probably. I don't remember."

"That's it exactly."

Kane set his drink down and his barstool creaked as he spun on it to address his friend.

"Rad, you're a wonderful and talented guy, but even you draw the line at cryptic. You hate cryptic. Cryptic is not your bag at all. What is what exactly?"

"Saw the wife yesterday."

"Ah." Kane's nose disappeared into his cup.

"Yeah, yeah," said Rad. He sighed. He was always like this after he spoke to his wife, or his ex-wife, or whatever the hell their relationship was. It was complicated and Kane wasn't interested much.

"She asked for a divorce," Rad said after a beat.

"Ah. You?"

Rad shrugged. "What do I care? Yes."

"So no problem."

"So no problem. But then we don't remember the good times, you know? Was it really that superficial and forgettable that we both forgot? I don't get it."

Kane gulped his drink and ordered another. "Dutch courage," he said, then he added: "Wartime, y'know?"

"Yeah, that," said Rad. He stared at nothing for a few seconds, then said: "We ready?"

Kane's face broke into a smile and he slapped the bar as he drained his fresh cup in a single gulp.

"You bet."

Rad glanced at the clock above the bar. Three o'clock in the a.m. and the rain was back. Perfect cover.

He nudged Kane. "Then our adventure begins."

"Good evening, gentlemen!"

Rad winced as Captain Carson clapped his hands together with little regard for the noise he was making. They were in a yard of some kind, sandwiched between warehouses in the disused part of the docklands. The surrounding buildings were empty shells and the empty lot was overgrown with weeds and scattered with twisted metal and other industrial junk.

The lot was a good choice, Rad had to admit. It was narrow and with the tall flats of the warehouses on two sides, completely out of sight of the naval base and factory. There was a concrete ramp that descended into the black water, allowing them easy access. Rad took off his hat and rolled it into an inside pocket. He wasn't looking forward to this, not one bit.

Kane walked ahead of Rad, greeting Carson with a handshake and shoulder slap, before taking the suit held by Byron. The Captain's servant must have been strong, holding the suit and helmet up in one hand. Rad could tell how heavy they were just by looking. If they were caught in them a chase – and an escape – would be impossible. They were huge, a mass of rubber and waxed leather, topped with a copper dome helmet. More copper – more weight – ringed the shoulders, elbows, every joint for reinforcement and articulation, and the middle chest was covered by a small metal breastplate.

Seeing Rad's hesitation, the Captain stepped forward and placed a reassuring hand on the detective's shoulder. Carson was already suited up, sans helmet, and the metal gauntlet felt like a lead brick on Rad's arm.

"Have no worries, detective. Don't forget I'm coming with you, and I trust this equipment with my life."

Rad *hrmmed*, and nodded at Byron. "And don't tell me, he likes it so much he wears it all the time."

The Captain's smile tightened at the corners. "Something like that," he said, then turned away from Rad to help Kane with his suit.

Realising his trench coat wouldn't fit under the diving suit, Rad let it slip off his shoulders. Glancing around, he saw a broken, curved half-barrel that he could stash it in to collect later. He shuffled forward, pulling the junk experimentally to one side, but Kane's hand caught him before he could do anything more. Rad looked up, and Kane shook his head.

"Can't risk it. Won't it fit under the suit?"

Rad looked Kane's suit up and down. It was baggy but stiff. Maybe his trench coat would fit, although Rad really didn't want it to cause a problem when they were on the riverbed. He wasn't hot on the idea of going for a swim anyway, and getting his long coat tangled around him inside the suit when trouble arrived made him feel dizzy with claustrophobia. He licked his upper lip.

"Anything the matter, gentlemen?" Carson called over, again in a voice loud enough to send a shot of adrenaline racing through Rad. "Detective, you're not dressed yet?"

Rad straightened up and Kane moved to one side as Carson and Byron walked forward. The Captain's eyes lit up in the dark and his wide smile glinted.

"Ah, a wardrobe malfunction, I see. Well, we cannot have a private detective without his hat and coat. Please, allow me. Byron?"

Rad passed his folded coat into Carson's outstretched arms, and the Captain nodded theatrically. Turning on his heel, he reached forward and unclipped something on Byron's tunic. A door opened, and the Captain carefully stashed the coat on a shelf inside, like he was packing a trunk for a vacation. Rad blinked. Maybe it was the dark, but it looked like Byron had a cupboard in his torso. It occurred to him that he should maybe be surprised at this, but after waiting a second, the surprise never came. Rad shrugged. Byron was a walking cupboard. No problem.

"Here, let me help you," said Kane, taking Rad's suit from Byron's outstretched arm.

Rad looked up, and saw nothing. The water was black and filled with stuff that floated. The lamp on his helmet shone a dull magenta, and the detritus that swam around them, kicked up by their metal-booted feet on the riverbed, reflected the light back as a bright pink. Rad had no idea where they were, or what direction they were heading, or how long they'd been down there. But now they'd stopped and the four of them were looking up.

After a few seconds he picked out an outline, a slightly darker, duller patch of black surrounded by the translucent darkness of the water. As he focussed on it, a long rectangle resolved itself.

"How far?" Kane's voice echoed between their helmets. Rad jumped inside his suit, banging his head against the roof of his helmet. It sounded like Kane was right on his shoulder. He looked around, his magenta lamp picking out his underwater companions nearby.

The Captain considered, and Rad thought he could hear his moustache bristling against the helmet microphone as he pursed his lips. "Should be thirty feet. Depends on how the ironclad sits."

Rad tried to turn quickly but succeeded only in a slow drift. "What, we're here already? That didn't take long."

"About a half hour I think," came Kane.

"I wasn't counting. So how do we get up?" asked Rad.

The Captain walked forward, still looking up, gauging the vessel above. "Ready, Byron?"

"Ready, sir."

"Jolly good. All aboard!" If Carson could clap his hands underwater, Rad was sure he would've. As it was, one gauntlet grabbed Rad's arm and steered him towards his servant. Kane followed, the three of them converging on Byron. The Captain took one of Rad's hands and guided it to Byron's shoulder.

"Hold on. Don't let go. Are you ready, Mr Fortuna?"

"That's an affirmative."

"Good lad. After you, Byron."

"Sir."

Byron lifted off the riverbed, dragging his three passengers up through the water. Through his helmet Rad could

hear a bubbling, and angling his head down as much as possible, he saw the water below them a whiteout of silt.
Looking up, the black rectangle of the ironclad increased in
size with significant speed.

The boat was quiet, but Rad wasn't convinced it was empty,
so he tried not to move too much. The suit creaked with every
motion, and when he'd put his helmet down on a nearby surface, the metal-on-metal clank gave him the fright of his life.

It didn't seem to bother the others. Byron stood immobile
and impassive, although that seemed to be about standard
for him. Rad couldn't take his eyes from the... man? A man
with a hollow chest and a helmet that never came off and
some kind of power system that allowed him to rocket
around underwater with passengers. He'd need to ask the
Captain about Byron. No, he'd need to ask Kane. He needed
to ask Kane about a lot of things.

His friends clanked around the deck without much concern for noise. The brass and copper boots of the suit felt like
bricks out of the water, and on the iron deck of the boat they
sounded like a bulldozer dropping its shovel with every step.

Around them the night was nearly total. The city was there
all right, but the fog had come in, rendering the cityscape
nothing but a red and yellow smear. Looking up, the city cast
an orange halo against the low cloud. Rad tried to remember
the last time he saw the stars, but couldn't. He shuffled a little, wincing at every sound. The water around them was as
black as the night and the fog really was pretty close, so that
even the cordon of smaller boats just off the ironclad were
practically invisible, a few dull solitary lights marking out
their otherwise invisible positions. Lights that were on the
ironclad side only, that you couldn't see from the city.

Kane clomped around and started talking to the Captain,
loudly. It was foggy and the air was still, which meant sound

would travel. Even assuming the ironclad was empty – and Rad wasn't entirely sure that it was – they'd be heard by the quarantine ships, and surely at any moment he expected spotlights to be thrown on them, and most likely a half-dozen police blimps descend through the cloud layer to pick them up.

"Ah, guys?" Rad's voice was drowned out by the sounds of Carson and Kane walking on the deck. They'd found a hatchway leading into the ship itself. The handle made the most horrendous screeching sound as Kane began to work at it. It looked stiff. Rad held his breath and walked across the deck as quickly as possible, with feet feeling like they were in concrete. Screw the noise. It was too late now.

"Kane!" he said, laying a gauntleted hand on the hatch-way handle. Kane stopped and looked at the detective.

"Found something?"

Rad closed his eyes and shook his head and waved a hand around. "Ah, no. Look, we need to keep it down, right? This boat might still have crew aboard, but also don't forget the quarantine ships are just off to port, or starboard, or what-ever. They'll hear us."

Kane frowned and glanced at Carson. Carson's eyes flicked between them, and he nodded sharply.

"He's right. It would pay to be cautious, young man."

Kane nodded. Rad frowned.

"Help with the door then," said Kane, grabbing the hatch handle in both hands. "Rad, grab hold. If we can do it quickly, maybe it won't make so much noise."

Rad nodded and took hold of the handle and on the count of three, the pair heaved.

So the boat *was* empty, and for that Rad was relieved. Some-where deep in the bowels of the ship they'd thought it safe enough to remove the suits and stow them somewhere obvious for the return trip. They'd been walking around for a couple of hours at least, checking doors, peering into cabins. Kane led the way with the Captain following, and Kane kept ahead by quite a mark. Rad and Byron took the rear, and Rad realised he had no clue what they were actually looking for. Kane was trying to find something, that much was certain. Clues? Evidence? Confirmation, Rad supposed, that the ship had brought back a passenger. Kane ploughed on, leading the way, apparently guessing his way around the ship rather well. He'd have to ask him about that too. For the moment, Rad felt as useful as Byron. Actually, less useful, as he didn't have a handy compartment in his chest to keep his hat and coat all nice and dry.

What about the Captain? A useful contact, sure, and he had the gear and the know-how and the experience, somehow. Those pictures in his house... Rad still couldn't quite get his head around it, but his subconscious had been working on them for a while now and they didn't seem quite so alien as they had at first. Something itched at the back of Rad's mind, but he couldn't work it out.

But on the boat, the Captain seemed to be following Kane's lead. He was at Kane's elbow, and had a lot of opinions to offer, but Rad wasn't sure Carson knew any more than he did himself.

Did it have anything to do with Sam Saturn? The girl was killed by a robot, a robot in the city, which was a unique event. Kane presumed it came from their mystery boat, which was logical given that ironclads were crewed by robots, and robots were found nowhere else. The arrival of the ship itself was another unique event, but Rad was wary of putting two and two together to get five. Coincidence didn't mean connection, and even though the fleet had sailed months ago, there would still be robots at the naval dockyard. In fact that made much more sense – presumably in the months between sailings, the navy was busy building more crew, along with more ironclads, to send away next time. So if a robot went wrong, somehow, malfunctioned during production and got out of the dockyard, it could wander around the city. Sam Saturn was just in the wrong place at the wrong time, met the robot in the alley, and *wham*, got a dumpster dropped on her. This was nothing to do with the ironclad in quarantine.

"Rad, you need to see this," called Kane.

Rad snapped out of his reverie. Kane and Carson were ahead of him, with the Captain standing in a hatchway along the corridor so only his back was visible. Kane was in the room proper, and had leaned out around Carson to call to Rad. As Rad approached, Carson turned and poked his head out of the door.

"Byron, stay here and guard the passageway, please."

"Very good, sir." Byron stomped to a halt behind Rad. As Rad approached the lip of the hatchway, Kane disappeared back into the room with the Captain. Rad hesitated at the threshold, then stepped through, holding his breath.

The room beyond was brightly lit, which unnerved Rad. He lingered at the hatchway for a moment, glanced back to see Byron standing stationary further down the corridor, then held his breath and stepped over the bulkhead.

The room was large, long, and narrow. Overhead, low girders hung, suspended from the ceiling by a riveted metal frame. At regular intervals, more metal framework hung down to roughly head-and-shoulders height, each terminating in a horizontal T-bar. Rad counted a dozen rows of frames spanning the entire length and width of the room. Rad blew his cheeks out, unsure what to make of it. When he looked down, he saw both Kane and Carson looking at him. The Captain's moustache bounced up and down as he rolled his lips, and Kane's big eyes reflected the strong light.

Around the walls of the room were similar T-frames, flattened against the walls but obviously hinged so they could be flipped out as needed. Rad spun in a circle, counting the frames. As he reached the corner of the room and turned back to face his companions, he blanched. Out of the corner of his eye he saw Kane nod, and as Rad stepped forward to examine the frames on the far side of the room, he felt the Captain at his shoulder.

Some of the frames were not empty. In one corner of the room, maybe from a third of the way along the far wall down to the end, stood a row of humanoid shapes. There were nine, the first of which was upright and undisturbed. As Rad counted in from the end, the condition of the figures deteriorated. The second was intact, but crooked in its frame. The third was badly damaged and the frame was twisted around its neck.

Robots. The ironclad sailors who crewed the ironclad ships. Nine of them, broken, hung like meat in the weird room. The fourth one along was in worse shape, tangled in the bent frame, metal armour drenched in a dark substance which glistened like honey. Rad had seen plenty of it over the years. The robot was covered in blood, and the next one along was missing half his head and a large portion of his torso. Even in the bright light of the room, the damage was nothing but a dark mess.

Rad took a breath. "What is this place? What happened in here?"

It was the Captain that spoke. He took a step backward and raised a hand to indicate the contents of the room.

"Storage locker," he said, as if he were back giving a guided tour of his strange house again. "The ironclad only needs a skeleton crew to pilot. Most of the robots are kept in rooms like this, asleep, waiting for battle."

"Asleep?"

Carson shrugged. "In a manner of speaking."

Rad indicated the blood-stained wreckage of the robots behind him with a jerk of his thumb. "I thought the crew were machines?"

The Captain coughed and looked at the floor. He met Kane's eyes, then looked away.

Rad felt Kane's hand on his shoulder and his friend's quiet voice in his ear. "So we've been told. But this is the evidence I've been looking for. We've been lied to about the war and about the ironclads we send off each year. The robots are only half machine."

"And the other half?"

Rad still had his back to the remains of the crew. Kane turned to stand in front of him, his eyes glancing around the room as he spoke.

"The robots are sailors. Real men. Volunteers, we think. Nobody knows anything about any conscription programme. We do know that people disappear into the naval dockyard and aren't seen again."

Rad tasted something hot and sharp in the back of his throat, and swallowed. He didn't want to turn around, but he knew he'd have to. He took a breath. The air was thick and stale this deep in the ship.

"What do they do it for?"

"Strength," said the Captain. "Stamina, intellect. A machine is harder to kill than a man. A machine is also better *at* killing. A sailor that is half machine, half man requires less food, less water, and less air." He looked away and fingered the straps hanging from one of the empty ceiling frames. "Makes sense really. Very efficient."

Rad almost swore, but when he opened his mouth he tasted bile again. He blew out, long and hard, and turned around. The nine dead half-robots hung grotesquely from their frames.

Kane stepped forward to take a better look. "Exposing the lies of Wartime is my next investigation." He laughed and looked back at Rad. "My ultimate investigation."

Rad frowned. He wasn't in the mood for jokes. "You know 'ultimate' means final, right? The Empire State will never let you print anything about this. Dammit, we'll be lucky if we're not collected in the middle of the night with black bags over our heads after this."

Kane seemed to pause, his eyes flicking over Rad's shoulder to Carson, then back to Rad. Then he relaxed. "You're right, Rad. But look, here's the proof connecting the iron-clad to your murder."

Rad raised an eyebrow, and followed to where Kane was pointing. One more frame, making a set of ten in total, but this one was empty. More importantly, the frame was bent outwards, as if the robot in it had forced the frame off as it struggled to get free.

Rad wasn't convinced. "One robot missing? It went haywire, got free, taking out the others, and then... what? Swam to shore?"

"It's possible." The Captain moved past the pair of them and experimentally tugged on the bent empty frame. It rattled and rocked on its hinges, but stayed in shape. "The naval robots are equipped for aquatic warfare. It could have walked to the shore, just as we walked to the boat."

"And then," continued Rad. "Still haywire, killed Sam Saturn? Which means..."

"Which means," said Kane, "It's still in the city."

In the passageway outside there was a clomping of metal on metal. Carson spun around and jogged to the door, then called out to his servant.

"Byron, stay in the passageway, please."

Byron said, "Very good, sir. But port authorities are approaching the ship, sir. We should depart."

Rad swore, for real this time. "I told you we made too much sound. You done here, Kane?"

Kane nodded. "Back to the suits. Can you lead the way, Captain?"

Carson nodded first at Kane, then at Byron, who turned to move off down the corridor.

"Very good, sir. This way, please." Byron walked ahead, the Captain close behind with Kane following.

Rad took a final look around the locker. They were in way, way over their heads. Maybe he should call it quits. His murder would be unsolvable and he'd have a disappointed client, but at least he'd still be alive. Kane's path was not one he wished to follow. If only he could convince his friend of this. Kane listened to Captain Carson, perhaps Rad should talk to him first.

"Rad, come on!" Kane reappeared at the hatch, and Rad nodded and followed.

THIRTEEN

EARLIER THAT NIGHT.

When Rex came to, his head was wet and there was a buzzing in his ears. No, not his ears, the sound was all around him, all over him. He blinked and coughed and wiped his chin, and discovered he was wet all over.

He sat up on an elbow, and the alleyway swam, so he closed his eyes again. He felt like his head was stuffed with cotton wool – he'd never really known what that expression meant, but this seemed a fair approximation. It was still raining, and a wet city makes a fair amount of sound, but it was muffled, like it was all coming through a crack in a closed door. He screwed his eyes tighter before opening them again, and the world came into focus.

Rex was lying against the side of the alleyway, and it was still night. He raised himself up again. He couldn't have been there too long, as he wasn't that wet and although the rain was no more than a misty drizzle, it was exactly the kind of misty drizzle that got you soaked to the skin in less time than you'd think.

His head ached. He must have hit it on the way down. Rex sat up, ignoring the uncomfortable tug of his trousers on his crotch as he shuffled his behind on the hard ground. He gingerly fingered the back of his bald head, and when the expected spike of pain didn't arrive, he ran his hands over his scalp. Damp and prickly and needing a shave, but nothing, no cuts, no sore spots, no bumps.

The buzzing kept up and his ears felt hot and gunked. An experimental pinkie in one ear brought a loud squelching. Rex sat up a bit more. It felt like he'd been lying in a hot bath for too long, but when he examined his little finger he found the tip a dark red almost to the first knuckle. It was too dark to see clearly, so he sniffed. The unmistakable aroma of earwax mixed with a cold familiar tang. Blood. He patted his cheeks and swore as his fingers traced the ooze of blood out of his ears and along the line of his jaw. What the hell happened?

The broad. Rex spun on his backside, twisting left and right with sudden urgency. He saw an arm, bare and thin, poking out from behind a yellow dumpster. Rex got up carefully and took a look behind the bin.

There she was. Unlike Rex, she wasn't getting up again. He coughed, five short dry bursts that made the fuzz in his head and the buzz in his ears pulsate. He rubbed the heels of his hands into his forehead, then stopped, realising that he was covering his face with his own blood. He looked down, suddenly aware that he was covered in the stuff, but that it surely couldn't all have been his.

Rex looked around. The alley was damp and dark, but he was standing in regular rain water, thin and slightly slicked with the grease of the city. Other than that, the ground was clean.

Rex was confused. No blood. But then, he'd only strangled her anyway. So what the hell was he covered in? He bent down to take a closer look at his victim.

She was... bent. The body wasn't just lying there, it was curled over like a gymnast warming up for a routine. Arms and legs at not quite the right angle, same with the neck.

The girl's head was exactly horizontal in a way that no vertebrae would ever allow.

Rex blinked. He remembered punching the girl, then clamping her face when she screamed, and then dragging her backwards in a neck-lock and squeezing, squeezing, squeezing. He hadn't injured her, he didn't think. Maybe something popped? He didn't really know what happened when you strangled someone to death. And he was a very large man and she was a very small girl. Perhaps he was stronger than he'd thought.

Rex rubbed his eyes, but the buzzing was beginning to smart, like his eyeballs were too big for their sockets and their every movement stung like Christ. He stopped rubbing and blinked again and again, trying to clear them. He'd never been that strong. He strangled her... OK, maybe he did the neck. But not the rest. And the blood! So much blood. His hands were covered in it, but the alley was clear and there was only a small amount beginning to pool out from underneath the body. The alley was wet from recent rain, and as Rex ducked down to a puddle to clean up, he glanced back at the body.

Holy shit. What did you do next, after you murdered somebody? He didn't do this kind of thing himself. Bootlegging was dangerous but it didn't usually run to killing the opposition. Rex stood motionless for a moment. There was nobody around, not a sound except for the gentle noise of the light rain. His hearing was still woolly and there was that buzzing driving him mad, but looking down the end of the alley, the main street was dead. He squinted, and rubbed his eyes again. The streetlights were an odd colour, too yellow. He shook his head and ignored it. He needed to clean up and then drink a lot of strong alcohol.

Was it murder? He looked down at the body. Squeezed behind the bin in a puddle of water and blood, the girl looked tiny, like a toy doll. How could someone so small and fragile be the world's greatest criminal mastermind?

Rex held his breath and gripped the girl's fine chin between finger and thumb. He tilted the head slightly, but with no neck support the shifting weight caused it to loll horribly. Rex recoiled, withdrawing his hand quickly. He stood up and looked at the girl's face, now pointing to the sky.

It was her. No doubt. The Science Pirate, the girl who had taken her mask off and revealed her identity to the world in some weird tantrum.

So it wasn't murder, it was execution. He felt dizzy and laughed. A New York gangster performing his civic duty. He was pretty sure the authorities had wanted the Science Pirate alive or dead. Dead it would be.

Rex released the breath he'd been holding for too long, and the horizon of the world flipped. He staggered up, supporting himself against the alley wall with one outstretched arm. The goddamn buzzing was murder. Stress, and excitement, and a bang on the head. Holy mackerel, did he need a drink.

The body. He couldn't carry it, he could barely stay upright. It was well hidden, although he didn't remember hiding it. But OK. Leave it. Come back later.

Rex pushed off the wall, but a headache the size of the Earth hit him like a rubber mallet and he stumbled, groping for the dumpster. The sharp rusted surface dug into his palms as he thudded into it, and it was twenty seconds before the buzzing died down enough for him to open his eyes.

The dumpster was on wheels, and had rocked when Rex fell against it. He glanced at the body. The arm still stuck out. He needed to do a better job, tidy her up.

Rad sucked in a cold, wet breath, ignored the noise in his head, and ducked around the bin. He flipped the protruding arm up, trying to ignore the way it flopped like a fillet of beef. Limb folded back, he gripped the dumpster and pushed the body with one foot. It slid with relative ease, lubricated by rainwater and spilled fluids. She didn't seem to have any intact bones and was easier to pack in behind the bin than he'd expected.

Rex tried shifting the dumpster, just to check, but could only rock it back and forth a few inches. No problem.

Rex patted his pockets down. No smokes, but his wallet was fat and he was thirsty. A drink or two would help his head, of that he was sure. And cigarettes, and another drink, and then sleep, and then he'd go straight to city hall. And then some kind of civil ceremony where he would get his medal and pose for photographs with the mayor and the Skyguard.

Buoyed by these thoughts, Rex turned and walked down the alley and into the main street. The buzzing in his head had settled to a low hum, and a drink would wash that away, easy.

The rain abated to a fine mist, and smiling, Rex turned left, down Soma Street, under yellow streetlamps.

FOURTEEN

THE PLACE DIDN'T HAVE A NAME, or a sign, and Rex supposed it was just plain luck that led him there. God only knew where he was. He'd lived in New York his whole life, but didn't recognise any of it, and now the buzzing was back. It was OK. Shock, probably. A drink and a smoke and then blissful sleep. If he could work out which direction home was.

The place didn't have a name on the outside, but as soon as he hit the bottom of the stairs he imagined it had a name on the *inside*, one only the regulars knew. He'd walked for most of the night, or at least it felt like most of the night, and had found nothing but empty streets lit in weird, dead yellow light. No people, no cars, no lights on in any buildings except one house down a side street, a big old brownstone. But also no restaurants, cafes, clubs, milk bars, not even any stores where he could get some cigarettes. Rendered in an uncomfortable yellow monochrome, this was a part of downtown that Rex vowed never to return to after he'd shown the authorities where the body of the Science Pirate was tucked away. It just... it felt wrong. He didn't recognise the *buildings*, let alone the streets. He was near the Hudson and the ferries, of that he was sure, but every new street he turned down presented a fresh surprise.

And then he found some people. Rex was nervous suddenly, so he hung back in a shadowed alcove for a while, watching. It wasn't many people, just a handful, walking back and forth across the street, coming up out of or heading down into a set of basement stairs hidden in pitch darkness. Some were casual. Some were trying to be casual, out for a night stroll but maybe swaying a little, or spending too much time trying to nonchalantly adjust a tie or do up a shoelace. There was no sound, no light from the black stairwell. But every so often, every now and again, there was a smell. Subtle but distinctive, a smell that dried Rex's throat out completely. He knew the signs all too well. At last, somewhere to get a drink.

At the bottom of the stairs and through the door, the place looked more like a cafeteria than a bar. Reasonably dark, lit mostly by small table lamps with old orange shades. The weak light filled the room with shadows, casting what few customers were present into an array of long silhouettes. It was also quiet. No music, just hushed conversation. Exactly how he liked it.

The man behind the bar had a blue towel slung over his shoulder, and regarded Rex with a fixed look, two fists clenched against the bar top.

"Can't sleep again?"

It took Rex a moment to realise the barman was talking to him. He smiled at him, but the barman's expression didn't flicker. Rex walked up and cast his eyes over the neat rows of teacups and saucers on the shelf behind. Right place, for sure.

"The usual?"

Rex rubbed his eyes, and nodded at the barman, who turned away before he could ask what the usual was. The seconds collected like peanuts in the bowl on the bar in front of him, and then the barman turned back around with a cup and saucer. Rex squinted down into it, but the cup looked empty. He turned it by the handle, and caught a rippled reflection. It wasn't empty and while he knew it wasn't going to be tea, the vapour coming off its surface was something much stronger than Rex was used to. He wondered who the supplier was and which gang's territory he'd accidentally crossed into.

"Ah...?"

The barman frowned again, then nodded. "OK, but I'll be calling it in at the end of the week."

Rex closed his mouth, and listened to the buzzing in his head as he lifted the cup and looked around. The only other person sitting at the bar was a young man with rakish hair hooked around to the left to frame his face. He watched Rex, his big blue eyes glittering in the pale light. The young man nodded a greeting, and sipped from his own teacup.

"Got a smoke?" asked Rex. "I'm out."

The barman hissed between his teeth, but turned away. The young man didn't say anything, but set his cup down with a gentle clatter. Rex glanced around the room, at the dozen or so people at tables, all with cups and saucers in front of them. The air was stale and had the tang of alcohol in it, but was otherwise clear. Nobody was smoking.

Rex turned back to the barman. "Hey, barman. Do you sell cigarettes?"

The barman's shoulders seemed to tense up before he turned around.

"Pal, you know better than that. Don't ask again." He turned back to his teacup polishing.

"Huh," said Rex, to himself mainly. He looked to his left, and saw an empty stool where the young man had been sitting.

He sighed, and took a sip of his drink. As soon as it came into contact with his tongue, his whole mouth seemed to catch fire. Rex gasped at the sensation, then as the warmth spread over his whole body, he tipped the cup and drained the moonshine in a single gulp. It sure was strong stuff, more like Harlem hooch than downtown refined.

"On my mother's grave," he swore, loudly, causing the people in the bar to pause their conversations for a second, before the background murmur returned. Rex ran his tongue along the back of his teeth, tasting the last stinging citrus of alcohol. He frowned. He didn't know anyone that peddled that kind of gut-rot. He'd have to look into it.

The world swayed left, then right, and the orange globes that lit each table seemed to flare suddenly. And then the buzzing stopped, just for a moment, before creeping back in.

The drink might have been industrial cleaner for all he knew, but it was doing the trick. Rex ordered another from the frowning barman, and drank until the buzzing faded and his eyes were filled with orange light.

FIFTEEN

IT WAS LATE WHEN RAD GOT BACK TO THE OFFICE, and he heard the phone ringing from down the hall as soon as he hit the top of the stairs. He stopped, drew a wheezing breath and used the air to swear loudly, then thudded down the corridor to his door. His fingers were hot and swollen slightly from the trip up the stairs, and he fumbled at the lock. The phone kept ringing.

It was always late when Rad got back home. This last week he hadn't seen any daylight. What was that thing you needed the sun for? Photo-whatsit? Vitamin something-or-other? Or was that plants? Huh. He was feeling pretty green himself. He needed light.

The door opened and the phone stopped, and Rad swore again, even louder this time. He slid his hat off the back of his head and tossed it like a discus onto his desk. Sleep. Sweet, sweet sleep. He glanced at the handsome grandfather clock in the corner, his pride and joy and the only thing that Claudia had let him take without any argument, but he couldn't work out which day of the week the time it showed belonged to.

There were a hundred questions running in his head. About Captain Carson and his peculiar manservant, about the underwater equipment and the ironclad. He wasn't sure who he could ask. Kane was up to his neck in it too, and now, for the first time in all the years that he'd known the young reporter, he was beginning to have doubts about whether he could trust him. Rad didn't like the feeling.

No, he was just tired. He needed sleep. Being upset with someone, a close and trusted friend, was a sign of sleep deprivation. That was all.

But still. How much did Kane know? And Carson's photos. Tall hills, jagged shards of a uniformly white material, the airship hovering over water. Rad wanted to ask the Captain about that. Or... maybe not. He waved a hand to nobody, dismissing the idea for now. Sleep. He closed the front door behind him, and headed for his adjoining one-room apartment.

The phone sprang into life suddenly. Rad froze, heart beating, then shook his head and darted for the desk. He grabbed the phone and leaned over the desk on one elbow. It wasn't comfortable, but then until he got his forty, nothing would be.

"Hello?"

The line crackled. It was bad, very bad. Rad thought of Katherine Kopek and what on Earth he'd have to tell her if she was on the other end of the line. My dear Ms Kopek, he rehearsed in his head. Your lover is dead and smashed to a pulp and we hid her behind a dumpster in an alley. Don't worry, we paid a corrupt cop to take her away before the rats got to her. Say, can you advance me another check?

The seconds fizzed away in Rad's ear, until he heard a breath being taken from somewhere very, very far away.

"Mr Bradley?" It was a man, and not a voice Rad recognised, although he couldn't really tell, the line was so bad. The accent was familiar though. It was strange, different from how everyone else spoke.

"Rad Bradley, private detective." He paused. "Who is this?"

The voice took another breath and made a sound that, if the line had been clear, Rad supposed might have been an "Ah!" of success.

"Mr Bradley, we have been trying to get hold of you for quite some time. And time is something that, due to our respective circumstances, we have a great deal of difficulty controlling."

Rad tapped the top of the desk and then stood up. He knew the voice now, despite the bad line. Deep, melodious, with a slow, clipped accent.

"Captain Carson?"

There was a tutting sound which could have been the phone or could have been the caller.

"My name is Nimrod. We haven't met, although I think you know two of my employees."

Rad curled around the desk and slumped into his chair. "*Sonovabitch*. Those goons were yours? You got a lot of nerve." He took a deep breath. "So what is this? The threatening call? The 'back off or the girl gets hurt' warning? The 'don't mess with the big boys' spiel? Standard fare in my game, Nimrod." Rad paused. "What kind of a name is Nimrod, anyway?"

The tutting came again, and Rad realised it was Nimrod's laugh, distorted by the appalling quality of the phone line.

"Mr Bradley, this call is indeed a warning, although not of the kind you are used to. Tell me, what do you know of nineteen fifty?"

Rad sat up and his eyebrows kept travelling. He stared into the empty middle distance of his cold office, remembering his encounter in the alley with the two goons in gas masks. He shook his head.

"If you sent your thugs to ask me that very same question, why bother calling me about it? Or why bother sending the heavies in when you could just have called?"

"Calling you is a considerable difficulty, Mr Bradley."

"That so?"

"Indeed yes," Nimrod said over a pop and a crackle. His voice matched Carson's perfectly. Maybe they were related. "I would have come personally, but that is not advisable under the current circumstances."

"That so?" Rad repeated.

"It is, Mr Bradley. Now, I want..."

"Oh, now look here, Mr Nimrod, or whatever you call yourself," Rad cut in swiftly. He was tired and had really had enough of mysteries, for possibly one entire lifetime. "Nineteen fifty what? Dollars in the bank? Flowers in the park? Number of times you're going to ask me what I know about nineteen fifty? It's late, I'm tired, and I don't appreciate your calling, and I certainly don't appreciate that little visit from your friends. If you have a job for me, then money talks and I'm all ears. Otherwise it's good night, I think. And don't call again."

Rad gripped the earpiece. His blood was boiling and he didn't have time for games, but he knew well what nuggets you could pick up on the end of a phone when the other person thinks you've gone. He waited, and as the gap in the conversation grew so did the static in the earpiece, expanding to fill the void. When Nimrod spoke again, his voice cut through the background roar with surprising clarity.

"I apologise, Mr Bradley, but we had to be sure."

"Huh," said Rad. "Sure of what?"

The tutting again. "That we had the right man. And it seems we did. Nineteen fifty means nothing, does it?"

Rad let a whispered curse slip out, happy for it to be lost across the bad connection. "*Criminy*... nineteen-fifty what, Mr Nimrod?"

The white noise grew again, but this time the voice came back quickly. "We must talk, Mr Bradley. Face to face. It will be difficult. Do you understand? Travelling to your city presents certain... problems to overcome. We will need your assistance."

Rad pressed the earpiece against his hot ear and drew the mouthpiece up until it was almost touching his lips. Finally, someone was talking.

"I'm listening," he said at last. "Tell me what to do."

SIXTEEN

RAD WAS NERVOUS, there was no doubt about it, but it
was amazing the difference some hours of sleep made. And
a stiff drink. He balanced the delicate teacup between
thumb and forefinger, and considered maybe that Jerry's
liquor was not the best breakfast beverage. But then it was
already six in the evening, and dark outside, and the rain
had returned, so Rad considered that maybe this was a pre-
dinner drink, and therefore perfectly acceptable.

He'd slept, and the sleep was the most glorious he'd ever
had. Rad was keen on sleep. He was a fan. Not just for the
addictive quality of it, the natural means of recharging
and refreshing that every human being needed. He was
keen on sleep because in his line of work – where days
were filled with loose ends and blind alleys, and leads
that go nowhere and questions that go unanswered – it
fixed things. With the conscious mind, with all its stupid
questioning and unhelpful, confusing thoughts out of the
way, out for the night, it was the subconscious that took
over, the *real* power behind the throne. Left alone and
unbothered by the waking mind, it could spend the sleeping hours collating and crosschecking data, filing
memories, analysing observations. The number of times a
case had been solved, or at least progressed to an appreciable

degree, thanks to nothing more than a good night's sleep, was high.

Although on this morning – afternoon, evening, whatever – Rad had nothing. The subconscious had been busy, that much he knew, but had been unable to piece anything together that was of much use. Rad tried not to let it bother him. He had a feeling that the case of now-confirmed dead Sam Saturn was going to involve Kane and his captain friend more than it should, but Ms Kopek hadn't called in yet for an update like she said she would, so there was time still to get some answers. The case was going to be handy for paying a few bills, which was a remarkable motivator. As Rad ordered a second drink, he carefully checked the contents of his wallet. With Jerry's open slate, poverty hadn't been as good for the soul or body as Rad had hoped.

Jerry passed a fresh cup and saucer, and took the spent one away with a tearoom clatter. "You're looking better."

Rad nodded but Jerry's back was turned. "Thanks, Jerry. Amazing what a little shut-eye is good for."

Jerry turned back with a smile. "Ain't that the truth? Don't forget I'm clearing the slates on Friday. You've got a few lines there."

"Ah," said Rad, vaguely, aware that his eyebrows had moved up entirely on their own, pushing his white hat high on his forehead. Jerry's eyes watched Rad's rebellious forehead, then he smiled again and shook his head.

"Friday, my friend."

"Ah," said Rad again, this time pushing his hat back down and nodding. "Good call, Jerry. No problem." He glanced down the bar. "You seen Kane?"

Jerry's lips pursed for a moment. "Yesterday, last night. Didn't you speak to him? He was sittin' right there."

"Didn't see him." Rad shook his head. "Doesn't matter."

The last thing Rad had thought of as he had drifted off to

sleep in his tiny bed the previous night – morning, afternoon, whatever – was what Nimrod had told him, and the
first thing Rad had thought of as he had woken up an hour
ago was to grab Kane and tell him all about it.

But Kane wasn't here, and the more Rad thought, and
the more Rad drank, perhaps there were some things that
he *didn't* need to talk to Kane about. Things like Nimrod's
little phone call. He ran the instructions over in his head.
They were specific and they were weird, but Rad wasn't
going to argue.

Rad drained the last of his drink. That settled it. It was nothing to do with Kane or the Captain or Katherine Kopek or
Sam Saturn or anyone. This was a private matter for a private
detective. His own personal case, in more ways than one.

"Thanks, Jerry," said Rad, waving one hand as he slipped
from the bar and stole up the stairs to the street above. Six
thirty-five. Time enough. He was expecting company, and
had some things to prepare.

SEVENTEEN

THE EMPIRE STATE WAS AN ISLAND, long and narrow, at the head of which the great naval dockyards lay, from where the great ironclad fleets sailed to fight the Enemy every Fleet Day. What lay across the water was difficult to determine. Most of the time the city was bounded with thick fog that stuck to the sides of the island like sticky cotton candy. Sometimes citizens of the Empire State reported lights in the mist, sometimes even sounds that came drifting over the water, but usually this was followed by a swift arrest for sedition, or breaking the Prohibition or whatever made-up charge seemed most appropriate. This was Wartime, and the Empire State was all, and there was nothing on the other side of the water. Only the brave ironclad crews left the Empire State to face the Enemy, and none of them had yet returned to tell of their journey beyond the fog.

At its height, tendrils of the stuff left the borders and crept into the city. Mist encircled the Empire State Building, the tallest structure on the island, and seemed almost to spread outwards from it, wrapping around the other skyscrapers and office blocks and civic buildings.

Above that, the cloud cover was low and thick, lit orange and yellow by the lights of the city at night, dark and heavy with rain yet to fall. Police blimps hugged the underside of the clouds, their distinctive twin searchlights probing the city below. Anything under the clouds was immediately visible. Anything above would be hidden, but nothing ever flew above the clouds.

The Enemy airship drifted sideways silently, then stopped. At this altitude the Empire State was just a brilliant orange smudge below cloud deck. The police blimps cruised sedately nearby, looking downwards, never thinking to look *upwards*, where nothing ever flew. The only structure that penetrated the cover was the spire of the Empire State Building, the very tip of its antennae, with the solitary red light blinking a beacon out to the nothingness.

The airship hovered for a while, safe above the clouds. It had no lights anyway, and was made of black iron, rendering it practically invisible in the night.

It was rumoured that the Enemy had an ironclad fleet of its own, but not one waterborne, one that sailed through the sky like the police blimps. But not mere patrol craft, a fleet of warships as powerful and gigantic as the ironclads, made of armour plate and piloted by an ironclad crew. But it was just a rumour, a story whispered in the speakeasies and late at night in the bad parts of town, out of earshot of the Empire State. It was impossible, of course. The police blimps were just helium-filled aerostats, a product of science. Anything else – anything like an iron warship that could float in the air as easily as the Empire fleet could float on the water – was just ridiculous, at best a bad bedtime story for naughty children, one that didn't scare but rather amused. Flying ships? Who would believe that?

The floating fortress, five thousand tonnes of iron and steel, dark and silent, hung in the air above the city, and waited.

EIGHTEEN

SOMEONE WAS IN THE APARTMENT. Rad knew it as soon as he got back. He hesitated at the end of the hallway for just a moment, holding his breath, listening. He was expecting company, sure, and he had his instructions, which he now ran through his head in detail, step by step. This wasn't part of the plan.

From the corner by the top of the stairs, he could see that his door was closed, but not locked. The building was old, and the door cheap, and when the lock engaged it sucked the door to its frame. When unlocked there was a hairline gap. Nobody would know it, unless it was their own door, and they happened to be a private investigator habitually looking for silly details.

Well, OK. He was expecting guests and he had his instructions from Nimrod, and while he thought they didn't include this, perhaps he'd missed a bit, or misunderstood something, or maybe Nimrod had left a step out.

Rad started walking down the hallway, and then stopped with a wince as the floorboard beneath the threadbare carpet creaked. He stopped and looked down, watching his shoes as if it would make any difference, and had another thought.

What if it was Kane? Well, he wouldn't break in, but sometimes he walked in like he owned the place, and the door was unlocked. Except Kane was the last person he wanted to see right now. He wanted to put the strangeness of recent days behind him and focus on his own little problem and his own little meeting that Nimrod had set up. If it was Kane, he'd have to get rid of him.

Another step, another creak, and another thought. What if it was Ms Kopek? She hadn't got in touch like she said she would, and surely was expecting news of her lover. Not for the first time, Rad wondered what the hell he would tell her. But it couldn't be her, because she wouldn't break in either.

But he didn't remember leaving the door unlocked, although it wouldn't have been the first time. Goddammit. Rad patted his coat, feeling for the bundle of keys in the pocket on his left breast, like that would make a difference too.

Breathing again, Rad shrugged, got the keys out – just in case – and moved swiftly to his office. He opened the door and stepped in without breaking his pace, closing the door smartly and quietly behind him before turning back to the room.

It was empty. Maybe nobody was here and he'd left the door unlocked, again, and maybe he needed to get his sleep rhythms back in check so he didn't have to walk around his own building in the middle of the night hallucinating about burglars and unwelcome guests. His hat hit the desk and his coat found its hook, and as Rad headed for the connecting door that led to his apartment, he remembered he'd used the last of this month's coffee ration just the other day. He swore loudly and began searching the cupboards for something else to drink.

There. Just as he thumped the last cupboard closed, there was another sound in the apartment. Tiny, just a creak, but not a sound that Rad made. He paused, still bent over by the cupboard, before slowly raising himself up.

OK, it made sense. Nimrod set the meeting up, and Rad had given himself plenty of time to prepare like he was told,

but given the circumstances it was logical for Nimrod's people to check the scene out ahead of time. No problem. Which meant Rad was supposed to just get on with it, apparently oblivious to the unseen watcher or watchers. Rad really had no idea where they could be hiding, but who knew what Nimrod was capable of. Maybe making two goons in gas masks invisible was just one of his party tricks.

OK, relax. Just make a coffee without any actual coffee and then get the room set up. Easy.

The drink was foul, a mix of hot water and something which Rad had thought was loose leaf tea in the back of another cupboard, but which he really wasn't sure of now he was actually drinking the stuff. But it was warming, and if he stopped breathing through his nose as he swallowed, he could pretend it was tea. He sat on the edge of the bed, and regarded his wardrobe through the haze of steam from his mug. Double doors, which opened out and folded back almost completely. Good. He set the mug down on the bedside table, flicked the side light on and then stood and killed the main light. The room went from hard white to soft yellow, the overhead strip light giving way to the shaded incandescent bulb of the table lamp. That was the first part. Minimise reflections. Rad checked this off on his mental list as he skipped over the single bed and closed the curtain over the large window that looked out over the night outside. Another reflection quenched.

Rad didn't have much stuff. Well, actually he did, but until he signed Claudia's papers they were held "in trust" by the Empire State. A nice insurance policy, or perhaps outright bribery. Rad had given up worrying about it, happy that he had his grandfather clock at least. For the moment he was also pleased he didn't have to rearrange things in the small room so much as he rolled the thin rectangular rug up to reveal old, worn, and quite wonderful floorboards.

Rad paused, smiling, and thought perhaps the boards were much nicer than the rug itself.

Step three. He clomped over to the wardrobe, his footsteps percussive in the small room and reminding him why he had the rug down. He unlatched the doors, and swung them open. A few minutes later he'd cleared the items – ties, suspenders, belts; all old and ratty – that hung from racks affixed to the backs of the doors and dumped them on the bed. The doors, and their two mirrors, were clear.

Rad walked backwards and sat on the bed as soon as he felt its edge against the back of his knees. He picked up his mug, checked his watch, and waited. There were twenty minutes to go.

Rad woke up with a jerk, and knew at once the biggest mistake he had made was the eight hours of sleep he'd treated himself to yesterday. They were sheer bliss, and when he'd gotten up he felt revived and invigorated and very happy. But sleep was like a drug. It was a physical addiction, and now Rad had fallen off the wagon. Now his body wanted it more than ever, and at every opportunity it would tug his consciousness down under the blankets to where it was soft and warm and dark.

And now he had a stiff neck from lying awkwardly on the bed. His legs were still bent at the knee, hanging off the edge of the bed from where he had been sitting, what, ten minutes ago? Rad didn't remember falling asleep. He sat up slowly and painfully, his body made of lead and his head made, conversely, of something approaching sponge. His fingers dragged his eyelids around as he rubbed them dry. He sighed, and looked at his watch.

"Hell in a handbasket!" He came to his feet even as he drew breath to curse, and looked wildly around the room. The wardrobe doors, so carefully cleared of random, musty business attire, were closed. Rad had slept for an hour. He had missed Nimrod's appointment.

Rad swore again, and paced the room looking for something to kick. With the few items of furniture neatly tucked away according to Nimrod's instructions, there was nothing within reach, so after a few seconds Rad settled for throwing the bent roll of rug down onto the floorboards. It hit them with a satisfying *woof*, sending a surprisingly large cloud of dust up into the middle of the room. Rad coughed; his eyes closed as he waved the stale particles away.

"Good evening, detective."

Rad opened his eyes and almost sneezed. Framed in the doorway connecting the back room to the main office stood a black shape with shining white eyes. The intruder filled the doorway almost entirely, shoulders rubbing on the jamb and the tall helmet leaving just half an inch to spare. When the figure turned his head, there was a creak of thick leather and a rattle, something metallic like chain mail. His cloak pooled across the floor like a small, dark lake.

The Skyguard. Rad's shoulders tensed. He'd tried to forget about his rescue in the alleyway, now knowing that the two goons were in the employ of Nimrod. Maybe there hadn't been any connection between his mysterious caller and the city's deceased protector. Maybe someone had just taken up the Skyguard's mantle and arty mask thing and had just interrupted Rad's mugging by chance.

But having slept an hour, having missed Nimrod, and with the wardrobe's twin doors shut (and it sure wasn't Rad who had shut them), and with the Skyguard as large as life in his office, Rad knew there had to be a link. Nimrod and the Skyguard, with Rad in the middle. This complicated things.

"Detective?" The Skyguard took a step forward, cloak swimming silently across the floorboards. "You don't seem surprised to see me. I apologise if I interrupted your plans.

But you don't want anything to do with Nimrod, trust me."
His voice was a hoarse, metallic whisper.

Rad laughed. It was an unhappy sound, and as he sat
back on the bed he was shaking his head.

"What is this? The 'Second Appearance'? You gonna pop
up three times and grant me a wish? Or is there some mys-
tic prophecy to fulfil?"

The Skyguard didn't react, but maybe there was a hiss of
impatience from behind the front grille of his helmet.

Rad's mouth was dry, but he was well used to that sensation. He looked up at the uninvited guest. The Skyguard was
just a black outline in the long shadow cast by the table lamp.

"Y'see," said Rad, talking more to himself than the Skyguard, "dead people tend to stay dead. And if dead people
turn up not dead, then they're not dead. By definition, if you
see what I mean. But when that happens – and believe me,
it happens – it means that the person who didn't die wanted
to make everyone else think they *had*. There are a variety of
reasons for that, all of them nefarious. Which gets me thinking: The Skyguard – the State's most notorious felon, no
less... well, after the Pastor of Lost Souls, but let's not go
there – has been in the clink since the beginning of time, and
then finally meets his maker in a State-assisted manner. So
we've got three options. The Skyguard wasn't executed and
it was all a big cover cooked up by the Chairman of the City
Commissioners. And I wouldn't put it past him. Number
two: the Skyguard, being all fancy with his gadgets and giz-
mos and amazing powers, can survive death and/or come
back from the grave. Until this week I wouldn't even have
thought of that option, but it's been a strange few days, so
I'm not putting that past him. Third, the sensible, sane option, is that the Skyguard *is* dead as advertised, and
someone collected his costume in an everything-must-go,
two-for-one offer."

Rad finished and rubbed his scalp. The room was silent, until the Skyguard or the floorboards, or both, creaked. When the Skyguard spoke, his low voice made Rad jump. It was unidentifiable, disguised by something fancy. Rad wondered who was inside the suit.

"Are you finished?"

"Huh," said Rad, and then after a second, "Yes, I've finished."

The Skyguard folded his tree trunk arms and in the low light Rad's eye caught the glint of metal and chain, and creases in the otherwise tight leather. He pouted. The design and material was familiar to him somehow.

"The truth, detective, is that this *is* the second appearance of the Skyguard, if you want to call it that. I've been watching you, just to be sure I had the right man. If Nimrod has been in contact, then I definitely have."

"Friend of yours?"

The Skyguard ignored the interjection. "You may not remember, or know it at all, but I'm the city's sworn protector. The City Commissioners will have you think otherwise. Nimrod as well. But I'm not in the habit of lying, and I haven't come into the open without good reason."

Rad was looking at the floor. He rubbed his chin. "Enemy then. Commissioners too."

The Skyguard paused, which made Rad smile. Rad might be mostly floundering in the dark, without much of a clue, but the Skyguard was... nervous? Maybe not. He was trying to *impress* Rad. So what did the Skyguard want with an average, mostly unemployed private dick like him? And what would make a hardened criminal – sorry, the city's protector – so nervous? Rad knew that if he kept pushing, maybe something would give. It was worth the risk.

Rad stood up, and walked towards the Skyguard. The Skyguard didn't move, but his costume creaked again as he straightened his back. Standing at just a few feet's distance,

Rad saw that the man was actually about his height, maybe just a little shorter. It was the helmet, armour and cloak that made him look so bulky. Like a cat that puffs up to scare other cats in a territorial war.

"What do you want, Mr Skyguard? I've got a murder case to solve, and I'm pretty busy really. I'm just a private detective trying to earn a crust, and quite frankly I can do without your brand of mystery."

Another sound came from the armoured man, and with the distortion introduced by the winged helmet, it took Rad a few seconds to work out what it was. The Skyguard was laughing. Rad felt his face flush hotly as his temper rose.

"This some kind of joke?"

The Skyguard shook his great head, the white eyes embedded in the helmet shining brightly.

"Mr Bradley, you are more important than you think. That's why Nimrod wants you. That's why I want you. I can help solve your murder case and I can stop Nimrod and his men from skinning you alive in the process. He's dangerous, Mr Bradley. If I hadn't been here, we wouldn't be having this conversation now, let me assure you."

Rad frowned and motioned towards the closed wardrobe. "You knew about all this?"

"Like I said, I've been watching you," said the Skyguard as he slowly walked around the room. Rad backed off a little, keeping a certain distance from the intruder as he moved about. "When I overheard your conversation with Nimrod, I had to step in. I apologise for the sleep gas, but it seemed to be the easiest option."

Rad had been saved for a second time, and he hadn't realised. He laughed, and shook his head, and rubbed his scalp, and went back to sit on the bed.

"And the information from Nimrod? Nineteen fifty?"

The Skyguard stopped, and if his face hadn't been hidden

behind the front of the helmet Rad could have sworn he was looking wistfully into the middle distance.

"Lies," said the Skyguard, quickly. "All lies. Nimrod himself is a lie. He is not who he says he is."

"Well, he hasn't exactly been clear on that matter." Rad nodded towards the wardrobe. "What about the instructions? They were a little kooky, to say the least."

The Skyguard went over the wardrobe and opened one of the doors. He leaned in, checking something, then closed it and repeated the motion with the other door.

"They were. You followed them to the letter. You didn't know they would lead to your death."

The Skyguard yanked the second door back. Rad shot up from the bed and balled his fists, ready for whatever the Skyguard had found. Instead, the Skyguard pushed a gauntleted fist into the back of the door. The mirror shattered and dropped from its frame in a rain of shards. The Skyguard flung the first door open, and did the same. He stood back, surveyed the broken glass on the floor, then picked at the remaining triangular fragments that were still stuck to the inside of the wardrobe doors. When they were free of any trace of mirror, he looked at his feet and began grinding the larger fragments into dust with his armoured boots.

Rad whistled. "I get the picture."

"Avoid mirrors. Avoid all reflections, if you can."

"Yeah, I got it." Rad relaxed a little. The need for drink and for sleep rose again, but he gulped down a trickle of saliva and focussed to clear his head.

"So, what, you're my personal protector now? What does Nimrod want? Hell, what do you want? How do I know I can trust you?"

"Nimrod and I want the same thing, although for different, opposing reasons." The Skyguard's helmet turned to Rad and the hero walked up to the detective. Rad stood, and barely an inch remained between his nose and the Skyguard's slanted, wickedly sharp mask.

"I need your help, Mr Bradley, to save the world. The Empire State may not be perfect, but it's in more danger than you can possibly comprehend. The city has only days left."

Rad's breath condensed on the front of the Skyguard's mask, throwing up a dull grey mist on the black metal that ebbed and flowed like the tide. "Days left until what?"

"You misunderstand, detective. The Empire State has days left to *exist.*"

Rad drank the water gratefully. He wanted – needed – something stronger, but that would have to wait. Water would do, lukewarm and sharp with rust from his building's decrepit plumbing.

The Skyguard hadn't moved for a while. Beneath his boots the pulverised mirror fragments crackled like frost as the Skyguard shifted his weight from one foot to another. Arms folded, he stood with legs astride the mess like the triumphant hero he claimed to be.

"An attack? Here?" Rad's question broke the silence. The Skyguard didn't reply but inclined his head to look at his host. Even the slightest movement was exaggerated by the elaborate shaping of the winged helmet.

"Yes," said the Skyguard finally. Rad sighed and gulped another mouthful of water.

"What do you need me for? Can't the city defend itself? Can't you *help* the city defend itself?"

"Your role will be revealed when it is safe to do so. Nimrod is still after you, probably more so now he knows that I've intervened again. For the moment, you should know that this is no ordinary act of war. An attack is coming, one that will end Wartime once and for all, but not to our benefit. The Empire State will, literally, cease to exist."

Rad nodded. "OK, fine, need to know."

"I'm glad you understand, Mr Bradley. You are connected. That's enough information for now. As for the attack, it will be subtle. The Enemy strike could be detected and prevented if only the city defences were looking. But they're not. Nimrod is not the only traitor here."

"Wait," said Rad, letting the empty mug hang from his hand. "The City Commissioners?"

The Skyguard nodded once. "They have helped plan the attack. They have betrayed us all."

"I must be dreaming."

"This is no dream, detective."

Rad closed his eyes and rubbed his scalp. He needed to shave his head again. Three days of growth had left it as rough as sandpaper.

"You said a subtle attack, under the city's defences? How can that destroy us?"

The Skyguard held up a hand. He turned and looked through the connecting door, then strode briskly to the window behind Rad's single bed. Careful to avoid reflections, he pulled the edge of the curtain back, covering as much of his mask as possible as he peered out into the street like an old nosy neighbour. He stood like this for a minute, looking at something on the dark street below.

"I have to go," he said at last, pulling the curtain closed. "I'll be in touch again. The city is against us, but we are its only hope, you and I."

Rad stood up from the bed and walked over to the Skyguard, his face set.

"Now look here. This better be the real deal. I don't have time for games." Rad flicked his hand at the Skyguard's chest, the back of his fingers slapping at the breastplate. It was leather and metal, and had a waxy texture. Rad frowned, his fingertips stinging from the hit.

The Skyguard and Rad Bradley stood together for a moment in silence. Then the Skyguard brushed Rad aside, and strode from the room. Rad stood still, listening to his heavy footfalls in the office.

"I'll be in touch, Mr Bradley." And then the office door closed.

Nine o'clock. Rad needed a drink, and he needed to find Kane and squeeze him about the ironclad, Sam Saturn, and Captain Carson.

And Captain Carson's mysterious equipment, including underwater suits made of waxed leather and metal.

NINETEEN

KANE WAS HOLDING UP THE BAR, several spent teacups before him. Rad wasn't sure if he was surprised to see him or not, but was just thankful he'd been spared a trek around the city. The yellow of the streetlights gave him a headache, and the constant drizzle gave him backache, and the two combined did wonders for his temperament. With the Skyguard putting in a second appearance, Rad desperately needed to put his friend in the loop and enrol his help. He was in too deep to go it alone now. He should have gone to Kane earlier.

Rad caught Jerry's eye. The barman nodded and poured him a drink even as Rad was walking across the floor, but as he rattled the cup and saucer on the bar he rubbed the fingers and thumb of his right hand together, holding them out for Rad to see.

Rad nodded briskly. "Yeah, Friday, got it." The barman turned his back, apparently satisfied. "Thanks, Jerry," Rad added. Jerry grunted and cleaned teacups.

"Been lookin' for you, kid," said Rad, picking his cup up and turning to Kane. Kane's eyes were closed and he was leaning against the bar heavily. "I got developments..." He paused and counted the number of cups in front of his friend, and wondered why Jerry hadn't cleared so many of them away. "Everything OK? How's the newspaper?"

Kane snorted, a sound Rad hadn't heard from him before. The reporter leaned back on his barstool and smiled lopsidedly at Rad. His big eyes were red and he stank of Jerry's rough liquor.

"Oh, the paper. Fine and dandy, I guess. I wouldn't know." Kane swayed back a little on the barstool, then leaned forward again on the bar. He was smiling, but not looking at Rad. The smile was empty, fixed.

"The what now?"

"I said I wouldn't know. Papa don't work there no more."

Rad heaved himself onto the neighbouring stool. "What do you mean, you don't work at the newspaper? You're Kane Fortuna, star reporter. Right?"

Kane frowned and gave a half-hearted, noncommittal shrug. "You'd think. Not any more." He swigged the last of his latest cup and finally met Rad's eye. "Nothing to do with me, anyway. This is the Empire State. The Empire State controls the media, controls the newspapers. Controls my newspaper." He raised a cup and gave a theatrical bow, as best as possible while sitting intoxicated on a barstool. "My services are no longer required, it seems."

Rad didn't speak but exhaled loudly. That seemed enough sympathy for Kane, who thumped Rad on the shoulder as he surveyed the multitude of empty cups before him. Then his eyes widened, and his hand returned to Rad's shoulder.

"Say, you need a partner? I mean an official one that gets paid actual money? See, I know this guy who's looking for work. Goes by the name Kane Fortuna. He's a dish."

Kane's expression was deadly serious for a moment, before splitting into another of his characteristically wide grins. "To business!" He held an empty cup up for a toast.

Rad couldn't help but laugh, but shook his head. "Let's talk when you're a little more... cogent, shall we say." He shuffled himself on the stool and hugged the bar with his not insubstantial stomach. He tapped the rim of his hat at the back with one hand and flipped it off the front of his head with the other. Kane was no use drunk. Might as well suck it up and enjoy himself. They could plan to save the city in the morning.

"Tell you what though," said Kane, slapping Rad's arm to get his attention. "Before I got the sack I was talking to my friends at city hall. You thought the ironclad was weird... right?"

Rad craned his head to the left and right, scanning Jerry's establishment. It wasn't even ten, the night was young, and the place was more or less empty. Even so, Rad wasn't keen on attention. He turned to Kane and leaned in on his friend, patting him gently on one shirtsleeved arm.

"What?" he whispered, hoping Kane would get the idea.

Kane leaned over. Rad held his breath to avoid being gassed by his friend's.

"I said, you thought the ironclad was weird, right?"

Rad raised an eyebrow. "Uh... yes, I did."

Kane leaned back quickly, smiling like a cat. He even winked, then leaned back in, only just pulling up before knocking foreheads with Rad.

"Well, there's more than that. There's something else in the city."

"What kind of something?"

Kane's voice was barely audible, even at zero range. "Something." Kane raised one hand and pointed up at the ceiling. Rad caught the motion out of the corner of his eye, but said nothing. Kane emphasised the point, stabbing his finger upwards.

"Something in the air. Arrived last night. Just outside city limits. Some kind of ship."

"An airship? What, like a police blimp?"

Kane shook his head, stopped, then nodded. "I guess. But it's not a police blimp, and it's *above* the clouds. Looking down."

"Now you're just making things up."

"OK, maybe not *looking down*. But there it is. Police haven't spotted it yet, probably won't. An Enemy warship. You know the stories about the Enemy? How they have their own iron-clads, but they fly, while ours are just big boats?"

Rad sneered as he sipped from his cup. "Yeah, I'm sure. Invasion by single airship?"

Kane looked unhappy, and swivelled around on his barstool. "Well, why not?" He sounded like a hurt child. "Who knows what those sons of bitches have up their evil sleeves."

Rad finished his drink, savouring the heat in his throat. Then he remembered what the Skyguard had said. His teacup hit the saucer hard enough to crack the china. He pushed it aside noisily, hopped off his stool, and grabbed Kane by his shoulders. He shook his friend, gently, and turned him on the stool so they were face to face.

"An airship? A single airship, and the city knows, but the police don't? *Goddammit*, Kane, we're in deep now. The whole city is."

Kane blinked, apparently unaware of Rad's urgency.

"How do you know?" Kane asked.

"The Skyguard told me. Had another visit. Was going to tell you about it. Damn it, how much have you had to drink? You need to think, boy. You got any coffee ration left?"

Kane rubbed his forehead. "Ah... yeah, plenty. I don't drink it. The Skyguard again?"

"Yessir."

"But..."

"The Skyguard is dead," said Rad. "Yes, I know. Just no-body has told him that yet. Come on."

Rad helped Kane off his stool, grabbed his jacket, and waved to Jerry as they headed up the stairs.

TWENTY

KANE FORTUNA'S APARTMENT was not what Rad had
expected. Although they'd been friends for, well, forever,
for as long as either of them could remember anyway, Rad
had never been to Kane's place. Kane had made himself
at home in Rad's office-apartment regularly, but only because it was close to the newspaper office and, given their
frequent collaborations, was an easy place to meet. That,
and it was close to Jerry's – and Rad hadn't been able to
find another speakeasy that was prepared to give him
quite as much room on the slate. Rad thought about this
as he helped Kane with his keys, blinking as his inebriated
friend breathed heavily all over his face as they hunched
over the door.

Kane's fingers eventually picked the right key, and the
key eventually found the lock. Kane spun the doorknob and
swung the door inward. The brass globe of the handle rattled until Rad stilled the vibration as he closed the door
quietly behind them.

Familiarity with the internal layout of the apartment
meant that Kane was able to stagger with remarkable accu-
racy around the furniture, despite his drunkenness. After
watching him for a moment to make sure Kane wasn't
going to fall over or walk into anything hard, Rad let him

do his own thing and paced the hallway slowly, taking in everything around him.

The front door opened directly onto the street. Behind the door was a short hallway, three doors leading off. The single light in the high ceiling cast a warm glow over the walls, which were festooned with pictures. Rad slipped his hat off and found his eyes crawling over the images, taking them all in. Colours and shapes punched out from the wall, and Rad realised they weren't just pictures, they were posters. Theatre posters, in bold and bright colours, showcasing the Empire State's finest artistes as they entertained a city locked in Wartime. He recognised a few of the more famous shows... *Zoo City Nights, The Boneshaker, Supergods, Forevermore*. But Kane was clearly more dedicated to the stage than Rad, which was not at all. There were dozens of posters, fliers and placards, some pinned naked to the wall, others behind glass or surrounded by frames.

A few caught Rad's eye and he peered closer. Well now, that explained a lot. Kane's wide-eyed baby-doll face peered back at Rad from the wall. Swirling cloaks, top hats and tails, wide suits and large hats. Never top billing, but frequently second or third. A couple of posters – older ones, it looked, the way the edges had frayed – showed Kane's likeness but he wasn't credited as far as Rad could tell, unless it was under a stage name. Seemed Kane had more than a passing interest.

Kane reappeared from around one of the open doorways and he smiled broadly. Rad's face split into a grin as well; he couldn't help it. The posters were impressive and unexpected.

"You've been keeping a secret, Mr Fortuna."

Kane laughed. "A man needs a hobby. Doesn't pay what you think it might." Kane leaned further into the hallway, hanging onto the doorway for dear life. "Detective, you're in charge of the coffee." He hooked a thumb over his shoulder.

"Kitchen and coffee. Make a pot, join me in here." He clawed himself back into the room.

Rad nodded at nobody, and walked to the kitchen.

After an hour, they'd drained the pot. Actually Kane had drank most of it – four cups in all. Rad nursed his own single cup, although the aroma of coffee drove him out of his mind. But coffee was a precious commodity in Wartime, and he'd made his bed. Kane's coffee ration belonged to Kane. Rad respected that, and knew that Kane was exaggerating when he said he never touched the stuff. But boy, did Kane need it now. Rad was more than happy to hold back.

They were sitting in what Rad could only think of as a cross between a parlour and a study. It was a room of browns and oranges, of old worn sofas swamped with rugs and tired cushions. There was a large writing desk against one wall, a huge roll-top number with about a million drawers ranging in size from a small coffin to a matchbox. It was covered with paper, and there was a typewriter centre stage.

The walls of the room were plastered with more theatrical posters. The large bay windows, which would have looked out onto the street, were hidden behind gigantic brown and red embroidered drapes. The room had a warmth that Rad found immensely comforting, and he realised how sterile and un-lived in his own makeshift accommodation was. Kane seemed to share a similar taste in old-fashioned decor as his friend Captain Carson. Rad mentioned this, and Kane agreed, although he found it far more hilarious than Rad had intended.

Kane sucked down the coffee and listened dutifully as Rad laid out the conversation he'd had with Nimrod and then the Skyguard. The coffee seemed to work. Kane was sobering. He kept his mouth closed, but his eyes rarely left Rad's. They were red and bleary. Occasionally he'd twitch his nose, which he held low over his coffee cup, inhaling the aromatic steam.

Rad sat back when he was finished, and took a sip of his coffee. It had cooled a little too much in his cup, but was still wonderful.

Kane didn't say anything for a while, but closed his eyes, breathing in the steam from his freshly poured cup, before draining it with a gulp and a gasp. He opened his eyes.

"Thanks for making the coffee."

"No problem."

"An interesting situation."

"Sure is."

Kane shook his head. "We need more information."

"That we do," said Rad.

Kane set his cup down on the low table between his sofa and Rad's armchair. "You're important. Both sides want you. Which do you pick?"

"Both sides want me?"

Kane shrugged. "Well, on the one hand you've got Nimrod and his men. On the other you've got the Skyguard." Kane held his hands forward, palms up, to illustrate the point.

"Well," Rad said at length, drawing out the vowel sound. "I'm not sure this all just isn't one load of hokey. Nimrod sounded like a nice guy, but his instructions to meet him were all kinds of weird. But this is the real world. I've seen a whole heap of oddness in my line of work – you too, star reporter – but you can't just get one crank woofing about the power of the atom in your ear and just believe it like that." He snapped his fingers, but they were too thick for the gesture and the intended sound was damp. But he figured Kane got the picture. Rad continued.

"And it's not the Skyguard, it's someone pretending to be him. Hell, you put anyone in that suit and you couldn't tell them from you or me. I appreciated his interference a few days back, but it's the same story. No manner of fancy hat and cloak will convince me that the world is about to end." Rad paused and then leaned forward. He stabbed a finger at Kane. "And, I might add, all that gear doesn't mean you can go waltzing into just anyone's apartment. Oh no!" He sat back, and folded his arms, feeling somewhat better.

Kane smiled, showing big teeth filmed yellow by the strong coffee. "Better?"

"Better," said Rad, and laughed, but the sleeves of his coat pinched as he folded his arms even tighter.

"But...?"

Rad sighed. "Yeah, *but* is right. The Skyguard said an attack would come, under the nose of the Empire State. An infiltrator, entering the city with the permission – perhaps even assistance – of the City Commissioners."

"The airship."

"The airship is damn right." Rad shook his head. "There have been too many coincidences in the last few days. There's a connection, has to be."

Kane leaned back, the leather of his ancient sofa letting out a gentle *foosh* as he sank into its deflated back cushion.

"The airship and the ironclad," he whispered. Kane ran the tip of his tongue over the very edge of his lips. As if to punctuate his statement, the wind gusted outside, howling faintly and causing the heavy drapes over the bay window to move.

Rad watched them settle. Must have been quite a breeze to shift them, he thought.

"'The Airship and the Ironclad'," Kane repeated. "Sounds like a good headline for the *Sentinel*."

"Or one of your shows," said Rad, nodding at the posters on the wall.

"I guess it followed the ironclad back. Some kind of scout, perhaps?" Kane turned on the sofa and drew his legs up to his chest. Kicking his shoes off, he stretched out horizontally on the leather and rested one forearm on his forehead. "So what do you want to do? Wait for the Sky-guard's next call?"

Rad nodded, although Kane was staring at the ceiling. "I guess. Avoid Nimrod."

"So no phone calls."

"You got that right. *Inbound*, anyway. I need to call Katherine Kopek and give her an update."

Kane's arm swung down and he turned his head to face his friend.

"What are you gonna tell her?"

Rad shrugged. "Nothing in particular. The fewer people we involve in this, the better."

"Good plan, Stan." Kane yawned and stretched his arms out. "Here's a thing. No more drinking, ever. Thanks for the coffee and the company."

Rad sat for a while, not saying anything, before summoning the strength to stand. He cast one more look around Kane's remarkable room, picked up his hat and waved it at his host. Kane didn't register, his chest rising and falling in the gentle rhythm of sleep.

"I'll let myself out," Rad said quietly to himself, and slipped out of the room.

A few seconds later, the sound of Rad's big feet marching down the hallway was followed by the front door clicking shut.

Kane counted to ten, and opened his eyes. He glanced around the room, happy that Rad wasn't hanging around. He swung his legs over the edge of the sofa and sprang up. He jogged to the door with precise agility, and just to be sure checked behind it. The hallway was empty, and the front door was closed, the deadbolt automatically engaged after Rad had left.

Good.

Kane went back into the study, closed the door, and put his hands in his pockets as he turned to face the bay window drapes. He coughed, and grimaced as the taste of the coffee filled his mouth. He hated coffee, but Rad needed to think he was helping to sober him up. And after a dozen cups of tepid water at Jerry's and just a single half-cup of alcohol to get it on his breath, he felt like he'd drunk half of the harbour.

"He's gone. You can come out now."

A black gloved hand separated the curtains, paused, and the Science Pirate stepped into the room.

TWENTY-ONE

RAD WAITED OUTSIDE, hand squeezing the doorknob with some force. Realising this, he loosened his grip a little, and pressed himself up against the door. Ear to the frosted window, he counted the rings of the phone on his desk inside the office.

He didn't know why the telephone always started up just as he got to the top of the stairs at the end of his hallway. It was becoming a regular occurrence, and then Rad realised that maybe Nimrod's men were watching him. Or maybe, somehow, Nimrod himself could just *see* what Rad was doing. Nimrod's tall tale returned fleetingly to Rad's mind, but he pushed it away with a frown and squashed his cheek into the cold glass.

Nineteen... twenty. The phone died. Rad counted a few more seconds off, then opened the door. He stood behind it for a while, looking around his office, then shook his head and *harrumphed* loudly.

Was he being cautious, or paranoid? He wasn't sure, but to save himself becoming a shadow-jumper he decided to stick with the cynical, straight-down-the-line approach. Fantasy didn't come into it. He couldn't afford to be fanciful, not in his line of work. Rad's back touched his closed office door and for a moment he remembered his earlier cases, jobs that, while not necessarily easy or simple, were at least logical when you came down to it. He rolled back the memories, revelling a little in the nostalgia of past days. And then his face creased and his forehead furrowed, and he opened his eyes. The effects of Wartime did odd things to the memory. He couldn't remember what his first case was about.

There was a knock on the door, the report loud in the dead office and enough of a surprise that Rad pushed himself off the door and clean into the middle of the room. With his back still to the door, he called over his shoulder.

"Who is it?" He was sure whoever it was could hear his heart thundering down to the building lobby five floors below.

"I tried calling, Mr Bradley," said a woman's voice. It was small behind the door. Rad turned and saw a shadow with a hat move behind the glass.

Rad turned and reached for the door. Ms Katherine Kopek stood in the hallway, looking at the floor, one hand tugging on the opposite sleeve of her tunic. The startling red outfit was gone, replaced by a sombre affair in royal blue. Still striking, still full of class and reminding Rad plainly how low his own income was. He needed more clients like Ms Kopek.

"Ms Kopek, please come in," he said, straightening his voice into something serious and businesslike. OK, so he'd have to magic up a great story for her about Sam Saturn and his investigation, but so long as his voice was low and level and his eyebrows folded into an expression of professional concern, she'd buy anything he said. He'd done it before, it was part of the job. Occasionally a case would go on for too long, or, more likely, would be wrapped up so quickly Rad hardly had any time to generate any expenses. Sometimes you had to stretch the truth.

Ms Kopek stepped smartly into the room, but as soon as Rad closed the door and turned to face his client, her hand pressed his breastbone firmly. He stepped back until he hit the door, watching her fingers curve backwards as she pushed on his chest. He opened his mouth to speak, but his lips just formed an instinctive O-shape as she brought up her other hand. In it, she held a gun, compact, all squares and rectangles, the perfect size to keep in a fashionable woman's handbag. But her hand was shaking, and Rad noticed the wavering barrel was actually pointing at the back of her other hand, currently on his chest. If she intended to shoot – and Rad could tell already that she wouldn't – she'd blow it off in the process. Rad relaxed and let himself slump a little on the door.

"Don't move!" she shrieked at his movement. Her voice was high and broken, as frightened as the hand that held the gun.

Rad didn't, although he let his head tilt a little from side to side as he tried to gauge the kind of state that Ms Kopek was in. She watched him, her eyes wide and face frozen almost in surprise. Would she calm down and lower the weapon after a minute or so? Or would her nerves ratchet up enough that she'd start shooting anything in front of her out of pure fright?

Fright. At first Rad thought she was frightened by the gun, and frightened at finding herself at a time in her life where she, a lady of distinction and taste, with a distinctive and tasteful and *extensive* bank account, had somehow found herself at the wrong end of town holding a gun.

But maybe she wasn't frightened by that, exactly. Both hands were shaking now and the shakes spread over her body as tears started to well in her eyes. The pupils were tiny nothings in her light grey irises. Her breathing was shallow and fast; she was racing on pure adrenaline and... something else?

Rad watched her for a moment. She'd never held a gun before, that was easy enough to tell. The weapon was unfamiliar, her grip was too tight on it. And while he could imagine that she might have had a weapon in that small handbag – bought no doubt on the recommendation of friends or relatives, who merely shook their heads as they said the city wasn't what it used to be – this particular gun was an oddity. Small pocket revolvers were what frightened ladies carried. This was small but it was a semi-automatic.

"Who gave you the gun?" he asked.

Ms Kopek snapped her wrist higher, and the barrel moved in the direction of his face.

"Don't say a word, or I'll blow a hole in you!" Her words were fast, garbled, her gaze unfocussed.

"Who told you to say that?"

Ms Kopek's shakes seemed to pause for a moment as she thought. Her mouth turned down at the sides and her wet, wide eyes narrowed, just a hair or two. When she spoke again, her voice lacked that panicky edge that worried Rad.

"What do you mean?"

"I mean," Rad began, carefully picking his words and speaking slowly and clearly before realising he'd raised his hands against the door. He gently began to lower them back to his sides. "I mean, who gave you the gun and told you to come see me with it? Who sent you?"

The gun grip slackened and then the barrel moved back down to Rad's chest. She let the other hand drop, and as it hung by her side Rad watched her flex the fingers, moving the life back into them.

"I... it doesn't matter. This is important."

He nodded. "I'm sure it is, Ms Kopek." As he spoke, she closed her eyes and rubbed her forehead with the back of her gun hand. His eyes were locked on the end of the barrel. Inexperienced and nervous and armed, not to mention most likely doped, she was an accident waiting to happen.

"No, no," she said, shaking her head. She suddenly looked tired, and when she brought the gun back to bear she seemed to rock a little on her heels. The adrenaline rush and effects of whatever she'd been dosed with had abated, and she was turning grey, exhausted.

"No what, Ms Kopek?" Rad turned the volume up a notch. She was losing it and he was regaining control of the situation. Easy, easy does it.

"You have to... to stop. Stop investigating. Stop looking for... for..."

Rad's hands were now down at his sides, out of Katherine's line of sight.

"Stop looking for what? Or who? Sam? You want to call it off, close the case?"

Ms Kopek nodded, her movements sluggish. The gun drooped, and Rad took his chance. He reached out and grabbed the top of the barrel, twisting her hand as he did. She let out a small sound but her grip on the pistol was limp, and in a second the gun belonged to Rad. He pocketed it in his trench coat without looking and then squeezed her shoulders with both hands. This snapped her attention back to him, and the white look of fear reappeared on her face.

"Who sent you, Ms Kopek? Who wants me to drop the case?"

She sighed, and collapsed. Then Rad sighed, and changed his hold on her shoulders, slipping his hands down her back and lifting her in his arms.

She was out for quite a while. Too long, Rad thought as he sat on his office chair, dragged in from the other room to watch over her on the bed. Long enough for him to find another ancient tea ration in the back of a cupboard, and make himself a vile cup, and drink it, and then after setting the empty cup on the floor beside him, eventually pick it up and rinse it in the washroom sink. When he sat down again, she opened her eyes. Her pupils were still small, but he thought they looked a lot better.

"Welcome back, Ms Kopek. I don't normally bed my clients on the second visit, but I hope you don't mind. The floor is mighty hard in this building. Old wood."

She smacked her lips and pushed the hair out of her face. Hitched up on one elbow, she looked at Rad with an expression that would have been hilarious if she hadn't pulled a gun on him just a half hour ago.

He waved a hand. "Never mind. You OK?"

"Mmmm," was all she managed. "Can I get some water?"

Rad shuffled to the washroom.

"You ever been drugged before?" he called out over his shoulder, then realised there were better ways of putting it. She didn't answer and when he returned with his mug half-filled with lukewarm water she was rubbing her face, apparently oblivious.

"Here."

She drank greedily. Rad watched the liquid trickle over the edge of the mug and down her chin, onto his bedspread.

"Can you remember anything, Ms Kopek?"

She nodded as she finished the last of the drink, then smacked her lips again. It was an unattractive gesture.

"I'm sorry. I don't have a choice. You have to stop the investigation. You're no longer being employed by me, Mr Bradley, as of right now."

They looked at each other in silence. Eventually, Ms Kopek sat up on the bed and began adjusting her creased tunic. She patted the pockets urgently and looked up at the detective. Rad smiled.

"Oh, don't worry about that. I've got it safe. Why don't you tell me who I should return it to? I'd like to pay them a visit."

The pulse juddered in Ms Kopek's neck, and her mouth opened like a beached fish gasping. Then she started to cry.

"Please, I have no choice. You have to stop."

Rad pressed the point, politely but firmly. "Who sent you, Ms Kopek? Who wants me to quit the case?"

She leaned forward suddenly, taking Rad by surprise, but it was only to grab his hands. She remained perched on the bed. Rad ran his tongue over the front of his teeth.

Was it an act, or was it genuine? He wasn't sure. He was sure that she didn't have a clue what she was doing, although desperation made a person do strange things. But she couldn't be desperate for him to stop looking for her lover, unless she'd been dishonest when she hired him. The collapse was real and the gun certainly was, and he was pretty sure even the very rich and very well connected, like Ms Katherine Kopek, didn't have friends in quite those places. He also thought she'd been slipped something to make her a little more... pliable, although that was pure guesswork. Then again guesswork was important in his line of work.

But as he well knew, there were no such things as coincidences.

He flipped his hands over and grabbed her wrists. She yelped, but seemed to relax.

"The Skyguard? Nimrod? Who was it?"

"Please, you must stop. The State... the State is in danger. You must stop."

He released her wrists, pushing her back to the bed. She fell backwards onto her elbows and stayed in that position, hair across her face again. Rad stood up and over her.

"The Empire State, is that what you're saying? The Empire State is in danger if I find Sam Saturn? Well now, ain't that interesting?"

"I... what? What's interesting?"

Rad turned his back and paced the room. His hand felt the small dense mass of the pistol in his coat pocket. A government issue gun.

"Oh, not much, Ms Kopek. Seems a lot of folk think the city is about to be hit by some mighty calamity. Seems it all centres on me too. This week ain't been no picnic."

"Oh," said Ms Kopek. When Rad turned back, she was sitting up on the bed, hands in her lap. The shakes had stopped entirely.

Rad sighed, and then apologised as she started at the sound. He helped her to her feet.

"Go home, Ms Kopek. You're not meant to be a part of this, you never were. But I think maybe Sam stumbled into something way, way out of her league. Out of mine too, maybe."

Katherine began to protest, but Rad shushed her.

"Go home. When they get in touch, you can tell them I'm off the case. Tell them you did what they said. But remember, I'll still be looking. You and me, we don't belong to anyone, least of all those motherless bastards at city hall."

He reached into his pocket and took out her semi-automatic pistol. Her eyes widened at the sight of it. He lifted her handbag without a sound, considered for a moment, then returned the gun to his pocket, shaking his head. Their eyes met, and Katherine Kopek nodded, and Rad Bradley nodded, and after showing her out of his office with a gentlemanly sweep of the arm, he closed the main door behind her.

Rad twisted the deadbolt to make sure it was set, and went back to his apartment.

TWENTY-TWO

DID IT EVER STOP RAINING in this fucking place?

Rex pulled his coat tighter and his hat lower, and hunkered back into the doorway. From his damp position, he looked down the street to the east, and up the street to the west. It was deserted, the wet street shining under hard yellow light. Rex blinked the rain from his eyes, savouring the cool feeling against his eyelids. It helped with the headache and the buzzing. That damned noise, right behind his eyeballs.

It was night. Rex wasn't sure what time, but it couldn't have been too late. It was hard to tell. With such a thumper of a headache, the daylight was too bright, grey and foggy as it was. He'd been lost a day, maybe two, hiding in alleyways, in basement stairwells during the day, coming out at night to try and find his way home.

It wasn't intentional. In fact, it was exactly what Rex didn't want to be doing. He was lost, but this was Manhattan. He knew Manhattan, had lived and worked in Manhattan all his life. It was just the shock of the... thing, was all. Rex closed his eyes and listened to the buzzing grow and nodded gently to himself. It was OK. Lesson learned. It had been a harder job that he had expected. No problem. He was OK now. He just had a bump on the head which had given him this goddamn migraine, and that plus the shock of the... thing, had sent him into a bit of a spin. No problem.

Rex felt better. He was thinking clearly, and that was good. Realising what had happened, the root of the problem, that was good. That was halfway to getting it sorted.

Rex nodded again, then jerked his head up. He blinked and found his face was still wet, and the rain was still falling, and the street was still empty. He'd managed to drop off. Good. How long, it was impossible to tell. The street stretched out like an abandoned film set before him. Rex folded his arms close, thankful at least that while the rain was very wet, it wasn't very cold.

So where the hell was he? Born and bred a New Yorker, Rex had to admit that he hadn't been down *every* street in Manhattan. That was one of the best things about living in one of the greatest cities in the world. You could live there all your life, and still be surprised just a few blocks from your own front door. Rex'd heard the same about London. If you're tired of London... or New York, you're tired of...

Rex knocked the back of his head against the stone doorway as he jerked back to consciousness. The damned buzzing abated when he slept, but it was that moment of wakefulness when it peaked, his head pounding like he'd been tapped with a baseball bat. A second later the sensation was gone. He needed to get home, get inside, get to his bed and sleep and take some aspirin. Sleep, and food and drink, and some pills, and he'd be ready to tackle the next item on his agenda.

Move the body.

He'd hidden it pretty well. This whole part of the damned city was a ghost town anyway, and Rex wondered if perhaps he could just have left her in the middle of the damned street and nobody would find her. But how long ago had it been? Last night? The night before? Last week? Time felt fuzzy. That was to be expected. Good. Another sliver of recognition. Rex felt like a private eye slotting the pieces of a case together. Tell me, Rex, where were you on the night of the fifth? He laughed. He was OK. He stood, and decided it was time to move.

Rex looked down to tighten the belt of his trench coat, and when he looked up again if there wasn't a damn *person* walking down the street. His pace was quick, his head hunched down, hands thrust in pockets, trying to dodge the rain as he clipped along the sidewalk. The rim of the man's fedora was sagging from the water, and the bottom half of his pale trench coat was a patchwork of water and oil stains thrown from the wet streets. The man kept a straight line, then turned down a side street.

"Huh," said Rex, to himself, as he fingered the brim of his own fedora. There was something familiar about the man in the rain. Perhaps he wasn't so far from his own apartment building, because he was sure – no, certain – that that man lived in the same building. Hell, hadn't they exchanged a polite hello each and every morning for the past... for the past forever?

Rex pushed his hat onto his bald head and skipped down the stairs two at a time. His feet hit the sidewalk and he turned in the direction the man had been heading. Head down, hands thrust in pockets, trying to dodge the rain, Rex set off.

Now he was lost.

He'd been trailing his neighbour for a half hour, but that buzzing, that damned-to-all-hell headache peaked and troughed and perhaps he hadn't been following his neighbour at all. It was still night, and the rain had eased to drizzle, and Rex stood in the middle of another empty street and wondered where the hell he was.

There were street signs, sure, but he'd never heard of any

of them. All of the buildings were featureless granite or limestone. There were no shops, no bars, no restaurants, no clubs, no market stalls, no newspaper signs, no billboards, no advertising, no cars or buses or bicycles. No people, no litter. Just wet streets reflecting the yellow lights, and a million buildings with locked doors and black windows.

Maybe he was somewhere in the banking area. One of those little zones where it was all stockbrokers and merchant bankers and lawyers, where you didn't need signs or plaques because everyone knew where they were going, and if you needed to know the name or number of a building or office, then you weren't supposed to be there in the first place. If he was in the financial district, maybe that explained the dead buildings. Rex sniggered.

There was a small park on the corner, raised up from the street. Rex pulled himself up the four or five steps and found himself on a bench-lined path that orbited a square lawn. Sitting on the nearest bench, he found the hedges all around blocked out the view of the lifeless street below, and the single large tree in the centre of the park, its branches extending broadly outwards, removed his view of the grey stone buildings all around him.

If Rex sat there, and let his eyes fall, just a little, he could pretend he was back in New York City. Because the thought occurred to him that somehow, bizarrely and impossibly, he wasn't in Manhattan. Maybe he hadn't fallen and hit his head. Maybe he hadn't been the only one down that dark alley that night. If he thought it was a good spot, perhaps other people did too. Perhaps McCabe had found him? No, if it had been that sonovabitch he'd be as dead as the girl now. Maybe, entirely without realising it, he'd walked straight into someone else's operation, and they watched him kill the girl and then removed him from the scene and dumped him in New Jersey or something.

No. It didn't make sense. They'd've just knocked him down too and he sure as hell wouldn't have got up again.

But somehow, he didn't feel like he was home.

He curled his legs up onto the bench. The whole park was tiny and mostly kept dry by the huge spreading tree. The night was warm and fuzzy, and if he lay down his head seemed to settle.

Rex fell asleep on the park bench in the warm night.

It wasn't until the fifth shake that Rex awoke. Both eyes snapped open quickly, his subconscious giving his conscious mind a kick, letting it know that something was going on and really he needed to start paying attention. Rex looked up and saw the leaves of the tree, glossy bottle green in the half-light, and the face of a man leaning over him and shaking him by the shoulders and speaking in a quiet, polite voice. Not a whisper, more a murmur, the low monotone employed when you need to tell something important to someone but don't want the people in the next room to hear. Rex blinked, and found his eyelids were dry. He could hear water hitting tarmac, so it was still raining, but the small park was dry thanks to the tree.

Rex blinked again and squinted. The man standing over him didn't *have* a face. Eyes, sure, and the bump of a nose, but all covered in white cloth that hung long as the man leaned over. If only he could think straight and see straight, he'd ask the man why he was wearing a napkin over his head.

"Friend, friend..." said the man with the napkin on his head, as he gently rocked Rex on the park bench. When he saw Rex's eyes flick open, he straightened up, and the white cloth moved like he might have smiled underneath it. Rex raised himself up onto an elbow, but when he raised his voice his head pounded.

"Hey, back off, buddy.. I ain't your friend," he said, and realised he couldn't get off the park bench. He'd lain on one leg, which was now numb and useless. Rex swore, and then heard the man in the white hood laugh.

"Welcome, friend, welcome." At regular volume his voice was rich and deep, the accent a strong and familiar Yankee twang. "You have led us a merry dance, but you're in safe hands now."

Rex closed his eyes again, thinking perhaps that would ease the buzzing in his head which had now returned, louder and heavier than ever, and that perhaps the weirdo in the mask would vanish in a puff of smoke. Sleeping on a park bench in New York City was exactly the right way to attract weirdos and worse.

"Buddy, I'm not interested." Rex made it to the sitting position and hammered on his left thigh, urging the blood to flow and the feeling to return. "If you don't quit it, you'll know what's coming." Rex looked up at the man, knowing his threat didn't quite make sense. But for all the confident voice and pose, the man in the hood was smaller than Rex. Rex was tall and broad, an ex-boxer run a little to fat. On purely a weight-by-weight ratio, he'd be able to floor the man without much effort if he didn't goddamn leave Rex alone.

The man reached to help Rex stand, but Rex shrugged the hand off his arm instantly. He made another threat, a more cogent one this time, although this just made the masked man laugh more. As he watched, Rex could see the hanging front of the cloth mask puff out with each expelled breath.

The man stood to his full height, and placed his hands in the pockets of his smart double-breasted suit.

"Rex, I'm here to help you. You'll understand that shortly, but I think we need to get you inside and cleaned up first. Come, let me help you up."

Rex pushed the man away for the second time, although now he managed to push himself up off the park bench to stand. He stood nearly a foot taller than the man in the mask, even as Rex swayed on his feet. He rubbed his eyes with the heels of his hands.

"How do you know my name? Who are you? What's with the get-up?"

"Allow me to introduce myself. My name will not mean anything to you, but people call me the Pastor of Lost Souls. And welcome to the Empire State. We have been expecting you for a long, long time."

TWENTY-THREE

THE MEAL WAS GOOD, but the Pastor hadn't joined Rex. He'd sat at the table – but hadn't touched his own food as Rex ate, and then stood and left as soon as Rex's plate was clean, saying only that he would be back shortly and that Rex should wait there. After a few minutes, Rex shuffled his chair over to the Pastor's spot and ate his meal too. It was cold, and under any other circumstances dreary fare, but for Rex, food had never tasted so good. He mashed the cold egg, cold half of a sausage, cold potatoes and hard bread together, the pain in his head and the buzzing behind his eyes lessening with each mouthful. When he was done he felt full and much happier. He sat back, and looked around the room.

They were at the top of a three-level house, in an office. It was virtually empty, with bare board floor and white painted walls. The only items that offered any colour were the dark mahogany desk, and the big red title on the front of the book sitting on it, although its dust jacket was a stark black and white that seemed to match Rex's surroundings.

Rex pushed his – the Pastor's – plate aside on the desktop, and reached for the book. *The Seduction of the Innocent*. Rex smirked, checked over his shoulder then, feeling faintly ridiculous, flipped it open at a random point.

Huh. Some history book or something. Nothing salacious at all, despite what the title promised. Although the man in the white hood had called himself a pastor, Rex knew very well the kind of books that men like him liked to keep hidden away in the vestry. But this book was hidden in plain sight, and looked like a disappointing read.

Rex heard voices downstairs. Hospitality of the Pastor aside, the house was a nutcase in itself. All the walls were white, and all the doors were open, and all the lights were on full. Each room was lit by round white bulbs, individually far too bright for the old building, and grouped together in wall settings of two, or chandeliers of a dozen, the effect was dazzling. White light reflected off white walls, with the open windows showing nothing but the black of the night outside. Rex could *hear* the world outside – the rain ebbing and pulsing, the wind picking up and funnelling between the tall buildings – but it was all invisible from inside the house.

The House of Lost Souls. That's what the Pastor had called it. Rex had been impressed from the outside, with the house lit like a goddamn beacon in the dark city, and he quickly realised where he was. A commune, some sort of weird religious sect. The Pastor was a nut. Wearing that freak show hood was bad enough, but the house was full of his followers. Young, all smiling, eyes refracting the light which reduced their pupils to tiny pinpricks.

Rex knew these kind of places existed, or rather, he had imagined they had, in New York City. But the fantasy in his head had been one of shadows and decadence and insubstantial, diaphanous clothing. Not a bunch of lefties sat crossed-legged on the floor listening to their beloved leader lecture them about moral turpitude.

Rex stood up, the cold meal sitting heavily in his stomach as he thought of another option. He whistled low, and scuffed the floorboards with a brown shoe. Communists?

Anarchists? Maybe Fascists, perhaps funded by one of those groups spreading out in Europe? Well, holy smoke, if he hadn't just found himself a gold mine. Not only had he single-handedly removed one of the primary obstacles to the growth of his business empire, which would put the mayor squarely in his pocket, he could lead the authorities to a nice little collection of crazy anarchist loons on the side. Maybe these last few days were starting to turn around.

"Rex, I hope you are feeling better."

Rex turned. The Pastor was standing in the doorway to the office; one hand in his jacket pocket, thumb out, the other holding another copy of the black-and-white-jacketed book.

Rex smiled and nodded, muttering a thanks for the meal. He had to play it cool, but his head was starting to hurt again. His eyes seemed to pop when they were looking in the Pastor's direction; glancing back at the two empty plates on the desk, his eyeballs didn't burn quite so much. It must have been the weird white light, and the knock on the head. He rubbed the back of his skull absently, wondering how many days' growth of stubble he had on his scalp.

The Pastor jerked into life, walking from doorway to desk and sitting in the chair behind it. He placed the second copy of _Seduction_ on top of the first, straightened the pair, then folded his hands into a steeple in front of his covered mouth, before gesturing to the empty chair in front of the desk. Rex waved a thank-you and sat.

"Nice little prayer meeting, Mr Pastor?"

"I can get you home, Rex."

Rex's train of thought was instantly derailed. He leaned in and rested an elbow on the desk.

"I should be OK, although if you could just give me some directions that would be mighty fine, thanks very much."

The Pastor clasped his hands together and raised an index finger, tapping his lips under the hood. After a few seconds of this, he clapped his hands together – then laid them palm-down on the desk. If Rex didn't know better he'd've said the Pastor had a short fuse.

"You misunderstand me, Rex," he said. "We are not in New York. We are in the Empire State."

When Rex leaned back, the chair creaked. He rolled his back into it, and it creaked some more.

"The Empire State? You mean New York State?"

"Not quite. Oh, it's close to New York. Manhattan, I mean. But it equally might be a thousand million miles from home. It makes no difference."

"Huh," said Rex. The word felt unnecessary, but it filled the gap that formed when he wasn't really sure what to say. The Pastor was a nut job, and no mistake.

"Don't worry yourself, Rex. I live in New York myself. Greenwich Village, actually."

"Very nice."

The Pastor paused, inclined his head, and continued. "But, like you, I find myself marooned, somewhat. The Empire State is home but not home, familiar yet alien, the city but not the city."

Rex scratched his cheek. Maybe it was the belly full of food and the warm dampness of the air, or the brightness of the room and the buzzing in his head that followed the outlines of the Pastor sitting behind his desk, but not a whole lot of what he was saying made sense. Then again he was a loon, this Rex had confirmed, and although he was used to dealing with unusual or difficult people, he hadn't really dealt with the genuinely insane before. He didn't really expect anything they said would make much sense. But what was the old advice? A madman must be humoured?

On the other hand, Rex wanted to go home.

"I don't follow. The Village can't be far. Ever taken a cab?" Rex said.

The hooded head shook slowly. "You misunderstand again, and I knew you would. Suffice to say, no matter where you walk, in whichever direction, for however long you choose, you will not find your home. The Empire State exists in isolation. There is nowhere else but the Empire State. The Empire State is all."

Rex had a thought which fought its way past the fug in his brain and made him sit up straight suddenly, then lean forward towards the desk. As the Pastor came closer in his vision, Rex ignored the increasing volume of his headache.

"Wait. This doesn't have anything to do with the Skyguard, does it...?" His mouth was suddenly dry, as were his lips. He stuck his tongue out and then sucked it back in and moved it around his teeth, but his mouth was dry, dry, dry.

"Or," said the Pastor, "the Science Pirate?"

Rex gulped, but the reflex just made his throat stick. He rubbed his fingertips against his sweaty palms. Keep it together. This preacher ain't got nothing on me.

"Well, it occurs to me, Pastor, that the Skyguard and the Science Pirate had an almighty fight, not too long ago, not too far from here. I'm no expert on whatever the hell foolery those two usually get up to, but they've done some mighty odd things in the past. Floated Manhattan up into the sky one time until the air was too thin to breathe. Electrified the Hudson. Hell, one time everyone with the surname 'Johnston' disappeared, then came back the next day. They say it was the Science Pirate and the Skyguard fighting."

The Pastor nodded. "You have a fine memory, Rex, although I imagine such events would be hard to forget. For myself, I only witnessed the first wonder of your list. From my office window I could see the stars, bigger and brighter and more colourful than ever in my whole life. Though that might have been oxygen starvation, I'm not sure."

The pair laughed, Rex nervously, but for a while afterwards the smile stayed on his face. He had another stab at figuring out what the Pastor was talking about.

"OK, so this Empire State, it's like some part of New York, some part that we're trapped in. Some plan of the Science Pirate's, am I right? So what, we wait for the Skyguard to break us out?" He thought of the broken body of the small, frail girl that had been the Science Pirate crushed behind the dumpster. For genuinely the first time, Rex wondered if he'd done the right thing. If she was dead, what if the Skyguard couldn't get them out of their... bubble, whatever it was.

The Pastor reached down and pulled a drawer of his desk open. Rex craned to see, but from his position across the substantial desktop it looked empty. The Pastor fished out a white rectangle of glossy paper, and placed it on the desk in front of Rex. He took his hand away, and closed the drawer, then steepled his fingers. Rex eyed the rectangle.

"You're right, Rex, we are trapped, and it is to do with the Skyguard and the Science Pirate. You're not far off the money, but now is not the time to explain the hows and whys of it. The fact is, we can get out. You and me, Rex, we *need* to get out. The solution is easy. You are the man to do it."

A beat. "Uh-huh," said Rex.

"Look at the photograph, Rex."

Rex coughed, covering his mouth politely with a clenched fist, although the action was merely a reflex brought on by uncertainty. He watched the blank white rectangle for a moment, almost as if he expected it would rise up of its own accord, then slid it to the edge of the desk on his side and flipped it over.

It was a portrait photograph, black and white, head and shoulders. The man in the picture was heavily built, skin almost as dark as his suit, with wide shoulders pulling at the jacket and waistcoat, spreading the pinstripe apart near the seams. A shirt and plain tie. A trim goatee beard surrounded a serious expression. A white fedora finished it off, pushed at a fashionable angle on the man's impressive, bald head.

Rex blinked, then his forehead creased in bewilderment and he rubbed his own goatee. He didn't remember the photo being taken, and he'd never seen it before in his life, but he recognised the subject. He was looking at a nicely posed photograph of himself.

"That man," said the Pastor, stabbing a finger in the air towards the picture in time with each syllable, "is a criminal and a threat to New York City. He's behind it all, and the only way to get out of the Empire State is to get *him* out of the way of *us*."

The Pastor stopped, and waited. Rex said nothing, and stared at the photograph.

"Kill him, and we can go home."

Rex's jaw worked and his head buzzed. "Ah... that's me... who is this?"

The Pastor's hooded head tilted to the side, just a little.

"Rex, meet Rad Bradley, private detective."

TWENTY-FOUR

KANE FORTUNA.

For the last five minutes, standing in the drizzle outside the salubrious, ostentatious, impressive frontage of the house in the Upper East Side, not feeling any more comfortable now than he did a few nights ago on the first visit, Rad repeated his friend's name over and over in his head.

No, that was wrong. He did feel more comfortable, if not with the setting or who he was visiting, but with himself. This time he was here on his own terms, without Kane to... to what? Lead the conversation with Captain Carson? Steer it in the right direction, keeping Rad at arm's length while he discussed whatever secrets he had with the inhabitants of the grand house?

Kane Fortuna. Huh, the night work was getting to him. Kane was his best friend, his only friend, in the whole damn city. He was trustworthy, he was on the side of the angels. And while he was sleeping off the effects of Jerry's finest, there was work to be done, and enrolling Carson into their merry band full-time seemed the best – the *only* – option.

But there was something about Kane that itched at the back of his mind. Rad huffed. The night work was getting to him. No problem.

He felt better, and puffed up his chest. He raised a hand to operate the black iron door knocker, only to stop as there was a huge *clunk* from behind it. The door swung open, held by Byron. The Captain appeared on tip-toe around his servant's shoulder, the grin on his face wide and, Rad thought, genuine. The older man clapped his hands, twice, and rubbed the palms together as though the night air was cold. It wasn't.

"My dear detective! For no fewer than five minutes Byron and myself have been waiting for you to knock." Carson winked at his servant, then gestured for Rad to enter. "Byron had suggested as many as ten minutes. I plumped for five, and I think that means Byron owes me something."

Rad looked from Carson to Byron, realising that he'd just decided, on his own, to visit the house of two madmen.

"Don't look so worried, Mr Bradley," said the old man. "I presume you are here for..."

This kick-started Rad's brain. "A second opinion, yes."

The Captain shook his head. "An explanation, dear boy. An explanation! Now come in, and wipe your feet."

Rad followed Captain Carson down the hallway at some distance from his host, who skipped along at a fine pace. Rad noticed white straps tied around Carson's waist, and another white loop at his neck. He hadn't seen it when the door had been opened, as Carson had been peering around the bulk of his servant in the doorway, but the Captain was wearing an apron, long enough to be scuffed by the toes of his shoes as he walked. Although the Captain's arms were being held in front of him – and hence out of Rad's eyeshot – he saw the sleeves of his shirt were rolled at the elbow.

"Not interrupting anything, am I?" Rad asked.

"Not at all, dear boy!" Carson called cheerily over his shoulder. He waved one hand up in the air, and Rad saw the bare forearm ended in a tight-fitting glove made out of latex or rubber or something. Also, Carson's forearm was covered in blood to the elbow. Rad blanched, and stopped. He heard Byron's footfalls stop just behind him, and heard a weird ticking from his chest, which was just about at head-height to him.

"Ah, you sure about that, Captain?" Rad said quickly, eyes wide. A few paces ahead, the old man stopped and turned. He walked back towards the detective, each passing hall lamp mounted on the old wood panelling strobing his face. Captain Carson was an old man, his hair and moustache – and *skin* – white as chalk. The vivid crimson on both arms, and splashed in some abundance across the front of his heavy apron, was in shocking contrast to the elegant surroundings.

The Captain stopped by yet another sepia-toned landscape, another mystery fantasy shot showing an empty, flat background, some men, and Carson's own airship. The nearby wall lamp cast a cone of light over the picture and left Carson's face mostly in an angle of shadow. Rad could see the Captain's mouth glittering as he smiled in the semi-darkness.

"I must apologise for my somewhat dishevelled state, but the truth is you *have* interrupted Byron and I in what you might call a rather delicate operation."

Rad nodded blindly, and managed a quiet: "Uh-huh."

"However, that is not to say your visit is unwelcome or the moment of it inopportune. Indeed, we both saw you approach up the street, and it was Byron that remarked upon the happy coincidence."

"Yuh-huh."

The Captain's smile flickered in the shadows, and then he raised his hands up into the light, examining the lurid mess.

"Ah... *hmm*..." he muttered, then looked over Rad's shoulder at Byron. "Perhaps we have done enough for one night, Byron. Please show our friend into the study, and I'll go and clean myself up." He turned to Rad. "Please, help yourself to a drink, and if you'll excuse me I won't be a moment. I have something interesting to show you."

With that the Captain turned and creaked down the hallway, elbowing a door open carefully and disappearing from sight. Rad heard Byron's heavy feet behind him, and he turned.

"This way, sir."

"And there we are!" Captain Carson took the minuscule glass of liquor from the tray Byron held, and joined Rad at the wall, where the detective was looking at more pictures. Carson pursed his lips comically as he sipped the deep amber liquid. Rad watched with interest, sniffing his own glass. Carson saw the look and chuckled.

"They call this 'sherry', my dear fellow. I have a small store of bottles." He paused, waiting. "Go on, try it. Much more flavour than the rotten potato juice you seem to prefer at Jerry's."

Rad sipped, and winced. It was sweet, like drinking hot sugar.

"So you know Jerry?"

"Not in the slightest. But I know where you drink."

"That so?"

"That is so, detective. We've been following you for some time."

Rad's eyebrows went up, and holding his breath he drained the sherry glass. "Uh-huh," he whispered, throat constricting at the unusual, heavy liquid.

The Captain ignored Rad, and instead walked past him, looking along the wall. More portraits, some paintings, some more of the weird fantasy scenes. Rad found them fascinating, but at the same time they somehow made him feel sick. He felt an emptiness, an ache in his chest, and a buzzing behind the eyes when he looked at them.

Carson was wearing a linen suit, smart but a dull dun colour. The apron was gone, and there was no blood. When he turned back to Rad, the detective saw his fine white hair was freshly combed and parted and slightly wet.

"Interesting, aren't they?"

Rad glanced sideways at the picture Carson was indicating. The Captain's finger was pointing at the weird white landscape, but his gaze remained fixed on Rad.

"Uh, yeah, very nice," said Rad. "If you like that kind of thing," he added, a best attempt at indicating – politely – how strange he really thought they were.

Captain Carson sipped from the crystal glass he held delicately by the stem. "You got a good look at my airship, in the old hangar, didn't you? Last time you were here, I mean, with Mr Fortuna."

Rad frowned. "Ah, yes. Very impressive." What was this? Was the Captain fishing for compliments now?

The Captain tapped his fingernail against the picture. "Shame it is in such a state. Byron and I are working hard on it, but you know, materials are difficult to get these days. Wartime."

"Wartime..." Rad repeated, nodding as had become the custom.

"There's a whole front section missing. An aluminium shell over a magnesium frame. Dashed clever."

"Uh-huh." Rad had no clue, and couldn't have cared less.

"You can see it in this picture here. Shame, shame. Lost the nameplate. Hand-engraved, hand-painted. Do you see it?"

Rad took a tentative step forward. He peered at the picture. Sepia browns swam before his eyes, and at half an inch away the image broke down into smudges. The Captain tapped his finger again, and Rad saw a light brown rectangle with dark brown markings. Frowning, he stepped back, trying to focus.

And when he could focus, he tried to speak, but found he didn't have anything to say, even if his throat had been moist enough to produce any sound.

"Yes, detective. Come, I have something else to show you."

The Captain finished his drink and handed the glass to Byron, who extended a long, thick arm instinctively and caught the glass on his tray. The two of them turned and left Rad at the picture.

Rad screwed his eyes shut. The buzzing in his head faded. He opened them again, and he felt OK, no, really, he was fine. He looked again at the nameplate of Captain Carson's airship and the dizziness returned.

Nimrod.

He needed another sherry.

The further into the house they went, the stranger Rad felt and the more he thought this had been a mistake. Wood-panelled hallways, winding staircases, hundreds and hundreds of the brown and cream fantasy landscapes. Faces stared down at him from all sides as he walked, strangers in impossible places. Groups of people, more often than not with Captain Carson standing proudly at the centre, the blond man at his side. Carson was younger, hair dark, but the old man leading Rad through the house bore the same broad shoulders and straight back as the young burly man in the photographs.

This was a mistake. This was just leading to more confusion, more fantasy. Someone was playing Rad, good and proper. He was at the bottom of a deep, dark well, the light of truth nothing but a tiny pinprick in the blackness above.

No. Rad caught his steps momentarily, falling further behind Carson and feeling Byron looming behind him. He kept walking. Rad was no schmuck. If he was at the middle of some conspiracy, some plan, someone's practical joke, he wouldn't be the stooge. Nor would he be the fall guy. A week of darkness and rain and nonsense. It ended here.

"Wait," he said, and stopped.

The old man continued a few paces, then stopped himself and retraced his steps back across the thick hallway rug.

"Detective?"

Rad puffed himself up and straightened his shoulders. He was a big man and, at a guess, probably half the Captain's age. But Carson was anything but old and frail, and even with chin held proudly, Rad only just matched him in height.

"I came here to get some answers, and by God, I'm going to leave with some." He raised his voice slightly. Carson peered down his nose at Rad, but Rad was sure his mouth flickered into the smallest of smiles.

"And answers you shall have, detective." The Captain thudded Rad on the right shoulder, twice, with his fist. "You're a good man. Can I take it that you are going to step up and lead this investigation like you should have from the very beginning?"

Rad was unsure whether Carson's tone was supposed to be condescending or encouraging. He decided it was both.

"Investigation?"

The Captain nodded. "Indeed yes. You are surrounded by riddles, so I would presume that if you considered this to be your own personal case, you would be busy finding clues and piecing them together. I will help as much as I can, of course. Byron as well."

Rad glanced over his shoulder, just to make sure the seven-foot-nothing servant was behind them.

"Point," said Rad. The Captain nodded and smiled.

"My boy, you will go far! Now, shall we continue? As I indicated before, there is something I must show you, but please, we can talk as we go. Begin your enquiry." He turned and padded down the hall silently. Rad and Byron followed, the deep red pile absorbing their footfalls almost completely.

"This is quite some house, Captain. I figured as much when I... well, when you showed me the hangar. How big is it?"

Captain Carson did not turn, but kept walking. He raised his voice so Rad could hear clearly, and it echoed dully from the dark oak that lined the passage.

"*Very* is as good a description as any," he said. "In fact, I own the entire block, and have over the years interconnected all of the buildings that were of use. Some are not; those are rented out. My family have actually owned this section of the city for some two hundred years."

Rad quickened his pace, so he was right at the Captain's back.

"What do you mean? That doesn't make any sense."

"Is that so?" Then Carson stopped and turned quickly. Rad brought himself up short just in time, then backed off as the Captain leaned in to him.

"What year is it?" asked Carson.

"Nineteen."

"Nineteen?"

Rad frowned. "You forgotten or something?"

The Captain ignored the question. "And what year will it be next?"

Rad's mouth turned upside down, but he decided that wherever Carson was heading with this train of thought, he'd promised to provide whatever answers he needed.

"Twenty," he said at last.

"Ah." The old man smiled quickly, then resumed walking. "By my count, next year should be approximately Nineteen Fifty."

"What did you say?"

Carson's hand appeared over his shoulder as he walked. He waggled his fingers in the air.

"Well, it's hard to measure. Byron and I have been working on the equipment, but it's not perfect. But Nineteen Fifty is about it."

The passageway finally came to an end at a sort of square porch. A wide, somewhat grand staircase rose from the right-hand side, leading up then turning at ninety degrees and continuing above their heads. Below this, a narrower staircase led downwards. The porch itself was filled with a few items of furniture – a chair and a bookcase – and several closed doors led off from it.

The Captain began to head for the descending staircase, but stopped when Rad laid a hand on his shoulder. He turned.

"Mr Bradley?"

"How can it be the year Nineteen Fifty? That doesn't make any sense."

"Hmm." The Captain looked Rad up and down. "How old are you?"

"Forty-four."

"And what year was it, oh, twenty-one years ago?"

Rad snorted. "Now I know you're crazy. This is only the year Nineteen."

Carson smiled tightly. It was an expression devoid of all emotion. Rad suddenly felt cold, and felt his heart race as adrenaline pumped through his body.

Oh, no... no no no no no...

"How then," said the Captain, slowly, "are you forty-four years old?"

Rad's mouth moved but no words came out. The Captain patted his shoulder gently.

"Come," he said. He turned, and walked to the stairs.

The narrow stairs were lined with more wood panelling for just a short while, before the walls turned to brick. This gave an impression of age – what Rad now knew to be an *impossible* age – and although he had the feeling the picture would be complete with dripping walls and darkness, he was surprised to find the large cellar quite dry and very well lit.

It was a laboratory. Rad had given up on being surprised at the contents of Captain Carson's home, but still had the capacity to be impressed. The room was lined with benches holding various apparatus, and above these, glass-fronted cabinets filled with bottles, jars, boxes, and the usual collection of scientific junk. Several large refrigerators hummed, while overhead long strip lights fizzed faintly.

Carson trotted to the centre of the room then turned back to Rad with an expansive smile, rubbing his hands. He stepped to one side, and Rad then understood what the Captain had been working on when he called at the house, and what he had been so keen for Rad to see for himself.

Two freestanding tables were spaced in the middle of the room with enough of a gap between them so people – Carson and Byron, presumably – could work back-to-back if needed. The benches were rectangular and wide, with a couple of high stools pushed against them.

One table was empty and clean, a blank, glossy white ceramic surface interrupted in one corner by a stainless steel sink and tall, curved laboratory tap.

The other table was covered in a slick liquid, dark and thick at the edges, brighter red towards the centre where it pooled around its source.

Sam Saturn.

The girl's body was naked, although it took a moment for Rad to realise this, as her skin was dirty with the grime and filth of the alley and the congealed paste of her own blood. Her chest, her whole torso, had been split down the middle, the two sides folded back like blankets. What had become of her innards, Rad couldn't tell. Sam Saturn's body had been straightened out on the bench, but the twisted joints and shattered bones were still obvious.

Rad had seen bodies before. Many bodies. It went with the job, especially – unfortunately – when he took on a missing persons case. Some bodies simply looked like still life, a person merely sleeping. Some, especially those fished out of the water after an indeterminate time submerged, hardly looked like people at all. Rad was used to it. No problem.

But seeing Sam Saturn, the subject of his own case, whose body he thought was lying in a police morgue at the other end of town, Rad felt nauseous. It wasn't the smell – in fact, there was hardly any odour in the Captain's laboratory. The body was wet but cold, and no doubt Carson had some miraculous disinfecting device which cleared the air as needed.

But Rad felt a connection to this girl. He'd been told he was the centre of a conspiracy, a movement to destroy the Empire State. Nimrod had told him, the faux Skyguard had told him.

He shook his head. If he was connected, then goddammit *she* was as well. An innocent – murdered, brutalised, hidden in an alley. There had to be a connection. He felt guilt and responsibility too. Guilty at keeping her body hidden out on the street where she died. Responsible for her death, because if he was the centre of the web, then he was the cause of it all. He held his breath and counted to ten, trying to disperse the unhelpful thoughts. If these facts were true, then he owed it to her to solve her murder and right this wrong.

"I can understand your hesitancy, Mr Bradley," said the Captain. He was standing to one side, hands clasped before him. Byron stood at the foot of the stairs, silent and impassive as always.

Rad closed his eyes. "I had a phone call, from someone who says he... *knows* you. Said his name was Nimrod. Like your ship," he said, turning the subject from the corpse to the bigger picture Rad felt was hanging over him like one of Captain Carson's fancy landscapes. He needed answers, and he needed to collect them in some kind of order.

Captain Carson twitched his nose, then rubbed it before he answered. "Yes, I thought he might call. I do hope you never have to meet him."

"I was planning on it, but my benefactor the Skyguard gatecrashed." Rad paused, thinking. "Have you met Nimrod? Do you know who he is?"

"In reverse order, yes I do, and technically no, but philosophically... perhaps." Carson gave a half-smile. "The Skyguard, eh? Interesting."

Rad held up a hand. "OK, that'll do me for now." Rad opened his eyes and stepped up to the bench. Close up, Sam Saturn looked even less like a person. Her skin was a pale greyish cream, like off milk, and webbed with residue spread by the rain and old, congealed blood. Her open chest was just a bundle of wet rags, glistening like wax under the strip lights.

"I thought the police had her? Kane said he arranged it." Rad's stomach flipped at the guilt.

Rad heard the Captain walk on the tiled floor behind him, and he reappeared around Rad at the girl's head. The Captain looked down at the broken, lumpy face.

"Yes. I must say I was surprised to find her still there, in that alley." Carson sniffed and looked at Rad. "She's been dead a couple of days now, and somebody was going to find her sooner or later. Fortunately the authorities are not particularly interested. You were careless."

"Kane said he was going to wire it in to the police, get them to handle it."

"Yes." The Captain smiled tightly.

Rad detected something in the tone. "But?"

"But he didn't," said Carson. "So I decided to... look into it, shall we say. Besides which, I wanted to do an autopsy."

"Why? And why would Kane lie about the police?"

"Well." The Captain's mouth flickered into a frown, and he tilted his head, looking down at the body. "Certain aspects of Mr Fortuna's evidence were... circumstantial at best. And then after that charade at the ironclad." Captain Carson laughed heartily, as if giving a high society after-dinner speech. He clapped his hands together. "Well, I mean, really!"

"Charade?"

The Captain met Rad's eye. Rad didn't like it.

"Oh yes," said Carson. "Didn't you notice anything?"

Rad thought. The whole trip had seemed like a lot of fuss for nothing. He clicked his fingers.

"He was looking for something, wasn't he? And nothing to do with the unfortunate Sam Saturn here either."

Carson nodded. "I don't know what it was, or whether he found it or not, but I suspect he also used the outing to judge your own position, Mr Bradley. Whether you were *in* or *out*, as it were."

"Huh. I thought you were Kane's buddy. His... fixer? He didn't tell you anything?"

"Nothing that he hadn't told you. And yes, perhaps I have acted in that capacity for him, but the truth of the matter is I have been worried by his behaviour in recent weeks. No, not his behaviour, perhaps... more his state of mind, shall we say."

"What do you mean?"

Carson began pacing around the bench, slowly, his eyes moving over the body as he did so. Rad's own eyes followed him as he walked, until the Captain walked behind Rad. Rad turned as Carson began a second circuit.

"Ever since he made contact with Gardner Gray – the *real* Skyguard – in prison, he has been... well, odd about it.

After his prison sessions interviewing the man for his newspaper, he would come and visit me. It started normally enough, a casual pop-in after dinner, a quiet chat about life and some shared thoughts and theories on the city's most infamous criminal. But then the visits starting coming later, at night, and becoming longer. Midnight. Two in the morning. He would sit in my study, and drink sherry, and talk about the Skyguard for hours. Sometimes I never spoke. He didn't notice. Sometimes he'd stop in the middle of his stream of consciousness, get up, and leave without so much as a goodbye."

Rad took off his hat, and rubbed his scalp.

"So... he became, what, obsessed with the Skyguard?"

Carson stopped walking and nodded, fixing Rad with his eyes over the body.

"Well, the late Mr Gray had a fantastic story. Kane felt I was the best person to discuss it with. I have a fantastic story of my own, similar in many ways to that of the Skyguard."

Rad's eyebrow raised. "That so?"

Carson smiled. "Yes, but that will come later."

"Answers, remember?"

"Indeed yes." The Captain nodded. "But one thing at a time, my dear boy."

Rad waved his hat at the Captain, then slid it back onto his head. He pushed it back as far as it would go.

"So poor Sam Saturn," Carson continued. "Kane's story was too convenient, based on little evidence."

Rad considered the remains on the table before him.

"He faked the footprints? What about the damage to the wall and the dumpster?"

Carson held a finger up. "One thing at a time, detective. But after he told me about the body I had Byron watch the alley for some time. No police ever came, although some came close. Kane never called the murder in, of that I am certain."

"So you collected her to perform an autopsy," said Rad. "You qualified for this kind of thing?"

Carson nodded and smiled, but his eyes were cold and black. "Oh yes. Oh yes."

"Cause of death?" Rad eyed the body. The pathologist's art was well beyond him. How you could tell anything from the remains was witchcraft as far as he was concerned.

"Strangulation, actually." The Captain leaned over the body and pointed to the woman's neck with an extended little finger. He was careful to keep his now clean jacket away from the blood. "Crushed windpipe, bruising characteristic of fingers and thumbs." He looked at Rad. "Human fingers and thumbs, I should point out. If a robot had attempted strangulation, I would imagine the results would have been complete decapitation."

"So our murderer is a human?"

Carson nodded. "Yes. There is also abrasion and bruising around her mouth. Her attacker grabbed her from behind, covering her mouth so she couldn't call out."

Rad looked up and down the body on the bench. The limbs were straight, but he could see bulges and bumps under the skin. Broken bones poked and pushed at the flesh, although none had actually broken through the surface, as far as he could tell. One foot sat square, toes pointing upward. The other flopped inwardly, horizontal to the bench top, on the snapped ankle.

"What about the rest of her injuries? Is a man strong enough to break bones like that? She was a small woman... but why go to the effort if she was killed by asphyxiation?" Rad looked back at Carson. "To fit her behind the dumpster? Could this have been caused by forcing her body into the gap between the dumpster and the wall?"

Carson stroked his moustache, nodding.

"Perhaps," he whispered. "There my expertise begins to

run dry. The injuries were inflicted after she was dead, that much is certain. After that..." He spread his hands in defeat. "It seems difficult to think that all of the breakages and contusions could have been caused by the murderer trying to hide the body, but then again, desperate men are capable of remarkable feats." He paused, and tapped his front teeth with the fingernail of his index finger. "There is another theory, of course."

"I'm all ears, professor."

"Well, while it may be difficult to imagine a human being having the strength to, well, *wreck* a body quite like this, if someone was to tell you that the crime wasn't committed by a human being at all, but..."

Rad's heart sank and his stomach flipped. The two seemed to meet in the middle and Rad felt bile rising in his throat.

"But a robot from an ironclad."

"Indeed," said the Captain. He nodded and his shoulders seemed to sink.

Rad was afraid to say it, but it seemed clear, to him at least. He had no idea *why*, but that was what he had to find out. This was his case, he was the private dick.

"Or," he said quietly, his mouth uncomfortably dry all of a sudden, "someone wearing a suit that gave him the strength of a robot." Rad was afraid to look up at Carson, but forced himself to, and when he did – the Captain was nodding as feared.

Two and two came together in Rad's mind, no matter how hard he tried to get around it to render the whole theory worthless. He felt a nauseous crawl from his stomach.

"Kane. He's the Skyguard. He got the suit, somehow. He killed Sam Saturn, made it look like a robot did it." Rad could hardly believe he was saying it. His voice sounded odd, alien, and he felt like he was watching the scene from far away. He looked around, found one of the high stools behind him, and dropped his behind onto it. He took his hat off again, and held it with both hands, fingers working the brim.

Captain Carson pursed his lips and looked Rad up and down. He turned back to the bench and looked down at Sam Saturn's body, then back at Rad. He watched as the detective rotated his fedora in his hands absently.

"Except the murderer left us some rather stronger clues than some footprints and broken brick."

Rad looked up, eyes narrow. "I... I don't understand. You saying Kane didn't kill her? Only... what? Messed with the crime scene afterwards?"

The Captain smiled. Rad's eyes widened. The world was getting dark and confusing, but if he could follow the Captain's inference, at least his best friend – his only friend – wasn't a killer. He replaced his hat.

"So who killed Sam Saturn?" He shook his head, unsure of whether Captain Carson could give him an answer or not. Then again, if he was so sure that Kane wasn't the one...

Carson returned his attention to the dead girl's neck. He nudged the head, which toppled sideways to face Rad. One eye was closed, one half-open, and the lips were stuck to the teeth in a parody of humour. Rad grimaced and felt ill again. The Captain muttered an apology, but pointed again with his little finger.

"The murderer didn't think to cover his tracks. For whatever reason." He shrugged. "Simple enough to get prints."

Byron plodded from the bottom of the stairs where he had been waiting, to one of the side benches. He fussed over something, then brought some narrow sheets of paper over to his master. The Captain nodded, and Byron turned and laid them out on the other, unoccupied table. Carson motioned for Rad to join them. Rad slid from his stool and walked over.

Arranging the sheets of paper on the ceramic surface, the old man stood back and smiled, clearly pleased with their handiwork. A set of fingerprints, in duplicate it seemed, were presented as evidence. Rad whistled. Whatever Carson had done, he had a better forensic technique than the Empire State police department. Prints off skin? Impressive.

Rad pointed a finger at one set of prints. The swirls and loops were smudged and wide, but clearly recognisable, rendered in dusty pale blue and grey.

"Can you match these?"

"Indeed."

Rad held his breath, then exhaled when Carson didn't say any more.

"Well?"

Carson looked at Rad, a tic moving across one cheek. The old man licked his lips, and his eyes moved up and down Rad's face, then flickered over to Byron, and back.

"What? Captain, you'd better spill. What did you find?"

The Captain smiled tightly and looked back at the table. He indicated the other set of fingerprint images. To Rad they looked like an exact duplicate of the first, only smudged in slightly different places.

"These prints I took from my own home. The hangar, actually, the hull of the *Nimrod*."

Rad sighed. "I don't understand."

"I was very careful where I took them from. You have very big hands, detective. As soon as I saw the size of the marks on poor Miss Saturn's neck, it occurred to me that you have more of a connection to this case than you think. Or are telling us."

Captain Carson's voice had dropped to a low murmur. Rad didn't like it.

There was a click. The laboratory was large, the floor tiled and the walls brick, amplifying the smallest sounds. The squeak of Rad's soles on the smooth floor. The rustle of the Captain's suit as he stroked his moustache, narrow eyes fixed on Rad.

The click of the gun in Byron's hand a second before the blunt barrel stuck square into the back of Rad's bare neck.

"These are your fingerprints, Mr Bradley. Those from the *Nimrod* match those on Miss Saturn's neck."

Rad gulped and felt hot. He wanted to say something, but his head was filled with nothing but white noise.

"I think some answers are called for, don't you, detective?"

TWENTY-FIVE

THE CHAIR IN CARSON'S STUDY was comfortable, and for that Rad Bradley was grateful. The sherry was strong and sweet, and while he gasped at the odd flavour, he'd never needed a drink more in his life. He drained the small crystal glass in a gulp, and held it up. Byron tilted the ornate decanter and dispensed another measure. This Rad also drank, quickly. He closed his eyes and focussed on the ball of warmth as it travelled down his oesophagus and into his stomach, and then, after a few seconds, spread across his chest. He ran his tongue around his teeth, savouring the remaining flavour where he found it.

"I apologise for my little trick," said the Captain, sitting opposite. His glass was still half full. He smiled happily over it as he watched Rad regain his composure. "But I had to be sure it was you. We must take nothing for granted."

Rad shook his head, and coughed. Byron leaned forward with the bottle, but Rad waved a hand over his empty glass.

"Well, you'll forgive me if I don't just sit here and practice some breathing for a while. I think my brain is suffering from oxygen starvation. You had to know it was me? What, have I got a double walking around?"

"Yes," said Carson. He sipped his sherry.

Rad stuck his empty glass out at Byron, never taking his

eyes off the Captain. Byron refilled the glass and Rad drained it in one gulp.

"Huh," said Rad, licking the sweet residue from his lips. "I could have sworn you just said 'yes'."

Carson laughed. "I did, my friend. You have a double. Your double killed Sam Saturn."

Rad rubbed his eyes. "I think I'm going to take you up on that offer of answers, Captain. Then I'm going home and I'm going to bed, and when I wake up, I'm going to laugh over this dream with my morning coffee before I do my taxes."

The Captain carefully set his empty glass down on the table next to his armchair, and steepled his old fingers in front of his face before taking a deep breath.

"This is no dream, detective. Please, allow me to explain.

"I used to work for the Empire State in a... scientific capacity. My own contribution to the war effort, shall we say. I have certain skills which were useful to the City Commissioners. You know of the Battery, of course?"

Rad nodded. "Sure. Downtown at the naval yards. Powers the whole place."

"It does indeed. But it is more than a mere power station. The Empire State draws energy from something very unusual indeed."

"Uh-huh."

"It is called the Fissure. It's a tear, quite literally, in the fabric of the world. We don't know what it is, exactly, but it is a tremendous energy source. Limitless, I would think. The city is literally plugged into it. It's what keeps everything going."

Rad wondered if he'd had too many sherries, or perhaps too few. He regarded his empty glass.

"So, it gives us light and power?"

"More than that," said Carson. He raised his arms up, apparently indicating the room. Rad's eyes flicked around the ceiling.

"It powers the *Empire State*. The city is all we know, because there is nowhere else. And there is nowhere else because we exist inside a bubble, as it were. A *protrusion* of a larger universe, on the other side of the Fissure."

"The Fissure..." Rad muttered. "A tear... a tear that leads somewhere else? Like a... hole in the world?"

The Captain clapped his hands. "Precisely, my dear boy! That other place, beyond the Fissure, is a whole world, and much more. This place, the Empire State, is like a pocket, a confined space, just large enough for the city. The space across the Fissure is infinitely larger. I call it the Origin."

"OK, say I'm crazy enough to buy this. But what does that have to do with me having a homicidal double?"

Carson steepled his fingers again. Rad could tell he was enjoying it.

"When I worked for the City Commissioners, I developed certain equipment which allowed us to look into the Fissure, into the Origin. We even made contact with those who live there. I called it the Origin for very good reason, detective. It *is* the original. The Empire State is a copy – a smaller, paler version of a city they call New York."

Rad sat back in the armchair. "And don't tell me, we're copies too. There's another me, another you, another everybody?"

The Captain gestured to Byron, who walked over and refilled his sherry.

"Yes, Mr Bradley."

Rad rubbed his scalp, and realised he must have left his hat in the laboratory, dropped on the floor when the gun was pulled.

"Don't tell me. Nimrod and his goons are from the other place?"

"Yes. He said nothing when he called?"

Rad shook his head. "I guess this is why he wanted to meet in person. It takes some explaining. But OK, so I killed

Sam Saturn. Only it wasn't *me* me, it was the other me, from the Origin. And people can cross over, from one place to the other, like the not-me and like Nimrod's goons."

"Indeed."

"And this," Rad looked around, at the walls and the ceiling, and spread his arms wide to try and indicate the house and everything. "This is... it's just a 'Pocket.' It's not real."

"Oh no, you misunderstand." Carson sipped from his refreshed glass. "There is no 'just' about it. This is real. The house, the city, you, me, Byron, Mr Fortuna, the ironclad in the harbour, the police blimps that fly above." He stopped and chuckled to himself. "The rain and the mist and the damned fog too, I'm sorry to say!"

Rad didn't quite share the Captain's joviality.

"Do you think there is anybody else here, apart from Sam's killer?"

"Well," said Carson, slowly. "Transfer from one place to the other is not only possible, but I think also not always deliberate. I doubt Ms Saturn's killer came here on purpose. I would imagine there are a handful of refugees from the Origin here. But our tests showed that the Origin and the Pocket are somewhat incompatible environments, and any who can or could or have crossed, shall we say, would have a hard time of it without... supportive equipment."

Rad nodded, then clicked his fingers ineffectually. "The masks Nimrod's goons were wearing?"

"Most likely, yes." The Captain interlaced his fingers on his stomach and leaned back.

The two sat quietly. After a while, Byron moved and Carson nodded, and his manservant left the room to perform whatever duties he normally performed in the small hours of the night. After another while, Rad's head jerked up, and he blinked, realising he had dropped off. The Captain was still, but awake, staring into the empty, cold black iron fireplace.

Rad wet his lips and checked his watch. It was nearly day-break, which meant, for him, bedtime. He wondered how to break his new nocturnal cycle. Maybe when all this was over, when the problem of the Pocket and the Origin didn't concern him.

Huh. Who was he kidding? Now he knew, it would sit with him for the rest of his life. He shifted around in his armchair and listened to the Captain's slow, heavy breathing. Maybe he was asleep, with his eyes open?

Had the old man been telling him the truth? It was too weird to make up, and there was no real reason to do so. Plus it tied with Nimrod's instructions and how he'd said how difficult it was to meet in person.

Rad coughed and said, "What do we do?"

Carson scratched at his moustache. He was wide awake. "Do?"

"Ah... do, yes. About all this." Rad gestured around the room again, as if it was an inconvenient problem to be eliminated.

"Oh, nothing we can do about that. How do you fight the world? More to the point, why would you? No, I think our – your – problem is more down to Earth. Pardon the expression."

Carson moved to the edge of his seat. He drew his legs under him, and leaned forward. At a stretch, he tapped Rad's knee with his fingers.

"Find the murderer, Mr Bradley. Solve your case. You are a detective, that's your job."

"Find... me?"

The Captain shook his head and clicked his tongue impatiently. "Don't think of it like that. For the purposes of your case, he is merely an impostor, a doppelganger. Find him, arrest him, whatever it is a private detective does."

"OK," said Rad. "I guess that makes sense. Start with what is possible, right? And then..."

"... Move to the *im*possible?"

Rad laughed. "That's your department, I think." He paused, and sat back, chin in his hand. "It does occur to me we have other issues going on in the city, sir."

Carson sat back as well. "Enlighten me, dear chap."

"Well," said Rad. "How did he get here? And Nimrod wants my attention. The Skyguard too."

"Yes, that had occurred to me."

Rad tried for a theory. He had no idea how any of it worked, but it seemed that this week, anything went. "Or maybe the barrier is weakening, coming down, making things... easier? Is that a danger to us and to New York?"

The Captain smiled and nodded, although he was now staring at the fireplace again. In the small light of the dark room, he looked old and sad.

"That could explain some things. Although I fear it would not be for the good of the Empire State. The Pocket and Origin cannot co-exist, for they are the same place. One cannot overlap the other."

Rad sighed. He found himself watching the black fireplace as well. "The Skyguard – Kane – talked about the end of the world. Could that be it?"

"The wall falling," Carson whispered. "The Fissure closing... or opening wider? Perhaps. Perhaps."

Despite himself, Rad yawned, long and hard. He rubbed his eyes. The study had windows with old heavy drapes, similar to those he'd seen in Kane's apartment. The curtains were not quite closed, and a sliver of pale dawn was shining in, lighting a small section of the baseboard. Rad watched it for a while, trying to remember what the sunshine was like on a hot summer's day. Then he realised the Empire State never had hot summer days. He wondered if the Origin did.

"If I'm looking for my alter ego killer, then I need some sleep." Rad stood. "If you'll excuse me?"

Carson waved a farewell without looking at Rad. Rad turned, and found Byron had re-entered the room. He was holding Rad's hat.

"Thanks, Byron."

The servant bowed but didn't speak. Rad took one look around the room and saw the Captain's eyes were closed. Perhaps he was sleeping now.

TWENTY-SIX

THE MORNING LIGHT WAS bright and hot against Rad's eyes, and it felt wonderful.

It was early, but already a few people were about, making their way to work, a few pushing handcarts or carrying briefcases, some with a crisp morning edition of the *Sentinel* under one arm. Sans any bylines by one Kane Fortuna, Rad thought.

He turned and looked back up the hill to Captain Carson's building. The regimented grey granite structure shone in the dawn light, the gardens in front glowing in the brightest colours Rad had ever seen. He laughed. The brightest colours he had ever seen since last week, at least. Existing as he had been almost entirely in the Empire State's night, he was used to the whole place rendered into a sick yellow monochrome under the streetlights, the only other colour the orange glow of the mist and fog bouncing the artificial light around.

The main street, with its steadily increasing foot traffic, was some distance below Rad. The Captain's house was on the crest of the hill, and as he trotted down the sidewalk with its bright green grass shoulder, Rad looked at the view before him with a newfound sense of wonder.

He couldn't see that far, but it was more than a usual city street. People were moving now as far as he could see, and more cars were passing. He could see directly down the street opposite for quite a distance, and while it was still crowded with tall buildings, they weren't the monster blocks of downtown, and allowed more of the mottled grey sky to stretch out before him.

Rad stopped, halfway down the hill to the main street. If he went to the top of the hill behind him, the point just beyond the Captain's house where the street met the apex of the rise, he'd be able to see the water, the docks and naval yards. The ironclad too, and its cordon of official vessels protecting the quarantine.

The sunshine filled Rad with energy, so he turned, judged the steepness of the street, and jogged up, mind already expanding with ideas he hadn't thought were possible and a sense of wonder about the city around him.

Whatever he had been expecting, Rad was disappointed. Sure, the view from the top of the hill was pretty good. He could see to downtown, the familiar spire of the Empire State Building dominating the landscape. On other sides, the lower, flat-topped buildings of Uptown. And in front of him, the street descended gently to the busy thoroughfares below, much as it did on the other side. Beyond, a great bulk of water the colour of steel. The morning air was hazy over it, but Rad could see the black rectangular silhouette of the mighty ironclad that he, Kane, Carson and Byron had stepped onto just a few nights before.

Rad shook his head, amazed that they'd actually made it there and back. Then he thought of Kane, and the fear returned. What was his friend up to? What was the connection to... to everything? Then it occurred to him. Did Kane know about the Origin and the Pocket? If the Captain did, Kane must, surely. What else did he know?

The ironclad was surrounded by a half-dozen smaller

shapes, the naval patrol boats. The water was calm, but Rad could see the flow of the current if he squinted.

What he wanted to see, though, he couldn't. Beyond the ironclad, the water vanished into a thick bank of cloud, the perpetual fog that surrounded the city.

For the first time in his life, Rad wondered what was on the other side. He'd never thought about it, never considered there was anywhere else. There was the Empire State, and there was the land of the Enemy, obviously. The ironclads steamed off into the fog and never returned, but... but that was just *how it worked*. That was what happened.

Rad had never thought about it, just like he had never thought about how he could be forty-four years old when the year was only Nineteen. How the city could have been built, founded before then. How he couldn't remember being married to Claudia, or remember why they were getting divorced.

Living in the Pocket, as Carson had called it, *did* something to you. He didn't really understand what the Pocket was or what separated it from the Origin, and he didn't think Carson really knew either. But just being in the Pocket, subjected to... what, its rules? Rad laughed. Maybe the world itself had its own laws, just like up was up and down was down and Jerry always asked for the slate to be cleaned on a Friday night.

The Pocket *made* you forget, *stopped* you thinking. Rad had heard people say that what the human brain couldn't understand, it just rejected. The entire population of the city lived and worked and played and just *existed*, happy that the war with the Enemy was being fought, happy that the Empire State looked after them, happy never to consider what was on the other side of the goddamn water because there was no other side. It was ridiculous and it made Rad laugh, but even as he did, he could feel it inside his skull. Pressure, a buzzing, almost a vibration. The Pocket fighting back.

Rad rubbed his eyes and swept off his hat to work at his tense forehead. He stood and looked at the fog bank beyond the ironclad, emptying his mind of dissenting thoughts. He began rolling his fedora in his hands and the headache started to recede.

Then he turned, and jerked back.

Two men were standing behind him, close enough to touch. Rad looked from one to the other, at their trench coats, fedoras and gas masks, and swore. Something moved, black and fast, and Rad dropped his fedora and hit the ground. Night descended once more.

i
7th AUGUST, 1930

"OH, MAX?"

Max stopped just short of the door, his hand reaching for the handle. Goddammit, now what? Like he didn't have enough to do. Like he wasn't already late for the next meeting, at which his plate would be piled even higher. He took a breath, and ran a finger around the front of his starched collar. He needed to talk to Dolores about their laundry. Maybe that was part of the problem. Oxygen starvation due to collars so stiff they may as well have been made of tin sheet.

"Yes, Mr McKee?"

McKee tapped his fountain pen on the blotter. Max cringed inwardly, counting the taps in his head. McKee's pens were expensive, and tapping did them no good at all.

"Have you seen Joe this morning?"

Max shook his head and clutched his open sheaf of papers close to his chest. He swallowed, causing his Adam's apple to bob up and down and catch on the top of the damn collar.

"No, sir, I haven't seen him since yesterday evening."

"Oh, no problem," said McKee. Finally he stopped tapping the pen, only to toss it onto the desk. Max winced. He didn't care if McKee saw it, which he was fairly sure he wouldn't.

"He was supposed to call earlier this morning, but he didn't, and he's not answering at home," said McKee. "Can you send someone downtown to run a message for me?"

Max nodded sharply. "Certainly, Mr McKee. In fact, he's due in chambers in..." He looked at his watch with a flourish. He wanted McKee to know he was now running late and that he had an awful lot to do before Joe arrived and it was all his fault. Not that McKee would realise, or if he did, he'd never show it.

"... Right about now, actually." Max raised an eyebrow at McKee, who sat there with that blank expression on his face, mouth slightly open, eyes almost unfocussed. How men like him got into offices like this he really had no idea on Earth.

Finally McKee seemed to snap out of it, nodded, and waved the clerk away. Max gulped again, but McKee was already looking at some papers. All Max could see was his superior's greased crown.

"Thank you, sir. I'll make sure to tell Judge Crater to call his office."

PART THREE
NEW YORK, NEW YORK

"I am just coming out of five years of night, and this orgy of violent lights gives me for the first time the impression of a new continent."
Albert Camus, 1946

TWENTY-SEVEN

WARM RED LIGHT. Shapes swam, crescents and arches and semicircles. They darted around his vision, the movements jerky. The red light pulsed, each change a physical vibration. It felt like someone trying to pull his eyes out with icy fingers.

Rad snapped them open, and lifted his neck, then let his head fall back with a yell.

Those bastards were torturing him. Drilling into his head while he was awake. *Psychopaths!* Rad yelled again, raining abuse on his captors, but his tongue was numb and it was just a sound, an animal moan.

He stopped, and the buzzing in his head died down, to be replaced by the characteristic pound of a killer headache. Rad bit into his numb tongue and rolled his head left and right, feeling a cold, sticky leather cushion underneath his skull.

He looked at the ceiling. White, brown, red, bright, dark. Nothing. It was a ceiling in a room, nothing more. There were lights. There were also shadows and black shapes. Two people, occasionally leaning over his face, occasionally standing next to whatever it was he was lying on. Talking to each other, passing instruments of torture over his body. Rad shouted again, perhaps clearer this time, but then the buzzing started. His eyes felt like they would burst like rotten grapes.

Then hands on his head. More than one, more than a
pair. One set of fingertips were cold, and pressed into his
scalp painfully. They pulled his head and held it, and the
more Rad tried to shake them off, the harder they gripped.
A second pair, warm and soft, moved over his face and then
the back of his head. They tugged, lifting Rad's head from
the surface. Then something else: cold and frightening,
pressing, slicing into the thick skin of his scalp. Rad shouted
again, but a big deep shadow blocked his vision. Abstract
shapes appeared in the darkness, two windows of light, and
something enclosed his chin and stuck to the sweat of his
forehead.

Rad gasped for air, and the buzzing stopped, and the
headache faded. His tongue regained life, and he licked his
lips. His eyes throbbed and his ears were filled with the
sound of a sea that he had never seen. He took another
breath. He tasted rubber and something else, something
chemical, hot and spiced.

He blinked, and looked at the two people standing over
him, through the goggles of the mask he was now wearing.
He raised his head, and found nothing to stop him. He tried
his hands, flexing his fingers, then moved his arms. They
felt heavy, but there was no pain, no impediment to the motion. His hands found his face, and moved across leather,
rubber and plastic. There was something heavy pulling on
the mask from the front. Rad couldn't see it, but he could
feel it. Connected to the mask, over the mouth, was a short
corrugated tube, leading to a large cylinder, the size and
shape of a soup can.

The two men standing over him were not masked. They
wore blue pinstripe suits of an odd cut, and had short hair,
shaved at the sides, longer on top. One was thickset with a
bullet-shaped head and hardly any neck at all. The other was
thinner, with a long face ending in a chin a mother could

only call "disappointing". Both had very faint red and white marks on their faces, and the chinless wonder's hair, longer than his colleague's ugly crew cut, probably parted quite neatly most of the time, was askew and stood up a little in random bunches. Bullethead frowned; Chinless smiled. Rad wasn't sure which expression made him feel better.

"Mr Bradley," said a voice – one which didn't come from either of the two goons, but from somewhere near Rad's feet. He raised himself up on his elbow, wincing as the bottom of the mask cut into the flab of his neck. Another man walked closer, moving to the left and stopping next to Bullethead. He leaned in, too close, peering at Rad through the mask goggles like he was some kind of specimen. It crossed Rad's mind that perhaps he was as he gasped for breath, pulling air through the mask's soup can for everything he was worth.

The third man was old (but he couldn't be old because it was the year Nineteen), and his accent was foreign (but it couldn't be foreign because there was nowhere else apart from the Empire State). A thick shock of white hair, properly combed. Moustache, also white, also thick, trimmed in perfect symmetry over a small mouth. The clothes were the same too, belted jacket, somehow out of place, with epaulets and silver buttons. The third man laughed at some triumph. The sound was high, short, and sharp; a staccato exclamation. After it came the smile, showing teeth straight but yellow and grey with age.

Rad felt his heart settle. "Captain Carson! What's going on?"

But the third man shook his head, the smile plastered on his features. "No, my dear chap, my name is Nimrod.

"Welcome to New York City."

TWENTY-EIGHT

NIMROD STROKED HIS MOUSTACHE. Rad had a great deal of trouble thinking of him as anyone other than Captain Carson. He was identical. The voice with strange clipped accent. The smile. The way his eyes shrank to slits when he smiled. The same grey and yellow patina across his front teeth. Identical, like Rad was identical to Sam Saturn's killer. That didn't make him feel any better.

Rad sucked in another breath. The mask was comfortable enough, sure, although the way the heavy filter pulled out and down was annoying. He could feel the rubberised edge of the mask stuck all around his face, forming a tight seal. The goggles misted just slightly, but it was no problem. He could still see fine.

It was the breathing that was the problem. If he sat still, and didn't speak, he could pull air into his lungs, and push air out. He could breathe, but it was a conscious effort. He had to take over the manual controls from his brain stem, and move the muscles of his ribcage himself. It was tiring, and somewhere in the back of his mind the seed of panic was sown. It was the same spark that entered the mind of someone being strangled, or drowned. People with asthma had it bad, Rad suspected. They'd get that spark every time they had an attack.

It was worse when he spoke. He had to time his breaths with his words, which resulted in strange pauses and broken sentences. He remembered his first encounter with the masks in the alley. The two goons – who now stood in the office, picking their nails and choosing their cigarettes with the greatest of ease – had not only moved with agility, they'd sucker-punched him good and proper, and had still been able to hold a conversation. Well, one of them had. Rad glanced at Chinless on his left and Bullethead on his right, trying to remember the voice and match it to the face. The man who had applied his fists to Rad's face and asked the questions had been the heavy man with no neck – Bullethead – while his friend had stood back and not done much at all – Chinless here, who Rad remembered the Bullethead had called Grieves when the Skyguard had dropped on him. Rad looked at their faces and thought he preferred them with their masks on.

Another breath. In, out. The intake felt like sucking on elastic, as if the rubbery air was resisting and would snap back into the soup can if Rad let up the pressure. Breathing out made the goggles mist, momentarily, and his eyes hurt as the pressure inside the mask increased, the foreign air, absolutely, positively refusing to be pushed back out into the atmosphere through the respirator.

Rad figured he'd get used to it. Perhaps it was a case of learning the rhythms of the mask. He imagined they would become second nature after a while. He didn't know how long that would take. He didn't want to find out either. He needed to get back to the Empire State.

Chinless lit a cigarette, wreathing his face in smoke. He put the cigarette to his lips, then pulled it away, holding it in mid-air while transferring thick grey smoke from his mouth to his nose. It wasn't particularly classy, but Rad was fascinated. The Prohibition in the Empire State covered tobacco as well as alcohol. While the latter was easy enough to distil and sell in places like Jerry's speakeasy, tobacco was another matter. Rad was then very glad of the mask. Before Wartime he'd been a chain smoker. Safe in his little rubber and glass universe, not a single whiff of the rich smoke was available to him. Then the thought occurred to him that maybe there was no "before Wartime" and that maybe he'd never smoked in his life, that the tingle in his nose the sight of the smoke produced – and the sharp craving that followed it – was another element of his life "reflected" from his New York City original.

"I apologise for the way my agents Mr Grieves and Mr Jones here were forced to manhandle you, Mr Bradley, but I felt it was really time for us to meet." Nimrod vaguely indicated the two goons as he spoke. Rad glanced at them again but neither seemed particularly interested in the conversation.

Rad shifted in his wooden chair, then regretted the motion as he struggled to pull a proper, full breath. He wasn't restrained at all, which was a pleasant feeling, even though he knew he wouldn't make it to the door without getting dizzy. They knew it too. That was why he wasn't restrained to the chair. He was restrained by the mask.

Rad managed, "They're making a... *(breath)*... habit of it. A bad habit *(breath)*."

Nimrod laughed, and clapped his hands. At this sign of humour from their boss, Chinless Grieves and Bullethead Jones smirked.

"My point being, Mr Bradley, that I was most displeased you failed to make our previous appointment. Getting in touch with you in the Empire State requires considerable organisation and expense. Travelling to the Empire State, even more so." Nimrod leaned over his desk on his elbows. The desk was covered with papers, in stacks, in file folders, in loose sheaves covering the blotter. The paper crinkled under his elbows.

"You have cost me a lot of time, and a lot of money." Nimrod paused, then sat back and folded his arms. "There is a lot riding on this. We can't let one unreliable factor ruin our plans. There is too much at stake."

"That so?"

Nimrod nodded in exactly the same way that Carson would nod. Rad's eyes flicked to some pictures on the wall behind Nimrod's head. A certificate or diploma, with a bright red seal. Something else that was also text, too small to read from his chair. But three pictures, sepia photographs, showing the impossible landscapes in white. Carson – no, *Nimrod* – as a young man; the airship; the companion with blond hair. Rad frowned.

If Nimrod could see Rad's eyes roving behind the mask goggles, he gave no indication.

"That is so, Mr Bradley. I'm not sure you are taking this seriously."

A hard-won intake of oxygen. "Oh, the end of the world seems pretty serious to me." And another. "That's what you said on the phone anyway."

Nimrod nodded.

"How did you call me, anyway?"

"We have the Fissure tapped for a variety of purposes. Communication is one. Monitoring and observation is another."

Rad nodded. "Carson explained the Fissure. A tear in the world, he called it. So, it allows travel too?"

"Yes," said Nimrod. "Although the two realms are not entirely... compatible, shall we say. The environment in each rejects material from its opposite." With one arm still folded, he pointed at Rad's face with the other hand. "The mask helps. The environment is not *lethally* toxic, but it is exceedingly uncomfortable."

As if to prove his point, Nimrod stopped speaking and the office was filled with the sounds of Rad's heavy, slow breaths coming through the respirator. Nimrod smiled. "You'll get used to it. You *acclimatise*."

"So you pulled me through the... Fissure?"

Nimrod's mouth turned upside down. "Not through the Fissure itself, but using its power. The Fissure is a single, physical location, but its influence spreads out across the whole city. A 'field' of sorts. If you can detect the field, *measure* it, you can tap it as a power source and use it for all sorts of things. You can even use that power to cross from *here* to *there*, using mirrors and reflections. Fascinating really, quite a trick. But physical transfer between the Origin and the Pocket is even more expensive than a telephone conversation. I'm going to have the department accountants on my back for this one, eh?"

Grieves and Jones sniggered. Grieves puffed his cigarette and said something back to Nimrod, although Rad couldn't catch it. Nimrod exploded with laughter, slapping the top of his desk.

"So if you're Nimrod, who's Captain Carson?"

Nimrod's laughter died. "I was hoping you could tell me. I am Captain Nimrod."

"His ship," wheezed Rad. "Carson has a ship, under his building. Like an airship, of some sort. Said it was called *Nimrod*."

Nimrod steepled his fingers. "Ah."

"Still no clue?"

Nimrod shrugged, then rotated on his swivel chair to face the back wall of his office. He looked up at the photographs.

"I was commander of the *Carson*, a hydrogen dirigible of experimental design, on an expedition to the Antarctic. Funded by the United States government, mostly scientific, partly military. I was recruited, you see, due to my not inconsiderable experience with Arctic exploration. It's in my blood. My father cut through the jungles of Africa in the nineteenth century, claiming lands and treasures for Queen Victoria. I followed in his footsteps, although I was no good in hot climes. The snows called me!"

Rad looked at Nimrod's back, ready to start with the questions, but took a breath and found the effort required to ask what he wanted was just too much. "No kidding," he managed at last.

"Of course," Nimrod continued, lost in his own personal nostalgia trip, "money was the issue, and funding seemed to come more easily from the United States. So we upped sticks and moved from London to New York in 1921. My family tree had some branches here already, including property in Manhattan, so it was not quite such a wrench as it may have been."

"Uh-huh."

Nimrod spun back around to face Rad, his face somewhere between delight and surprise. A beaming, open-mouthed smile, forehead creased and narrow eyes as wide as they could go, which was not very.

"*Extra*ordinary," said Nimrod. "You really have no idea what I'm talking about, do you? London? England? Africa? No? The Arctic and Antarctic? Polar ice caps?" Nimrod shook his head, paused, then frowned. "Even New York City? Manhattan?"

Rad shrugged, because it was easier than speaking. He saw Grieves finish his cigarette and laugh silently, shaking his head. Jones said nothing. Rad figured that he probably hadn't heard of any of these places either.

Rad wasn't sure what to make of it. The Empire State was the Empire State. Polar ice caps? Sounded weird.

And yet... something, something stirred in his mind. He thought again of Claudia. He had no memory of their wedding day, like he had no knowledge of what London was.

"I'm in New York City, apparently," he managed. "You said so yourself."

"Yes, yes, I did." Nimrod went back to stroking his moustache. "The name may be different, but I feel you will recognise New York. Manhattan, at any rate. The Empire State was born out of New York City, and takes its image, more or less."

"You said 'we'. You and these two beauties?" Rad managed to nudge an arm in the direction of Grieves and Jones. Grieves straightened against the door, like he wasn't quite sure whether he was being insulted or not. He looked at Nimrod for support.

Nimrod met his agent's eye, then turned back to Rad.

"Alas, I am at the mercy of the State Department when it comes to staff. When I say we, I mean myself and my companion, Keats." Nimrod leaned back in his chair and tapped one of the photographs on the wall behind his head with a fingernail. Nimrod the younger and the blond man. Nimrod held his head up, pulling the loose skin of his neck tight, and sucked air through clenched teeth.

"Keats was my batman and engineer on every voyage. On our last expedition, there was an... accident."

Nimrod's eyes narrowed and he gulped. He kept his head up and was staring at the wall behind Rad. Rad didn't like where the story was going. The old man cleared his throat.

"Keats was injured. Very badly. We brought him back home, and I even managed to fashion... *devices*, to help with his breathing and alleviate at least some of his discomfort. A 'life-support', you could say. When the position was offered here, they also offered to take care of Keats, to help him rehabilitate and even regain something of his former life."

Nimrod coughed again and lowered his head. He glanced at the top of his desk and shuffled some papers. Rad kept quiet.

Nimrod lifted a single sheet of paper and pretended to read it. He didn't look at Rad as he spoke.

"We came by ship, but Keats died during the crossing. I had been reading his favourite book to him as we travelled, as it seemed to ease his pain. After he died... well..." Nimrod tapped his breast pocket, which Rad could now see was filled out by something flat and rectangular. A small book.

Rad tried to nod, but the soup can just slapped his chest. "I understand."

Nimrod put the paper down and smiled at the detective. Rad wasn't sure whether his eyes were wetter than they were usually.

"He always had an affinity for the great Romantics. Always claimed he had been named after John Keats." Nimrod's eyes went far away again. His fingers found the book in his breast pocket and tapped against it again. "*Don Juan,* by Lord Byron. Have you read it?"

Rad sat up and coughed. Nimrod leaned forward in concern, his glazed eyes clearing and his hand automatically adjusting his tie, as if he was suddenly aware that he had said too much. Rad recovered after a moment and ran a finger along the rim of the mask under his chin.

"Can't say that I have." He cleared his throat. "Any chance of a drink? Can I take this mask off?"

Grieves looked at Nimrod, and Nimrod nodded and waved at the door. The agent pointed at Jones, who shook his head without taking his eyes off Rad. Grieves left the office and closed the door behind him with a click. In the brief moment it had been open, Rad could hear footsteps, voices, and typewriters. Wherever Nimrod had his office, it was a busy workplace.

"A capital idea, Mr Bradley," said Nimrod, clapping his hands again as he was fond of doing at regular intervals. Just like Carson. Rad actually found it easier to think of

Nimrod as Carson, or maybe Carson's brother. The personality and manner were identical. Nimrod, captain of the
Carson. Carson, captain of the *Nimrod*. After his personal
journey back through difficult memories, he had appeared
to regain his composure. Rad wondered how many times
the agents had heard the story of Keats. They sure hadn't
shown any interest on this occasion.

Rad cleared his throat, looking forward to his drink. The
air pulled through the mask was smelly but completely dry.

"Its *image*, you say?" he asked.

Nimrod nodded and said nothing.

"An image of the city. New York City – this place – what?
Reflected? Reflected through this Fissure thing. And the
people in it. You, for example? Nimrod and Carson, two
sides of the same coin."

Another clap of the hands and the expansive smile. "We
will make a private detective of you yet, Mr Bradley. An excellent deduction." He paused, and leaned in, voice low. "Or
are you merely, how can I put it, 'playing' with me? You
are accepting the facts somewhat easily. Have a care, Mr
Bradley. This is no elaborate practical joke."

Rad shook his head, exaggerating the otherwise natural
movement so it would be clear with the rubber hanging off
his face.

"Hey, I've given up fighting." He waved a hand dismissively
as he took a long breath. "Carson had a theory about doubles
and the Empire State being some kind of Pocket. That runs
with your tale. If my city is an image of your city, then this
makes New York the Origin. That's the word Carson used."

"Interesting nomenclature. Pocket is quite accurate. The
only place you know of is the Empire State, because the
Empire State exists in a pocket. There is nowhere else."

Rad laughed. "Just the city and the fog. Explains why I could
never figure out what was on the other side of the water."

Nimrod *hrmmed* to himself, and there was a tap on the glass of the office door. Grieves was a grey shadow behind the bubbles, hunched over a tray. Nimrod glanced at Jones, who sighed, nodded at his boss, and opened the door with complete disinterest. The tray wobbling in Grieves's thin arms held four cups and a tall, narrow pot. Steam rose from the spout, and Rad wished he could smell what it was. He was still smarting from using up his coffee ration prematurely.

"Thank-you, Mr Grieves," said Nimrod, as his minion set the tray down on the most stable stack of papers on his desk. Nimrod busied himself with the cups, and inclined his head towards the detective. "Help him with the mask, would you? I think we can afford you maybe ten minutes of the freshest air New York City has to offer!"

Rad gripped the arms of the old wooden chair. He didn't quite know what to expect as Grieves rolled his knuckles and approached. Rad saw Jones smile behind Grieves, then laugh into his fist. He didn't like the Bullethead. This wasn't going to be good.

Grieves yanked the mask, the straps catching behind Rad's ears. Rad yelled, and instinctively raised his hands to them, then stopped. A wave of relief flooded over him as breathing suddenly became effortless and automatic. He smiled at Grieves, who just shrugged, then looked at Nimrod. Nimrod, at least, returned the smile, and pointed to the jug.

The aroma, the sweet, sweet smell of coffee. Richer, deeper than he had ever experienced it. Rad could almost taste bitterness at the back of his throat as he took a deep breath, wide nostrils flaring even more. Even with a full coffee ration, it had never smelt like that.

Rad smiled, licked his lips, and leaned in towards the desk. A second later, his head cracked its edge, and he toppled from the chair onto the cheap carpet of Nimrod's office, white foam bubbling at the corner of his mouth.

Rough hands with short fingers gripped Rad under the armpits and hefted him back into the chair. Cold hands with long fingers slapped his cheeks lightly.

Rad opened his eyes, looked around with a narrow gaze, then widened his eyes in shock. He managed to get his hands to his chest; Nimrod barked something at his agents. Rad's eyes closed and he felt his head pushed backward. A shadow passed over his reddening vision, and when he brought his head to the upright position, he was looking at the world through the steamy goggles of the mask. Each hard-won breath was a battle, tainted with rubber and a chemical odour that stuck in the back of his throat. Each was a blessed relief, easing the buzzing in his head and the knife-hot pricking behind his eyes and the stabbing pain in his chest.

Nimrod looked relaxed, at ease, sitting back in his reclining office chair, fine porcelain saucer in one hand, fine porcelain cup in the other. He was holding the cup just in front of his mouth, nostrils flaring – as Rad's had done as he enjoyed the rich aroma.

Rad sighed, coughed, then took a laboured breath. "No coffee?"

Nimrod shook his head, but he was smiling as he sipped his own drink. Rad closed his eyes and focussed on not coughing.

"What happened?" he asked at last.

Nimrod sniffed loudly and set the cup and saucer down on the desk. His chair snapped back into the upright position with a clatter of old springs.

"This environment takes some getting used to." Nimrod almost sneered as he looked Rad up and down. "For some it takes longer than others." The sneer broke into the grey-yellow toothed smile.

"What exactly did you want to... *(breath)*... tell me in person anyway?"

"Nothing that couldn't be relayed via the telephone, but I always like to meet my agents for a face-to-face interview, and I thought it was important you saw me *in vivo* so you could be sure I was who I said I was."

Rad nodded. It was a fair point. While his week had been odd, to say the least, he was pretty certain that he never would have believed any of it unless he'd been dragged through the Fissure himself to meet Captain Carson's alter ego. He wondered whether the offer of a drink was just a ruse, another demonstration that he was telling the truth about the "incompatibility", as Nimrod had put it, of the Pocket and the Origin.

"When I went to visit Carson," Rad huffed, "I went looking for answers. For days I've just had hints here and there of something big happening, with me smack in the middle of it all." He paused for breath and raised a hand, indicating to the others that he was not finished. "With Kane not only acting up, but not being around most of the time, Carson was the obvious choice. And I was right, he knows about the Pocket and the Origin."

Nimrod nodded. "He would, yes."

Rad shuffled in his chair with impatience. "That's just it. How would he know? He said he had 'probed' the Origin through the Fissure, but he seemed to make some pretty good guesses. How is the Empire State related to this... place, whatever you called it."

"New York City."

"Right." Rad nodded and sat back. It wasn't that he hadn't ever heard the name before, it felt like he'd known it well, in childhood, and hadn't heard it for thirty or forty years.

Which was impossible, because it was the year Nineteen and he was a forty-four year-old man with no childhood.

Grieves turned his back to Rad and moved around Nimrod's desk. Nimrod looked up, and leaned his ear towards Grieves as his henchman whispered something quickly. Rad couldn't hear behind the wheezing of his mask, but Nimrod's eyebrows moved around on his forehead as he took the information in. Grieves stood back, and Nimrod nodded, chewing his lip. For the second time, Grieves left the office and closed the door with an almost inaudible *snick*.

"Time is short, Mr Bradley," said Nimrod. "One of the... side effects, you could say, of the Fissure. Time does not necessarily run in parallel between the two cities. We must get you back to the Empire State."

Rad shook his head vigorously and summoned the strength to stand. He slid his lead-like legs towards the big desk, and practically fell onto his clenched fists. Nimrod jerked back instinctively as the respirator hanging from Rad's face swung towards him with the movement.

"I'm a detective. I have a case to solve. If I'm a pawn on someone's chessboard, fine and dandy. Just tell me which side I'm playing for. Black or white?" He sucked in a lungful of stale, flavoured air. "What's the deal, Nimrod? What is the Empire State?"

Nimrod stared at up at Rad leaning over him; Rad could hear Bullethead Jones peeling himself from the wall and moving around until he was directly behind him. Nimrod watched his henchman over Rad's shoulder, and shook his head. Looking back at Rad, Nimrod felt his stomach with his right hand until he located a small pocket in his tunic. He extracted a pocket watch, a gold half-hunter, and flicked his eyes towards it.

"Very well. We can return you home via the Fissure itself. That will lessen the risk of time dilation, although may not eliminate it entirely. Besides, perhaps you might like to take a look at it for yourself? It will give us a little extra time."

Nimrod stood and smiled coldly as he looked down at the detective bent against the desk.

"Crossing the Fissure itself is something we try to avoid." A pause, a beat. "But you're a big strong man. You might just survive."

TWENTY-NINE

IT WAS NIGHT AGAIN, but a night unlike any that Rad could remember. Or maybe he could, locked somewhere deep in his nineteen year-old mind filled with memories that weren't his. A memory, an image, reflected through the Fissure from the Origin to the Pocket, from *his* New York equivalent. Because like Carson and Nimrod, he had a double, an original, too. Rad's heart fluttered, just a little.

The killer.

He had no idea how it worked, or why it worked, or why it was, but he was hoping to find that out.

Grieves and Jones had helped Rad walk. They were still rough, still thugs, but obviously Nimrod trusted them, and they seemed pretty good at obeying his orders. They were government employees, after all, and even governments need tough guys sometimes.

Nimrod's office was full of people, a large central open-plan area filled with desks and people typing. Around the periphery were private offices like Nimrod's. Rad noticed that the clothes people wore were a little strange. Different cuts, different styles that he didn't like. Then he remembered Nimrod's claim about how time moved differently in the two cities. If it was 1949 or 1950 here, and Nineteen at home, how did you convert? Did that make it nineteen years since the Fissure had opened? He'd been in New York for a few hours, but Nimrod was eager for him to return home. If the timelines weren't parallel, how long had he been away from the Empire State?

Rad sat in the back of the black car as it cruised the city. Even through the mask and the tinted windows of the government limo, Rad was transfixed. The city was brighter, lighter than the Empire State. He recognised a lot of buildings, and didn't recognise a lot of others, but he was amazed at the lights. So many burning in the night, so many colours. With no fog or mist, he watched Manhattan in crystal clarity. It was alive with people and cars – although he wasn't sure what the time was, it couldn't have been that late. There were shops too, restaurants, corner stands; buildings and doorways and windows blazing with light.

It was bright, and busy, and noisy, and it felt like home. The Empire State was cold, grey, fogbound and as quiet as a grave. Rad realised now that his city, his home, was merely a shadow of New York, a bad knock-off, a worn-out second-hand copy. Rad felt odd. His chest was tight, not just from the breathing. His mask goggles steamed more, and he recognised the feeling. Sadness. A profound, deep emotion. He hadn't felt this sad since... well, since he couldn't remember.

And if he was a fake, an image, a reflection, a copy, a duplicate, with memories that half belonged to someone else, maybe his emotions were copies and fakes too.

New York City made him unhappy. Rad wanted to go home. He was afraid, now, that'd he'd been away too long. Perhaps Nimrod had the same thing in mind, as he leaned forward from the back seat to tap Grieves on the shoulder and urge some speed. Grieves nodded and the car rocked on its back wheels as he increased pressure on the accelerator.

Nimrod squeezed closer to Rad, and tapped him on the shoulder to drag his attention away from the passing view outside the window. Rad turned around awkwardly.

"The Fissure is located in Battery Park, at the bottom of Manhattan. We own the whole area now, and access is tightly restricted."

Rad nodded. "We have the same. It's called the Battery."

"Really?" Nimrod smiled at the name. "That's appropriate. The Battery. The power source of the Empire State, quite literally."

"As Carson said. He didn't seem to know much about how it worked."

Nimrod nodded, and rolled his hands around each other then took a deep breath.

"The Fissure is a tear in space-time." Nimrod paused and squinted at Rad. "Space-time?"

Rad shook his head. Nimrod waved his hand.

"Doesn't matter," he continued. "The United States of America – that's the country that New York sits in – was once protected by a, well, a freelance law enforcement agent, shall we say. You'll know the name, I think."

"The Skyguard?"

"Correct! But the Skyguard had an opposite. Perhaps his equal, perhaps not. He called himself the Science Pirate." Nimrod paused, waiting for a response. Rad shrugged.

"The Skyguard has been in jail for... forever, I guess," said Rad. "Never heard of a 'Science Pirate'. Sounds kooky."

Nimrod touched a finger to his lips. "Fascinating, quite fascinating. Some aspects reflected, some aspects translated. Some even translocated. Some absent altogether."

"Trans-what now?" Rad asked.

"The Fissure was opened when the Skyguard fought the Science Pirate over the construction site of the Empire State Building, back in 1930. A sort of last stand, you might say. There was an explosion. The Skyguard's body was never recovered, and the Science Pirate fled, but was not seen again.

"There were strange events that night, according to reports both official and unofficial. At the same time as the explosion, the Statue of Liberty suffered a colossal lightning strike. The lightning was *green*, Mr Bradley, according to the newspaper report. Strange sounds were heard and lights seen all over Manhattan. Over Queens, the stars in the sky – and I quote – 'danced like fireworks on the Fourth of July'."

Rad huffed inside his mask. "Very poetic for the *Sentinel*."

Nimrod's moustache bounced around as his mouth twisted into a frown. The old man leaned back a little, as though terribly offended by Rad's comment.

"The *New York Times*, old chap."

Rad blinked. "OK," he said, slowly, before changing tack. "So why were you looking for me, anyway?"

Nimrod smiled, his attitude changing instantaneously. Rad wondered if eccentric was quite the right word for him.

"We weren't, my dear detective. We were looking for the Science Pirate and your doppelganger, a man called Rex. A small-time gangster, ran a minor Prohibition racket in Midtown. No one of consequence, although there were numerous warrants for his arrest and he was also required as a witness in another case presided over by the New York Supreme Court."

Nimrod stopped, the smile plastered over his features. Rad could see he was enjoying this far more than he should have been.

"But...?" Rad prompted.

Nimrod's eyes flashed. "But! At the same time as the Skyguard vanished and the Science Pirate fled, there was a car accident at the scene. The body of one of Rex's associates was recovered, but not Rex himself. On the night that the Skyguard and the Science Pirate vanished, so too did our fugitive, Rex."

Rad shook his head with effort.

"I don't get it," he wheezed.

Nimrod leaned closer. "We can detect the trails that people leave, in this world and in the *other*." He jabbed one index finger to the left and the other to the right as Rad watched. "The Skyguard vanished from New York, but once we knew of the Pocket and how to look into it, we picked his trace up immediately. But of the Science Pirate, there was no trace, here or there. Until now. Likewise your twin, Rex."

"How long ago was this fight?"

"Nineteen years," said Nimrod.

Rad sighed. "I figured. But why Rex? Why was he important?"

Nimrod frowned and he shrugged with some difficulty in the back seat. "Maybe he isn't, but his trace was difficult to follow at the *nexus*. Tangled, distorted, but detectable. It is possible he had something to do with the Science Pirate's disappearance, or was at least tied to it. Find him and perhaps he would lead us to the Pirate's trace."

Rad nodded. "OK." Anything Nimrod said. He looked out the window again. Lights, people, *life*. He felt his heart sink again.

"So, what about Battery Park? How did you find the Fissure, exactly?"

Nimrod rubbed his hands together, a clear indication yet another story was forthcoming. Rad kept his eyes on the wonderful, mysterious world outside.

"Well, those reports of strange occurrences were not just from the night of the fight. The area of the explosion was sealed off for a time, for cleanup and investigation, and so on, but opened soon enough. Then, days later, came strange reports from downtown. Battery Park. Things appearing, disappearing. People, police. Even cars and a horse! The park was kept open, but soon people stopped going there. Stories spread that it was haunted."

Rad laughed, then coughed at the lack of oxygen. He took

a breath that was like pushing mashed potato through a sieve and turned back to Nimrod.

"Ghosts?"

At Rad's comment Nimrod laughed as well, the sharp sound ricocheting around the inside of the car. Even Jones's bullet-shaped head seemed to shrink slightly into his shoulders like a man-sized turtle.

"But you took it seriously?" said Rad. The laughter died and Nimrod looked sheepishly at nobody in particular.

"Ah, well, yes."

"So the Fissure..."

Nimrod met Rad's eyes through the steamed goggles. "So the Fissure," he repeated, as if it were a profound statement. "Indeed. A crack that opened in the world, in the middle of the park, leading from New York to an *alter* dimension. We don't know *how* it was opened, but the whole city appears to be seated on a weakness, so to speak. The Skyguard's battle with his nemesis sent shock waves outwards like a boulder dropped in a lake. Perhaps in the park reality was at its thinnest, and tore." Nimrod shrugged. "You know the rest."

"Believe me, I don't. Are you saying the Fissure, what, actually created the Empire State? Created me, created Carson. Created the war and the Enemy?"

Nimrod *hrmmed* loudly and his face creased into a frown. "Not sure about the war – what do you call it? 'Wartime'? Well, there's nothing like that in the United States. As for creation... well, we don't know. I don't know. The Pocket is an accurate name. It's an extension of here, the Origin, but it's small. New York City is in America, and America is in the world, and the world goes around the sun, and the sun... well, you get the idea. The Origin is vast, unimaginably so. The Pocket is just that – a pocket. A protrusion."

Rad snorted. "I live in a hernia. Great."

"Ha! Oh really, Mr Bradley!" Nimrod was greatly amused for some minutes, and continued sniggering to himself as they drove at speed. Rad remained silent, concentrating on his breathing, watching the miraculous view outside. Then the lights changed, and he realised he was looking at the water. The night air was clear, invisible. And there, on the *other side*. More lights, and the outlines of buildings. Some lights were moving too. Cars. Cars and people.

Nimrod saw Rad pressing the mask to the glass of the car's window.

"That, my friend, is Jersey City. Smaller than New York City by quite a margin, but, aside from the separation of the Hudson River, more or less part of a single conurbation."

Then Nimrod rested a hand on Rad's shoulder. Rad flinched, but didn't take his face from the window. "I'm sorry, my boy," whispered Nimrod. "I was forgetting."

Rad's head shook, the loose ends of the mask straps clacking their metal-capped tips together as he did so.

"What do you want me for?"

Nimrod shuffled back around on the narrow bench seat so he could see out of the front windshield again. "Although we can trace people, follow and watch them, in a way, intervention is more difficult. For my agents to be in the Pocket is a great risk, one which I must limit whenever possible. Far easier would be to have someone from the Pocket act on our behalf."

Rad swung back, the respirator knocking Nimrod's nose. The old man raised a hand to protect his face from any further contact.

"What do you mean?"

"Jones and Grieves have been very busy on your side of the Fissure. We have been following the Skyguard – the new Skyguard – for some time. He is going to destroy the Battery – your side of the Fissure. He must be stopped. I would presume he thinks that by destroying the Battery, it will cause the Fissure to collapse and return everyone to New York City."

"But... the Empire State is not New York? We don't come from New York. We never did."

"Top of the class, Mr Bradley. Destroy the Battery on your side and certainly the Pocket will collapse. It'll be the end of the Empire State, and everything and everyone in it. Skyguard included."

"Aha."

Nimrod ran the edge of his index finger along the underside of his moustache. "Am I right in thinking you may know the identity of the new Skyguard?"

Rad drew a breath, making the respirator whistle.

"You think right. You don't know? You said you were following him."

Nimrod shrugged tightly in the small space of the back seat. "Not constantly, and whoever is wearing the suit now is covering his tracks very well. In all honesty his actual identity is probably not that important to us."

Nimrod squared up to Rad as they squashed together in the back seat. "I'm hoping, detective, that this little visit would be enough to remove any last remaining doubts from your mind. The Empire State is in great danger, Mr Bradley, but the stakes are higher. The two cities, yours and mine, the Pocket and the Origin, are *tethered* together by the Fissure. Instability in one destabilises the other. The connection *cannot* be broken. Therefore, if anything should happen to the Fissure on your side..."

Rad held up a hand. "Got it. Lights out for everyone. I'm with you. What's the plan?"

"That," said Nimrod, "is your department. Stop the Skyguard. Do what you must."

"OK."

"OK it is."

The car slowed and turned, then stopped. A small ceiling light flicked on in the front seat and Grieves's thin face appeared like a spectre in the reflection on the inside of the windshield. Nimrod, Rad and Jones were shadows in the background, but the light caught the goggles of Rad's mask, picking them out in the reflection in front of him. Rad shuddered.

Time to save the world. Rad stopped and considered. Two worlds.

Nimrod tapped Rad's knee like a friendly uncle. "We're here, Mr Bradley."

Rad nodded. "Show time. Shazam."

Battery Park in New York City did not differ significantly from the Battery in the Empire State. The signs came first, warning the public that the area ahead was restricted. Then the streetlights were replaced by large white floodlights, illuminating the high fence ahead of the limo. The fence was divided by a manually operated boom painted in yellow, with a giant warning sign covered in tiny print hanging from it, offering a selection of imprisonment options for the discerning trespasser. A small hut on either side was manned by a pair of soldiers each, their white helmets etched with "MP" in heavy black letters in sharp contrast to their regulation khaki from the neck down. Their guns were large but thankfully slung over their shoulders, barrels skyward. As the limo slowed, Grieves wound down a window and offered one of the approaching MPs a pass. The barrier was raised and the car waved through without even having to come to a complete halt.

They stopped in a large parking lot half occupied with green trucks with canvas-covered beds. Nimrod helped Rad from the car, and the pair followed Grieves and Jones ahead, the agents already negotiating passage through a second barrier ahead with a single guard hut, leading to a floodlit

path cut through a stand of tall trees. The remains of the public Battery Park, thought Rad. There were more signs ahead,
also in the infuriatingly small and precise military lettering.
Grieves and Jones waited for Nimrod and Rad to catch up,
then Nimrod skipped to the head of the party and led them
off into the woods.

The Fissure was close. Maybe it was because he was
charged with a mission. Maybe he was getting acclimatised
to the new universe, but Rad felt full of energy and had to
stop himself walking ahead of his host. Maybe the Fissure fed
him energy or something airy-fairy, mystical-magical from
the Pocket, Rad drawing current like a lightning conductor.
Rad eyed a few of the signs as he walked. NYCF Secure Area
Alpha. Rad allowed himself a small smile. Here be the Fissure.
Come one, come all, step right up, ten cents a peek. Keep off
the grass and please don't touch.

After a few paces along the wide path Rad felt that the
mask was a hindrance. He wouldn't need it back home, anyway. So he stopped, took it off, and as he did so realised his
hat was back at Nimrod's office. Nimrod stopped and turned,
waiting patiently while Rad first rubbed his scalp, then
scratched his chin, then examined the mask in his hands. All
the while, he was aware of his chest rising and falling with
each breath, aware of the movement, the arching of his ribs
and contraction of intercostals, aware that it no longer required conscious thought to control his breathing. He looked
up at Nimrod. The old man smiled, the hard floodlights
bleaching his already pale features to chalky whiteness.

"Come," he said, and turned and walked briskly down
the path.

The New York night was different to the Empire State
night in more ways than one. No fog made the air clear, invisible, but also cold. The chill was unfamiliar to Rad, who
was used to the cloying humidity and warmth of Empire

night, not to mention the perpetual orange glow of the fog
lit by the city lights. As he walked, Rad tried to imagine this
city in the daylight. Would it be hot? And how far could he
see? If he went to the top of the tallest building – the Empire
State Building, he assumed, if they even called it that here
– how far would he see? If Jersey City was on the other side
of the Hudson, as Nimrod had called the body of water,
what was on the other side of Jersey City? And what about
the east side of the island?

Rad walked on, not paying attention to his surroundings,
lost in a newfound wanderlust. He had to come back, had
to. He gripped the mask hanging by its straps from his left
hand. He'd take it home with him. It would be needed for
return trips.

Because he had to come back.

The white light of the path began to change, becoming
steadily overwhelmed by a blue glow from up ahead. The
blue light shone through the trees around them, casting
long shadows back along the path. Rad jogged ahead to
match Nimrod's pace, and when he caught up with the old
man Nimrod smiled and winked.

The path turned, and the trees vanished. They were in an
open clearing now, a large circular zone of poured concrete
perhaps one hundred yards across. Armed MPs crawled the
perimeter; three stationed closest to the end of the path approached the group and Grieves revealed his pass again. The
MPs nodded briskly, saluted and stood aside to let them pass.

Rad's eyes fell on the object at the centre of the disc, and
he slowed his pace a little, letting Nimrod get ahead again.
The thing was metallic, individual plates fashioned into
curved, overlapping slats to create a giant egg perhaps
twenty feet high. Despite the bright floodlights that ringed
the clearing, the whole area was lit in a flickering electric
blue, escaping from the seams of the egg-like structure. As

Rad got closer, he shielded his eyes from the brightest emanation and as the contrast dropped, he could see the thing was painted in a dark matte green, just like everything else owned by the military. The structure was mounted on a four-tiered pedestal, surrounded on three sides by army crates in wood and metal with lids ajar. Cables of various thicknesses spooled around the crates and the steps of the pedestal, the thickest pair disappearing into a large black multi-port box inset into its base, their opposite ends snaking away to the periphery of the disc on the opposite side, where a prefabricated cabin with one long, wide window looked out onto the clearing.

Nimrod stood with his hands clasped behind his back, looking at the green egg, peering at it until his nose was almost touching the surface. Rad gingerly trod the four steps to the base of the egg and raised an arm to knock, experimentally – but before his hand was halfway there, Nimrod grabbed his wrist in a lightning move. Rad didn't resist, but was still surprised at the strength hidden in the old man's biceps. There was a loud clatter from behind them as several MPs raised their rifles and jogged from the edge of the concrete disc to the central structure.

"Have a care, Mr Bradley," murmured Nimrod.

Rad lowered his arm and eventually Nimrod let go, his small dark eyes locked on the detective's. Rad frowned and turned his attention back to the egg.

"This is the Fissure?"

Nimrod nodded. "The Fissure itself is protected by this shielding, which in turn protects New York from the energy radiated by it."

Rad raised his eyebrows in quiet admiration. He was right about the Fissure having power, then.

Nimrod looked at him for a moment, and *hrmmed*. He then turned and waved at one of the MPs, who departed from his station on the concrete disc at a fast trot and headed towards the cabin.

"The Fissure itself is a fragile space-time event. Like a tear in a piece of cloth, it can grow, change shape. And I needn't remind you of how important it is for both our cities that no change comes to it."

Rad craned his neck up to look at the egg, the top of which curved away out of sight.

"So, what, you open this thing up and I step through the magic door?" Rad patted his stomach. He was just over six feet, and was wearing a suit and shirt both somewhere comfortably in the region of *extra*-large.

Nimrod's lips pulled together into a pout, then he chuckled. "Oh, you'll fit, don't worry. You might even lose a few pounds."

Rad's eyes widened but Nimrod had turned around to face the cabin. Nimrod raised a hand and pointed a finger skywards, and moved them in a fast circle. A helmeted figure framed in the cabin window gave a thumbs-up and leaned over, and a few seconds later a series of dull thuds sounded from somewhere deep in the concrete foundations under Rad's feet. He felt Nimrod's hand on the bend of his elbow and allowed himself to be pulled back a few yards, down the steps and onto the concrete disc proper.

The surface of the metal egg began to move. Rad saw that the whole pedestal was a rotating platform, itself made of concrete but a completely separate structure to the large disc. The egg appeared to turn an arbitrary number of degrees in the clockwise direction, slowly, then stopped. The ground vibrated again as more deep, unseen machinery was set into action, and the shell split in two, the twin halves moving out slightly in separation, then telescoping into themselves until they were just two stumps on either side of the Fissure itself.

Rad hadn't known what to expect. He had imagined the Fissure as a sort of bright, fiery object, tall and thin, crackling at the edges with the magic of the universe, tendrils of energy curling from it like the perpetual fog of the Empire State. He expected light and sound; something dangerous, beyond the understanding of men. So he was a workaday private detective in a bad part of town. At least he had an imagination, he thought to himself.

As it happened, Rad saw he was right. His mental image of a roaring red inferno was wrong only in that the Fissure was rendered in shades of blue, from dark indigo at the very edge to almost white at the centre. The Fissure was a pillar of flame like an out-of-control gas jet, ten feet tall, two feet wide, vaguely elliptical, although the corona spilling from it made it hard to focus exactly on its size and shape. Rad felt the buzzing behind his eyes again. His fist closed in a reflex movement on the straps of his borrowed mask.

The Fissure wasn't hot. In fact, Rad couldn't feel any change of temperature at all. Looking up, he saw spiralling smoky fingers of light and energy spilling out, streaming from the centre and around the concrete clearing. They looked like fast moving clouds against the night sky. If he wanted to, Rad could have reached out and touched them, but he thought better of it and kept his hands to himself. He was about to get intimately acquainted with the Fissure anyway.

Nimrod watched the flicker of the miraculous space-time event, his pale features now bleached baby blue by its light.

"Magnificent, isn't it?" Nimrod had to shout. Rad realised that the buzzing sound wasn't just in his head, it was in the air, halfway between a hurricane and a swarm of bees. Nimrod pointed at the Fissure, as if it wasn't the most obvious and awe-inspiring sight that Rad had ever, ever, ever seen.

Nimrod smiled in the blue light. "Any chance I get, any excuse to see it with my own eyes."

Rad licked his lips. "Very impressive." Keeping one eye on the Fissure, and one on his companion, he said: "You sure it's safe?"

Nimrod nodded vigorously. Rad could see the whiskers of his moustache bristling in the invisible wind emanating from the crack in the universe.

"It will be uncomfortable, so be prepared, but it will be safe. The influence of the Fissure actually spreads for many miles around, and we have other, more convenient methods of harnessing its properties and effecting a transfer between the Origin and the Pocket – travel via mirrors, as I said – but direct transit via the Fissure is possibly the easiest to understand. You go in here," he pointed at the Fissure again. "And you come out again *there*."

Rad shook himself, and rolled his shoulders. He took a series of long, deep and easy breaths. Maybe when he came back he wouldn't need the mask. Maybe he'd acclimatised to the Origin. Then it occurred to him that if he had adjusted to New York, would that mean he was now incompatible with his own dimension? He dismissed the idea from his mind. Home was home.

"Ready when you are, chief." Rad hopped up and down like a champion sprinter waiting for the call to get ready.

Nimrod held his finger up like a school teacher. The smiles had gone, and his white eyebrows curved downwards to nearly meet in the middle as he frowned.

"Find the Skyguard. Find the Science Pirate. Stop them. The Battery must not be shut down. One side of the Fissure depends upon the other. Close it and the Empire State goes." He clapped his hands to emphasise the point; the sharpness of the sound made Rad jump. "And New York goes with it."

Rad looked over his shoulder. Grieves and Jones were loitering at the bottom of the stairs, idly chatting to an MP.

"They not coming?"

Nimrod shook his head. "As vital as your task is I have the upmost confidence in your ability. Unfortunately, as I said earlier, I cannot place my agents in the Pocket for the time required. But we will be watching, Mr Bradley, have no fear."

Rad nodded smartly.

"Captain Nimrod, always a pleasure." Rad made a casual salute.

Nimrod laughed as he clasped Rad by the forearm and shook his free hand vigorously.

"Good luck, old man. Until we meet again."

Rad winked, and held his breath, and ran towards the blue inferno before them.

There was a cracking sound like a peal of thunder under-water, and Nimrod was alone on the platform.

ii
19th AUGUST, YEAR 1

IT WAS AMAZING HOW DIFFERENT the city was at night, how a city so familiar, a city you had been born in, grown up in, could suddenly become so different, so strange and weird. So foreign.

New York City. Population: nearly seven million. Area: almost three hundred square miles. Population density: over twenty-three thousand per square mile.

The Skyguard considered this as he took another wrong turn, into another blind, vacant lot sandwiched between office blocks.

The edges of his vision clouded with mist again and he tilted the front of his helmet up, wiping the condensation off the inside of the mask. His suit's systems had gone down when the Science Pirate had ploughed them both into the ground, but it was too risky to remove the helmet. New York City was a busy place, even late at night, and he had a secret identity to maintain. And with no rocket boots to jet into the sky, he was stuck with travelling on foot. He couldn't ditch the suit completely and come back for it later either, it was too valuable to stash in a trash can for later collection. God knew what the damage was. The Skyguard hoped he could put it back together again. He had contacts, friends with the necessary skills. He could do it, given time. He presumed the

Science Pirate had been the lucky one, as there had been no sign of her when he climbed out of the crater.

In fact, he hadn't really seen that many people at all. With no power in his suit, he didn't actually know the time, but it was still night and it was still raining. How long he'd lain unconscious at the bottom of the smoking hole he could only guess. Maybe a couple of hours, maximum, but then all those people and all those police wouldn't just have left him there, would they? Or did the Science Pirate scare them off? Or worse?

The Skyguard shook his head, and his helmet rattled. The drizzle had passed, but a thick fog had rolled in. Even out in the open streets it was hard to get a bearing, as all major landmarks – the Chrysler Building, the half-finished Empire State Building – were obscured. Several times he thought he'd seen something he knew and picked the right direction, but then a building loomed in the wrong place, and a street turned where it never had before. It was disconcerting and frightening.

Bingo. Concussion. That was it. The Skyguard wobbled his head and listened to the rattle in the helmet again. Something was loose, and while he felt OK – sore, bruised perhaps, a headache like a jackhammer – he must have taken quite a punch. Concussion and shock, leading to confusion and fuzzy vision and getting lost in the city of his birth that he'd sworn to protect for the last ten years.

The Skyguard leaned on a lamppost, and after a few seconds noticed a vibration. It was nothing, just traffic... except he hadn't seen or heard any of that either. No one was around, so he flipped the hinged mask on the front of his helmet back up again to get a breath of fresh air.

With no power in his suit, his helmet had been muffling the sound of the outside world. He'd been walking around almost deaf without realising it, and as soon as the mask was up a roaring filled his ears. He let go of the lamppost, but by now the ground itself was shaking.

There was a *clunch* as a searchlight was switched on, travelling for just a second over the ground before pinpointing the Skyguard. Startled, he instinctively turned to look up at the source, shielding his face. Behind him, his torn cloak billowed like a sail as the small lot was filled with what felt like a mini tornado.

He couldn't see properly. He swung the visor back down, but the blaze of the searchlight just turned his vision almost completely opaque as it illuminated the condensation inside. Streaming behind him, his cloak tugged strongly on his neck, and he overbalanced and toppled backwards. As he impacted the ground, he used the momentum of his fall to help slide his helmet off. This was no time to worry about disguises.

Something had flown into the lot. Something elliptical, a little larger than a city bus, but looking like an upside-down boat with curved hull stretching upwards with the cabin hanging from the underside, two searchlights mounted at the front. As the Skyguard moved his arm around to screen out the light, he could see a long, curved window in the front of the hull, lit a dull red from inside. There were two figures in the cabin, nothing more than black cut-outs.

The PA barked, "Gardner Gray."

The Skyguard felt the adrenaline punch a hole in his chest. He crawled backwards a little, almost instinctively, on his armoured elbows, but the heel of one boot got caught on the trailing edge of his cloak and his neck jerked backwards painfully.

A hundred thoughts crowded his mind, chief among them was how they – *anyone* – could possibly have known his name.

"Gardner Gray," the PA barked again. "Stand down!"

The voice reverberated around the hard stone borders of the empty lot, amplified beyond the roar of the engines of the thing, and the rush of air that whirled around the Skyguard. Four large jet nozzles attached to the rear of the cabin and also higher up, on the sides of the boat hull above, were angled downwards, blasting hot air into the lot. It was some kind of airship, a dirigible or something. The Skyguard knew well what they looked like – German Zeppelin were frequent visitors to New York – but he'd never seen anything like this machine. It was small and agile, nothing like the giant hulks he was familiar with.

Gardner Gray, the Skyguard, managed to scramble up, and detached the cloak from his neck, pulling the clasps that held it across the top of his shoulders. Freed from the awkward helmet and cloak, he bounced on the balls of his feet, ready for action, ready to fight for his life. The suit was unpowered and very heavy, but was otherwise undamaged, articulated joints moving smoothly and easily. He could put up a defence, for a time. He checked the available exits. There was just one, directly behind him.

The craft dropped, coming to around ten feet from the ground. At close range, the searchlights had to pivot to their maximum angle to keep the spots on Gardner, but they were not very manoeuvrable and he sidestepped the beams easily. Keeping out of the main beams, Gardner got a better look at the mystery machine.

It was an airship of sorts, certainly, but Gardner could only marvel at the design. It drifted to a halt at a slight angle, allowing Gardner to see the huge, six-foot-high letters stencilled in white on the lead-grey hull.

POLICE.

Gardner gasped. Since when did the police fly airships – of any kind – around the city? Since when did the police know who he was?

EMPIRE STATE

268

He smelled conspiracy, betrayal even. The Science Pirate. It had to be her. Ten years of crime-fighting partnership, ten years of happy marriage. Now this, sold out to the authorities.

The Skyguard knew the law. Resisting arrest or trying to fight would, in the short term, just provide more dirt in the conspiracy or plot against him. But in the long term, if the Science Pirate had arranged something, organised some master plan to pitch the very city which the Skyguard had sworn to protect against him, then he had to fight from the *outside*.

With more mechanical grinding, a door on the side of the airship's cabin slid open and two steel rope ladders were flung over the side. The cavalry was coming to take him down.

The Skyguard lunged backwards, pushing off with his toes to get maximum speed and spinning in mid-air as he sprinted for the lot's exit. Behind him he could hear nothing but the roar of the engines and the wind. Ahead, the alley-way was an inky black void.

And then, at the other end a light clicked on, as powerful as the searchlights behind him, enveloping him in endless white. The light swayed a little, revealing the bottom of a second small airship as it dropped into view, its front search-lights swinging around as they locked onto their target.

The Skyguard slid to a halt, nearly tripping. Escape route blocked, no rocket boots. He was trapped.

He turned back, but they were on him already. Six officers, clad in helmets and heavy body armour, each carrying a nightstick that was too long and flared at the end like no weapon the NYPD ever carried. He raised one armoured fore-arm to protect his face, but the first blow nearly broke his ulna. The second hit ricocheted off the edge of his shoulder, the head of the nightstick rebounding to clip him on the back of the head. The Skyguard dropped like a stone to his knees and then onto his stomach. Lips sucking on the flagstones, he dragged in a difficult breath that tasted of water and dirt and machine oil and blood.

"Gardner Gray, also known as the Skyguard."

Gardner Gray – also known as the Skyguard – craned his neck upwards. The searchlight was on him and he couldn't see anything except the black shoulders of the police around him. The PA burst into life again with scarcely a crackle.

"You are hereby ordered to stand down and surrender yourself to the City Commissioners. It has been hereby decreed that you are a felon and an outlaw and are due to face justice at the Chairman's leisure. So it has been proclaimed in the first year of the Empire State."

Gardner Gray closed his eyes as the booted feet of the riot police, or whoever they were, closed in around him. He felt an armoured knee grind into the small of his back as his hands were yanked backwards and cuffed, and then gloved hands caught him under the arms and he was on his feet.

He blinked. Pain zigzagged up the back of his skull with every heavy heartbeat. He saw the airship and the police, silhouettes in the light, swimming in front of him, before his knees gave way. Before he blacked out, his mind swam with images of New York and bewilderment that he could have got lost – in a city he knew like the back of his hand.

But in the first year of the Empire State, Gardner Gray, also known as the Skyguard, felon and outlaw, wasn't in New York City anymore.

PART FOUR
SHAZAM!

*"The Empire State and even New York City are about
due for some agitation on this subject."*

William Anderson, 1914

THIRTY

THE PASTOR OF LOST SOULS made the final adjustments, then stood back. The hood nodded, and he walked back to his desk.

Rex fingered the lapels of the suit. It was hideous, chocolate brown with a heavy cream pinstripe, double-breasted. The shoes were OK, black shiny leather, and at least the white spats were a touch of class. The ensemble was finished with a fedora in white felt and, using the closed window as a mirror, Rex experimented with a few different angles until he thought he looked more or less passable. He opened the window again like he was told and turned, walking stiffly back to the Pastor's desk, limbs straight like he was soaking wet. The hooded man laughed.

"You'll never make an actor, Rex."

Rex frowned. He really wasn't sure about this. "I thought there wouldn't be any acting required?"

"Of course there won't. You just need to look the part, enough to get in, get close. Once the target is eliminated and there is no danger of mistake, you can go back to how you were."

"You're damn right I will." Rex sat, wincing as the uncomfortable suit fabric creased under his knees. He reached forward and picked up the photograph of Rad Bradley from

the desk. It was remarkable. Dressed in a more-or-less approximation of the detective's favourite outfit, Rex was
identical. He adjusted the hat a little to match the photograph. Bingo. Then Rex snapped his fingers.

"Hey, I've seen this guy. I remember the hat. He was
walking downtown."

The Pastor ignored him. He reached down and slid a
drawer on the right side of his desk open, reached inside,
then dropped something small and heavy in front of Rex.
The Pastor withdrew his hand, then reached forward with
the other and pushed the snub-nosed pistol towards his
guest. Rex looked at it for a moment, then covered it with a
meaty hand and dropped it into a pocket of the ill-fitting suit
jacket. Even sitting down, the weight of the gun pulled the
jacket down on one side. Rex felt immensely stupid in this
get-up, but he glanced at the photo again. It was perfect. Rad
looked immensely stupid as well.

Rex took the hat off. A white fedora? What was this guy
thinking? He shook his head at the Pastor, who inclined his
white hood to the left, as if inviting Rex to spill his thoughts.

"You're kinda assumin' a lot here, preacher."

"Am I?"

Rex felt his face flush hotly, his hair-trigger temper set off.

"What do you think I am, some kinda hatchet man? I'm
a bootlegger, sir. I don't go in for murder usually. If I need
someone knocked off, I hire a gun. Why get me to do it?
Why wait all this time for me to arrive to take out this guy?"
He flicked the photograph on the desk. It skidded across the
top and spun towards the Pastor, landing the right way up
for him to regard the portrait quite by chance. This coincidence seemed to galvanise Rex, who sat back with an
alarming creak and folded his arms so tightly the seams of
his jacket parted just a little.

The Pastor's eyes, the only features visible through his

hood, roved up and down, between Rex, squeezed into the chair in front of him, and the photograph of Rad Bradley on the desk. He clacked his tongue.

"The likeness is remarkable," he said quietly, paused, then added: "But you *are* the same person. Still, remarkable."

Rex huffed. "I still don't get it. You want me to do it because we look the same? Like I said, I don't usually get my hands dirty."

"Ah, Rex," the Pastor began. "Perhaps a gun is not your style. But strangulation is? Bare hands are more satisfying. You really know you've got the job done when you can feel the bones grinding under your fingers."

Rex blanched. Goddamn. The Pastor knew. Rex feigned ignorance, barking a "What?" that was too loud, too quick, redolent of guilt.

"You killed Sam Saturn," said the Pastor. He shrugged as he spoke, as if he was disregarding a minor misdemeanour. "That very act brought you here, because you and she, and she and Rad, are connected to this place."

The Pastor stuck his elbows out at ninety degrees, holding his forearms horizontal in front of him. He interlocked the fingers of each hand to emphasise his explanation, and made a show of a one-man tug o' war.

"You killed Saturn. You must kill Bradley. It is not so much my decision as a preordained event. It is inevitable. You must kill him. As the death of Saturn pulled you here, so the death of Bradley will pull you back. It is your path to New York City. Home. And my path too."

Rex sighed and felt hot pinpricks on his forehead. He rubbed his fingers on his scalp, and found it slick with greasy sweat. The Pastor was a nut, a loon in a white hood living in a white house, he was sure of that. But something in what he said made sense. Little else did about the whole situation, although Rex had long since given up on the idea that he'd wake up, or snap out of it, finding himself back home in his own bed, the Empire State a fading dream. Then he thought of the girl's body breaking in his hands, so easily, and the blood, and the smell of the blood, and the buzzing in his head.

No, it was real. The Empire State was real. And what he wanted now, more than anything, was to escape, to go home. If the Pastor knew what he was talking about – and why wouldn't he? He'd been here longer than Rex, he knew how it worked, he knew about the girl, knew how to get home – then all it would take is one simple job and they'd be back in Manhattan. And this Rad, he wasn't real anyway, he was just some stooge, a lookalike, a pale shadow of himself. Rex wasn't anyone's schmuck. Give him a job, he'd do it. He reached into the pocket with the gun, and ran his fingers over its machined surface. The metal wasn't cold as he'd expected. It was warm, smooth.

"Do you understand me, Rex?"

Rex nodded.

"Do you want to go home, Rex?"

Rex nodded again.

"Then play your part. Eliminating the detective is but the first step. Relax, I'll have some coffee brought up while I tell you the rest."

Rex nodded a third time. He wanted to say something else, but wasn't sure what, so closed his mouth as the Pastor headed for the open door. Rex turned and watched, noticing one of the Pastor's zealots sitting on the stairs, a surprisingly elegant woman in porcelain makeup and a royal blue dress, apparently having heard the entire discussion. But the woman just smiled at Rex before turning her attention to the Pastor as he approached. The two shared a brief, whispered conversation, then the Pastor turned and walked back towards the desk. The woman at the stairs looked again at

Rex. She smiled, then delicately and carefully headed down-stairs on very high heels.

The Pastor sat.

"To business."

Dawn was just a handful of hours away by the time the Pas-tor left the brownstone with Rex trailing close behind. The pair stopped at the base of the stairs that led back up to the front door. Almost the whole street was illuminated by the white lights inside the house, and Rex didn't like to dawdle in what was practically a spotlight. He fidgeted, and shifted his weight from one foot to another, and the Pastor asked again whether the instructions were clear.

"I got it, dammit," Rex snapped. Then he sighed and apol-ogised, but not without looking over his shoulder towards the darker part of the street, which he could barely see out-side of the glow of the Pastor's house. His new employer tilted his head at the outburst, the hood hanging in a straight edge towards the man's shoulder.

"I am trusting you, Rex," the Pastor whispered. "I do hope you can fulfil your appointed task."

Rex held a hand up. The Pastor nodded and rested a hand on his shoulder.

"Go."

Rex nodded and departed at a trot, relieved to be out of the Pastor's company and out of the light. The damn city was strangely quiet, but he wasn't going to take any chances, so he hit the shadows as soon as he could.

The Pastor stood and arched his shoulders like a weightlifter stretching out before the snatch and grab. Straightening the hem of his jacket, he slid out of the light and headed down the street in the opposite direction from Rex.

He stopped around the corner, in a shadow cast by a

raised set of stairs leading into one of the many anonymous dead buildings.

He stood in the dark for a while, watching the street. There was nobody there and as he stared ahead, the yellow streetlight opposite seemed to flicker and blur. The Pastor tried to blink it away, but it just got worse. After thirty more seconds his vision split almost completely into two overlapping images, the yellow streetlight beginning to slide and spin in his mind.

The Pastor sucked in a breath, bringing his hands to his face. When he pulled them away, the white hood came with them, which he folded neatly like a large handkerchief and placed in his inside jacket pocket.

Stepping out of the shadow, the man from under the hood straightened his hair, adjusted his tie, and headed north, towards the Empire State Building.

THIRTY-ONE

SPREAD OUT BENEATH THEIR FEET, the Empire State was a glittering jewel in the night, the perpetual misty haze blurring the city lights, turning the city into a black and grey canvas studded with a million multi-pointed stars.

It was beautiful, peaceful, and even romantic, and before he'd even realised it, Kane had composed a poetic – if purple – chunk of copy perfect for an op-ed piece in the *Sentinel*. He shook his head. That was his past life. Kane Fortuna, star reporter, had ceased to exist.

"Something wrong?"

His companion's rockets flared as their burn was adjusted. The Science Pirate bounced a little in the air; Kane watched the blue jets flash orange momentarily as they stabilised.

"No," said Kane. "Just nostalgia for a past life. How's the suit?"

The Science Pirate bounced in the air again and made some further adjustments to a set of manual controls hidden under a cover on one gauntlet. After a moment the Science Pirate closed the cover, but it didn't quite sit flat. Something slightly too large blinked with a blue light underneath it.

"Power flow is still erratic, but that might just be the new levels. I could tune it a little if we had time, but we're good to go." The Science Pirate flexed the gauntlet. "Thanks for the actuator. I could never have got the suit working again without it. Make it yourself?"

Kane raised his own hand and flicked open a similar panel on his wrist. Another actuator, blue light glowing, was wired into the suit. It was inelegant, a cradle of wires that looked confused and fragile, but clearly a similar component.

"No, that one I... acquired from a boat, shall we say. Electricity has slightly different properties here. I'm lucky I had a friend to help with my suit, otherwise it would have been as dead as yours. The actuators are a weak point for us now, but it's only a temporary fix. We won't need them where we are going."

The Science Pirate looked down at the city far below. The wind picked up and tugged noisily at the huge cloak streaming out behind. Kane watched, impressed by the rocketeer next to him, also aware that from the ground, he would look exactly the same. He began to run more newspaper copy through his head, then wondered if he'd ever be able to kick the habit.

"It's like a prison," said his companion.

Kane opened his eyes, suddenly aware that he'd been lost in a dream. The Skyguard's helmet picked up the Science Pirate's words over the wind.

"What is?" Kane asked.

The Science Pirate pointed down at the city. "This. The Empire State. You're trapped in one city, that's all you have." The rocketeer paused, and the helmet shook slowly. "Poor bastards."

Kane smiled. His ally was right. It was a prison. A tiny, inescapable world. The Empire State.

"Your Empire State Building is pretty fancy." The Science Pirate pointed at the tall structure a mile away. It dominated the city. "Ours isn't finished yet."

"I think it might be done by the time we get back. Don't forget time passes differently between here and there."

"Yeah, you said. Thank Christ," said the Science Pirate. "Maybe I can make a home in a more enlightened time."

The pair floated in the light breeze for a few minutes. Lights winked below, stars slowly rotating through the fine mist that clung to the concrete and glass and steel of the place.

Finally Kane spoke: "A more enlightened time?"

"Forget it," said the Science Pirate. "I'm just looking forward to going home."

Kane folded his arms. As he raised the heavy gauntlets, he noted the tempo of the actuator's blinking indicator had slowed slightly. Suit power was down a notch, but no problem. They had plenty of time.

"So what happened?" he asked.

The Science Pirate drifted a few inches away from Kane and turned towards him. The Pirate's helmet tilted to the left slightly as the response was pondered. "I was hoping you could tell me."

Kane clacked his tongue, the mask turning it into the sound of someone trying to open a particularly stubborn can of beans with a wrench. He shrugged.

"I don't understand the how and the why. But I was just curious."

The Science Pirate rotated back around slowly, and looked down at the Empire State.

"Not much to tell. There was a… fight, with you. The Skyguard." The Science Pirate paused, and looked Kane up and down. "The *real* Skyguard. I thought I had him, but there was an explosion. Light and sound, and colours… *weird* colours, y'know? Anyway, when the fireworks stopped I was at the bottom of a hole, alone. There was no sign of him, and suddenly the place was crawling with cops. A real scene."

The Science Pirate stopped, and Kane waited, but no more came. They hovered for a minute or two, then the Science Pirate shifted in the air and spoke again.

"Maybe I did something stupid then, I don't know, but I panicked. It was some kind of trap, I was sure, so I took off. Up, up and away.

"It must have been only a couple of seconds later. I was over the Brooklyn Bridge, and I lost everything. All power, all rocket burn. But it wasn't just running out of juice, or some system failure. It was like flying into a brick wall, or maybe flying straight into the heart of a tornado. Everything died and I fell – or, rather, was *thrown* – back to the ground. Ditched into the Hudson. I made it to the shore but it was nowhere I recognised. I thought maybe it was concussion, or perhaps I'd been thrown further than I thought and washed up in Hoboken or somewhere. Nothing worked, so I hid. A few days in empty warehouse. I worked on the suit, but it was dead. I couldn't even get out of it. But finally I got the emergency line on. God knows why that was the only thing that had any juice. Then I got your signal, loud and clear." The Science Pirate tapped the side of the flanged helmet. "And here we are."

Kane nodded, understanding a little more. He reached down and pulled his flapping cloak aside to reveal a small, flat box attached to the belt above his right hip. He squeezed something and a light flicked on and started blinking.

The Science Pirate made a huffing sound, which might have been a laugh, and nodded.

"Receiving. So how do we get out of here, exactly?"

Kane paused and turned off the signal box. He pointed at the Empire State Building.

"You fell out of the sky in New York nineteen years ago. It might only have been yesterday for you, but it's nearly two decades for everyone else. You understand that, don't you?"

The stony huffing sound came again. "Like I said," said the Science Pirate, "maybe it'll be a more enlightened time. So what's the secret?"

Kane lowered his arm, then folded his arms again.

"The Empire State is linked to New York by something called the Fissure. It's a gateway, like a corridor connecting our two worlds."

The Science Pirate nodded. "OK. So we go through the gate. Easy."

Kane shook his head. "Not that easy. You're not the only prisoner here. Down there, in the city, are others from New York. We have to return them all home."

The Science Pirate's helmet turned to Kane. Kane wondered who was behind the sculpted mask.

"And how do we do that?" his companion asked.

"Collapse the Fissure. The Empire State folds up and takes everyone through to New York."

"And how do we do *that*?"

Kane laughed.

"What?"

"Oh, that's the easy part," said Kane. "I thought you were the scientist?"

The Science Pirate turned away, but didn't say anything. Kane wondered if his companion was thinking or offended. He was about to continue when the Science Pirate spoke again. Thinking, then.

"Energy input?"

Kane wagged his gloved finger. "Got it in one."

The Pirate said, "There's nothing in your tiny little world to provide it though."

"Right again, but we've got something that's not from this world, exactly."

"Explain?"

Kane pumped his rocket boots, lifting higher a little. He

looked down at the Science Pirate, then beckoned with a hand.

"Come with me. We've got exactly what we need, waiting above the clouds."

Kane throttled his rockets and shot skyward, his blue and white jets fanning out over the Science Pirate as he vanished through the cloud deck.

The Science Pirate watched him rise, then raised one arm straight up and followed.

THIRTY-TWO

THE EMPIRE STATE BUILDING, the seat of the City Commissioners, was a fortress. At one hundred and two stories,
over fourteen hundred feet high, it was the tallest building
on the island, and sat at the heart of the city, a shining beacon that the citizenry were justly proud of. Scared of as
well, for it was an inescapable reminder of the tight control
the City Commissioners had over them. Keep yourself to
yourself, do as you were told, and they'd leave you alone.
Step out of line, and it was you versus the Empire State.
And you weren't going to win.

One hundred and two stories of reinforced, armour-clad
stone and steel. Each level as secure as a prison, each of the
hundred or more departments contained within protected
not just by thick walls but by a whole platoon of heavily
armed Empire State police. The Empire State Building was
an impregnable citadel and a symbol. So long as the Empire
State Building stood, the Empire State would prevail.

At 4.05am, all contact was lost with the last police covering floors one through fifty. The building commander in the
operations deck on the one hundredth floor ordered security
sections from floors fifty-one through seventy-five to take
positions on the fifty-second floor, with the remaining police
to dig in at ninety-nine. Above the operations deck was the

commissioners' boardroom, and above that the Chairman's private quarters. The Chairman needed to be protected at all costs. Nothing could get past floor one hundred.

The attack, it seemed, had come from street level. The entire ground floor had gone black, but by the time the staff in the operations deck had worked out it wasn't a power cut or glitch in the system, word came from the second and then the third floor. Something was coming. More confusion, more hesitation followed. Security coverage of the building stretched several blocks in every direction, and nothing had been seen aside from the usual smattering of authorised early morning traffic. It was only when the emergency channel from the fourth floor finally sprang into life – relaying the screams of the dying to the Building Commander – that he fully realised the trouble they were in. The Empire State was under direct attack. For the first time the Enemy had struck home.

By the time the building commander gave out what were to be his final orders, it was too late. Floors fell, one by one. Operators lost radio contact with section leaders while the building commander demanded to know why they hadn't seen the strike force coming. The police blimps on routine patrol all over the city were called, but they only confirmed what the building surveillance teams had already said. There was no strike force, no army. Not even a crack team of commandos or saboteurs. The blimps had seen nothing. The city was quiet.

The navy was called at the waterside bunker. Peering out into the fog over the water, they kept a constant watch. Nothing. The perimeter was secure, and the ironclad in the harbour was under guard, so what the hell was going on in the Empire State Building?

To his credit, if the building commander had known what he was dealing with, he might have been able to formulate a plan of defence. But there was no way he could ever have predicted in just what form the attack would come, and perhaps he didn't even believe what he was seeing with his own eyes when death came to take him while he was still sitting in his command chair. After the crew of the operations deck were massacred, the combined sections on the ninety-ninth floor held out for nearly ten minutes, but when they fell, there was nothing between the invaders and the commissioners.

Two blimps launched from the roof, carrying the four deputy commissioners skyward. The craft drifted upwards, negotiating the ring of a dozen police ships that now orbited the building, called in by the emergency signals broadcast from the operations deck. As the blimps powered away into the clouds, the emergency signal went dead, and in the first blimp Deputy Commissioner Warren watched as the building's lights went out, turning the elegant, tapering tower into a featureless black shadow, a void in the heart of the Empire State. Warren's mind raced. They needed to regroup, quickly, and gather their forces. Perhaps the fleet could be called back, but they'd never been able to re-establish contact with it after it entered the fog. And who would be the Chairman now? The great and noble leader of the Empire State had ordered their evacuation, and armed only with a revolver, had decreed that he would hold the boardroom, the symbol of the city governance, by his own hand for as long as possible. He'd said it was his moral duty.

On the one hundred-and-first floor, the Chairman stood by the vast, floor-to-ceiling, wall-to-wall plate glass window, watching the twin blimps sail upwards and vanish into the orangey clouds. Other shapes, other blinking lights swam around in the night sky, several of the police blimps breaking off from the cordon formed around the Empire State Building to escort the deputy commissioners safely away.

The boardroom was cavernous and austere, its marble floor and columns designed to convey an atmosphere of solemn importance. The meeting table itself, a single slab of black marble, could have seated two dozen with room to spare, but looked tiny and isolated in the centre of the enormous room.

Although the building's power had gone, the boardroom was suffused by the light of the city from the glass wall. But standing in the shadow of a marble column, the Chairman was practically invisible to anyone entering the room. When he heard the double doors of the chamber swish open and solid, echoing footsteps approach, he allowed himself a smile. The revolver hung loosely in his left hand, the hammer gently rocking back and forth, back and forth, under his thumb.

"Welcome to the Empire State," he said, taking a step backwards from the window and turning on his heel to face the new arrival. He carefully placed the revolver on the tabletop with a *clack*, hammer safe, and sat down. Relaxed, he steepled his hands in front of his face.

"Report, please. What did you find?"

The intruder had stopped in the shadow of a pillar, but at the Chairman's invitation walked into the light, each hammer-on-anvil footstep accompanied by a whirring of gears and the ticking of a clock.

The Chairman watched as the robot walked towards him, taking smooth, oiled steps in a horrible parody of human movement. Its monotonous voice ground from somewhere within its metal chest.

"Orders, sir."

The Chairman tapped the table and stood, rubbing the tip of his nose as he walked back to the window. Behind him there was a click, and then another, and then the robot spoke again.

"Orders, sir."

But the Chairman wasn't listening. He looked down on the city, lost in thought.

Seconds, minutes, or hours passed. The Chairman didn't know. The clock inside the robot ticked time away. It was... hypnotic. Comforting. The Chairman shook his head and sighed, and glanced at the machine.

The robot had joined him at the window. When, the Chairman couldn't remember. If he didn't know better, he could have sworn that the thing was actually *looking* down at the city. Could it remember? Could any of them? Was there anything left inside the copper and pressed steel shell that could *think* independently, remember what had happened to it, how it had happened. Remember its past life? The machine was motionless, and silent except for the clock, tick-tock.

The Chairman coughed, surprised at his own nervousness. It wasn't fear, not really, it was anxiety, that low grade of growing panic familiar to everyone at some point in their lives. Times of danger. The need for self-preservation. Fight or flight.

The robot was taller than he was and it didn't move when the Chairman stepped closer. He wanted to touch it, to feel whether its machined surface, tarnished now after its fight up from the street, was hot or cold. Would the robot even feel it? He raised a hand, but before his fingertips even made contact, the Chairman jerked his arm back as if shocked. There was whirring again from the robot, but still it didn't move, although maybe its head had shifted slightly, imperceptibly. The Chairman couldn't really tell.

The robot's clock continued to tick. Time. Not enough of it, and how much had been lost in a daydream the Chairman didn't know. People would be coming soon. Once they'd judged it safe enough to enter the building, lots of people with guns and armour of their own would come to rescue the Empire State's highest official. Time pressed on the Chairman's mind like a dead weight.

Guilt, as well. There was no one left in the building, he knew that. The robot had killed them all. It had to, in order to reach him. Nobody could know of the plan, so there was no alternative. The Chairman regretted it and the regret blossomed into guilt, but he knew there was more to come, much, much more, and he knew he would regret that too. Untold destruction. Apocalypse. Holocaust. But it was worth it. It was all part of the plan. The ends justified the means.

Only... only standing and staring out of the window, if that's what the robot *was* doing, watching the city below was *not* part of the programming. What if it had gone wrong? What if the plan, after all these years, was going to fail? What if the very purpose of the City Commissioners, the Chairman, the Empire State itself, was to come to nothing?

No, no. Panic, anxiety, guilt was driving the Chairman's thoughts, and he knew it. Everything had been planned. Everything was in order. This was it, the final moment.

The Chairman of the City Commissioners took a deep breath, calming himself. He rolled his shoulders and shook his arms and walked around the robot until he was behind it. He turned away from it, and very gently leaned against its back. The robot was warm, hot even. He pushed against it, straightening both legs against the floor and pushing as hard as he could against the machine. But the robot didn't move, didn't even rock on its feet. It was like leaning against a stone pillar. The Chairman felt safe, at least, having the robot with him. Perhaps, if the police came too soon, before they were done, the robot would protect him.

"Orders, sir," the robot intoned. Its voice was human, male, but it sounded far away, and was lightly dusted in static. The Chairman closed his eyes, wondering if the man inside the shell knew what had happened to him after he volunteered for the fleet.

"Report," the Chairman whispered.

THIRTY-THREE

THE AIR WAS WARM, AND CLOSE, and there was a creeping dampness underneath Rad. The back of his head hurt like all hell, and when he moved to feel the damage, sensation suddenly returned to his whole body like he'd put his finger in a wall socket. The ground was hard, grooved somehow. His hand found wet wood underneath him, past the bump at the back of his head.

Rad opened his eyes, and saw an orange-tinged sky, dark with lighter patches drifting on the wind. His view was obscured by something black and moving. He sat up.

He was lying on a park bench in a small park, laid with grass, ringed with hedges, with a tall, spreading tree in the centre, its leafed branches swaying in the slight breeze. The sound was, Rad imagined, that kind of peaceful, almost melancholic rustling, a tiny sliver of natural, organic sound in the heart of the industrial city. Except he couldn't hear it over the buzzing in his head. He blinked, and moved his eyes. It felt like someone was trying to scoop them out with hot spoons.

He closed his eyes, screwing them tight and drawing balled fists against them by primal instinct. Rad moaned, and curled his legs up to his chest. One roll to the right and he collided with the ground in front of the bench.

Something snagged on the narrow edge of one of the wooden planks of the bench. It pulled Rad's left arm up awkwardly, and as his conscious mind fought against the wreath of pain that had suddenly enveloped it like boiling water around a coddled egg, his subconscious worked on getting his hand free. After a few minutes of waggling the appendage, without success, Rad finally realised what it was. One of the looped straps of his mask was caught over the edge of the bench. Rad stared at the mask as it strained on the end of the strap, using it as a focal point. He pulled himself to his knees, eyes narrowed on the glass goggles glinting in the orange night air, and sucked in wet air across clenched teeth, lips pulled back in a dog-like scowl. His head buzzed and his chest hurt and his teeth throbbed as the air was drawn over them.

How long he could last, he wasn't sure. He'd been awake a minute and already his vision was spawning black clouds at the edges. The park bench swung sideways before him, but he couldn't be sure whether that was because the whole world was spinning as his inner ears gave up the ghost, or because he was heading back to the ground.

He got the mask free, wrenching it from where it had been hooked and pushing it onto his face. Forgetting about the straps, he let momentum carry him backwards, mask held firmly with one hand. The path around the park was narrow, and Rad was a big man, but he was grateful his head hit the damp grass rather than the edge of the abutting flagstone.

Rad lay on the grass, and breathed, and breathed, and breathed. After a minute, the buzzing began to fade. After two, it was gone, replaced by the sharper sting of the split on the back of his scalp. But that was just pain, good old regular pain, unpleasant but familiar. The buzzing was an alien sound, a foreign sensation, one that would drive you to panic if you didn't know what it was. Rad did. He'd had it in New York. He'd had it close to the Fissure. He was now incompatible with the Empire State, at least a little bit, at least for the moment.

Rad opened his eyes to see the tree branches waving above him. The breeze had picked up, bringing with it a warm, slippery drizzle. Rad watched it spot on his goggles, and listened to the rustling of the leaves. Beneath the mask he smiled as he drank in the rubbery, filtered air.

He didn't know where he was, or why he hadn't come directly out of the other side of the Fissure, but he was home, of that he had no doubt. He let go of the mask with one hand and ran the other over his chest, sides, neck, wherever he could reach while lying on his back and not moving a whole lot. He was all there. Aside from the crack on his head and a developing headache, nothing was broken, damaged or missing. He'd survived passage through the Fissure. Lying under the tree, the night was quiet, warm and wet, with floating fog and the orange glow of the clouds above. This was the Empire State all right. Home sweet home.

He coughed into the respirator and drew another forceful breath. How long had he been in New York? Just a few hours, he assumed. What did that equate to here? More time, or less? Given Nimrod's concern, he assumed it was likely to be more.

Well, the city was still here, so the end of the world hadn't quite happened yet. Of course he might still be too late. Perhaps the Skyguard would take out the Battery in the next thirty seconds, and Rad's world would pop out of existence. Rad laughed at the thought, then regretted it, and closed his eyes as he focussed on his breathing for a while.

A minute passed, maybe two. Rad opened his eyes. He was still here, as was the Empire State. Which meant there was still time to do the job he'd been sent back to do. He pulled the mask straps around his head and pulled the tags to secure the respirator. Hopefully he wouldn't need to wear it for very long, maybe an hour or so, until his body had reacclimatised to the Pocket.

The Pocket. It sounded ridiculous. The Empire State was a city, a huge, sprawling industrial complex, full of people and architecture, and streets and buildings. An impossible city with no history. A city with no resources and an impossible economy. How much air was there in the Pocket? Where did the food come from? The power? Maybe it really was magic, a side effect of being tethered to – being *a reflection of* – the Origin – what the Origin had made or produced, so this was reflected through the Fissure.

Rad gave up as his head began to pound again. The Pocket stopped you thinking, and perhaps for a good reason. Rad rolled his head and stood, flexing as many joints as he could while he got his bearings. He didn't recognise the park, but it was no more than a tiny walled lawn set up on a street corner. A short set of stairs would take him down to street level, and with the tree out of the way, he figured he'd be able to recognise some landmarks.

The street was dead and washed in yellow light. Rad thought back to New York City. So much life and energy. In the Empire State there wasn't actually an official Wartime curfew, but people tended to stay indoors after dark. Rad's new nocturnal lifestyle was becoming a drag. He was a loner, and he enjoyed his own company, sure, but even he had to admit it had been good to see the hustle and bustle of New York.

Looking around, none of the street names meant anything to him, but ahead, down a wide boulevard that curved away to the left, came a different sort of light. A white glow: fairly bright even in the yellow street glow, diffused by the low-lying mist. The Pastor's house? Could be. At least from there he knew where he was, which was a start.

Stop the Skyguard, Nimrod had said. Well, OK. Stopping the Skyguard meant stopping Kane, and for that, a little help would be required from Captain Carson.

But perhaps Kane didn't know Rad was onto him. Perhaps he could be convinced, shown the error of his ways, told the truth about how the Pocket and the Origin were linked together. Perhaps he could solve things peacefully, sensibly.

Two places were obvious starting points – Kane's apartment, and Jerry's speakeasy. And Rad really, really needed a drink.

Footsore and with a thirst, Rad headed downtown.

Rad walked into Jerry's, then turned around and walked back out. Taking a breath, he slid the mask off, and shoved it under his trench coat. He sniffed the air experimentally. It was OK, easier in fact than using the mask. But almost immediately his head began to throb, and a buzz-saw vibration behind his eyes started up. Rad had no idea what was in the soup can on Nimrod's fancy masks, but it wasn't an ordinary respirator. Still, he felt could manage a few minutes. If Kane was in there, he'd pull him out quickly, get the mask back on, and then take him back to his office to talk. The mask would be a giveaway, but Rad hoped that Kane was still, at heart, the reasonable young man Rad had always thought he was.

Rad held his breath as he headed to the bar, but his head thundered with each beat of his heart, forcing him to release the air and gasp for a moment as soon as his fingers hit the bar. Jerry, never far away, gave him a dirty look and reached into the pocket of his apron. He slapped his hand down on the counter in front of Rad, making the detective jump. When Jerry removed his hand, Rad saw a white slip of paper on the bar.

"I said Friday, bub. You can't run out on me. Pay now, or you're barred. You and your friends."

Rad focussed on the note. The dim light made the writing swim a little; Rad picked it up and drew it closer to his eyes, adjusting the focus by moving the paper back and forth like an old man.

"You said Friday, Jerry."

Jerry leaned over the bar, and twisted a finger into his own temple. "You got, what, a deficiency or something? You're late, pal. Late!"

"Wait," said Rad, glancing behind the bar in case a calendar would magically appear behind the endless shelves of cups and saucers. "What day is it?"

Jerry leaned back, too far, as if he'd got a whiff of something particularly nasty. "You playin' the game with me, Rad? I'm not interested. You got the money, I'll take the money. Problem solved."

"Easy, Jerry, easy." Rad patted the sides of his trench coat until he found his wallet. It was fatter than it was normally, and then he remembered. Katherine Kopek's advance on Sam Saturn's missing person case. Shit. As ludicrous, as *criminal* as it was, he'd forgotten about the dead girl and her bereaved partner. He knew how the pieces fitted into the puzzle now, but his mind raced as he tried to think of a way to handle it with the mourning Katherine Kopek.

"Jerry, what day is it?"

"Boy, you really do need a rest," said Jerry, eyeing the notes Rad flipped out of his wallet.

"I ain't playin', Jerry!" Several patrons looked over at the bar from their tables. Jerry closed his eyes and shook his head. This kind of scene was not needed in an illegal basement bar.

"Just tell me," said Rad, waving the money under Jerry's nose. Jerry sighed and took the cash. There was too much, but as Jerry peeled off a few notes, Rad waved a hand. "Put me in credit."

"Well, I'll let it pass this time. But Jesus, Rad, I gotta business to run. Anyway, it's Monday. Now go home and get some sleep. You're working too hard, boy."

Monday. He'd left on Thursday. He'd been away half a week. Rad whistled, then coughed. His head was beginning to smart real bad and the buzzing behind his eyes was turning his vision black. He had to be quick.

"OK, I apologise, Jerry. Call it overwork. So, you seen Kane recently?"

Jerry shook his head, nice and slow. "He ain't been here. Thought you two ran off together."

"You're a comedian. Thanks, Jerry."

Rad pushed himself off the bar, stumbled slightly, then righted himself under the glare of a nearby table of drinkers. Rad touched a finger to his forehead in apology, then half-walked, half-ran to the door. In the stairwell leading up to the street, he paused, leaning against the wall, then took the mask from inside his coat and pushed his face into it. He held it there for a moment, taking deep and difficult breaths, until the pain in his head and the pins and needles in his limbs subsided.

Flipping the mask straps over his head, Rad headed for Kane's apartment.

Rad was too wet for his liking by the time he got back to his office. Kane's apartment had been a negative. It had been open, but dark, and Rad had snooped only a little to confirm his friend wasn't in. The three-room apartment was so cluttered it was impossible to tell whether there was anything amiss or not, although the bed was neatly made. Leaving the room, Rad's foot crunched on something brittle. Looking down, he traced the few tiny crumbs of broken glass to an old dressing table, an elaborate affair in several different types of wood that wouldn't have looked out of place in the star dressing room of a fancy theatre. The dressing table had a plain wooden panel that tilted on arms. It used to hold a mirror, but it had been cleanly removed. There was no sign of broken glass anywhere, except the tiny, cuboidal fragments hidden in the carpet, but there was a fresh cut in the front of the dressing table, the newly revealed wood under the lacquered top bright and pale. Kane had taken the mirror out and dropped it, damaging the dressing table and chipping the edge, and breaking the glass. He'd cleaned up, but not perfectly.

Happy with the small piece of detective work, but unhappy with what it suggested, Rad had headed home. The third stop would be to see Captain Carson, but once he had filled the old man in on his journey to New York, there would be no going back. They had to find the Skyguard and protect the Fissure. He needed Carson's help, and they'd either succeed, or fail.

Rad's naked head was wet and itchy, the rain trickling off it making the stubble bristle. The straps of the mask were also starting to bite – even though they were buckled at maximum length, Rad's head was still a little large for it. And if it was going to be battle stations, all-for-one, do-or-die, he needed to clean up and get out of the mask. As he turned the key in his office door, he hoped that it had been sufficient time to acclimatise back to the Empire State, and that trekking around the city blocks from Jerry's to Kane's to his office hadn't impeded the process.

The key turned loosely in the tumbler, but Rad wasn't sure if that was just the slight numbness in his fingers. He swung the door open, closed it behind him, and reached for the light switch without looking.

The light came on, and Rad stopped. His hand was still inches away from the switch, fingers only just beginning their crawl up the wall to find it. Rad turned his head, far too slowly.

There was a man standing there, in his office, in a white hat. Rad recognised him somehow – a large black man, his goatee beard surrounding a scowling mouth. The man's arm pistoned forward oddly, the butt of the gun in his clenched fist connecting with the side of Rad's head, behind the protective rubber seal of the mask.

Rad moaned, hands at his ear, and toppled sideways to the floor. Before he passed out his last sight was an image of himself, in his brown suit and white hat, looking down at him, skin slicked with sweat, spittle clinging to the lips pulled back in a vicious grin.

And then Rad surrendered to the rubbery darkness.

"I said wake up, you sonovabitch."

The slap was like a firecracker, a hot, dry sound in the small office. Rad's head snapped back and he opened his eyes. He looked at himself looking at him, and began to cough. He looked past his own self, standing there, and saw the mask discarded on the floor near the front door. Rad tried to gesture to it with a hand, but his wrist was jerked back by a tightly tied rag. Shaking his head to fight the buzzing, he tried to assess the situation.

He was tied to his office chair, which had been pulled around to the front of the desk. His feet were not tied, but his legs felt as heavy as granite, and without his mask he didn't think he could hurt a fly, let alone fight... himself.

The man *was* him, he was sure of it. The goatee was a little rougher, the suit wasn't exactly the same as his own, and the way the man held himself didn't seem quite natural for Rad. But these were details only he could pick up. To anyone else, it was Rad Bradley, the private detective. Standing in front of him, holding a small snub-nosed pistol.

Except it wasn't him. Or rather it *was* him, the original. The man wanted by Nimrod, Rex. *Rad* was the copy, the reflection, an after-image burnt into the fabric of the universe by the final battle between the Skyguard and the Science Pirate.

Rad wasn't sure what he felt, looking at his original, *the* original, the source of the fingerprints on Sam Saturn's neck. The killer, standing there with the gun. He felt as alive and kicking and real as anyone, yet he knew that the man in the white hat had memories stretching back forty years or more. Rad wondered whether Rex could remember why he split from Claudia, or whether he was still married to Claudia, or whether he'd ever met Claudia in the first place.

Rad sighed. More than anything, he was just pissed off. Life was what you made it. Tomorrow is the first day of the rest of your life. Other such smug platitudes wandered through his head as he eyed the wicked smile behind the barrel. The gun wavered, just a little, and Rad realised he was rocking back and forth on the office chair enough to make it tap-dance on the floorboards. But the rags held tight.

"Don't try it, buster," said the original. "You and me gotta date with someone real important, see."

Rad frowned. Did he really sound like that? He sure as hell didn't talk like that. Then again, perhaps the original didn't either. Maybe this was all new to him. For the second time in just a few days – give or take, considering his holiday in New York – Rad was in his own office being held at gunpoint. Maybe if the universe didn't end he'd think about looking into another line of work.

"Who put you up to this?" asked Rad.

"Shut your mouth, boy, or you're history."

Rad chuckled. "Nice cliché. You ever thought about becoming a private dick?"

The original's smile tightened. "Detective, huh?" He looked

around the office, gun still pointing dead ahead. "Shitty office you got here."

"Gee, thanks." Rad decided to try something. "They don't teach you any manners in New York City?"

The man's smile vanished. In its place, his lips pursed together like he was sucking a lemon, the skin around his mouth pulled pale and ugly.

"What do you know about New York City?"

"Oh, it's a nice place. Might take me up an apartment there. You know, somewhere upmarket."

The man raised an eyebrow. "Nice idea."

Rad asked again, "Who put you up to this?"

The man shook his head. "I gotta job to do, pal. Nothing personal."

"You want to go home, right?"

"What?"

"Home," said Rad. He nodded his head sideways at the wall, not pointing, just pressing his point. Not here, but *there*.

The man put on the sick smile again and raised the gun.

"Oh, you betcha bottom dollar."

"The name's Rad, by the way. Rad Bradley." Rad looked the man up and down. The gun was wavering again, just a little, maybe just enough.

"Colour me impressed."

"Aren't you going to introduce yourself?"

"What?"

"You deaf too?"

"Rex," the man said. "Rex Braybury. Ain't that just hilarious?"

Rad nodded. "Hilarious," he said, voice flat.

Rex twisted his gun hand just enough to check his watch. His eyes flicked from his wrist to the wall behind Rad's desk, over Rad's head. Rad craned around as best he could, but saw nothing except his desk and the corner of the big window, blinds down.

"Don't move, sucker."

Rad faced front. "Whatever you say, boss."

Then the telephone rang. Rad jumped in his chair and closed his eyes, convinced that Rex had pulled the trigger out of pure fright, and that he was now bleeding to death in his office. He opened his eyes after a second, realising that the gunshot he'd heard was only the sound of his heart thundering against his throat at the surprise.

The phone kept ringing. Rex stood over Rad, gun hand jogging up and down as he shifted his weight from his right foot to his left then back again. He looked worried, very nervous, and glanced at the phone on the desk out of the corner of his eye, showing big scared whites to Rad.

"You gonna answer that?"

"Shut up!" The gun stabilised.

"Might be the landlord. Sees us here, he'll want two rent checks."

Rex snorted. "You're a real comedian."

"Hilarious," Rad said again, voice still flat.

The phone rang for a long, long time. Rad tried counting the rings but lost it as soon as Rex started pacing the floor, his footsteps unconsciously in sync with the telephone. When the phone wouldn't stop, Rex disappeared from Rad's sight, going behind the desk. Rad stared at his office door, wishing for a heroic rescue by... hell, by anyone, right about now. Behind him, Rad heard his captor rip the blinds up to the top of the window. Rad sniffed. With the light on and it being the dead of night outside, the window would be nothing but a mirror. Rex wouldn't be able to see a thing.

The telephone stopped ringing. Rad heard Rex swear, and there was a buzzing, electric sound. A light came on, a light from *behind* Rad, casting his shadow on the front of the office. Rad saw his own silhouette, tied to the chair, and Rex's outline, complete with hat and gun, stumbling. And then two

more shadows, at first long, as if cast from two people standing at the opposite side of a football stadium with the
floodlights on them. Then smaller, resolving into two shapes,
men in hats. There was something odd about the shapes of
their faces – they were bulky, bulbous, angular, with a weird
bobbing soup can in the front.

Rad yelled and tipped his chair over, spinning himself
around on the floor to face the window, just in time to see
Grieves and Jones step out of an opaque white void where
the solid glass had been and grab Rex by the arms. Grieves
yanked on the gun; Rex struggled and the hand went skyward and the trigger was pulled. Rad blinked at the report,
then saw a meaty fist belonging to Bullethead Jones fly forward and take Rex out under the jaw. Rex went rigid and
flew back at least a foot, before hitting the floorboards cold.
Grieves and Jones took two steps further into the office,
backlit by the white rectangle that was Rad's office window.
Then the light flickered and snapped off, and the window
reappeared, black and mirror-like against the night outside.

Black brogues stepped into Rad's floor-level line of vision,
and hands sheathed in leather gloves gripped him by the elbows and pulled him, and his chair, upright. Grieves made
to slap Rad on the cheek, but Rad pulled his head away.

"I'm all right, jackass!" He tugged on his hands. "Get me
loose."

Jones was down on one knee, checking Rex's pulse. As
Grieves bent over to untie Rad, he called back to his companion for an update.

"He'll live, but he'll have a headache when he wakes up."
Jones poked at Rex's lower jaw indelicately. "And a sore
mouth for a month." Bullethead's voice matched his head exactly. Ugly and gravelly, like a retired boxer turned to drink.

There was a coughing sound behind Rad's head, and it
took him a moment to realise it was Grieves laughing inside

his mask. The two agents really were thugs. Rad wondered how Nimrod could possibly put up with them. On the other hand, he could see how the two heavies would be useful in a corner.

The rags loosened and Grieves stepped back. Rad pulled the last of the knot apart and brought his arms around so he could check his wrists. They hurt like heck, but were otherwise uninjured. He rubbed the circulation back into them.

"I appreciate the entrance, gentlemen," said Rad. He looked at the office window. It was intact, completely unblemished. He shook his head and whistled. "And what an entrance it was."

He stood and exercised his stiff knees, walking over to where Rex lay snoozing on the floor.

"But what's the occasion? Nimrod said you guys couldn't make the party. Were you actually watching what was happening, from the Origin?"

Grieves thrust his hands in the pockets of his trench coat and joined Rad to look down at Rex. "Something like that. Not see exactly, but detect. It's not like we sit there watching you like you're some kinda game show on TV. But Captain Nimrod has some tricks up his sleeve. He said you'd come into your office twice, and then you didn't answer the telephone. Looked like a problem. Then you, or rather, he, opened the blinds and let us in. 'Transition via projected reflection'." Grieves shrugged. "Mr Nimrod has some tricks, I told you."

"OK. Appreciate it." Rad knelt next to Rex. It was weird, seeing himself lying there, and to begin with he didn't want to touch Rex. But maybe he was carrying something, anything that might be a clue as to who sent him. Rad began to pat the body down, checking pockets, grimacing as he did so. Was he really that big? Were his arms really that flabby? Rad held his breath as he went, and realised he was doing fine now without the mask. Good. He had reacclimatised.

Rex's pockets were empty save for a couple of spare buttons sewn onto a little fabric tag. The suit was thin and cheap, not like Rad's own tailored number. It was also fairly new. The hat was the real deal, however; there was only one store in the city that sold white fedoras. He slipped it off Rex's unconscious head and checked the size. It was a half size too big, although it had seemed to fit the crook perfectly. So, there were differences after all. The hat would do for now; Rad felt a little better already with it on.

"Someone dolled him up to look like me," said Rad, standing up. "Seems a lot of effort if it was just to come here and shoot me in the head."

"He'd need the get-up if he was going to meet one of your contacts, no?" Grieves stood over Rex, who sighed and began to move his head from side to side.

"I guess," said Rad. "Fortunately that's a short list. Kane is the Skyguard, which just leaves Carson."

"You been in touch with him since you got back?"

Rad looked at Grieves, eyes wide. Carson was locked in his house on the other side of the city, and had Byron to protect him, but even so...

"No, I wanted to work on Kane first. *Goddammit.*" Rad watched as Rex stirred. "You think this sonovabitch was sent to, what, assassinate me and then Carson?"

Bullethead Jones spoke from where he was standing by the office door. "They're taking out anyone who could throw a spanner in the works."

He had the door open a crack, and was peering into the deserted corridor. Standard practice, Rad thought, although nobody ever came to his floor that wasn't a client. Or – looking down at Rex – someone trying to kill him.

Grieves kicked Rex in the ribs gently, but enough to make a point. Rex opened his eyes and moaned and tried to rise, then seeing Rad and the masked agent above him, swore and settled back down on the floor.

"If Carson knows as much about the Pocket, the Origin, and the Fissure as we do, he's gotta be the prime target," said Rad. "My not-so-friendly twin here said he was taking me to meet someone. Which means he's working for someone else. And that someone else has dolled him up as me, using him as a stooge to get in, see what Carson knows, then put him to bed."

Rad stopped and shook his head. "But why send my master copy from the Origin here, with all the theatrics of tying me up, making threats? The Skyguard could waltz in here anytime and take me out. Last time we met, he tried to recruit me."

"Maybe they need you alive," said Jones from the door. "Maybe the Skyguard is otherwise indisposed." He shrugged. "What am I, psychic?"

Rex fidgeted on the floor. Grieves bent down to help him up. He offered no resistance, and peacefully allowed himself to be placed in the office chair which had so recently held his counterpart.

"Look," Rex said, focussing on Rad. "I just wanna go home, back to New York. They said this would do it. I don't want to hurt no one no more. Not again." Rex shook his head and looked at the floor. "I just want to go home." His shoulders slumped. It was either a good act, or the man had broken.

"Can you take him back to New York with you? Arrest him or something?" Rad asked.

Grieves shook his mask, the soup can swinging comically. "Seems our friend here knows something. Our first priority is to protect the Pocket and prevent the Skyguard shutting off the Battery."

He looked at Rex. "Hey, buddy!"

Rex looked up. His expression was slack, like the muscles of his face were just hanging off his skull. It was the kind of expression worn by someone who had gone beyond fear and into total abject surrender. It was pathetic. Rad felt sorry for him. Rex just wanted to go home. Rad thought back to his glimpse of New York City, and knew that being sucked into the Empire State would be quite a shock. Rad's mood turned black. Someone was manipulating Rex in the same way that someone was manipulating him. Both were victims, pawns in an indecipherable game.

"Where's the Skyguard?" asked the agent.

Rex blinked wetly. "The Skyguard?" He paused, and cleared his throat. He was trying very hard to give the right answer.

Rad thought perhaps Grieves could lose the attitude... but then Rex had pulled a gun on him. And Rex was a hood: the opposite profession, in a way, to Rad's. And as with most tough guys, he seemed to be breaking when the odds were stacked against him. Self-preservation. All criminals were cowards at heart. Rad's sorrow was replaced by a feeling of anger.

Rex fumbled for an answer, and when he spoke the words tumbled out too quickly. "He's dead, isn't he? Disappeared in the fight. The fight that started all this."

Rad and Grieves exchanged a look.

"So you know about the Skyguard and the Science Pirate, and how the Fissure was created?" Rad stroked his beard as he posed the question.

Rex shook his head. "I don't know nothing about no 'fissure'. But I got the story of this place, how it's like New York, but it's not New York. He gave me the job to do, said when it was done we could go back home."

"Who's 'we' and 'he', Rex?" asked Grieves. "The Skyguard and you?"

"No, no." Rex licked his lips. "The guy in the white hood. Some kind of preacher. He's from New York too. He knows how it all works."

Rad clicked his fingers and nodded, threads of evidence slowly stitching together. Grieves looked at him; Rad could see the thin man's eyes blinking in the deep glass goggles of his mask.

"Mean something?" Grieves asked.

"Sure does. There's a guy, wears a white hood. Runs some kind of underground cult. Calls it a church, but it's not the kind of Sunday service I've ever seen." Rad walked around to his desk and pulled his copy of *The Seduction of the Innocent* from the drawer. He tossed the hardback to Grieves, who stared at the cover for a while, but didn't open the book.

Rad pointed at it in Grieves's hand. "That's his book. Pretty dull stuff. That copy belonged to Sam Saturn, the girl whose disappearance – and murder – I was... am... investigating."

"And he's from New York?"

Rad shrugged and inclined his head towards Rex. Grieves turned back to the man slumped in the chair and repeated the question. Rex nodded.

Rad leaned over Rex's chair, placing his hands on each arm and peering at the man's face. It was weird – *wrong* even – to be looking at himself like this. Rad closed his eyes to clear the thoughts, which were unhelpful and illogical, then fixed Rex with a hard glare normally reserved for the most difficult parts of his investigations.

"Why tie me up? Why not just shoot me? You expecting someone else to arrive?"

Rex shook his head, his heavy cheeks flapping with a faintly wet sound. Rad grimaced.

"No, no, I had to keep you busy, then when I got the call, head across town and pick up someone else, an old guy in a big house. Y'know, play the part. Then show him how I caught the killer and together we take you over to the Empire State Building. He said we'd go straight to the top, he'd cleared the way."

Rad stood up and frowned. "To the City Commissioners?"

Rex shrugged. "I don't know," he said, quickly. "I'm just doing what I'm told. I don't know what's up there."

"You came here first?" Rad pulled on the lapel of Rex's jacket. The material was sharp against his fingertips, a poor imitation of his own suit.

"Straight here. Do the thing, get the guy, then we go. That's it, I swear it."

Rad turned away and paced the office space between where Rex was sitting in the chair and the front of his desk.

Bullethead Jones closed the office door with a click and joined them. "We're wasting time here. Let's go."

Grieves shook his head. "We call Nimrod."

"Trust me," said Jones. "We gotta act." He jerked a thumb towards Rex. "We take the schmuck here to the Empire State Building, see what the jazz is. Sounds like our targets might all be there."

Jones paused. Nobody said anything. Grieves seemed to be considering behind his mask, then Jones reached out and punched him lightly on the chest in impatience.

He said, "Come on, we ain't got no time for any of this. Let's go."

Rad nodded, mouth curled upside down. "We've got to find the Skyguard somehow. Sounds like the Pastor might know a thing or two about him. Sounds like the whole gang is going to be there."

Grieves ground a gloved fist into the open palm of his other hand. "OK," he said at last. "Let's go."

He held out the pistol that belonged to Rex, offering it to Rad. Rad looked at it, but shook his head. He heard Jones sigh through his mask before the agent snatched it and slapped it to Rad's chest, then Jones drew his own weapon, the odd fat-barrelled revolver. He jogged Rex's shoulder.

"Come on, let's move."

The four of them left the office, Rad and Grieves in front, then Jones following Rex in the middle, gun in the centre of his back.

THIRTY-FOUR

"CONTACT HAS BEEN ESTABLISHED," said the machine.

It had worked! The Chairman smiled and almost turned around to face the robot, then caught himself and thought better of it. He pushed his back against the robot again, reassured by its unyielding solidity.

"What did they say?"

A pause, then: "What do you require of them?"

"Peace," said the Chairman, excitement creeping into his voice. "An end to Wartime. If the war can end, I will be able to leave the city."

The robot paused, as if it was considering.

"The contact wishes peace and an end to Wartime."

The Chairman's eyes lit up. He clasped his hands together, rolling his fingers around his knuckles. It was perfect. With Wartime over, he'd be able to leave the Empire State, and return home. It made sense. He had been sent here for a purpose, a mission, and with that mission complete, he would be sent home.

Praise the Lord, amen. The Chairman unlocked his fingers and one hand found its way into a pocket. His fingers curled around a large, folded white cloth, something like a napkin, stuffed inside.

The Chairman thought again about the police. Outside the

night was black and orange, the city spread out underneath his feet. There was movement, blimps gathering. Keeping their distance, but always moving, moving, moving, slowly like drowsy bumblebees on a cold morning. Spotlights played hesitantly across the Empire State Building; no sooner did a beam of bright light stab into the boardroom than it was snatched away again, like a cat pawing at cotton thread. The Chairman considered again how long it might be before they had the courage, or numbers, to storm the building and "rescue" him. They were probably working out what to do, knowing now that one machine had single-handedly killed an entire building full of people, and would have no trouble taking out a handful of police, no matter how heavily armed they were. They would have to wait for more robots and hope that no more would go rogue.

It didn't matter to the Chairman. Nothing mattered. Wartime was going to end, the Empire State could return to normal, and he could go home. He slid down the robot's back, and landed with a thud on the floor. The machine's legs were not as comfortable a support as its smooth back, but they were just as solid and unmoving.

"Tell me about the Enemy," he whispered. "Tell me about the war."

The robot whirred, as if accessing the memory required a mechanical action deep inside its armour. The whirring stopped, and then the static-laced man's voice spoke. Unlike the previous responses, this voice was emotive, more human, rising and falling in excitement as it told its story.

"We set sail in the summer of Eighteen. Oh, the crowds, so many people. I saw my family there, down at the docks. They were in the second row, in a crowd of, oh, thousands of people. Clarke and Zachary were laughing and shouting, and waving flags. Pa was smiling, but he was quiet-like, you know? And Ma. Ma was cryin'. Pa ignored her, didn't even have his arm around her shoulders. She just stood there and cried, and I don't think she was even looking at the fleet as we sailed away. Then she turned and pushed her way into the crowd, and I lost her. Pa didn't even move. But his smile, it wasn't real. He was putting it on. Perhaps he knew.

"My name is Rating six-three-eight-nine-oh-five, and I don't remember my family any more than that. I am a part of the ironclad crew, for the glory of the Empire State. We sailed to the Enemy to take the war to their door, yessir.

"We steamed away, all of the ships. It was a splendid sight, sir, a splendid sight. So many ships, as far back as you could see, as far in front as you could see. Why, you could have walked from the docks right across the water to the other side without getting wet. If there was another side."

The machine paused. The Chairman opened his eyes. He was surprised at the voice. This was the story of the man inside the shell, who was no longer a man, who had walked into the naval factories on his own two legs with a smile on his face, and left carried out on a rack, his batteries charging and a metal guard where his jaw used to be and a rubber pump where his heart used to be. The Chairman closed his eyes and wept.

"And then we hit the fog," the machine continued, the ghost of the sailor whispering in awe at the memory. "I imagine the fog was cold, sir, except I don't know, I don't feel the cold any more. We stood on deck, all hands. We were told that the battle would begin as soon as we passed through. None of us had any idea the Enemy was so close – right on the doorstep of the Empire State! They were there, had been there all the time, just a few miles on the other side of the fog. Just waiting for us to send in the fleet and fight.

"The fog took forever to get through. Hours, or days, or maybe it was months. I don't know. None of us did. Our internal chronometers went haywire, but the ship's clock hadn't moved hardly at all. When the fog began to clear the commander came around and manually adjusted our chronometers back to ship time.

"The first thing I saw was the light. It was orange, a glow, like flames hidden in smoke. And then as we got closer, the fog bank thinned, and lights shrank, focussing into points, like stars on the water. They were close too, so close.

"And then we were there, all at once. The fleet was steaming up a river, into a harbour. On our starboard side was a city, a huge floating city, with tall buildings and low buildings, and lights. A city on an island, docks and wharves pointing right at us. Our radios went wild, we all started chattering. We'd got lost in the fog, we'd somehow got turned around and steamed back home. We were looking at the Empire State.

"Then the commander gave an order for radio silence, and we all manned our battle stations. I was a marine, and had to get ready for a landing, but before I went below decks – to charge up in the battery room with the other soldiers – I stood by the deck rail and looked out at the Enemy. My logic gates flipped a few times, I can tell you. The commander gave orders to make ready the guns, but it didn't make no sense. We weren't looking at the Enemy, we were looking at home."

Rating 638905 stopped, and whirred again. The Chairman opened his eyes.

"Continue."

"I stood by the deck rail and looked out at the Enemy, but it wasn't the Enemy, it was *home*. It was the Empire State. It was night, and the lights were bright and the city had the mist, like always, but I could see the Empire State Building, and others, all familiar. And things were moving too, tiny shapes like ants, all moving and stopping at once, like someone was winding a clock with a broken spring that refused to catch. They were people, I suppose, or cars or something. Didn't make no sense. But it was my home, after all. It was the Empire State. Except... except the night was darker than I remembered, and the mist thicker. Our clocks had been reset, but I couldn't tell if it was late or early.

"The commander ordered us below, and then the deck guns started up. They were firing, round after round after round, the big guns designed to hit enemies broadside on the water.

"But they weren't aimed right. They were firing into the *air*. I looked up, and above us was *another* fleet. Lord above, ironclads like us, matched in number one for one. But these could fly, really fly, and they steamed through the air, their chimneys threading the orange fog with dirty grey and brown. They were upside down, the hulls above, the guns and decks hanging underneath. And as we fired up, so they fired down, with the same huge deck guns. Ma, what dream was this?

"Well, I didn't need to hear an order twice. I went below deck, and plugged in, and waited for the landing."

The Chairman bit into his fist. Afraid, overwhelmed with sorrow, the magnitude of the situation threatened to overwhelm him. His teeth drew blood from his knuckles; the copper taste snapped him out of his reverie and he withdrew his hand to look at the injury, then returned it to his mouth to soothe the bite with his tongue.

"The landing?" he asked as he sucked.

"The landing. The landing." The machine paused, as if the voice were a recording stuck in a loop. There was another whirr, and the Chairman felt the robot shift a little behind him. Then with a burst of static, the voice began again.

"The landing... there *was* no landing. Plugged into the battery room, we watched the fight through the eyes of the commander. For every shell of ours that found its mark up above, one of theirs hit an ironclad. We thought we were winning for a while, but really it was an even match. It was perfect, like we were fighting our own reflection, floating up there in the clouds."

The Chairman hissed.

"Your orders... What about your orders? If you didn't land, how did you make contact?"

The robot tilted its head in the glare of the latest spotlight, as if the human brain inside the shell, augmented with valve-powered electronics, was trying to make sense of what had happened.

"What about your orders?" the Chairman repeated.

"I didn't make contact... the Enemy made contact with me. Maybe that explained it, explained how they could match us shot-for-shot, boat-for-boat, so perfectly. The Enemy could patch into our radio, talk on our channels and listen to the ironclads whispering. There was a voice, speaking to me, telling me it had been ordered to contact me and offer a deal to end Wartime. It was like it was reading the orders out of my head. Contact was established and terms negotiated. Only..."

"Terms? Go on."

"Only there were no terms. Its orders were the same as my orders. Everything I said, it agreed with. The Enemy wants whatever we want. If we want an end to Wartime and the beginning of peace, then that's what they want."

The Chairman pulled his hand from his mouth, trailing a thick worm of saliva from his knuckles. It snapped and collapsed onto his chin, and hung there in the shadow behind the machine, until the Chairman licked his lips and wiped it away with his other hand. He nodded to himself, finally understanding, the robot's story confirming his own theories about the Empire State, the nature of the Pocket, and more importantly, the nature of the Enemy.

The machine's voice took on a more formal tone as it completed the report.

"Once contact was established and terms agreed, I fulfilled the second part of the Chairman's orders and commandeered ironclad twenty-seven fifty-nine and returned to the Empire State. Anchoring in the harbour, I disembarked to report to the Chairman of the City Commissioners of the Empire State. Forced entry was required." A whirr, and a click. "Report ends."

Rating 638905 fell silent and the Chairman drew his knees up to his chest, and rocked gently against the immovable metal legs behind him.

He was right. Carson's experiments at probing the fog had given the most outlandish, obviously incorrect, results. Something to do with the fog, some factor or property that made it impervious to analysis, twisting all data carried through and throwing it back as a garbled reflection.

Except it was not so. Carson's data was correct, and the Chairman's theory of the Pocket, and the Empire State, was correct.

There was nowhere else but the Empire State, and there was no Enemy.

Or rather... there *was* somewhere else. The Pocket hadn't been created by the fight between the Skyguard and the Science Pirate. They'd torn open the Fissure, and had created the Empire State, but the Pocket was a pre-existing space, an interstitial nothingness between the real universe and... and whatever else. Only it hadn't been empty. Like lights reflected on calm water, *something* was there. An after-image of the Origin, a semi-formed, reflected impression of New York. It must have been there from the beginning, from the birth of the Origin's universe, forged in the maelstrom of creation, a shadow, a blank silhouette of the "real" world.

But when the Fissure was opened by the Skyguard and the

Science Pirate, it provided a direct connection, a conduit for data, for information. New York City was *reflected* and *projected* into the Pocket. An imperfect copy, not a parody or caricature, but a broken, incomplete model. The Empire State.

Only there had already been a reflection of New York in the Pocket. The amorphous, pale sketch, mirroring the Origin but not existing, as such. Nothing more than a shadow crossing the dimensions. The Empire State usurped it, pushed it out as it made space for itself.

Pushing it beyond the fog, beyond the impenetrable, impossible walls of the Pocket. As New York was reflected in the Empire State, so the Empire State was reflected in the Enemy. The Enemy *was* the Empire State, but another copy, another image, another generation down, the imperfections and incompleteness increased by an order of magnitude. Not so much a place, but a state of being. With no independent existence outside of the shadow of the Empire State, it merely mirrored its own origin, the raw data that had been the original shade of New York solidifying and taking form beyond the fog.

The Empire State had been fighting itself. Every ironclad manufactured in the naval dockyard was matched by its counterpart across the fog, only the imperfect reflection created great floating airships instead of water ships. No matter how many ironclads were built, no matter how many citizens of the Empire State were converted into armoured sailors, no matter how large the fleet, they were matched, one for one, by the Enemy. Equal and opposite. Total, perfect, mutual annihilation.

The Chairman wept. He was responsible. Pulled into the Pocket without warning, without choice, finding himself leading a version of New York that wasn't New York, locked in a forever war with the nation beyond the fog. But he didn't know. How could he? But God knew. God had shown him the way. He reached into his pocket and fingered the folded white cloth, not quite remembering what it was for.

And Carson, not a refugee from New York like him, but another reflection, a copy of Nimrod from the State Department. Someone with expertise, know-how.

Martial law had been Carson's idea. Prohibition had been Carson's idea. The ironclads and robots and blimps and airships were his design.

But the war was the Chairman's responsibility. Sending the fleet and thousands of men to extinction had been entirely his decision. And when Carson left and locked himself in his house on the hill, realising that the data from his fog probes were correct, the Chairman kept building the ironclads, sending the fleets.

How many deaths?

And so the Chairman wept. He pushed himself away from the robot and hugged his knees, rocking back and forth as he cried. Eyes screwed tight in misery, he failed to notice the party of four that stepped into the boardroom.

"Sonovabitch!"

The Chairman's head snapped around, Rex's exclamation echoing loudly around the marble-floored boardroom. Rad turned to him, furious, but Rex pushed him off and stepped forward.

"So that's where you've been hiding."

Rad laid a hand on Rex's shoulder. He grimaced at the touch. It might have been his imagination, but his fingertips seemed to numb, just a little, at the contact.

"That's the Chairman," said Rad. He nodded to the man sitting on the floor. "What's the matter? You recognise him?"

"You bet I do." Rex took another step forward and looked at the man, who glanced up and pulled his knees even tighter to his chest.

"He's the 'Missingest Man in New York'."

Rad looked at Grieves and Jones. Grieves shrugged but Jones raised his gun.

Rex stood over the Chairman, who flinched away from his look.

"Joseph Crater, Associate Judge of the New York Supreme Court," said Rex. "I got a bone to pick with you."

THIRTY-FIVE

KANE SLIPPED THE HELMET OFF and placecd it carefully on an area of the control deck clear of levers. He sighed and waved a gloved hand over the panel.

"Any of this make sense to you?"

His companion paced the small bridge slowly, almost casually, dragging fingertips across the control panels that lined the walls. The metal-tipped gauntlets made a hollow, metallic sound like glass marbles rolling on pavement.

"Yes and no. Patience," said the Science Pirate.

Kane frowned, and turned back to the panel in front of him. Switches, levers, dials. That was fine, what he expected. But the language was odd. To be perfectly honest, he'd expected English. It had never occurred to him that it could be anything else, that *there could be* anything else. The letters were slanted, twisted, faded even. The whole ship felt old, worn out. Yet it floated above the Empire State's perpetual cloud deck without so much as a sound.

"You'd better work this out, because if I start pressing buttons, who knows what'll happen."

The laugh that emanated from the front grille of the Science Pirate's helmet was a deep, hard basso, the pitch artificially lowered to frighten people, Kane suspected. It was the same with the Skyguard's helmet, as he had discovered, but he couldn't stop himself flinching as his companion spun around to face him.

The Pirate said, "You want to crash this thing, don't you?"

Kane's eyes widened. "Generally, yes," he answered, taking a step towards his mysterious ally. "But not just anywhere. And not with us on it, preferably."

That laugh again. Kane watched the Science Pirate's helmet bob up and down. The helmet was similar to that of the Skyguard, although more austere and compact, with fewer flourishes. He decided he liked the look of his helmet better.

"Relax, pal. I can work it out. It's all going according to plan." The Science Pirate reached out and pulled a short lever downwards without looking. The airship shuddered, and there was a whining noise coming from somewhere high above them. Kane's big eyes searched the ceiling of the dark bridge.

"OK, I've got it." The Science Pirate turned to the control panel, and after a few minutes and a few more shakes, Kane saw the view outside the front window change. The airship was rotating about its axis. Kane watched his companion at work, the armoured frame hunched over the alien controls. After a while, the Science Pirate slid one glove off to get better precision on a panel of buttons, and then moments later took the other off as well.

Kane leaned forward, jaw flopping like a wet copy of the *Sentinel* fished from a gutter. He was about to say something when the Science Pirate sighed mechanically and began fiddling with a hidden strap under the helmet's chin. There was a click as a buckle and popper were undone, and then the faceplate pushed up and the helmet came off, swept off the back of the Pirate's head. Long hair, deep brown, spilled out from it as the Pirate pulled the helmet free, then balanced it on the top of the control deck.

Kane stared.

"You're... a woman?"

The Science Pirate laughed, this time in a beautiful, haughty female voice. She shook her hair out and swept it out of her eyes with her long fingers, and turned to look at Kane.

"Surprised, pal?"

"Ah... a little, yes."

The Pirate turned her attention back to the control panel.

Kane stood dumbfounded. OK, the Science Pirate was a girl. A woman. That was fine. In fact, that was more than fine, that was... alluring. He smiled as he watched her work, his eyes undressing her cloaked, armour-plated body.

He shook his head. There was something... familiar about her. She was slim, the armour bulking her dainty frame deliberately as part of the disguise to make her look like a man. It made sense – a female hero, protector of the city, wouldn't be taken seriously. Kane was sure she was a surefire hit, but really, during their partnership policing the skies of New York City, how much of the heroics had been down to the Skyguard and how much down to... *her*?

Partnership? Kane smirked. Maybe that was just what it was. What were they? Boyfriend and girlfriend? Lovers? Husband and wife? Was it a lover's tiff that split them apart and turned the Science Pirate against the Skyguard, and against the city? Gardner – the *real* Skyguard, the refugee hero from the Origin – had never said anything about his home life and had never gone into detail about the big fight. This had been a major hole in Kane's newspaper story leading up to Gardner's execution, an important omission, but one he'd had to gloss over with his best journalistic purple prose, distracting the *Sentinel*'s readers with tales of the Skyguard's wondrous exploits.

The Science Pirate hadn't got a mention either. It had taken some fancy and creative writing, but he'd excised the other half of the duo from the newspaper stories. Kane wanted to keep that part a secret. When the Science Pirate arrived in the Empire State, he wanted him – her! – to himself.

Her voice interrupted. "You going to help me with this, or just stand there looking handsome and heroic all night?"

Kane blinked. The Science Pirate – *she* – had both hands on a large lever, something like a railway track switcher, rising up out of the deck as part of a row of big controls. She was leaning on it, and looking back at him over her shoulder, clearly requiring help even with her powered suit. Kane's mouth twitched into a smirk. She was awful pretty. She smiled back, and her hair, all loose and natural, dropped over one eye. Kane studied her face. It was small, finely boned, exquisite in every detail. Although it was hard to tell in the dim light of the airship control room, her eyes were a brown so dark they were almost as black as the pupils. Her face was… familiar.

Kane stopped short, his expression hardening suddenly. The Pirate saw his change, her own face reflecting something else. Confusion, and alarm.

She raised an eyebrow and looked Kane up and down. "So, tough guy, a little help?"

Kane darted forward, grabbing her arm. She cried out – it was a high, harsh sound.

Kane looked into her face, at her chin, the nose, those deep eyes. He swore.

"So who the hell are you?"

"What?"

"Because I sure as hell know you're not Sam Saturn. Because Sam Saturn is dead."

The Pirate pulled her arm away, her face dark.

"I don't know what you're talking about."

"I'm talking about the fact that we found Sam Saturn's body lying behind a dumpster in an alley down there, in the city." Kane punched a gauntleted finger towards the airship window. He repeated, "So who the hell are you?"

The woman raised an eyebrow and went back to heaving on the lever. She grunted, then stopped, letting out a breath.

"I don't know who Sam Saturn is, but she's no relative of mine. My name is Lisa. Lisa Saturn. Isn't that a hoot?" She stood up and rubbed the raw pads of her hands. "And this Ms Saturn is very much alive and well and trying to move this lever. So the question still stands."

Kane leaned back against the panel, arms folded.

"What question?"

She smiled.

"You gonna stand there looking handsome and heroic, or are you going to help me crash this goddamned airship?"

THIRTY-SIX

RAD WATCHED REX CIRCLE THE CHAIRMAN – Judge Joseph Crater, the Missingest Man in New York – mindful of the hulking figure of the nearly seven-foot-tall robotic sailor standing just a few yards away. The machine wasn't moving, but it had killed hundreds of people to get into the office. When Rad and his companions had arrived at the Empire State Building, they'd found the street-level entrance a deserted war zone. The police had taken to the air in their blimps, orbiting the building many stories up, regarding the street level as perhaps too dangerous. As they entered, a blimp spotlight played over them for a second before they could dart into the smashed entrance. Rad hoped they'd been quick enough to escape detection, but then he didn't really care. It was time to end the farce. The Empire State would either fall tonight, or would survive. And if it survived, it would never be the same again. The power was still on, a fact Rad had been thankful for as they moved up through the building in the unbearably slow elevator; as they rose, the four of them standing in silence, Rad considered which would be the better option.

What would happen if the Empire State survived? Would anything change? Would the city still be at war, or was the return of the ironclad somehow signifying a change in policy?

Even if Wartime passed, would the population accept that? Rad now knew that Wartime had existed from the very beginning of the Empire State. Nobody – including himself – had a memory of peace because there never had been peace.

And now this. The devastation of the Empire State Building, a direct attack on the city's seat of government. Deliberate, planned, the first attack by the Enemy on home soil. This would frighten the citizens of the city and galvanise them to support the war for a very, very long time. At least, that's what it would look like. That all this was due to the actions of a single Empire State robot, the first hero to return from the war in history... that would be too much to bear.

And if the Empire State survived, what would happen to Rad? Would he still be a private detective? Maybe his role in all this would be unnoticed, forgotten, and he could slip away and go back to his old life.

But there was a more important question. Did he *want* to go back to his old life? In "peacetime", would the city be any different? It was still an incomplete, pale reflection of New York City. There was nothing beyond the fog, nowhere to go.

While Rad wished he wasn't connected, hadn't got involved in all of this, had remained blissfully unaware of the lie of the Empire State and the existence of Origin, Pocket and Fissure, he could live with it, if he had to. It was another case. A strange, messed-up-all-to-hell case. But there was something else, something which made Rad angry and upset. Something which would be hard to live with.

He wished Nimrod hadn't taken him to the Origin. In the short journey from Nimrod's office to the Fissure, he'd caught a glimpse of New York City. Just a glimpse, just lights and people from a dark car window. But it was enough. The Origin and the Pocket were all very well in theory, but having *seen* New York itself, even a tiny slice of it, crystallised everything in his mind. And, my God, he'd seen across the river. There was no fog. There was *somewhere else*. Just the concept frightened and excited Rad in equal measure.

So if he and Rex and Grieves and Jones failed tonight, the Empire State might very well blink out of existence. Would that be so bad? What was the point of it existing anyway? It was a fake, a forgery, a bad copy. The city, and everyone in it, were they real? If it was all just a mirage, an accidental after-image created by a freak of nature, would it matter if it just blipped out? Rad wondered if it would be so quick and easy, just the click of a light switch and "pop", darkness. Rad wondered if maybe Nimrod was wrong and the tether would just snap and New York City wouldn't feel a thing.

Keeping his eyes fixed on the robot, Rad elbowed Jones on his left to get his attention and whispered out of the corner of his mouth.

"You know who the Chairman is? He someone on the run from New York?"

Grieves answered from Rad's right before Jones could reply. "Judge Crater. Looks like him, not that I can remember it well. Big-time judge, got tangled in some mob business, so they say. Went out to dinner with a lady friend and was never seen again. Big news I think. A while ago now. I'd only just joined the department." Grieves shrugged. He didn't seem too bothered.

"Huh," said Rad, then he clicked his fingers softly. "The case Rex was involved with?"

Grieves tilted his mask. Rad wasn't sure if Grieves was agreeing with him or just trying to scratch his nose against the rubber.

So, people could transfer permanently across the Fissure from Origin to Pocket. And maybe from Pocket to Origin. Rad scratched his beard.

"So now you've found him."

Grieves turned his masked face to Jones, who nodded, then stepped forward, gun raised.

"Judge Joseph Crater, I am arresting you on a criminal charge on behalf of the City and State of New York. You will accompany us to the office of the district attorney to answer. Do you understand?"

"What the hell are you doing? I thought you didn't know him?" Rad looked at Grieves, at Jones. This was putting a spanner in the works. He stepped up to Jones. Rex moved closer, watching the pair of them

"Seems he's behind all this." Jones adjusted his grip on the gun. "You got a better idea?"

Rad spluttered. "What, you decide you want to do this by the book now?" He waved a hand around the expansive boardroom. "You maybe forgotten where you are? You ain't in New York. You're in the Empire State, which, if you re-call, is in imminent danger of fizzing out and taking New York with it. Hello?"

Jones didn't move for a second, like he was thinking it over, then Rex pulled away from them both and quickly turned, a small snub-nosed pistol in his hand.

"Back off, buddy."

Rad swore and grabbed at his pockets. The gun Jones had given him was gone, obviously. It was now in Rex's hand. Rad felt sick and foolish all at once.

Jones kept his heat pointing level at the Chairman's head, doing his best to ignore Rex.

Rad pulled at Grieves's shoulder.

"Goddammit, call up Nimrod. Seems he's the only one with any sense, and he ain't even here."

Grieves flicked the belt of his trench coat loose and began pulling a collection of small objects out of his inside pockets. The gun in Rex's hand moved between Jones, Rad and Grieves, uncertainly.

"What are you doing? Don't move!" Rex cried out.

Grieves ignored him. "Phone?"

Jones gestured with the gun towards the far end of the boardroom table, where a solitary telephone sat next to a blotter and an empty upside-down glass. Rex nearly jumped back a foot at the movement. Grieves nodded and went to move towards it.

A whirr, and then a click. "Cease or I fire," said the robot.

Grieves stopped short, just as the robot jerked into life. Rex, spooked, moved back even further, quickly flicking the gun to cover nearly every object in his line of sight.

The robot paused, and first turned its head then it rotated at the waist and walked towards Rex, obviously judging him to be a greater threat than the armed, but otherwise motionless, Jones. The robot's movement was fast and fluid, but somehow nauseating for Rad. He'd seen robots before, everybody had, lined up in the big parade downtown as they marched onto their ships on Fleet Day. But that was rigid, regimented. This was a robot in combat, at close range. It was insectoid, unnatural, and it creeped the hell out of him.

Rex fired, four times, into the robot's chest. The boardroom was cavernous with a ceiling that vanished into the darkness of the Empire State Building's upper reaches, but with shiny glass walls and hard marble floor, the sound was deafening as the shots ricocheted around them. Rad fell into a crouch, hands pressed against the sides of his skull. Even the stoic Grieves and Jones, ears exposed behind the rubber seal of their masks, flinched. Ears ringing, Rad heard another sound under the thunk of the robot's feet. The Chairman was crying... no, *laughing*. Both. Had his mind gone? Rad watched as he fumbled with a large, dirty white hanky in both hands. It looked familiar, but Rad's attention was drawn away as the robot moved again.

The robot shot an arm out towards Rex, but Rex, all three hundred pounds of him, managed to dodge out of the way, the force of his reflex action throwing his balance off and sending him skidding backwards as he tripped and fell against the boardroom table. As he fell he squeezed off another shot towards the ceiling.

"Stand down!" The robot's voice was remarkably human.

Rad tried to imagine the person inside, wired up permanently to the exoskeleton. He shuddered at the thought but, with the machine distracted by Rex, Rad scooched along the floor to Jones's side.

"Come on, man, we've got bigger fish to fry, and when the Skyguard gets here we're going to be outnumbered, if we aren't already." He turned to Grieves. "Call Nimrod, now!"

Just as the tip of Jones's revolver dipped, the Chairman leapt to his feet. Jones was perhaps more surprised by the hissing sound the Chairman made, letting out a yelp as the city's leader powered into him, hand wrenching the lapels of his coat and face pressed up against the mask. The Chairman was staring deep into one goggle, then with a dog-like bark started kicking and punching. Taken by surprise, Jones let the gun get pulled from his hand.

Rad grabbed at the Chairman's back in an effort to get Jones free of the madman, and succeeded, only to find the Chairman now holding the fat-barrelled revolver. The Chairman scrabbled backwards, and raised the gun directly to the centre of Jones's forehead, lips pulled back in a rictus grin. With his free hand, he pulled the dirty handkerchief roughly over his head. As he dragged the eye holes into place, his back straightened, his demeanour changing. His breathing slowed and the hissing stopped. Rad suddenly recognised the brown suit.

The Chairman of the City Commissioners, the Missingest Man in New York. The Pastor of Lost Souls.

They were all the same man.

That explained why the Pastor's madhouse had never been raided and shut down, despite the warrants out for the cult leader's arrest. It also meant that the man in the white hood was far more dangerous than he had assumed.

The Chairman – *the Pastor of Lost Souls* – thumbed back the hammer.

Rad tensed on the balls of his feet, trying to judge the best moment for a desperate lunge to disarm him. He watched the gun shake in the Pastor's hand, slowly at first, then the involuntary movement crawling up his entire arm to the shoulder. Any second and the gun would fire, whether by conscious intent or not. Rad licked his lips, ignoring the imposing form of the robot as it turned from where it had pinned Rex on the table and walked towards the Pastor.

It was now or never.

Rad sprang forward, only to find his momentum instantly impeded by a huge shock wave as the glass wall exploded, filling the boardroom with lethal, transparent shrapnel. Rad fought to keep his vision level, and watched as Grieves was likewise knocked from his feet. A huge, knife-shaped shard of glass connected with one eye of the agent's goggles, breaking into smaller pieces as the fragment split on impact, thankfully only cracking the protective lens. Rad hit the floor and was sent spinning on his back like the hands of a clock and, gliding to a halt against a corner pillar of the large room, he felt a hot, wet sensation on his leg. His hands reached down and found a tear in his trousers, his fingers coming away red as stabbing pain shot through his calf.

"Oh hell," he shouted, to himself mainly, as he was sure his voice wouldn't carry across the cacophony that had exploded into the room. Glass and fragments of metal window frame fell like deadly confetti as Rad held his breath and reached for the gash in his suit trouser leg. His fingers found the piece of glass, about the size of a dining room table at a rough estimate, and pulled it out. Rad felt a brief pang of nausea as the edges of his wound slicked together, but the sensation was replaced almost immediately by a deep, pummelling pain in the muscle, as if someone was hitting his leg with a baseball bat. Gritting his teeth, he touched the wound. It hurt like all hell, and was making a fine mess of the remains of his suit, not to mention the floor all the way from where he had fallen to where he had landed against the pillar. But it wasn't too deep. He'd had much worse. More of an immediate problem was the rib he was sure was now cracked. He gingerly examined his side, gasping in shock as he fingered the bruised area. There was no time to worry about it now.

Rad blinked away the dust, and took stock. Grieves and Jones were up already, dust-covered but apparently intact. Rex was too, although unconscious in the broken "V" of the boardroom table, the marble slab split cleanly in two by the explosion. The Pastor himself was not only unharmed but hardly even dirty, having been shielded from the blast by the bulk of the robot's frame.

The robot was a pair of legs with no body. The torso, head and arms were all now in separate corners of the room, and with a grimace Rad saw blood sprayed in an arc away from the window, covering the floor and nearby pillars nearest the metal legs. Whatever had hit the side of the building, the robot, nearest to the window, had taken the full force of the impact, square on. If Rad didn't know better, he would have said that was the intention. But the police wouldn't have lifted a finger, they would have happily circled the building in their blimps all night before anybody suggested they actually do anything, too terrified not of harming their Chairman, but of incurring his wrath. Rad doubted they had that kind of firepower anyway, unless a blimp or airship had crashed into the side of the building.

There was a crackle and whine, which would have been deafening inside the boardroom if Rad's ears weren't already deafened and ringing from the explosion. A PA sprang to life, and a familiar voice cleared its throat before speaking.

"Gentlemen, please remain where you are."

Captain Carson.

Rad rolled over with a wince and looked at where the glass wall had been. A stiff, ice-cold wind whipped around the edges of a large airship that hovered just a foot or two away from the lip of the precipice that fell one hundred and one stories to the street below. It was no sleek police blimp. This was a battered, bent, beaten mishmash, rusted and riveted, metals of different colours clashing as panels and patches overlapped each other.

Rad smiled. Someone had been busy while he'd been away. The *Nimrod* was shipshape once more.

The voice barked again. "I am sending my man across. Please do not move. You will each identify yourselves." In the window of the airship, Rad could see a vague outline of two men. One, a huge silhouette, began to move. Byron. The other remained still, bent over a control panel.

The Pastor watched Rad, and followed his line of vision. Then he stood, broken glass tinkling to the floor from his body.

"Captain Carson," he said.

Rad turned to see him raise Jones's fat-barrelled gun.

"Traitor!" He squeezed the trigger and his hand jerked back in recoil as the gun fired with a cloud of blue smoke.

THIRTY-SEVEN

GRIEVES, PARTIALLY HIDDEN UNDER a small amount of debris in front of the Pastor, leapt up, his shoulder square on his target. As the Pastor fired, his aim was knocked off true and the bullet impacted the metal patchwork above the *Nimrod*'s bridge window. Rad saw Carson duck instinctively, then wave a hand.

"Stand clear," came his voice over the tinny speaker.

There was a *whoosh* of compressed air, and a cable fired from the *Nimrod* and embedded itself in the rear wall of the boardroom. Retracting on a motor and pulley, Carson used the anchor to pull his ship snugly into the hole in the glass wall, causing what remained of the plate glass window to bulge alarmingly and sending another cascade of debris crashing down. But with the gap plugged, the chill wind was blocked, and Rad felt able to stand without being blinded by swirling dust.

More noise, more industrial scraping of metal on metal, and Rad watched as the nose of the *Nimrod* unscrewed anticlockwise, partially, and swung open as a huge, airtight hatch. From within the craft, Byron stepped into the building, one hand pushing a gigantic hatch wheel almost a yard in diameter.

The Pastor twisted in Grieves's grip, but the masked agent's hold was firm.

"Carson! Carson, get your traitorous carcass out of here or I'll throw your gutted corpse off the roof myself." The Pastor's white hood puffed out from his face as he spat each word. He struggled continuously.

Byron walked towards the Pastor, and seemed to regard him for a moment behind the opaque glass window of his faceplate. Then Byron walked over to check on Rex and Jones: the latter on his feet but battered, the former beginning to stir in the smashed cradle of the table. Apparently satisfied, Byron made his way over to Rad.

"Do you require assistance, sir? The Captain is most keen to remove you from this situation and prevent the closure of the Fissure."

Rad looked up at the voice, into the empty black window on the front of Byron's helmet. He stopped himself recoiling in fright, the story of Nimrod's dead batman at the forefront of his mind. Eventually he nodded and, leaning on Byron for support, walked stiffly with him towards the airship in its makeshift dock. Carson himself appeared in the airlock hatch, welcoming the detective with open arms.

"My dear chap! Let Byron see to your injuries. I had begun to think you'd met a sticky end."

Rad laughed, then stopped and straightened as he looked at Carson's face. It was amazing, truly amazing. Carson and Nimrod were the same person, clearly, identical right down to the bristling white moustache.

"How did you know we were here?" Rad asked.

The Captain's grey and yellow-toothed grin zipped open across his face.

"You've been absent for a few days. We thought you'd perhaps encountered trouble, so Byron and I decided that action was required. We repaired the *Nimrod*, keeping one eye on the city in case Kane or anyone else reappeared. Once airborne we could monitor things a little better and we saw your little group travelling across town." The Captain jerked his thumb back towards the *Nimrod* jammed in the window. "That was more good luck than anything. We followed you until you entered the building, then just kept an eye on the boardroom."

Rad nodded. He patted Carson's shoulder in thanks, then looked back at the others.

"You're gonna have more passengers. The guy on the table is our murder suspect. You might want to check his fingerprints against the ones you took from me. And bring the Chairman, Pastor, whatever the hell he is I think he might be our main villain."

The Captain smiled tightly at this, and nodded. "You leave the Chairman to me. I know all about him," he said, and strode briskly past Rad and into the middle of the room.

"You must be Grieves and Jones," Carson said, nodding to each of the masked agents. "I've spoken to Nimrod. His temporal calculations indicate Fissure collapse in just a few hours. Are you able to assist? With Mr Bradley injured, we may require additional manpower."

Jones walked up to Carson, stopping just a few inches from the old man's face. He brought his mask in close, moving his head around Carson's as if the Captain was some kind of statue or mannequin.

"You look just like Nimrod," Jones said in his smoker's drawl. Carson smiled, and indicated the semi-conscious form of Rex.

"Fascinating, I'm sure. Just like our Mr Bradley's doppelganger there." The Captain turned his attention to Grieves. Judge Crater now hung limply in the agent's grip, so limp that if Grieves were to let go the prisoner would surely drop to the hard floor like a stone.

Carson pursed his lips. "Are we agreed?"

"It's dangerous for us to stay here too long," said Jones.

Carson's head snapped around. Jones flinched and turned to his fellow agent.

Grieves looked at Jones, and then nodded. Jones held his hands up in surrender. Grieves jerked his head at Rex. Jones grabbed him by the shoulders and dragged him to his feet, then hauled the semi-coherent man to the airship in a fireman's lift.

Grieves remained where he was. Carson walked over to the Pastor, who snapped his head up. Carson sighed and pulled the hood off, revealing Judge Crater's face. The man looked up at Carson with an expression of insane, blood-vessel-popping rage.

"Good evening, Judge Crater," said the Captain, quietly.

At this the Pastor – Crater – jerked into life, rocking Grieves on his heels but remaining in his vice-like grip.

"You'll pay for this, you traitorous shit. I'll kill you easy, old man."

Carson raised a hand to his mouth and coughed, almost politely. "Aside from the threat, I rather think that is the statement I should be making to you. We know that the Fissure will close in a few hours. How are you planning to do it?"

Crater looked like a surprised child for a few seconds, then his face cracked into a wide grin.

"What am I going to do? Nothing. Nothing at all! You're looking in the wrong place, old pal o' mine. I'm not who you should be worried about." Crater began to laugh, long and hard enough that his eyes screwed up into tiny, tight creases. Then he took a huge whoop of breath and screamed "Hallelujah! Amen!" at the top of his lungs.

Carson frowned, and nodded at Grieves, who adjusted his hold on the prisoner and dragged him to the airship. The Captain stood in the boardroom, stroking his moustache and surveying the damage done to the room.

Rad limped over to the Captain, left calf tightly bound in a cream-coloured bandage below the rolled-up leg of his suit.

"Problem?"

"Hmm?" Carson shook his head. "No, my boy, we are in *crisis*. 'Problem' as such is not an appropriate descriptor for our current situation." He went back to stroking his moustache and dropped his eyes to the floor, clearly lost in thought.

Rad sighed. "If we're moving, we need to go now. Those police blimps aren't going to hang back forever. They may be a bunch of scaredy cats, but your ship is a sitting duck, stuck in the wall like that."

The Captain considered, then nodded, patting Rad on the shoulder. "Yes, you are correct." He paused, and then said, "Did you hear what the Chairman said?"

Rad nodded. "He said he's not the guy. Every crook says that when they get caught."

"This is true, but I don't think he was trying to lay blame elsewhere. It wasn't a ruse, it was a boast."

"You said Nimrod told you the Fissure was going to close in a few hours? How does he know, if it hasn't happened yet?"

Carson nodded. "The Fissure will close. There is a time distortion between here and the Origin. It's hard to predict, and it can run in both directions, and sometimes, just sometimes, you can catch a glimpse of the future, or maybe a possible future..."

Rad stopped him. "Yeah, the time thing. I know. I was in New York for a few hours, and it was a few days here."

Carson met Rad's gaze with his own watery dark eyes. He smiled and dropped his voice to a whisper.

"Yes... yes, of course. Magnificent, isn't it? So much space, so much life."

"You been there too?"

"No," said the Captain, shaking his head. "But I've seen it. I used to work for Judge Crater and the City Commissioners. I had the necessary expertise, and together we probed the Fissure and saw past it, into the Origin."

"You know Nimrod is you, the 'you' of the Origin?"

"Yes. We had a long chat. He mentioned your little visit."

Rad closed his eyes and rubbed the memory of his visit away.

"So what's going on? The Fissure is going to close. The Chairman set something running? Something to do with the robot. It came back on the boat from the Enemy... did it come back to kill the Chairman? Some kind of revenge, or reprogramming by the Enemy?"

"Or reprogramming by the Chairman. But returning for what, I wonder?"

"You can't be serious? The robot killed the entire building! The Chairman would do that?"

"It depends," said the Captain, "on what the end result is. For the Chairman, the ends may well justify the means. The entire police force is out there in their blimps. The Chairman had placed naval officers in command of each. More robots. The curfew has been extended. The streets are deserted while the citizens quake in their homes. And this building is surrounded."

Rad nodded slowly. "So if someone's going to attack the Battery, it's going to be now."

"Indeed."

"Was he going to use the robot to do it, somehow?"

Carson brushed his moustache. "Possibly. But I think not. The robot may have been an intelligence gathering operation. Crater was obsessed with learning the Enemy's secret. Perhaps he needed to be sure..."

Rad shook his head. "If the robot wasn't the tool in the box, then..." His eyes widened. "Kane said an Enemy airship had arrived, above the clouds. And guess what? Kane can fly now. Rockets and everything."

Carson looked at Rad, forehead knitted in thought. Rad nodded.

"And the Skyguard is strangely absent from our little party," he said. "Didn't even RSVP."

The *Nimrod*'s PA sprang into life with an electronic squall. Byron's voice, already mechanised by his suit, echoed oddly around the boardroom.

"Gentlemen, there is another ship approaching the city."

Rad and Carson looked at each other.

"Police blimp?" shouted Carson back to the *Nimrod*.

"Negative. Instruments suggest a large vessel, descending through the cloud deck. Destination estimated to be the Battery."

Rad grabbed Carson by the sleeve of his tunic. "There it is. There's our Enemy attack. And I got a bad feeling about who's flying that thing."

Carson raised an eyebrow, then nodded. "The Skyguard."

Rad shook his head. "Kane Fortuna."

"Byron," called the Captain. "Haul anchor and set full reverse!" He grabbed Rad and began to walk towards the hatch. "Your leg patched?"

Rad nodded. "Byron's quite the expert."

"He is indeed. Come, we have an airship to intercept."

Rad entered the *Nimrod* first; Rad paused at the bulkhead just inside the hatch and Carson waved him on. Ahead of them, at the end of the short airlock passageway, was a ladder that led both up and down through hatchways.

"Quickly, detective! Up!"

Rad glanced past the Captain, back into the Empire State Building. The ship shook as the engines were throttled in preparation for departure.

"What about the hatch?"

Carson shook his head and waved again. "Byron can close it from the bridge when we pull out of our temporary dock. Now, go!"

Heading up, the ladder took Rad into another dimly lit, steel-lined passageway which led back towards the front of the craft, where the cockpit sat above and slightly behind the protruding nosecone which was currently wedged into the side of the Empire State Building. As Rad stepped off the ladder, his weak leg gave out and he fell into an uncomfortable crouch in the corner next to something beige and soft. Curious, he moved his hands over the shape. Behind, he heard Carson clamber up the ladder and down the passage to the cockpit. The *Nimrod* shook again and Rad winced as the horrific sound of twisting and scraping metal reverberated inside the metallic interior of Carson's polar explorer as Byron attempted to reverse it away from the building.

The beige shape moved under Rad's hands. He blinked, and pulled at one side, rolling the form over. As it moved, a flap of fabric flopped away, the corner of the trenchcoat sliding off to reveal a gas mask with one cracked goggle.

"Grieves!"

Ignoring his throbbing leg, Rad helped the agent pull himself to a seated position. Grieves moaned and clutched his head.

"Crater escaped. Bastard was strong as an ox."

Rad swore and glanced down the passage towards the cockpit. The *Nimrod*'s control room was darker than the passageway, but he could see the back of Captain Carson's khaki jacket. It seemed he and Byron were concentrating fully on extricating their ship.

"Hey!" Rad called out. Carson turned and Rad could see the Captain's eyes widen as he took in the scene.

"Where's Crater?"

Rad shook his head and the Captain's moustache bristled. The *Nimrod* shook again.

Grieves grabbed at Rad's sleeve.

"The hatch... Crater will be heading for the boardroom."

"Ah, shit," said Rad. He swung himself onto the ladder and rattled down to the airlock passage. He turned as his feet hit the decking, but it was too late. The great airlock hatch was swinging slowly shut; beyond, the ruined facade of the boardroom's outer wall began to recede as the *Nimrod* pulled away.

Carson's voice crackled from a PA horn in a corner near the hatch.

"Too late, Mr Bradley, we are away. Quickly, come up the ladder."

When Rad returned to the cockpit passageway Grieves was standing, leaning against the grilled wall as he rubbed the back of his neck. He looked up at Rad as the detective approached. Rad saw the agent blink behind his mask.

"You OK?" Rad asked.

"Apart from feeling a damn fool, sure."

Rad patted Grieves on the back. If he was honest, Rad was happier not having Crater on board. The man was unhinged and very dangerous. He might have been the key to the whole mess, but the Enemy airship took top priority.

"Come on," said Rad, heading towards the cockpit. Grieves followed.

The *Nimrod*'s bridge was a large compartment, although the only seats were the two positioned in front of the main window for the requisite crew. Byron's expansive frame nearly took up both positions, leaving Carson to lean on the back of the second chair and peer out of the window. Rad followed his gaze.

"Son of a *bitch*," he said.

The breach in the side of the boardroom wall dwarfed the stick-like figure of Crater. He stood on the very lip of the opening, buffeted by the wind.

Carson and Byron muttered to each other and the airship began to swing in closer, the pair clearly trying to negotiate the craft back in to collect their ex-prisoner. But then the figure was gone. Everyone in the cabin jerked forward for a better view out of the window, but there was nothing to see, no movement, no falling, spinning dot, no body carried on the wind as Crater apparently plunged to the Earth.

Rad grabbed for Carson's shoulder.

"Come on, leave him. There's not going to be much left of him to scrape from the sidewalk if he fell."

Carson looked at him silently. Rad tried to read his face but he'd already learned that the Captain was pretty good at keeping his feelings hidden.

To Rad, it was obvious. The Fissure was going to close, very soon, and not by any natural means. It hadn't happened yet, hadn't even started to happen, but in the Origin, Nimrod had seen it. The Fissure vibrated space and time in all directions on this side and on the other, and whatever fancy gadgetry Carson's doppelganger had set up, he'd been able to... Rad struggled with the concept. Predict? No, it was not a prediction, it was a certainty. Foreseen? Nimrod, the Science Prophet? No, it wasn't mysticism, even if it was, essentially, looking into the future. *Measured*. That was it. Nimrod had measured the closing of the Fissure, hours before it had even begun.

"Airship at five miles, closing. Altitude decreasing, descent accelerating." Byron shifted in the pilot's chair. There was an urgency in his tinny voice that made Rad imagine a furrowed brow, and a mouth downturned with concern inside the helmet. Hell, for all he knew, perhaps that's exactly what was behind the smoked glass.

Carson met his servant's unseen gaze, then nodded. He sprang up, galvanised into action.

"Very good. Set course for intercept. We must catch our prey before their speed is too great." He turned to Jones, who was squeezed under a bulkhead at the back of the bridge, the conscious but unhappy-looking Rex firmly in his grasp.

Rad tried to keep his distance from his double, but it was difficult in the cramped space. Rex made him feel... strange. The thought that Rex was somehow more real than him was nauseating. Rex was violent and cowardly, two aspects of his own character that Rad knew full well he possessed, but that he kept in check, utilising them only for self-preservation in the line of work.

Huh. His work. His years of experience as a private detective – Rad now knew that the reason he couldn't remember his first case was that he hadn't had a first case. He'd sprung into existence, fully formed, agency in tow, when the reflection of New York had crystallised in the Pocket.

Rad felt hot bile rise in his throat. He swallowed, and grimaced, and turned his attention to the window. Outside, the city spun as Byron corrected their course. The cloud deck was close by, at this range a deep, powerful orange ceiling just above them. Rad wondered if it was just the reflection of the city lights, or whether the cloud, fog, mist, whatever, possessed orange light of its own.

Carson said, "Gentlemen, take your prisoner and secure him aft. You should find a suitable compartment, all can be locked from the outside. Return quickly, we will need to be ready." He paused, looking the pair up and down. Grieves seemed to have recovered from Crater's violent escape, although it was hard to tell behind the mask.

"Are you both armed?" Carson asked.

Jones flexed his wrist to indicate the fat-barrelled gun,

which he had trained on Rex's kidneys. Grieves nodded and patted his left side, under his arm.

Captain Carson clapped his hands, his moustache bristling over his grin.

"Capital, gentlemen, capital! Now, quickly. Byron will bring the *Nimrod* around."

Jones jabbed Rex in the guts with the gun, but if he was hoping to get a reaction, he was disappointed. Rex moved without any persuasion, ducking under the support girders that laced the ceiling at irregular intervals, and disappeared through the oblong hatchway that led to the main body of the ship. Grieves followed close behind.

With more room to manoeuvre in the cramped bridge, Byron shifted over in his seat, allowing Carson to slip in beside him into the co-pilot's chair. Rad moved between the two seats and leaned down on his elbows to get a good view out of the window. His leg smarted like all hell when he knocked it against a lever protruding from the floor, but the wound itself had settled into a steady, dull throb. Carson mentioned action, and Rad knew he'd hold up, but – if he survived, if they survived, if the Empire State survived – he'd be sore tomorrow. His breath wheezed a little from his damaged rib. He ignored it. He'd had worse.

"What's the plan, Captain? Any clue on how to stop the other boat?" Rad lifted his hat and scratched his scalp.

The Captain tutted, and kept his eyes fixed out the window as he spoke.

"The airship is the Enemy's equivalent of an ironclad. I assume Kane can't actually fly it, not if it operates on the same symbiotic control as our fleet. The robots are plugged directly into the system, *becoming* the ironclad in a way. But I suspect it would not be difficult to crash, if he had the know-how. Byron's calculations here show it *en route* for the Battery."

Rad whistled low. "A crash landing? That would do the trick. If it's as big as an ironclad. And I think I may know who is giving him the technical help."

The pair glanced sideways at each other and Carson's eyes flashed. "The Science Pirate," he said with a chuckle. "Nimrod provided a description. Oh, most interesting. Quite the cunning plan. The tools *and* the expertise."

"So what are we going to do? Can the police shoot it down?" Rad straightened and looked around the bridge. "Can we shoot it down?"

"This is not a military or police vessel, Mr Bradley. The *Nimrod* is an explorer, nothing more. Our only weapon was perhaps the emergency rocket flares, but they were spent creating the hole in the Empire State Building. However, we may have the advantage on the other ship. We are fast, agile. And I suspect the Skyguard will not wish to deviate from his collision course."

Rad frowned, then clicked his fingers.

"You mean...?"

Carson grinned, his wet eyes glinting.

"Exactly. Prepare to board the Enemy, Mr Bradley! I propose a little aeronautical piracy!"

THIRTY-EIGHT

THE AIR WAS COLD AND AT THEIR SPEED it was snatched away before he got a chance to take a breath. The shallow, quick gasps he did manage were enough, but they made him giddy. The cold air also stung his eyes, so he had to squint, but that didn't stop them from tearing.

Crater, AKA the Chairman of the City Commissioners, AKA the Pastor of Lost Souls, lay in the Skyguard's arms, his ears filled with the sound of the rocket boots and his nostrils filled, despite their slipstream, with the thick tang of kerosene. Unable to communicate with his saviour, he looked up at the Skyguard's chin, which jutted outwards like the prow of a ship.

Crater looked down. The river and dockside spun underneath them, a blur of lights and reflections, and he could feel the contents of his stomach sloshing to the left and right as the Skyguard sped towards a suitable landing spot. A moment later the rockets roared as the Skyguard braked. When Crater finally managed to open his eyes and scratch away the dried tear tracks, he found they were standing together on an empty street under yellow lights, the Skyguard striking a suitable heroic pose, hands on hips, legs apart. Then again, thought Crater, with all that armour and equipment, perhaps that was just comfortable. He giggled. At the strange, shrill sound the Skyguard tilted his head and gazed at Crater with his shining white eyes.

"Are our plans affected?"

Crater's laugh settled into a grin, which he kept for a while as he looked at the Skyguard. Then he seemed to snap out of his reverie, his cheeks dropping the smile in a second.

"No," he said. "I thank you for the intervention, but I had acquired the necessary information from the returned robot." He held up the push-button signal box, a slightly fatter version of the one on Kane's belt, and flicked the large switch to the "off" position. A faint beeping, inaudible to Crater during their flight but now present at the edge of his hearing, ceased from somewhere inside the Skyguard's helmet. Crater looked up at the night sky. He glanced at the orange-tinted clouds, here and there. The Skyguard followed his gaze, but said nothing.

"Is the ship ready?" asked Crater.

The Skyguard lowered his head to look at his employer.

"Yes. The Science Pirate has locked the controls. I need to return, there are still tasks to perform."

Crater nodded, slowly at first, then faster and faster until his cheeks and lips flapped with the motion.

"Good... good. I need to move the final pieces to the board." He glanced around and caught sight of a street sign. They were on the corner of Broadway and Soma. Crater smiled.

The Skyguard's boots clattered on the sidewalk as he prepared for take-off. But he hesitated. Crater tutted.

"You have something to say, Mr Fortuna?"

Kane stepped closer. He'd been working with the Chairman for months, ever since he first made contact with the Skyguard – the *real* Skyguard – in prison. It was thanks to Crater's efforts that he was allowed such free access to the Empire State's most notorious criminal, and thanks to him that he was able to take the Skyguard's suit from the police vault.

But standing here, in the warm street at night, as their grand plan unfolded, for the first time the Skyguard wasn't sure about his master. What had happened in the boardroom with the robot? And with Rad and his cronies from the Origin? Their interference was endangering everything.

Kane decided to start small.

"Did the robot complete its mission?"

Crater looked at the Skyguard again, his eyes distant, as if he hadn't been listening – although they were the only two people in the silent street.

"Oh yes. It is as we suspected. The Enemy is moving to us. They will take the Battery first, and with the Fissure secure, will then take the Empire State. There will be no escape for us if that happens."

Kane nodded. Crater had promised him a life in the Origin, in New York City. Crater had allowed him to see into the Fissure, just for a moment, just a glimpse of the unimaginably large world beyond, in the Origin. That had been enough. Kane wanted to leave the Empire State more than anything. And that meant destroying the Battery and collapsing the Fissure so he and Crater could enter the Origin and not be taken back.

The Empire State wasn't real, anyway. It was just an illusion, fake.

Kane decided to disregard the fact that, by the same logic, the same applied to himself.

Crater patted Kane on an armoured elbow, then jerked his finger up towards the clouds.

"Go back to the ship. Make sure all is ready. I will see you in New York, my friend." Head bowed, he walked away, towards Soma Street and the glowing white light at the end of it, just around the bend and out of sight.

Kane, the Skyguard, watched him for a while, then fired his rockets and shot up into the night.

• • • •

Around the street corner, Crater stopped, one hand deep in a trouser pocket. He pulled out the white hood of the Pastor, which he'd managed to slip out of that fool Carson's hand, pulled it on, and headed to the House of Lost Souls.

THIRTY-NINE

CARSON HAD BEEN RIGHT, THOUGHT RAD. The other airship, the mysterious hulk from the Enemy, was exactly as he had surmised. It was the airborne equivalent of an Empire State ironclad. Long and rectangular, the vessel looked like it was upside down, with guns, rails, cabins and the equipment of war on the bottom of the thing, hanging downwards in a series of black lumps and bumps silhouetted against the clouds. The bulk of the vessel was the hull itself, which bulged outwards in a series of geometric planes, then tapered inwards, coming together in a sharp crest that ran the length of the airship.

It was a remarkable sight, even without fine detail yet visible at their distance. Remarkable that something so massive and solid and heavy was able to fly.

Rad pondered. Did physics have any part to play? If this was, *literally*, a twisted reflection of the ironclad still quarantined in the harbour below, did it have to be logical? Or did it merely "exist" purely because it had to, float in the air because that was the opposite, apparently, of how the Empire State ironclads operated.

As the *Nimrod* moved closer, Carson reached for the searchlight control and the twin beams were projected out into the night before them. Rad traced the wide, white beams as they lit the misty air up in front of them. A few seconds later the *Nimrod* was close enough to the Enemy ship for the lights to splash against its side. Carson leaned forward a little and pointed at something.

"Look, gas lines."

Rad squinted, but had no idea what the Captain was referring to.

"Remarkable," Carson continued. "The entire hull must be filled with hydrogen. Although that can't be the only lift. It must have an up-thrust as well."

That answered Rad's question and another he had been forming in his mind. The ship did obey the laws of physics, it just looked weird. It was not the kind of ship any sane designer would actually draw the blueprints for, or that any shipyard would actually weld together. But it worked. It flew.

Hydrogen. Rad knew all about that. The gas balloons of the police blimps used to be filled with the light, highly flammable gas. It had only taken two minor disasters for the city to switch to the heavier, but safer, helium. Rad wondered how much of the two gasses even existed in their pocket dimension. Perhaps it didn't matter.

But if the Enemy airship was filled with hydrogen, it would make quite a bang when it hit the Battery. The size and weight of the thing was enough, Rad had thought, not considering the possibility of giant gas tanks. The mass, plus ammunition, plus fuel, would have been enough to level half the city. Add to that the gigantic hydrogen tank, and nothing was going to survive the impact.

The *Nimrod*'s front window was wide but very narrow, and with nothing to get a fix on, their target looked like it was hanging motionless in the air. When Rad glanced down at the controls in front of Byron, he saw two dials spinning, one slowly, one so fast it was unreadable.

"We going down?"

Carson nodded, but it was the pilot who spoke. "If we are to force a dock we must match speed and course exactly," said Byron impassively, then added: "Projected impact in four minutes."

Rad gasped, and he was sure he heard Carson suck in a breath of air with somewhat more effort as well.

"Captain, please tell me you programmed Byron with a sense of humour?"

Carson stood and swung out of the co-pilot's chair.

"My friend, I didn't programme Byron with anything, he's as alive as you or I."

Rad waved a hand impatiently. "Point taken. But I feel I should point out that we're about to hit something very big and very hard in the time it takes to make a sandwich. That thing being the Empire State. You might have heard of it."

The Captain barked a laugh, just a single expulsion of sound, and clapped his hands. "Then I suggest you don't dawdle, detective. Byron?"

The pilot operated several controls in a quick sequence, causing the *Nimrod* to shake to high heaven for a few moments before settling. Carson's companion extricated himself from the cramped pilot's position, and through the window Rad saw that the Enemy airship had vanished. He opened his mouth to ask the obvious, but the Captain called out to him even as Carson vanished through the inner hatch.

"We're locked alongside. We'll cut in through their hull and board. Come on."

Byron hurried after his master, Rad dashing behind. Each time his left foot made contact with the metal plating of the floor, his calf felt like someone in very heavy, steel-capped boots was giving him a kick, but as the adrenaline began to surge the sensation faded.

Grieves and Jones appeared at the other end of the passageway that led from the *Nimrod*'s bridge back to the ladder that led both up and down into other regions of the craft. Carson walked swiftly towards them and swung himself onto the ladder and went down, followed quickly by Byron, the two agents and Rad.

In the airlock passage, there was a small gap between the ladder and the rear wall where an access hatch was set. As Rad touched down on the decking, the Captain opened the door and led them down a flight of thin metal stairs into what Rad assumed was the main hold of the explorer. It was a large room, as high as it was wide, occupying the entire stern of the *Nimrod*. Looking at the framework on the walls and the floor, Rad could see how the space had been fitted out to carry a few large pieces of equipment, all tethered to racks that could be rolled on and off the ship with ease. To assist this, the rear and both sides of the hold appeared to be mostly comprised of large doors, which slid back like a concertina. Their structure was a little thinner than that of the hull proper, and the noise in the hold was deafening as the doors rattled and pulsed with the wind outside, the harsh scraping and banging mixing with the roar of the *Nimrod*'s giant fan engines.

The Captain drew Rad, Grieves and Jones to one side as Byron walked directly to the port-side hold doors. The servant reached up and quickly unclamped the basic clasps that held the door fast in flight, and yanked it open. The door folded into itself, opening a gap that ran along the entire length of the ship. Immediately the wind roared in, not just from their slipstream, but pushed into the hold by the port engine fan, which hung above the opening on the outside of the ship, tilted directly downwards to provide stationary lift.

Rad was glad that Byron seemed to be following some pre-agreed course of action, as the exposed engine fan so close made communication almost impossible. Rad tried blocking his ears, but found he needed his arms free to maintain balance in the driving wind. Grieves and Jones had grabbed some dark webbing that hung from the wall, while Carson stood, leaning into the wind with apparent practice, watching Byron's actions. Thanks largely to his impressive bulk, the *Nimrod*'s pilot seemed unaffected.

There was some equipment still stowed in the hull – two large, cannon-like instruments, each the size of a small ironclad deck gun and clearly intended to be mounted somewhere on the outside of the vessel. Byron unhitched one from its rack and held it with the "stock" under one armpit. The guns appeared to be preloaded at manufacture with something, as the barrel opening was sealed with some kind of foil wrap. Byron pulled a red cord on the seal and tore it off, then positioned himself at the very mouth of the hull door.

The cannon bucked under Byron's arm. Rad couldn't hear it, but he could feel a dull concussion wave hit him in the chest. Byron was knocked to his knees, then dragged forward as the grapple hook and cable he had just fired found its mark in the side of the Enemy airship. Byron reached forward to grab the cable with his free hand and pulled.

Rad saw the damaged side of the other ship buckle as the claw, which had penetrated its armour and then presumably expanded into a proper hook, yanked at the plating. Byron, on one knee, with one hand, tugged the two moving craft closer together. Rad watched Byron's arm bulge as he heaved, then leaned back to pull again.

Carson had said that Byron was as alive as he was, but Rad had only ever seen that kind of strength in one other kind of "human" before. The ironclad robots. He made a note to ask Carson about that later. If they survived.

Two minutes passed. The ships were now less than a yard apart. The *Nimrod*'s port engine shook in its housing as it was squeezed against some jutting structure of the other ship, out of sight beyond the top of the hold doors. Rad felt the floor of the *Nimrod* tilt slightly away from the other ship, as the two were pushed together and *Nimrod*'s engine got in the way, forcing their craft into an angle.

Byron stood, still holding the cable in one hand. He let the spent grapple cannon drop to the floor and roll away, and took one step forward. He punched his free arm through the armour of the Enemy ship right to the shoulder. A few quick jerks back and forth, up and down, then out, and the entire riveted panel came loose and was pulled free. Byron tossed it into the *Nimrod*'s hold, then stood and stepped to one side, keeping hold of the ragged edge of the makeshift door. Although the two ships were tethered, the cable stretched and slackened, the two vessels clanging together in the air as they plummeted towards the city. Byron grabbed the cable, pulled it taut, then began winding it around one of the empty frames dangling from the *Nimrod*'s ceiling.

Carson turned to the two agents from New York City, leaning in to shout so he could be heard.

"Go in first. You're both armed. Head forward, take the bridge. The ship might be empty, might not be. Expect anything. Go. Byron will follow, but he's our only pilot. Protect him."

Bullethead Jones touched his gun hand to his forehead in a makeshift salute and the two of them ran to the gap between the *Nimrod* and the other ship. Braced against the wind, they hopped the ever-changing gap with no hesitation and disappeared inside the Enemy craft. Byron immediately followed. Carson held Rad's arm for a moment.

"You can stay if you want to." The Captain pointed to Rad's leg. Rad waved the concern away.

"Let's go. No point staying, this thing is heading for the ground as well."

"Good man," said the Captain, who then nimbly crossed the deck and entered the other ship. Rad ignored his complaining leg and followed.

• • • •

The Enemy ship was lit in an angry red that provided ample light – but somehow still had the close, oppressive atmosphere of total darkness. Rad didn't like it.

They'd had it. Rad was sure. How much time was left? A minute? Less probably. Presumably the ship's bridge was close by, but would Byron be able to operate the controls? Wouldn't they be locked on the collision course, or something? And that was assuming there was nobody on board. Any resistance on the way would cost them any time they had.

Rad saw nothing but red and black shadows and the curve of Captain Carson's back as he followed him through the narrow corridor. The old man was slower than Rad, who could have reached out and touched him with his fingertips. Their footsteps clanged on loose metal grating; up ahead, the heavy stomps of Byron and the lighter patter of Grieves and Jones.

Then, gunshots. Three, a pause, then another two. The sound startled Rad and he slowed, while Carson accelerated towards the sound and sped away from him.

That settled it. *Now* they'd had it. Rad, Carson, Byron, Grieves, Jones. Rex, Rad's double, locked in the *Nimrod*. The Empire State. New York City. Shazam! All gone in the blink of an eye and, Rad imagined, by some kind of giant intergalactic lightning bolt.

The corridor expanded into a square room. Rad caught a glimpse of bulkheads, hatchways open and closed, shapes moving in the ink-thick red. Something large, black and rectangular swamped Rad's vision, and he pulled to a stop with a protective arm across his face. Something cannoned into his side, and he fell against the wall. His cry of surprise was masked by another gunshot and the shape moved away.

It was Grieves. His gun was pointing at the ceiling, being held in the raised position by the huge gauntleted hand of the Skyguard. The two were locked in a struggle, Grieves's

neck in the grip of the other hand. And Grieves was losing,
no mistake. He was being bent backwards as the bulk of the
Skyguard pushed him towards the floor, Grieves lacking the
strength to fight against Kane's powered armour.

Rad blinked, the red light flashing behind his eyelids, and
looked around for Jones. He turned to the left as he heard a
thud, just in time to see Jones throw a punch at another armoured figure. This one was as big as the Skyguard, and
wearing just as much armour. The Science Pirate, Rad
thought. With two armoured rocketeers to fight, he wondered
how bad the odds really were. But Bullethead Jones wasn't a
small man and he had been able to fell his opponent, who
scrambled on the decking, but caught his heels in his ridicu-
lously large cloak. Jones seized the advantage and landed a
kick against the struggling form's side, then reached down and
pulled him up by the neck, ready for a second punch.

"Carson!" Rad lifted himself from the corner. The old man
was nowhere to be seen. Jones might have been putting up
a fight, but Grieves was outmatched by the Skyguard, and
Rad wasn't sure he was much help. He limped forward and
tried to lunge for the Skyguard's arm to relieve the pressure
on Grieves, but with an injured leg he was a fraction too
slow. The Skyguard lifted his elbow at just the right time,
forcing Rad's grab to miss and connecting the armoured
forearm with Rad's chin. The detective hit the deck again,
although he managed to tuck his head into his chest to
avoid cracking it on the hard metal.

The ship shook, then tilted. Rad rolled on the floor, and
saw Carson through an open hatchway, at the end of another corridor. The ship rolled again, in the opposite
direction. Beyond Carson, a bulkhead door swung open, revealing the bridge. Byron was at the controls and was trying
to prevent the catastrophic collision with the Battery.

The motion of the ship was enough to let Grieves get free,

although as he used the yaw of the ship to push the Sky-guard off him, his gun clattered to the floor. It slid on the deck grille; Rad didn't hesitate, and pushed off the wall with his feet and dived across the room, flicking the gun towards Grieves with outstretched fingertips. Once he'd gripped it securely, Grieves got to his knees, then to his feet.

A third pitch of the ship separated the combatants yet again. Jones and Grieves fell against one wall; the Skyguard and his companion against the other. The two sides faced each other, concentrating first on maintaining a firm footing. Rad was more or less in the middle, but with both sides wearing masks it was impossible to tell who was sizing up whom.

The Science Pirate pushed off the wall and fell towards the hatch that led to the flight deck, Carson and Byron. Rad called out, then found the Skyguard's hands grabbing the lapels of his suit. The Skyguard brought the winged mask close enough to Rad's face that he could feel his breath condensing on its cool metallic surface.

"Whose side are you on, Rad?" Kane spat, his voice a low, harsh growl. "We're trying to save the city. I thought you wanted that."

Rad croaked a little, but Kane clearly had no intention of loosening his grip. Rad felt his back being dragged up the wall of the room as he was lifted off his feet. His chest caught fire as the cracked rib within flexed around the fracture.

Rad huffed, trying to get a breath. "You're not saving any-one but yourself, Kane," he managed. Another breath, and then: "You're right. The city needs to be saved. Both cities."

At that, the Skyguard released Rad. Rad slid back down the wall, jarring his injured leg against the floor, but he ig-nored it. The pain was keeping him awake, alert, and was making him angry. Rad knew he could use this to his own advantage, directing his anger and pain towards fulfilling their mission, at any cost.

"They've locked the bridge." The Science Pirate came back down the corridor. Kane turned to Jones and Grieves, just in time for Jones leap towards him, pulling the armoured man away from Rad. Rad rolled against the wall and into Grieves. Face to face with the agent, he saw the broken lens in his mask was now missing altogether. The agent blinked at Rad, his breathing laboured.

"You OK?"

Grieves nodded. "I'll manage," he said, before pushing off the wall and locking both arms around Kane's neck. But in the Skyguard's suit Kane was twice the size of Grieves, who just clung uselessly to his back.

The Science Pirate aimed a mechanically augmented punch at Grieves, but Rad got there first. He ran as fast as he could up the sloping floor, shouldering the rocketeer square in the chest. Rad connected with hard armour, but he felt it give underneath, and he heard the violent, metallic wheeze behind the helmet as he winded his opponent. The action distracted Kane, who finally succumbed to Grieves's efforts and, with the help of a piston kick to the stomach from Jones, toppled backwards to the deck. Grieves rolled free.

"Carson!" Rad bellowed.

Jones looked down the corridor, which was now dark. "Door's closed."

On the floor, the Science Pirate began to get up, but was stopped by Rad slamming the heel of his shoe into the Pirate's wrist. Something sparked and there was an oily, burnt smell.

"Rad!"

The detective turned at Jones's warning, diving out of the way as Kane powered down the corridor to the bridge. Jones and Grieves shot after him; Rad made to follow, but his ankle was caught by the Science Pirate and he tripped. Rad managed to twist himself before he hit the floor, avoiding a broken nose. He swore, kicked at the Pirate, and scrambled forward on his hands and knees. Once out of reach of the prone Pirate, Rad pushed himself to his feet with his palms and ran down the corridor. He made it just a few yards before a heavy hand grabbed his shoulder, pulling viciously. Rad cried out in surprise and fell, raising his arms over his face instinctively for protection, but no hit came. Instead he bounced on the decking as the Science Pirate ran past in his heavy metal boots.

Rad sat up. The door to the bridge ahead was still closed. Rad expected the Skyguard and Science Pirate to be fighting at the door to get it open, but Rad found himself alone in the corridor. He stopped to get his bearings, and saw in the red darkness an open hatch immediately to his left. Through it he heard multiple pairs of feet pounding on the metal decking. He followed the sound.

Two more turns and he was assaulted by a blast of frigid air. It blew at him with enough force to turn him against the corridor wall. Carried on it he heard shouting and more scuffling. The corridor had a rail running down the opposite side to where Rad leaned, so against the wind, Rad reached and grabbed the rail, and used it to help pull himself forward.

The hatchway was larger than those he had already been through, taller and wider, with a fat, reinforced rim. Rad grabbed the thick edge and pulled himself through.

He was standing on a walkway that ran around the edge of a large open space – a hold of some sort. Steep, angled stairs led down from the walkway at intervals along each wall, and in the centre of the ledge Rad found himself on, just ahead, a large ramp led down.

On the floor below, Grieves and Jones were fighting Kane and the Science Pirate. The two armoured combatants were relying on augmented strength, but Nimrod's agents were obviously highly trained and extremely agile. For every powerhouse punch thrown by Kane, the agents would duck and weave, and land short, sharp taps to vulnerable areas on the armour. Kane and the Science Pirate had strength on their side, but they were slow and awkward, trailing the huge cloaks that tangled and threatened to trip constantly.

Rad guessed it before he saw it, and started to run down the ramp. The Skyguard and the Science Pirate *knew* they were slow and that the two agents had the advantage. They knew it, because they'd managed to turn the fight and started to force Grieves and Jones back towards the gaping chasm of the open hold door.

The door was a floor-to-ceiling, wall-to-wall shutter, the size of half a football pitch, and it was open. The wind howled in, dragging mist and engine exhaust into the ship in spiralling grey eddies. The air was cold enough to take Rad's breath away, the wind strong enough to buffet him in surprising ways as he ran towards the fray. The hat he'd borrowed from his double lifted off his head and sailed out into the night outside the ship

The Science Pirate saw Rad, and pushing Grieves towards Kane, ran towards the detective, fighting against the billowing cloak that threatened to pull him out of the hold. Kane turned to look, the movement distracting Grieves and Jones. It was enough. Kane turned back and pushed the two agents backwards. Their feet lifted from the ground as they were thrown backwards and vanished over the lip of the open hold door.

Rad shouted something, he wasn't sure what, but his voice was snatched by the wind. He saw Kane fire his rocket boots and launch into the black night beyond the hold door, just as the Science Pirate collided with Rad's chest. The pair fell, but the Science Pirate was surprisingly light despite the armour and Rad managed to push him off – enough to get his feet on his attacker's chest, just as his back hit the deck. A blinding pain shot through Rad as the edge of a vertebrae cracked on the metal grille, then with a yell he forced his legs straight. The Science Pirate was thrown backwards towards the hold door. His cloak twisted in the wind and he slid backwards as he tried to stand. The cloak inflated like a spinnaker and dragged him back again even as he got to his feet, bent double against the pull.

Rad stayed on the ground, trying to get both breath and strength back. He watched the Science Pirate for a moment, expecting him to disappear into the night like Kane had. The Science Pirate continued to pull forward, but made no headway. Then Rad realised he was reaching out for help.

When the Science Pirate spoke, shouting against the wind, it wasn't the metallic ringing basso, altered and amplified by the helmet. It was quiet and dull, like someone shouting in another room. Rad didn't even register it at first. It was a woman's voice, far away.

Rad jumped up, hesitated, then ran towards the Science Pirate, steadily sliding closer to the door. He – she? – was still shouting. Rad stretched and grabbed her gauntlet with both hands. He winced as the hard metal edges of her glove bit into his flesh, but he squeezed his jaw shut and pulled as hard as he could. After a second, he let go with one hand and pointed furiously somewhere behind the Science Pirate.

"The cape!" he shouted, hoping his gesture would be understood. "Lose the damn cape!"

The Science Pirate nodded briefly, then fumbled with something under her chin with her free hand. Her faceplate drooped forward a little, then her helmet, cloak attached, was yanked off her head as the cloak caught the wind again and pulled it into the void. Suddenly free of resistance, Rad fell backwards, taking the Science Pirate with him. For the second time his back hit the decking, and the Science Pirate landed on top of him. Rad yelled as the weight of her suit compressed his cracked ribs painfully. Face to face, Rad blinked and spat as her long brown hair swirled around them and into his mouth.

"What in the hell?"

The Science Pirate rolled off before Rad could grab her. She hit the wall and stood, then sliding along reached a panel of levers and glowing buttons. She jabbed one button and threw one of the levers up, and with a rocky grinding that drilled into Rad's skull, the hold door began to close. The clang as the two edges met was deafening, and was followed by near total silence, as far as Rad could tell with the tinnitus in his ears.

Rad opened his eyes, and pulled himself to his feet. He shook his head and instinctively pressed his hands against his ears, trying to judge whether there was any permanent hearing damage. He could hear the squishy sound of his palms as he pushed them against the side of head, which was enough to satisfy him that the partial deafness was at least temporary.

The Science Pirate was slumped over the control panel, her back heaving as she panted for breath.

Rad walked towards her, then stopped. Call him old-fashioned, but he hated it when the bad guys were bad girls. He frowned. Whoever she was, she was not only a co-conspirator in the Skyguard's plan to destroy the city, but was responsible for the death of Grieves and Jones. Rad wondered whether Nimrod had been able to watch, up here in the clouds.

He reached out to her shoulder, but she turned before he touched her. Rad jerked back a little then, when she brushed the hair out of her face, he took another step back, and swore.

"That's nice," said the woman. She wasn't smiling.

Rad lifted an eyebrow, then stepped closer to her as he felt his temper ignite. Without the helmet, he could see how the armour inflated her bulk and height. Out of it, she would have been a very petite thing.

He said, "You're awfully alive for a dead girl."

"Nice *and* charming. Are all men like this in your grey excuse for a city?"

Rad frowned.

"Don't tell me, you like to call New York your home?"

The woman looked Rad up and down, an expression of sour distaste on her otherwise handsome features.

"I don't like to call New York anything, but it's a darned sight better than this wet shithole."

"Got a smart mouth too, lady."

"Lady?" A smile appeared. "Oh my!" she said, sarcastically fanning her face with one hand.

Rad grabbed her arm at the elbow. She pulled away, but without power the dead armour was heavy and she couldn't struggle much. After a few seconds she stopped pulling, and her arm went limp in Rad's grip.

He said, "New York or the Empire State, take your pick, you can be tried in either place, or in both places. I imagine we can work out an extradition treaty."

"What are you, some kind of cop?"

Rad nodded. Now it was his turn to smile. "I'm a licensed private investigator, so that means yes. And apart from terrorism, conspiracy to commit genocide, and a dozen other crimes I'm sure I can think up, I'm holding you responsible for the death of those two agents."

The woman smiled again. It was an unpleasant expression. Rad's eyes narrowed. His leg was hurting, and he knew he was in danger of blowing his stack the longer he stood here pissing in the wind with the Science Pirate. He thought of Grieves and Jones and wondered how long it would have taken to hit the ground. He wondered again if Nimrod had been watching.

The floor tipped, throwing Rad onto the woman. She yelped and punched him weakly in the chest, but Rad righted himself quickly and yanked her arm again.

"Come with me. Carson will want to see this."

• • • •

The door was open. Carson and Byron were at the bridge controls, gazing out into the darkness. Rad entered, dragging his prisoner behind him, then he stopped, and stared.

The entire city was laid out in front of them as they hovered, apparently stationary, just under the cloud deck. It was bright and surprisingly symmetrical, the spire of the Empire State Building forming the tall central spoke from which the illuminated city blocks radiated out into the characteristic oblong island. Rad watched as bright white spots moved around the city's heart like flies. Police blimps orbiting the damaged one-hundred-and-first floor of the Empire State Building.

"We safe?" he asked.

"In all practical aspects, yes." Carson didn't turn around. Rad noticed that neither he nor Byron were moving. The detective stepped up behind the Captain, who turned at the sound of a second pair of heavy footsteps clattering awkwardly on the metal grille decking.

Carson continued: "Sam Saturn, I presume? Or rather, her New York equivalent."

The Science Pirate jerked her arm free from Rad's grip.

"Lisa Saturn. Ms Saturn to you. I kinda guessed you'd be here."

The Captain turned fully towards Rad and Lisa. His moustache bristled as he grinned widely and clapped his hands like he was trying to keep warm.

"Actually, I don't think we've met. My name is Captain Carson. I believe you have me confused with someone else."

Lisa Saturn shrugged like she didn't care and looked Carson up and down with an expression of distaste.

Rad tapped his knuckles on the bulkhead impatiently. He nodded at the spectacular city view out of the main window.

"We safe?" he repeated.

Carson's smile tightened, and he wrung his hands together. He then pursed his lips, and glanced over his shoulder at Byron.

"Status?"

Motionless at the controls, Rad saw that one of Byron's arms was up to the elbow in an open panel underneath the main control deck. Rad swore he saw something flash inside Byron's helmet, but it must have been a reflection of something outside.

"Safety margin at thirteen minutes," said Byron. His voice was even and calm, as if he were offering brandy from a tray back at Carson's hilltop mansion. "Allowing for clearance, I estimate approximately twenty-one minutes."

The Captain turned back to Rad, and smiled, which Rad found infuriating. He looked out of the window again. They were way off the Skyguard's intended target, out of range of the city by at least a couple of miles.

"Twenty-one minutes until what?" Rad prompted.

"Until, Mr Bradley, this airship ditches into the water." Carson glanced back at the control panel. "Time we were leaving, I think." Carson headed for the door, pausing to glance at Lisa.

He said, "Does the armour function without the helmet?"

Lisa looked from Carson to Rad, then at Byron. She winced as she looked the exposed wiring connecting Byron to the control panel, then turned back to the Captain.

"Yes, but my actuator is gone, thanks to your friend. There's no power coming from the cell."

"Ah," said Carson. "Always a weakness, I thought, making the entire power system dependent on a single component, but some people just wouldn't listen. No matter, it should be easy to fix. Can you carry three?"

Lisa snorted, sending a fleck of spit arcing through the air.

"Like I'm going to lift a finger to help you, pal."

Carson smiled tightly. "You are most welcome to meet your fiery doom on board this craft, young lady. However, I had not intended to end my days in a hydrogen explosion.

I would not like to speak for Mr Bradley here, but I would presume he shares my view."

Rad folded his arms, staring at Lisa. "Hell no," he said.

Lisa poked a tongue into her cheek and moved her jaw like she was chewing gum. She looked Rad up and down, her eyes stopping at his waistline. "Landing might be rough, but we should be able to get to the city."

"I think our landing may be rougher if we remain here," said Carson.

Rad held both arms up, palms facing outwards. He closed his eyes and took a breath.

"Folks, hold on. We're still going to crash? What about the *Nimrod*?"

The Captain shook his head. "The *Nimrod* is the only thing holding this contraption afloat. Our young friend here is going to have to rocket us to freedom."

Rad blinked. "We're leaving Rex to crash?"

"No, Rex is coming with us. Go and collect him, there's a good chap. And hurry. Meet us in the hold. I'll fix the actuator of Ms Saturn's armour."

"What about Byron?"

Carson shook his head and pointed. Rad leaned over Byron's shoulder, then understood. Byron wasn't so much keeping hold of the controls, he was wired into the airship's system.

"It was the only way to override the system," Carson said quietly.

Byron said: "Eleven minutes, Captain."

Rad sighed, and felt the Captain's hand on his shoulder.

"Fetch Rex. Hurry."

FORTY

RAD PRESSED HIS LEG WOUND, and his hands came away spotted with blood, but perhaps less than he had expected. The landing had been rough, but they were in one piece. The grass was wet, as was the air.

Carson stood, hands in the pockets of his jacket, at the end of the park. There was a concrete wall, then a drop to a black-shingled slope which descended into the still water. Ahead of them, the fog barrier that surrounded the Empire State was clearly visible. Against the orange glow, higher, the misshapen collection of outlines that was the *Nimrod* tethered to the Enemy airship was silhouetted.

"I thought it was going to crash?"

The Captain half-turned at Rad's voice, then looked back at the two ships. Their altitude was dropping, but they still had some height and were moving away at a steady pace. Carson clicked his tongue.

"Byron is piloting the ships as far away from the city as possible. There are several million cubic feet of hydrogen in the iron ship, and a smaller but still substantial amount in the *Nimrod*." He paused, and rubbed his moustache. The conglomeration of ships was very close to the fog barrier. "I wonder?"

Rad saw it too. "He's gonna get through the fog? What happens then? He crashes into the Enemy city?"

371

"Perhaps. Who knows? The physics of beyond the fog are shaky. At least the Empire State will be safe."

The fog barrier popped around the two airships, then after a few seconds all that remained was a greyish swirl bruising the otherwise dark orangey wall. Rad and the Captain continued to watch, looking at nothing, for the best part of a couple of minutes.

"Gee, I'm all cut up." Lisa broke the silence. Captain Carson appeared to ignore her, but Rad turned, fists clenched at his side. Lisa was standing, arms folded, just behind them. Behind her, Rex sat cross-legged, looking at nothing, his face blank.

"You got a nerve," said Rad, taking a few steps towards Lisa. He towered over her, but she just looked up into his face with a smirk. "Add another murder to the list, shall we?"

Lisa hissed through clenched teeth. "Not sure you can murder a machine, can you? Not a hunk o' junk like that thing."

"Hmm!" It was the Captain. He was still looking out to the water, but his shoulders moved with the exclamation. He turned, walked towards Lisa, smiled – then punched her in the jaw. Rad flinched as there was a sharp crack, which he was pretty sure came from the old man's hand, but Lisa fell onto the soft ground on one elbow, smile wiped from her face. She touched her lip as a trickle of blood ran from the corner of her mouth, her cheek a livid scarlet from where Carson's punch had landed. She spat on the grass, but didn't get up. The Captain bent double over her, sticking his nose in her face.

"You are a particularly unpleasant young woman. I am not a vindictive man, but I will hold my rage in check as I know – and you know – full well that you will not escape justice. Whether it be in New York, or at the hands of myself and Mr Bradley here."

Someone coughed. Carson kept his attention on Lisa, but Rad turned. Rex shuffled uncomfortably on the ground where he was sitting.

"Someone want to tell me how a dead girl can be walking around and flying through the air and stuff?" he asked.

Rad and Carson exchanged a look. Rex made to stand up, but Rad pushed him back down with a foot to the shoulder.

Rex sighed. "Please, get me out of this nightmare."

Carson straightened, and rubbed his fist with his other hand. He shook it, and flexed the fingers. All seemed to be in working order, Rad saw.

The old man said, "If only it were that simple. You don't get out of a murder charge so easily. Your victim is still dead, lying on my mortuary slab." He looked down at Lisa. "Care to fill in our friend, here?"

Lisa spat blood again. "Go to hell, Nimrod."

The Captain laughed. "You really don't pay attention, do you?"

"I think I know," said Rad. Carson gestured for the detective to speak.

"Sam Saturn went missing from the Empire State, landed in New York, swapped places with her." Rad pointed at Lisa, who just scowled. "Rex found her in New York, thinking she was the Science Pirate, and killed her. Her death sucked both Rex and the body back to the Empire State, but didn't touch the *real* Science Pirate, who was stuck." Rad paused and pulled at his bottom lip. "Why'd you kill her, anyway?"

Rex glanced at Rad, then looked away like a petulant child.

"She got in my way. Goddamn city will give me a medal."

Rad sighed. "Huh. You may have to do better than that at your trial."

Carson stroked his moustache. "Fascinating. So the Science Pirate and the Skyguard opened the Fissure and were pulled through at the same time, but while the Skyguard arrived shortly after the Empire State had been established – just long enough for Crater to have anticipated his arrival and arrange his detention anyway – Ms Lisa Saturn got catapulted forward nineteen years. Sam Saturn was likewise sent *backwards* nineteen years. Right into the path of a killer."

Rad sighed. "Tricky-dicky." He nudged Lisa Saturn's leg with his foot. "How did Kane contact you?"

Lisa rolled her tongue behind her lips, sighed, then gave in.

"I've been here about a few days. Maybe more, it's hard to tell. I thought this was something planned by the Skyguard, some kind of trick. But my suit didn't work properly. I tried to fix it, but the only thing I could get working was the emergency receiver. That's when I picked up the Skyguard's signal. I followed it to him. He said we were both trapped in this place, that it was some kind of mirror of New York and that he knew how to get us back home." She paused, and rubbed her eyes.

"Except it wasn't the Skyguard you knew, was it?" Rad prompted.

She shook her head.

"Because the Skyguard from New York was dead in jail in the Empire State," said Rad.

Lisa tried to stand, but Rad shifted his foot and stood on her calf. It wasn't enough to keep her on the ground, but she got the point and instead drew her knees up to her chest and wrapped her arms around them.

"This guy was wearing the Skyguard's suit – not a copy, the real thing. I should know, I helped build it. He was the same, but... younger, different. Said he'd been given the mantle of the Skyguard."

Carson *hrmmed* loudly, and folded his arms. He looked at the ground, as if he was embarrassed about something. Rad rolled the story back in his mind to pick up on a loose thread.

"Rex killed Sam Saturn, thinking she was Lisa Saturn. So how'd they both wind up back here?"

The Captain looked up. "We don't understand the links between the Pocket and the Origin. Every event, every person is threaded through both worlds. Perhaps..."

"There was a flash." Rex broke into Carson's theorising. "I thought I'd hit my head in the fight, but you know, she didn't fight at all. She was like a rag doll, small, thin. She... she broke in my hands. Dammit, I didn't know it would be like that. But when I woke up, I was in the same alley, but in a different place." He looked up at the night sky. "Here." He shrugged.

Rad rubbed his prickly scalp. "So the very act of Sam's murder pulled her – and her killer – back into the Pocket."

Captain Carson nodded. "Sam Saturn did not belong in the Origin. Perhaps the Pocket was just bringing her home."

Rad continued: "So the Skyguard was arrested as soon as he arrived in the Empire State. He's always been in jail, right from the beginning."

"Crater arrived before he did, and knew that if the Skyguard arrived, he'd be a threat," said Carson.

Rad stopped rubbing his head. He missed his hat, badly.

"Crater doesn't make any sense." Rad knocked the toe of his shoe into Rex's side. "You said he was a judge, and he disappeared?"

Rex huffed and folded his arms, but he was getting the hang of the confession gig. "A couple of days before the fight. Vanished into thin air, big news."

Rad crouched on his haunches. "He vanished *before* the fight?" He looked at Carson, who just shrugged.

"Time dilation," Carson said, not very convincingly. Rad frowned. It was the same term Nimrod has used in New York, but it was clear that nobody knew what the hell the Fissure was or how the two parallel worlds worked in relation to each other.

Rad *hrmmed* loudly. "And he arrived here, walking into the role of the Chairman without so much as a how-d'ya-do?"

"The Empire State was created with a vacuum at the heart of it," said Carson. He interlocked his fingers and flexed them as he considered. "It was *made* for him, I suppose. Together with the House of Lost Souls, I imagine." He pulled his hands, the locked fingers tugging at the knuckles but not separated. "Interlocked."

"If Crater is here, where is his double in New York? Nimrod said he could trace people somehow."

Carson met Rad's eye, and let his hands drop. "I'm not sure he has a double."

Rad raised an eyebrow, then it came to him. He puffed his cheeks, held his breath for just a second, then exhaled.

"Is that possible?"

Captain Carson's eyes widened, but he said nothing. Rad gave a low whistle.

"Crater is the Chairman, *and* the Pastor. And one is the original, and one is the… copy, double, whatever. Except they're not doubles…" Rad struggled with the concept, then shook his head after a few moments. Carson watched, and nodded.

"It may be possible. Who knows. It would explain a great deal. The Chairman and the Pastor as doubles, but forced together into a single existence. He and his Empire State reflection did not switch places, they merged."

"Giving him one hell of a headache."

"Giving him," said Carson, with a tight smile, "a dual personality. Two minds, one body. Crater, the original, and the reflection. Trapped in the same body, fighting for control."

Rad shook his head. "Poor bastard." He turned back to Rex and the Science Pirate. Both sat on the damp grass, silent but both watching.

"So how did Kane get the Skyguard's gear?" Rad asked.

The Captain coughed. "Ah, I'm afraid I may have something to do with that."

Rad looked up at Carson, and then back at Lisa, who was now smiling. She held the tip of her tongue between her teeth, her grin showing the spark of arrogance.

Rad stood, eyes wide. He backed away from Lisa and turned to the old man, stomach doing a loop-the-loop.

In the dark Rad saw the Captain smile again, but it was a nervous look that wasn't pretty.

"I encouraged him," he said. "I was able to influence the Chairman, get him access to the prison. It was no different than the usual tricks he asked me to pull. I'm a reflection of Nimrod, I was fashioned with the Pocket and have influence here as he does in the Origin. And then when I heard about who the prisoner was, where he was from, I was able to find the suit. I gave it to Kane and helped to fix it."

Captain Carson held his hands out in a gesture of apology.

"I didn't know then what I know now, and for that I am sorry. Whatever my role, the important thing is that it revealed the plans of the Chairman."

Rad kept silent and kept looking at the Captain. He was waiting to hear the good reasons. So far, he'd only heard the excuses of an old man.

"Rad," said Carson, quietly. "Crater would have found someone else. And if he had, we might never have found out about the Origin and the Pocket, and we might not be standing here now, debating it. The Fissure might already be closed. New York and the Empire State might not even exist anymore."

Carson was right, and Rad knew it, but after having his world turned upside down, and inside out, after finding out that they were some kind of shadow of the "real" world, like that meant they weren't important or something, to find out that his best friend – his only friend – was the enemy, his week was getting long and old. Rad was tired. He needed a drink and to forget about everything he knew.

Rad turned away from Carson, leaving the old man's jaw working as he tried to think of something else to argue his point.

"Kane's lost the airship, so he'll be at the Fissure, trying to do some damage another way."

Rad walked to Lisa, and kicked her in the leg, hard. Her armour protected her thigh, but she swore anyway.

"Get up," he said. "We've got to stop Kane destroying the world. Yours *and* mine."

FORTY-ONE

THE CHAIRMAN, THE PASTOR OF LOST SOULS, the Missingest Man in New York, Judge Crater, opened his eyes. He'd had them closed so long and clamped shut with such force that the brightness of the room was almost painful. He flinched, and blinked, untangling eyelashes that had adhered together with dried tears and other secretions. He rubbed at his left eye, but this made purple spots dance in his vision, so he stopped.

He looked around the room from where he was sitting, behind a dark wooden desk, practically the only thing with colour he could see. The lights overhead fizzed, the bulb wattage higher than the fitting recommended. They bounced a harsh white light over the spotless painted walls.

He looked around, and blinked, as his pupils contracted and the features of the room came into focus. There was no doubt, no doubt about it at all.

He was still in the Empire State.

He sat for a few minutes, slowing his breathing down, not because he was angry but because he'd been holding it for as long as he'd had his eyes closed. His chest popped with each breath, and dizziness came and went.

The room's door was open as it always was. From where he sat, Crater could see a girl's hand curling around the old twisted banister rod of the stairs. Someone was standing, waiting to enter. The hand shifted a little as its owner bounced on the balls of her feet.

Crater licked his lips under the hood. Maybe it was the warmth of the night, or maybe it was the naked bulbs burning against the white walls. The room was hot, he was hot. Maybe it was fear and panic threatening to crush out all rational thought from his mind.

He was still in the goddamned Pocket. Perhaps this was his destiny. Perhaps he'd got it all wrong, everything about the Pocket and the Origin and the Fissure and how to get back home. Perhaps he was dead, and this was some kind of Hell. Hell with a capital "H".

He coughed, and saw the hand on the stair move again.

"Come in!"

There was a sigh from beyond the door, and this time the hand slid down the rod as the girl took one step backwards down the stairs. Crater felt his throat tighten as he shouted. He hadn't meant to. He couldn't help it.

"I said, come in, damn it!"

Whatever the girl said, he couldn't hear. He yelled again, at the top of his lungs. Loud enough for the whole house to hear his rage.

"Your face," said the girl from the stair. "I must not enter."

The Pastor of Lost Souls sat still behind the desk in the white room, staring ahead, his palms flat on the blotter before him. He felt hot, his face burned, and there was pain in his temples. The purple spots hadn't quite gone from his eyes.

And then, of course! What was he thinking! He smiled, relaxed, and casually reached forward, taking the hood from the desk and slipping it over his head. He caressed his cloth-covered face lightly with his fingertips, and closed his eyes, drawing in a deep breath. The room seemed to stop spinning, and when he opened his eyes, everything he saw was suddenly sharper, clearer.

The Pastor stood, calling to the girl to enter. She came in quickly, glanced at his hooded face, then stared at the ground. Her blue suit as immaculate as her flawless white skin, Katherine Kopek knelt before the desk.

The Pastor laughed, and walked around the desk. He ignored the girl, and stopped at the open window. The room was so brightly lit that everything beyond the frame was an inky blackness, but a warm breeze swept past. He closed his eyes, feeling the air play at the front of the hood.

No, this wasn't Hell. It was Purgatory, with a capital "P". And he well knew that there was an escape from Purgatory. It was nothing more than a holding cell for those who needed to expiate their sins.

"What is it, my child?"

Katherine turned on her knees towards Crater standing at the window, but she did not raise her eyes from the floor.

"Father, we heard... we heard shouting. We were afraid."

"Ah, my child," said Crater. He turned from the window and walked up to her, reaching down to pull her head up by the chin until she was looking at his hooded face. "There is nothing to fear. Tell the others. Tonight we will cleanse our souls and those of this new Babylon. Tonight I will show you all Heaven. Go."

Katherine's eyes widened, and she smiled.

It was good. It was exactly as he wanted. He controlled their minds. He had almost one hundred followers who would obey his orders or die trying.

The Fissure was going to close. The Skyguard had failed, clearly. Rex too, otherwise Crater would have opened his eyes in New York City. But he didn't need the Skyguard. He had all he needed in the house.

"Go," he said. The girl almost curtseyed, then ran from the room.

The Pastor of Lost Souls turned back to the window, closed his eyes, and laughed.

"Alpha and omega, I am the beginning and the ending," he whispered to no one.

"This city shall fall."

FORTY-TWO

THE EMPIRE STATE FISSURE was similar to the one in New York City, except the concrete disc was in the centre of a large hangar instead of outdoors. Rad knew the building as the Battery, part of the restricted naval zone that occupied all of the southern tip of the island. As far as he could remember – and he knew how reliable his memory was concerning his home town – this place had always been called the Battery, and now he knew why. He had no idea of the origin of the name of the New York City equivalent – Battery Park – but here, the Battery held the Fissure, and the Fissure powered the Empire State. Not the city itself, but the entire Pocket. Close the Fissure, close the Pocket. The Empire State would snap out of existence in an instant, pulling New York City along with it thanks to the transdimensional tether. The Battery was, literally, powering the very realm in which the Empire State existed.

That was the flaw in Crater's plan, and Rad suspected he knew it. Close the Fissure and erase the abhorrence to nature that the Pocket represented. He'd fooled Kane and Rex into thinking he could take them to New York City, using this as leverage to get them to do his bidding. But they'd vanish along with their insane employer.

Rad wondered how many people had been switched

between the Pocket and the Origin, exactly. Rex and Lisa were here by accident. So was the Skyguard, the original, but he was dead. Crater had been the first to arrive, assuming control of the newborn city. But who else? How many people had walked down one street at home and turned into a street in the other place? How many missing persons in New York City and the Empire State did transference across the two universes represent? Sam Saturn had walked into New York City and ended up dead. There must have been others. Perhaps those who had found themselves in New York were the lucky ones. They'd found the escape route into the Origin, into a universe of possibilities. For those who found themselves in the Pocket, it would have been like going to prison, trapped forever in a tiny, wet, fog-shrouded city in the grip of Wartime restrictions. Poor bastards.

The Lost Souls. Rad pondered Crater's alter ego as the Pastor, and thought back to his visit to the old brownstone. Was everyone in the Pastor's "church" a refugee from New York? Sam Saturn wasn't, and yet she'd been drawn there. Maybe Crater preyed on those who *thought* they were refugees, those lost in the Empire State not because they were from New York, but because they knew, deep in their very being, that something was not *right* about their world, about the Pocket. And perhaps at night, when they dreamed and saw through the eyes of their counterparts in the Origin, they felt they didn't belong.

Rad sighed to himself. Nice theory. Might fit. New York was nice, but... but it wasn't the Empire State, no matter how much it looked like it. The Empire State was full of people and life – it might have been created as a poor copy of New York, but it was real, and he was real, and the people in it were real, and it was worth saving. Rad smiled. What was this? Patriotism for his damp home town? Well, hot dang.

Rad felt a touch on his shoulder and twisted around. He

was down on his haunches behind a scalloped concrete wall, one of several that stood freely at the periphery of the central Battery disc. His injured leg was smarting, as were his ribs, and as he looked at Carson, he couldn't stop himself from wincing at the movement.

"We ready to go?" Rad asked.

Carson ignored the question, and looked into Rad's face for a moment. The detective bristled. His mouth was dry. He needed a drink. In fact, he needed to go back two weeks. What he wouldn't give for drinking moonshine out of a teacup at Jerry's, listening as Kane gassed about his day at the *Sentinel*. Other times. Happy ones.

"You're thinking about the Origin, aren't you?" said Carson.

"What?"

Carson smiled and pointed at the eggshell around the Fissure. To Rad it looked the same, although the blue light leaking from the joins wasn't as bright as it was in the Origin, it was still enough to turn the white floodlights that lined the hangar a faint baby blue. Rad looked over his shoulder at the Fissure, and then glanced around the Battery itself. Unlike New York, there were no guards here, and the Captain had led the group in unimpeded. It seemed that despite his retirement he had kept all the right keys.

"The Origin, detective," said Captain Carson, his face lit by the faint flicker of the Fissure. "A whole world lies just on the other side of *that*, Mr Bradley. New York is just the beginning of the journey. Think of it!"

Carson dropped his voice to a whisper. Rad felt his forehead crease as he listened.

"A whole world to explore. People and places, life writ large. Think of it."

Rad frowned. He was trying not to.

"And wars and disease and death, and crime, and pollution, and waste. Cruelty, tyranny, pain and hate," he said.

Carson stiffened his back, drawing himself up behind Rad.
"Indeed. A world of good, but of evil also."

Rad laughed. "Just like here then." He turned and looked over his shoulder, up at the Captain. "Come on, we've got two cities to save."

The Captain chuckled and slapped Rad's shoulder.

"Good man."

In all honesty, Rad was surprised that Rex and Lisa were as quiet as they were. He could see the deep dejection in Rex's face and the dull resignation in Lisa's. They had to help, or face extinction. Jail time in New York sounded like a good deal, all things considered.

Rex was a puzzle. The man was a killer and a gangster by his own admission. He'd killed Sam and wasn't bothered. And now he was sitting on the ground next to Lisa, his actual intended victim. Yet he ignored her. He sat on the ground, his face empty, staring around the side of the wall at the Fissure. Lisa ignored her would-be assassin as well. Rad wondered what trick she was planning to pull on his double once they were through the Fissure and home. Revenge? Justice? Maybe Rex deserved it. She'd been one of the good guys once, apparently. Rad turned back to Rex.

Rad jumped as Carson spoke, his voice right in Rad's ear.

"Rex is afraid. He's also a simple man – you and he share much less in common than you may suspect. He's simple, and he's afraid, and he wants to go home. He wants to run into the Fissure and disappear. He's waiting for us to help him."

"Huh," said Rad. He rubbed his goatee. Carson sure had a gift for reading people, a gift Rad had no doubt the Captain shared with his counterpart in New York.

"And her?" Rad asked.

Carson inhaled, sucking the air through his teeth, the sound sharp enough to make Rad jump again. Lisa had folded her arms now, and was looking out around the hangar, her eyes flicking here and there.

"She's waiting too," said the Captain. "Waiting for the Skyguard to come and get her. The unpowered armour makes an effective pair of handcuffs, as it were. She can't get out of it without our help, and she can't fight against us very effectively without power."

"So what do we do? They just gonna sit there? When Kane shows, something's going to happen."

"You're right. But he's here already."

"What?"

Rad shuffled around. Carson had stood up. Behind him, hidden in the shadow cast by the concrete wall, stood a tall, wide, black silhouette. Something metallic flashed as Kane moved his head, his white eyes blue in the glow of the Fissure.

The Captain smiled. The Skyguard stepped around the old man, and stood by his side. Rad took a step back, looked down, and saw the Captain holding Jones's fat-barrelled revolver. It was held low, and pointed at him.

"Well, I'll be damned."

"I'm sorry, detective. I'm leaving."

Rad swore, then felt a blinding pain shoot from the base of his neck, out across his shoulders and down each arm. He yelled and fell to his knees. As he toppled over, he managed to turn. The last thing he saw, before the night sky closed in like a curtain over his vision, was his own face – Rex's face – leering over him, a wet Cheshire cat grin splitting it from ear to ear, shaking the fist that had just whacked the back of Rad's neck.

Somewhere behind a woman was laughing. It echoed like a gunshot in a cathedral as Rad succumbed to the black.

When Rad opened his eyes, he saw blue-tinged shapes. He blinked, a lot, each flutter of his lids changing the shapes and shadows into new forms. The eggshell barrier had been folded down and the light from the Fissure was dull and washed out, but still felt wrong, like it was part of a spectrum of colour that wasn't supposed to be seen by human eyes. The Fissure in the Origin had been powerful, awe-inspiring. In the Pocket it was weaker, angry. Yin and yang. Whatever that was. Rad thought he should know, but he didn't.

He moved, and winced. He was lying on his back, on the concrete disc not far from the Fissure itself. His hands were tied or cuffed behind his back, and had been completely numb until he moved. Now pins and needles, combined with a scrape against the rough concrete, seared along the fatty edge of both hands. Rad focussed on the unpleasant sensation to help wake himself up.

"Welcome back, bud."

A new shape now. Blocking out the blue glow of the Fissure it was just a lumpy blackness, but as his eyes adjusted, he saw Rex standing over him in the cheap copy of his own suit. He stood, legs astride Rad's body, both hands clamped on the fat-barrelled revolver which was pointed at his head. His white teeth shone electric blue in the light of the Fissure.

Someone said something Rad couldn't quite hear – and Rex looked up, his body language at first tense, then disappointed. He switched the gun to just one hand, and still aiming it at Rad's face, he swung one leg over Rad so he was just standing beside the detective rather than over him.

Rad smiled to himself, and struggled into a sitting position. Rex was still at the bottom of the pecking order. That might be useful.

Might be, if Carson hadn't been a traitor all along. Rad shook his head. How could he have been so stupid? Events moved from point A to point B so cleanly that they had to have been controlled by someone. Carson, at the centre of his web, was the one with the knowledge and the technical expertise to get everyone back to New York City and to close the Fissure. So, had everything he'd been told – about how the closure of the Fissure would snuff out both cities – been a lie? What about Nimrod? Perhaps he'd been in on it too, a conspiracy that crossed two dimensions.

Rad looked around. Rex had the gun on him. Carson and the Science Pirate were hunched over stacks of equipment which, like the equipment in New York, spilled cables that snaked away in every direction around the concrete disc. The Empire State was, quite literally, plugged in.

Something hard dug into the small of Rad's back, so he shifted, craning his head around. Kane stood above him, looking down through the Skyguard's impassive mask.

"Give it up, Kane," said Rad, looking away. There was a *clink*, and when Kane spoke, it was with his own voice, the helmet hanging in one hand.

"He told you, did he?"

"Nothing I didn't already know and wouldn't have worked out anyway. It's called deduction. It's my job."

"Oh yeah, because you're the world's greatest detective. Sorry, I forgot."

Rad laughed. "How else would you get access to the prison and to Gardner Gray, huh? You needed someone on the inside, but not just anyone. Someone high up. Someone with the ear of the Chairman. Because the Skyguard – the *real* Skyguard – was a very special prisoner. Solitary confinement, no visitors."

It was Kane's turn to laugh. "Was it that obvious?"

"Not obvious, but careless," said Rad. "The suit was the clincher. Of course it would be kept somewhere in storage, but it didn't work in the Pocket, did it? Something to do with the incompatibility. But Carson could fix it, even though he'd never seen it, because Nimrod had helped make it back in the Origin. What Nimrod knows, Carson knows."

Kane walked around Rad, who was still sitting, facing away. As Kane's boots moved into view, Rad looked up. He didn't want to give Kane the satisfaction of stubbornness. Rad could face his enemies and look them in the eye.

"Handy, ain't he?" said Kane.

"Carson? Sure. But he doesn't just have Nimrod's knowledge, does he? He has his *memories*. Nimrod was an explorer. Carson's house is full of Nimrod's life. I've seen New York – I've been there, and just for a few minutes, I got a glimpse of that world. It's a wonderful thing, Kane. It's hard to resist. For Carson, the temptation is too much. A whole world to explore, to see with his own eyes what he only knows from the second-hand memories of someone else."

Kane laughed, and behind him Rad saw the Captain crawl backwards out of a tangle of cable, then stand up and brush himself down.

"Well," said Carson, "Kane was right. You *are* a detective, Mr Bradley. Very astute conclusions, I must say."

Rad smiled. "Oh, I don't blame you, Captain, not for a second. There's a lot to see over there, in the Origin."

"How very magnanimous of you."

"Thanks. But I'm a little disappointed you had to fall in with murderers to do it. These lugs might just be stooges who have only killed a few people while following their orders. But the Chairman? He's nuts. He thought the way to return home was to blow up the Empire State. Remember that?"

Rad looked at Kane, who was standing, arms folded, next to Carson and Rex.

Rad said, "So what happened to that plan, Kane? You seem to be missing an airship."

Kane looked at Carson, who smiled at him with that perpetual, infuriatingly smug grin. Carson knew more than anybody about, well, everything in the Pocket, and he clearly liked to show it.

"A minor setback," said the Captain, "but fortunately I have formulated an alternative arrangement."

"Plan B?" Rad asked.

Carson dropped into a crouch so he was eye level with Rad.

"As you say, 'Plan B'. A somewhat less drastic course of action. I can get them all back, and close the Fissure. Problem solved." The Captain spread his hands.

The corners of Rad's mouth turned down as he nodded in mock appreciation of the new plan.

"I like it. No messy explosion. Tidy."

The Captain barked a laugh and with some effort raised himself to his feet.

"Oh, there will be explosions enough for you, detective."

Kane scraped a boot on the concrete. "Energy input?"

Carson clapped, and rubbed his hands together. "Energy input," he said, nodding.

Rad pursed his lips. "But isn't the Empire State still going to fizz out if the Fissure is closed?"

"Indeed, yes. But then it's not really real, is it? It isn't even supposed to exist."

"Ah," said Rad. He smiled. "Well, don't forget to raise a glass to us once in a while, as you're cruising the world in the *Nimrod*. Oh, I mean the *Carson*. Say, won't that get confusing?"

Carson ignored the jibe and turned away, perhaps bored by the conversation. He rejoined Lisa at the pile of equipment, and resumed his tinkering. Kane stood still, arms folded, alternating his watch between the pair at the Fissure and Rad on the ground.

Rex bounced lightly on his feet and started to pace, slowly at first, then quicker and quicker. Still the weak link in the chain, thought Rad.

"So," said Rad. Rex stopped and jerked his head towards the detective's voice. "How many guards do you think the Skyguard had to kill to get access to the Fissure?"

Rex frowned. "What?"

Rad nodded into the darkness around the Fissure. Although he'd never seen the Battery, he knew it was in the heart of the military establishment down near the naval dockyards. Not surprisingly, it would have been the most highly defended piece of land on the whole island. The city, quite literally, depended on the Battery and the Fissure within it. Rad didn't know anything about how the navy ran the joint, but the absence of guards surely wasn't normal. He took a bet and hoped he was right.

"You're standing in the middle of an army base, jackass. Or do you think anyone can just waltz up to the Fissure and poke their head through for a quick look at New York?"

"I... what are you talking about?"

"Ignore him," said Kane. "Just keep still, and keep the gun pointed at him, and shut up."

Rex looked at Kane, eyes wide. They remained like that for a few seconds, gazes locked, then Rex turned away quickly and raised the gun again.

Rad raised one eyebrow. Kane smiled.

"You'd be surprised how much of a fuss the attack on the Empire State Building caused. Not just for the police, either. *Everyone* was called over there. Nothing but a skeleton guard left here. Easy enough to eliminate."

He looked out at the periphery of the circle, Rex and Rad following his gaze. What Rad had previously ignored, taken to be bundles of cable or more bits of mysterious equipment sucking power out of the Fissure, were actually long low mounds, the edges uneven. Bodies. Several, spread around the circle, hidden in the dark behind the lamps.

Rex made a sound in the back of his throat, the barrel of the gun dropping a little as his concentration moved elsewhere. Kane gave the man a disgusted look, then turned away.

"Shut up, Rex."

Rex turned back to Rad, gun now steady but aimed not quite as well as it had been. His face was shiny with sweat, reflecting the blue of the Fissure brightly. Rad tried to make eye contact with his Origin counterpart, tried to make some connection with someone who was, ostensibly, himself. But Rex wasn't looking at Rad. Rex's eyes were unfocussed, looking somewhere past him. Rad knew he was a gangster, yes, but he thought it was unlikely Rex was accustomed to killing on such a scale and to situations so complex. Everyone had their limits.

Rex's mouth opened in silent surprise and the gun moved from Rad's face to the empty air over his shoulder. Behind Rex, Kane turned and then whistled at Carson and Lisa, who turned away from their work with some complaint.

Rad heard a sound behind him. A rustling rumble, low and complex, consisting of many parts. He struggled to remember where he'd heard that kind of sound before, and then realised it was the last time he'd been up during the day. When the city was busy and full of people going about their business. It was people. Lots and lots of people.

He turned. At the edge of the concrete disc nearest the hangar doors, coming into the light of the Fissure, was a crowd of people. Young men and women, their features and clothes bleached blue with the alien, electric light. In front, a man in a brown suit, his white hood glowing as bright a blue as the New York side of the Fissure.

"You failed me, Skyguard," Crater called out.

Rex twitched the gun. Rad wondered how good a shot he'd be. At a distance of a hundred yards or more, he'd have to be pretty good.

Kane stepped forward, closing the distance between the Fissure and the Pastor's group. He stopped at a midpoint on the concrete disc, tilting his unmasked head.

"I don't think we've had the pleasure."

Crater laughed.

At the corner of his eye, Rad saw the gun wobble in Rex's outstretched hand. Rad glanced at Carson, who stood watching, his face unreadable.

"Your boss Crater was cracked in more ways than one, eh, Kane? Seems we each have a double. Me and Rex. Sam and Lisa. Carson and Nimrod. Maybe even you and Gardner Gray, eh? But what if the two people, the original and the copy, were forced together into the same time and space? Two minds – the same, but different – in the same body." Rad whistled. "That's quite a condition. Must be crowded in there, Crater. Sorry, Pastor. I mean Chairman."

Kane listened to Rad, his face creasing as he tried to follow the logic. He turned back to the Pastor.

"Go home, preacher. Take your flock with you. Go and pray in that white house of yours, or whatever it is you do."

"Get out of the way, mister!" Rex shouted.

Kane turned. Rex had taken a step further forward, the muscles in his gun arm so tense they shook. Kane raised his hands slowly, clearly recognising that any sudden movement, no matter how inconsequential, would give Rex's frightened mind all the excuse it needed.

"Do you want to go home, Rex?" Kane asked.

Rex dropped the gun's muzzle a little. Kane stepped back towards him.

"I can get you home. We can all go. Right now."

The Pastor laughed, or at least Rad thought it was a laugh. It was long, high and harsh, like he was gasping for breath. Rad figured his throat must have felt like hell afterwards, but also figured that the madman wouldn't even notice.

Carson's split personality theory explained a lot. Judge Crater vanished from New York, but he didn't switch with his counterpart in the Empire State. He merged with him somehow, walking into the mantle of the Chairman of the City Commissioners because that was how it always had been in the Empire State. The two minds fought each other for control, creating the Chairman and the Pastor, two sides to the same coin. One trying to run the city and bring peace, thinking that would enable him to go home. The other driven to religious insanity, thinking that he'd been banished, punished. The solution? Atonement. Sterilise the wound with fire, and return to the old life.

The Chairman wanted peace. The Pastor wanted destruction. With neither in full control, stalemate, for nineteen years. Until Kane took the Skyguard's suit and Rex arrived. Kane, working for the Chairman, finally providing the power he needed to take action. Rex, working for the Pastor, providing the impetus to eliminate any opposition.

Two sides of the same person, both working for and against each other. Rad blinked. It was impressive, remarkable, and batshit crazy.

"Don't give me that crap!" Spittle flew from Rex's mouth. He waved the gun between Kane and the Pastor, gesticulating with every word. "The preacher and I had a plan. He explained it all to me. Every action has an equal and opposite reaction, ain't that right? That's how it works. He told me. There's only one way back. I gotta do the opposite, cancel it out." Rex moved the gun to settle on Rad, and thumbed back the revolver's hammer.

The light changed. The blue flared to white, then altered, still blue, but darker, and tinged with orange. The same orange perpetually reflected in the clouds which surrounded the Empire State on all sides.

Rad spun around as quickly as he could while sitting on hard concrete with his hands tied. Rex turned as well. Kane took the advantage and kicked forward, knocking the gun clean out of Rex's hand and felling the man with a punch to the jaw. Rad saw it out of the corner of his eye, but his attention was on the Fissure.

Lisa Saturn walked backwards, away from the Fissure. With both hands, she was holding a dark cable as thick as her forearm and capped with a pronged metal ring. She kept backing away, letting the cable drop from her hands.

The Fissure had changed colour. It hadn't changed in size or shape, at least as far as Rad could tell. The pointed ellipse, perpendicular to the ground, still rippled and fizzed, the edges curling and glowing blue. But perhaps it was rippling a little more than it had been a moment ago. The orange light was weird, artificial, but not as alien as the electric blue. It was a colour that belonged to the Empire State and to the Pocket itself. Whatever the Science Pirate and Carson had done, the Fissure was turning inside out, destabilising, just a little.

The Pastor's laugh died, replaced by a scream that Rad could only think of as blood curdling. The scream of a madman.

"What have you done?!" he cried.

The Captain clapped his hands, and turned to smile at the assembled crowd. He and the Science Pirate exchanged a look. She was smiling too.

"Well, hasn't this been a jolly outing? My friend and I will be leaving now. See you in New York!" Carson paused, and put a finger to his lips as if he'd just thought of something. "Oh, actually, no – I won't." He drew the finger away from his mouth and pointed at Kane, and then back over his shoulder at the Fissure. Kane nodded and jogged over. When he reached the Captain, Kane held his wrist out.

The old man bent over the armoured gauntlet for a moment. Kane's back blocked Rad's view, but after a couple of seconds a beeping started, before Carson clapped a hand on Kane's shoulder and stood to one side. Kane nodded again and skipped up onto the platform and stood before the

Fissure, arms extended outwards. On his left wrist, Rad could see an open panel and a blue light winking in time with the beeping. Unless it was his imagination, the beep's tempo was steadily increasing, the tone of it heading slowly up the musical scale.

Rad shuffled on the ground, making a desperate attempt to free his hands. But it was no good, the knot was too tight. He rocked on his behind and managed to get himself standing without falling on his face.

"What are you doing? Destroy the Fissure, you destroy everything! Kane?"

Kane turned. As he did, tendrils of energy curled out from the lip of the Fissure, attracted to the suit like lightning to a conductor. The fingers of power were smoke-like but bright. Kane stumbled slightly, and took a step backwards. When he spoke, it was with some effort and through a grimace of pain.

"You're wrong, Rad." Kane shook his head slowly, eyes narrowing in discomfort. "We can all go back to where we belong."

Rad took a hesitant step forward, but the movement sent a static shock up his leg. He stopped and became aware of a peculiar sensation, like walking face-first into hot cotton candy. Whatever was happening to the Fissure, it didn't feel healthy.

"We don't belong there, Kane," said Rad. He stood tall against the pressure wave pushed out by the Fissure. "We belong here. The Empire State is our home."

Kane stepped back again. The energy tendrils flared an angry red and seemed to wrap around his outstretched arms like a neon octopus. Kane's head snapped back and he was pulled back further, until he stood across the Fissure's horizon itself. The Skyguard's cloak was yanked violently backward, sucked into the void behind him by an alien wind. When he managed to pull his head back, his face was plastered with a vicious grin. He pulled an arm out of the Fissure's fluctuating corona like it had been stuck there with molasses, and pointed. Kane laughed.

Rad turned his head quickly. The light streaming out of the unstable Fissure threw shadows long behind him, the high contrast making it difficult to see. But something had changed. The Pastor stood at the edge of the concrete disc, illuminated in blue, alone. His followers were gone.

Rad looked, tracing the edge of the disc. There was nothing around them but a total blackness. And then the blackness lightened, greying up and then turning a dirty orange over the course of a few seconds. It was the fog, the damned, cold, perpetual fog. The borders of the Empire State had collapsed onto the circle, surrounding them.

Crater fell to his knees and screamed. The sound was primal, animalistic, and powerful enough for Rad to feel sick.

Someone called out. Too late, Rad saw Rex roll on the ground. Rex scrabbled on the concrete, scraping nails against the rough surface, until the dropped gun was within his grasp. He then tore forwards on all fours, slipping and striking his knees, even his chest, against the ground as he crawled towards the Pastor.

Rad felt a tugging on the bindings that held his wrists behind his back. He moved to turn his head, but someone breathed against his ear.

"When I say run, run. No questions."

Rad nodded, not turning, mind racing as the Captain lightly patted his back. Rad pulled on his wrists, and the bindings unraveled the last few threads. With the pressure relieved and his wrists free, Rad slowly flexed his fingers, getting the feeling back into them.

Crater knelt on the ground, unmoving. He had both arms outstretched, and his hood was pointed up at the orange, cloudy ceiling. Rex crawled closer and pawed at his jacket.

Crater didn't move, but his eyes, wide through the holes the hood, moved to look at Rex.

Saliva dribbled down Rex's chin. "You promised me. You said we could go home, that all I had to do was kill the detective. You lied, didn't you? You were going to go home, but not me, right? Am I right?"

Crater moved his head slowly from side to side, but Rex also shook his head at the same speed. He pushed off the ground and stood in front of the Pastor. Rex raised the gun up and pressed the barrel against the white cloth-covered forehead. The hammer was pulled back again.

"Aren't you going to stop this, Kane?" yelled Rad. "Aren't you the Skyguard, the protector of the city?"

Rad turned around, back to the Fissure. Kane was still stuck like a fly in jam, a Vitruvian Man in a superhero costume and cape. Rad gasped in desperation. He turned to Carson. The Captain was watching Crater and Rex, his face blank. Beside him, Lisa Saturn stood, arms folded. She was smirking, like she was enjoying a night at the theatre.

"Captain Carson! What…"

Rad was cut off as the air cracked. A second later Crater, the Pastor of Lost Souls, toppled backwards, his white hood no longer white. Rex stood where he was, shaking, the gun still smoking in the air before him.

The Fissure crackled, and Kane shouted over it.

"I can get you home, Rex. Come on. There's not much time."

Rex let the gun drop with a clatter onto the concrete. He turned around on his heel, slowly, looking at his feet. He glanced at Rad, at Lisa, at Carson. Then he stepped forward and looked up at Kane.

"You can get me home?"

Kane nodded.

Carson stepped forward. "We can all leave, Rex. Come with us."

Rex looked at Kane. His eyes narrowed, and even in the weird orange-blue light, Rad could see his face darken. Rex's mouth curled into a scowl.

"You sonovabitch, liar!" Rex yelled, his voice echoing off the hard ground. He pushed Carson to one side and ran at the Skyguard, bent down into a football tackle. Rex's right shoulder collided with Kane's chest, but Kane barely moved. Whether it was the Skyguard's armour or the energy from the Fissure keeping him upright, Rad couldn't tell.

Rex was pushing at Kane, but Kane was in the way, blocking the portal. The beeping from his wrist had become almost a steady whine. Rex slid back, and brought his fists down on Kane's chest. Finally Kane pulled his arms down, and grabbed Rex by the neck. The Fissure protested, rippling with a thundercrack as the tendrils of light whipped around the pair.

"What did you do, Carson?" yelled Rad over the cacophony. "What did you do?"

It was the Science Pirate who answered. She'd taken a step or two back, and had unfolded her arms, holding them instead at her sides. The palms were facing back and her hands tilted slightly out, like she was ready to take off on her dead rockets.

"Energy input," she said simply, and looked at Carson. Carson nodded.

"Energy input." He turned to Rad and pointed at the struggling figures silhouetted against the transdimensional maelstrom. "There is more energy in the Skyguard's power cells than in the whole fuel tank of the Enemy airship. By overloading the suit on the threshold, the Fissure will absorb the leaking energy. A much more efficient solution."

Rad pulled his hands free and stood. Lisa watched, her face twisting into a scowl as she saw their prisoner had been freed by someone, and it wasn't her.

Rad grabbed Carson by the front of his tunic. As his fingers made contact with the fabric, he felt another static discharge, powerful enough to make his back molars sing in sympathy.

"More efficient? You want the world – both worlds – destroyed?"

Carson didn't struggle as Rad shook him around. Instead he met the detective's eye and smiled.

"Not destroyed, no. Overloading the suit is far more controlled. The Fissure will feed off the energy and stabilise even further. The Empire State is quite safe, as is New York. In fact, the tether between the Pocket and the Origin will be stronger than ever."

Rad relaxed his grip. He stared at the Captain's face, as if he was trying to read the old man's wrinkles like a street map. His mouth opened but his brain wasn't quite done processing the information, so he just stood there for a while, slack-jawed.

"No!"

Rad and Carson turned as one to Lisa Saturn. The Science Pirate was backing away, her mouth as open as Rad's in surprise. Her eyes were wide and wild.

"Skyguard," she cried, "it's a fix. You've been tricked!"

Kane and Rex were still wrestling, almost in slow motion in the rippling chasm. Tendrils of energy tore themselves off the portal, wrapping around the pair before shifting and evaporating. They were becoming more and more obscured by the light, apparently oblivious to anything happening down on the concrete disc.

It wasn't quite the stalemate it looked like. Kane was held firm by his armour and by the power of the Fissure, but Rex was winning. Rex was a desperate man.

Kane turned his head, and looked into the heart of the abyss behind him. The centre of the portal was black, and when Rad blinked, it flashed violet. Kane turned back, his eyes wide in fright. He pushed back against Rex, harder now, grunting with the effort as his arms locked onto Rex's shoulders. The two stood, balanced at the threshold between one universe and another.

The Science Pirate was on them in a second, although as she ran closer to the Fissure her movement seemed to slow. Rad wondered whether this was an effect of the time dilation, as Carson and Nimrod had called it, spilling out from the Fissure as it reshaped and rebuilt itself from the Skyguard's energy. Rad almost made to ask, when he felt Carson's hand on his shoulder and his hot breath in his ear.

"Do you remember your instructions, Mr Bradley?"

Rad turned, his face half an inch from Carson's. It was like talking inside a tornado, he thought.

"I surely do, Captain."

"Then I suggest you act upon them as soon as it is practical for you to do so. At my estimation, I would say now would be most appropriate."

"Anything you say."

The Captain winked. "Run!"

Rad turned to run, and saw Carson do likewise, before the both of them were knocked to the ground by a shock wave that pulsed from the Fissure as its border stretched and snapped back like tight elastic. Rad's shoulder hit the concrete and he shouted in surprise and pain. Ahead, he saw the orange fog convulse as the shock wave hit it and continued through into the nothingness that, apparently, now filled the Pocket. It seemed to Rad that the Empire State, the whole Pocket itself, was being eaten by the Fissure rather than strengthened. He hoped Carson had got his calculations correct.

Rad shuffled backwards quickly, pushing the ground with his palms. The air vibrated, filled with a buzzing that drilled into his skull. He remembered the feeling well. It was the feeling of incompatibility he'd experienced in New York. The Origin was reabsorbing the Pocket. The Empire State was crumbling. Carson had got it wrong.

Another shock wave, enough to push Rad and Carson down for a second time. Rad saw Kane and Rex framed in the Fissure, still wrestling, a third form clinging to Rex's back, arms locked around his neck, trying to pull him free of Kane. The Science Pirate's suit was unpowered but the weight of it on Rex's frame was just enough. The combined strength of Kane and Lisa were succeeding, and freed slightly from Rex's grip, Kane pulled his fist back, ready to launch an uppercut at his assailant, probably with enough power to kill.

There was a flash, blinding blue. Rad felt himself sliding back, the rough concrete biting through his suit and into the fat of his buttocks and legs as he was pushed backwards by a colossal gust of wind. The Fissure crackled and buckled, and someone cried out. Shielding his eyes against the flare, he saw the three struggling figures silhouetted against the portal, now a brilliant white. Then more movement as the Fissure flickered. Two shadows appeared, solidifying until they became opaque, moving shapes, gradually increasing in size until they resolved.

Two figures. Their black outlines easily distinguished – hats, flapping trench coats. Weird gas masks with soup-can respirators bouncing.

Agents Grieves and Jones ran out of the Fissure at a sprint. They collided with the Science Pirate, one on each side, collected her by the arms and carried her forward as they shot out of the Fissure and onto the concrete disc. The Science Pirate screamed and struggled, but Grieves and Jones had her firmly. They slid to a halt and turned, holding the squirming Science Pirate between them.

Kane and Rex stopped fighting, just for a moment, and looked out into the Pocket. The white light flared around them, blinding Rad and melting their silhouettes into indistinct shapes. Then the white light flickered, changing to a deep orange.

Kane made his move, dropping his fist and instead kicking Rex's feet out from under him. Rex cried out and began to fall backwards, and Kane raised his leg and again and pushed with his foot, sending the gangster tumbling backwards, down the short stairs and onto the concrete.

The Fissure growled, and licked at Kane with a tongue of electric blue light. Still balancing on one leg, Kane wobbled. The energy played around him, regaining its grip. Kane's eyes were wide as he tried to rotate his arms to get his balance. He was going to fall.

Rad didn't think, he just acted. He got up and ran in one clean and fast movement, fuelled by adrenaline and chaos and desperation. He practically jumped two stairs to the top of the dais, and pushed forwards through the storm of energy with Kane at the centre. The Fissure spat and fizzed and Rad felt his goatee prickle and get hot. He ignored it, and ignored the sharp tug on his unbuttoned trench coat as the Fissure reached for it and pulled the flapping ends towards the portal like the Skyguard's cloak.

"Kane!" Rad reached out, fingers stretched wide, grasping for something – *anything* – on the Skyguard's suit to grab hold of. His fingers skidded across Kane's chest until he made another step forward, enough to get both hands on a bicep. He hung on and pulled backwards with all his weight, attempting to arrest Kane's slow-motion fall into the void.

Kane screamed something Rad couldn't make out, and with a colossal effort dragged his head around. Kane's face was wild, his eyes wide and mouth pulled into nasty, tooth-filled crescent.

"Get off of me!"

Rad ducked as Kane dragged his free arm out of the Fissure's suck and swung it in an attempt to clip Rad's head. The movement loosened Rad's grip on Kane's arm; sensing this, Kane flicked it outwards with a yell, throwing Rad off and backwards.

"You don't deserve to go home. We tried to help you, and you fought us!" Kane yelled, spit collecting at the corners of his mouth.

"I'm not Rex, you lug! It's me, Rad!"

Kane snarled and kicked out, his boot touching Rad's shoulder enough for the detective to instinctively jerk even further away.

The beeping from Kane's wrist finally became a single tone. Rad could hear something else too. The Captain, shouting something from behind him. But behind the curtain of energy pushed out by the Fissure, Carson may as well have been shouting in New York.

Rad got to his feet, teeth gritted in effort.

"Kane!" he spat, and reached out once more. "It's me. I'm trying to help."

Kane's expression collapsed. Rad didn't look behind him, but wasn't sure whether his former friend was able to see past the pyrotechnics and out into the hangar. He hoped he'd seen Rex lying on the ground near Carson.

"Rad?" Kane reached out with one arm.

"The world's greatest detective, here to help." The recognition was all the motivation Rad needed. He moved forward easily, and grabbed the offered hand. At his touch, Kane's fingers hugged Rad's forearm below the elbow, and Rad pulled. As Rad rotated his arm to get a better grip, his fingers nudged the half-open panel. Something inside the gauntlet felt hot.

Kane's hand slipped and suddenly their hold was precarious.

The Fissure was alive and jealous, greedily drinking the energy leaking from the Skyguard's suit, grabbing and grasping at its prize, unwilling to surrender it so easily. Kane's body moved back another half-foot. Rad managed to crawl his hand up Kane's wrist a little more, but he realised this tug-of-war could not be won.

"Kill it, Rad!" Kane turned his hand a little and jerked his head towards the gauntlet panel. There was the flashing blue light, in a nest of cables. Neatly done, but not perfect.

Rad understood. He ground his teeth and pulled on the arm, succeeding only in dragging himself closer to the Fissure rather than Kane away from it, but that was his intention. Holding Kane's forearm so hard his fingers felt like they would snap like dry twigs, Rad grabbed at the cabling with his free hand and pulled. Some gave, the blue blinking light went out, and the whining stopped instantly.

Rad's loosened his grip. He wasn't sure what to expect, but the Fissure's hold on Kane seemed to slacken.

Then the portal convulsed. It was a liquid, organic motion, as the glowing, fizzing ellipse turned inside-out for a fraction of second, then rebounded. The wind buffeted and the buzzing in his head was agony. The whole world was a nauseating mix of blue light, orange fog, and sound. Rad squinted, trying to see more clearly, but was lifted off the platform entirely. He caught himself on his hands and rocked forward onto his knees.

The Fissure had stabilised, back to the vertical ellipse, faintly glowing blue. The air felt lighter, somehow, and Rad sucked on his tongue as his mouth was filled with the sharp tang of vinegar.

"Rad?"

Kane stood in the centre of the Fissure. His cloak was slack and its torn edges dangled gently around his ankles. He looked exhausted and as Rad stood and stepped forward,

Kane's eyes unfocussed and he fell backwards into the blackness. In a second, he was gone.

"Kane!" Rad stumbled forward, but there was a weight on his shoulder. He pushed against it, not knowing or caring what it was, but it pushed back, and he fell sideways onto the concrete.

"The son of a *bitch*!" It was Rex. The gangster was on his feet and running towards the Fissure even as Rad recovered his footing to follow.

"You ain't cutting on me like this, you bastard," Rex yelled and, without pause, ran directly into the Fissure. There was a faint buzzing, and he was gone.

Rad spat onto the ground, but his teeth hurt and his head was on fire. The Fissure's glow filled his vision.

Somewhere, a long, long way away, a woman screamed obscenities and an old man shouted something. Someone called Rex's name, or it might have been Rad's, or it might have been Kane's.

Rad closed his eyes and let blue-white light consume the world.

FORTY-THREE

WHEN HE OPENED HIS EYES, Rad noted that for the second time in one night he was flat on his back on hard concrete. This time the back of his head didn't hurt and it occurred to him that perhaps he'd landed on something else for a change. For this he was thankful. It was dark, although when he blinked, he saw stars.

No, when he blinked, he saw darkness. When his eyes were open, he saw stars. There was a hole blown clean through the hangar roof, and through the ragged gap the night sky was dotted with lights, just a few, but they were there. The clouds were patchy and still covered most of the sky, but they were clearing.

He sat up. His head still buzzed, until he realised he was sitting very near to the pile of equipment that Carson and the Science Pirate had been fiddling with earlier. To his left there was something like a large junction box, dark green with pipes and grilles. It hummed like an angry wasp. Rad backed away as he stood up. It looked like he shouldn't be near it.

Ten yards away stood the Fissure. It was a faint blue outline, curling at the edges to reveal a brighter border around a black centre. It was quiet, and stable.

"Well done, that man!" Captain Carson walked over to Rad, and reached down to help him up. Rad hesitated, trying to remember what had happened and who was who, then accepted the offer. However, as soon as he was upright, he shook the arm off. The Captain said nothing, just let go and stood back, smiling. Rad glanced past him, and saw Grieves and Jones standing nearby. Lisa Saturn was on her knees, hands clasped to the top of her head. Jones held the fat-barrelled gun to her temple.

Rad rubbed his scalp, then gingerly touched the back of his head. His fingers stuck to something tacky, and he winced. The headache was already beginning. He had landed on his head after all.

"Where're Kane and Rex?"

Carson turned to Grieves, who just shrugged.

Grieves said, "Nobody came through the other side, according to Nimrod. Looks like the Fissure wasn't completely stable when they crossed over. What happened to those two, I have no clue. You're the expert, Captain."

Rad looked at him. The Captain opened his mouth, but Rad started speaking first.

"Nice trick there, old man. Plans fall through, eh?"

"My dear detective, I don't like your tone."

"Oh, really?" said Rad, lowering his voice as his head thumped. He looked at Grieves, but could see nothing behind the dark glass of the mask goggles. Rad turned to Captain Carson, his voice a low whisper.

"You were going to go to New York, and let the Fissure close, and damn the consequences."

The Captain's laugh barked out. Rad shook his head, but Carson laid a hand on his shoulder.

"Me, leave the Empire State? You misunderstand. We have a city here of several million people. *Real* people, detective. A real city. And now that Wartime no longer applies, and the Chairman is no longer in charge, this city can breathe easy. The Pocket may be small, but don't underestimate it, dear boy. It's my home, and yours. Forgive my trick, but I realised we could turn the situation to our favour, and *strengthen* the link between the Pocket and the Origin. For that to happen, I had to... ah, *deceive*, as it were. Only temporarily, of course." Carson chuckled.

Rad frowned. "And Kane? Expendable? The ends justified the means?"

The Captain's laugh stopped and he looked away. "Not at all. Once the Skyguard's powerpack was drained, that should have been that." He looked at Lisa. "But interference was inevitable, I suppose. I'm sorry." He stood silently for a while, eyes fixed on the Science Pirate. Grieves and Rad exchanged a look.

"Nimrod was watching?" asked Rad.

Grieves nodded. "Pulled us out of the Pocket when we fell from the airship. Took us a while to recalibrate and come back through, looks like we arrived just in time." He flicked a button open on his trench coat and reached inside. His hand reappeared holding something white and cylindrical, which he offered to Rad. Rad took it and smiled.

"Much obliged," he said, unfurling his fedora and carefully putting it in its rightful place. "Mine?"

Grieves nodded. "It was cluttering the office."

"Impeccable skill, your Captain Nimrod," said Carson. He turned back to the pair and smiled, but this time it was tight and sad.

Rad looked around the Battery. The orange fog had gone, revealing the empty hangar.

"So the Empire State is safe? I thought it had been wiped out for a second, believe you me."

"I will admit there was a risk involved," said Carson. He pointed at the junction box. "The Pocket is supported by the connection with the Origin. Crater knew this, and used the power of the Fissure to build the city. Or rather, to help crystallise the natural reflection of New York. For the Fissure to absorb the energy from the Skyguard's suit, it had to be destabilised manually, as it were. Unfortunately I needed this unlovely lady's help with that. But now the Fissure is reconnected and the Pocket more stable than ever." Carson gestured to the junction box, and Rad saw that the fat cable was back in its port. "There may be some damage to the outer reaches of the Empire State. We shall have to see."

"We?" said Rad.

The Captain puffed up his chest.

"Well, I say we, I suppose I really mean me. I will assume control, I presume, in the absence of a Chairman. There will be a lot to do. Informing the populace of the end of Wartime, obviously. Lift Prohibition." He tapped Rad on the chest with the flat of his hand. "Not a bad idea, eh?"

"What about the people? The Pastor's crowd went zip, gone. Hell, the whole city did for a while."

Carson tapped his lip. "With a stronger connection to the Origin, I think the Pocket will have returned to the status quo, reset, as it were. We can but hope."

Rad looked over at Jones, holding the Science Pirate.

"What about her?"

Grieves walked towards their prisoner. "She doesn't belong here. We'll take her back to New York." He turned to her. "You're in for a shock, miss. You've been away nearly twenty years."

"And the Fissure?" Rad asked.

"Well," said Carson. "Nimrod and I have much to discuss. I hope we can share much knowledge about it, and the Pocket. The Empire State needs it, but then so does New York City."

The Captain laughed again.

"Come on, detective. Allow me to buy you a drink – the first legal one of the new age, my friend! Agents?"

Grieves shook his head, the soup can wobbling.

"We need to get back," said Jones. "The time dilation between here and New York is a problem and we gotta get her to Nimrod."

The Captain nodded. "Indeed, that is something to discuss with Nimrod." He turned to Rad. "Come on. You can introduce me to your friend Jerry. I hear he runs quite a remarkable establishment."

FORTY-FOUR

RAD PULLED THE BLINDS BACK, and slumped into his office chair. The dawn cast a bright yellow shard of light across his desk like a giant slab of butter. He leaned back and closed his eyes, enjoying the warmth on his face. When he opened them again, the sun had risen a little more. Far out on the water, Rad watched the current ripple. If he squinted, he even thought he could see the other side. Perhaps.

Something scratched by the office door. Rad swivelled in his chair in time to see a shadow duck away behind the frosted glass. Footsteps hammered quickly down the corridor.

There was a brown envelope on the floor, slid under the door by the visitor. Rad eyed it for a moment, then stood and walked over wearily to collect it. He and Carson had had quite a few drinks, and as he bent down the room spun a little. At least he'd forgotten about his sore leg and sore head. And then no sooner did he think of them, than they throbbed back into painful memory. He hobbled back to his chair, clutching the letter.

It was from Katherine Kopek. The envelope was stuffed full of notes, too much money for Rad to count properly. Her note was short. It just said thanks, and noted that Captain Carson had invited her to his hilltop mansion later that day. Rad's commission was over, and here was his fee. So, she'd survived the Pocket collapse. That was something. Maybe the city had been undamaged.

Rad tossed the letter onto the desk and leaned back. The chair creaked in protest.

He thought of Sam Saturn, lost in New York, killed by his counterpart.

He thought of Katherine Kopek, who had lost the love of her life, only to be brainwashed by the Pastor, pulled into his evil little game, using the very death of her beloved as leverage to get Rad involved.

He thought of Kane Fortuna, his friend. Had he really hated the Empire State that much? Or did he see it as his duty, trying to help the refugees from New York return home with Crater, no matter what the cost?

He'd never know for sure, but maybe a sense of duty was no bad thing. He'd been tempted himself, of course. Bright lights, big city.

As Rad drifted to sleep in his office chair, the morning sun streaming through the picture window, he dreamt of New York.

And he dreamt of the Empire State, the city that was his home, that he had helped to save. A city that was as real as New York and just as important.

No. More important.

The Empire State was his home. A home he'd never want to leave.

Rad's snooze was interrupted by the phone, jerking him rudely awake. He rocked his chair forward with a jolt, then grabbed the earpiece in one hand and the stem in the other. Leaning back into the warm sun, he closed his eyes.

"Rad Bradley, private detective."

A pause, then a voice, small.

"Hello, detective."

Rad's eyes flicked open. "Claudia?"

"Hi."

Rad returned his chair to the upright position.

"What are you...?"

Claudia breathed heavily down the phone. Rad's heart pounded.

"You free for a drink tonight, Rad?" she asked.

Rad gulped.

"Ah... yes. Hell yes."

"Jerry's OK?"

Rad laughed and nodded. "Of course."

"See you at eight."

Rad paused. He could hear Claudia move the phone against her hair.

"What about Declan?" he asked.

Claudia laughed.

"What about him?"

The phone went dead with a tiny click.

Rad replaced the phone on his desk. He leaned back again, allowing a smile to spread across his face. Suddenly the sun was all the warmer and perhaps the Empire State was not so small and grey after all.

ABOUT THE AUTHOR

ADAM CHRISTOPHER WAS BORN in Auckland, New Zealand, and grew up watching Pertwee-era *Doctor Who* and listening to the Beatles, which isn't a bad start for a child of the Eighties. In 2006, Adam moved to the sunny north-west of England, where he now lives in domestic bliss with his wife and cat in a house next to a canal, although he has yet to take up any fishing-related activities.

When not writing Adam can be found drinking tea and obsessing over DC Comics, Stephen King, and the Cure. He is also a strong advocate for social media, especially Twitter, which he spends far too much time on avoiding work.

adamchristopher.co.uk

twitter.com/ghostfinder

ACKNOWLEDGMENTS

It's been said before, but I'll say it again: writing is a solitary exercise; creating a book is a group effort. *Empire State* is my debut novel and a lot of people helped get it into your hands. If I've left anyone out, I beg forgiveness, but believe me when I say it's not intentional.

My thanks to Jennifer Williams, the best writing buddy anyone could hope for. We've known each other for years and she's the one person I can go to, day or night, when the writing is going well or (perhaps especially) when it isn't. Not only is she the perfect critic – honest, reliable, one who pulls no punches – but she's a natural talent and a truly great writer herself. Jen, I owe you one. You can find her online at *sennydreadful.com*.

Jen was also one of my trusted team of early readers, and my thanks also go to Amanda Leena, Mark Nelson, Sharon Ring, Amanda Rutter, Kate Sherrod, and Taylor B Wright. Authors live with their novels for so long that its easy to get lost in the fog, but these guys provided much needed guidance, encouragement and direction. See, I even resisted cracking a lighthouse joke there.

The founding members of the Manchester Speculative Fiction Writing Group were of great help in critiquing the early chapters of *Empire State*. Specifically, I am indebted to

Quint Bass, Saxon Bullock, Rob Cutforth, Kate Feld, Dave Hartley, Benjamin Judge, and Craig Pay.

My fellow Angry Roboteers are an amazing community of writers and creators, and for support, encouragement, and late night conversations about zombie rock bands, my thanks to Aliette de Bodard, Lauren Beukes, Matt Forbeck, Dale Halvorsen, J Robert King, Mike Shevdon, and Kaaron Warren. I couldn't have wished for a warmer welcome to your hallowed ranks. Also, my thanks to Chuck Wendig, who has been not only a valued friend I can rely on for a quick second opinion on everything from grammar and style to the anatomy of compact handguns, but also someone I owe an immense debt of thanks to for reasons we both know very well. And then he went and signed with Angry Robot himself, showing that our publisher really has the very best taste.

My thanks to Chris Cawthorne and Diana Steinway, photographers extraordinaire who were responsible for my official mugshot. Never has sitting in the snow outside a railway tunnel in Levenshulme been a greater pleasure!

To all the wonderful people who provided endorsements for *Empire State*, my heartfelt gratitude. As I'm sure any new writer knows, sending a book out into the wild unknown – to some of your literary heroes, no less – is a somewhat alarming prospect. But I'm glad *Empire State* was enjoyed by all, and knowing that I was able to give back at least a little of the entertainment they've provided me over the years was a surreal and wonderful experience.

To Lee Harris and Marc Gascoigne, the Angry Robot Overlords themselves – thanks for giving *Empire State* a shot and for giving this author his break. And Mur Lafferty, who set me on the straight and narrow so many years ago, and who I now have the pleasure of counting as a friend and, with her administering the WorldBuilder project, a colleague. The gin, oh mighty one, is on me.

And to my agent, Stacia Decker, whose unbridled energy and enthusiasm is a *constant* delight. You make me feel like the luckiest author in the world.

New York during the Prohibition is a fascinating slice of history, and for research I relied heavily on the excellent and very readable *Dry Manhattan* by Michael A Lerner (Harvard University Press, 2008). The quotes from *The New York World* and William Anderson that open Parts Two and Four, respectively, of this novel were sourced via Dr Lerner's superlative text.

Finally, to my wife, Sandra, whose unending, unfaltering support and patience have made this all possible. I'm glad to have you with me on this adventure, and I cherish each and every moment.

Now, what instrument does a lighthouse keeper play? A fog horn. Thank you, I'm here all night...

ADAM CHRISTOPHER
in conversation with Chuck Wendig

Okay, EMPIRE STATE reader, you have now reached the official end of the book, but guess what? We're not done. Let's tear the narrative asunder and let its author, Adam Christopher, rise from the rift – or should I say, the Fissure? – and give some of his thoughts on the book, from where his ideas come from to the novel's genre-stylings to just who would play these characters on the big- or small-screen.

Let's get to the interview, shall we?

The amount of awesome stuffed into the pages of this novel is jaw-dropping. Superheroes, detectives, robots, blimps, threads of noir, alternate realities, weird science, Prohibition, and on and on. Where did the idea for all this come from?

Y'know, it's one of those things where a whole bunch of different ideas sort of accumulated over a long period of time, collecting and aggregating until they reached some kind of creative critical mass. There's three separate events I can remember well enough: a flight to San Francisco with a copy of *The Big Sleep* by Raymond Chandler, which I thought was the most amazing book ever and in that weird kind of haze of a long haul flight thought wouldn't it have been great if Chandler had written the Philip Marlowe books with robots in them; a misheard lyric from a song by British Sea Power, which I became convinced was about the mysterious (and non-existent) polar explorer Captain Carson – as it turned out they were singing about a type of bicycle, by as they'd written an ode to an Antarctic ice shelf it all made perfect sense in my mind; a mistyped query on Amazon that gave birth to a new pulp detective hero. Those were the main story seeds, each potentially a separate novel initially, none particularly connected to the other.

The rest of it came from a few pet obsessions – the Prohibition, the Golden Age of comics, and the retro-science of something that wasn't quite steampunk but which meshed with the noir of pulp detectives to produce some vivid imagery – fedoras and gasmasks, superheroes powered by rockets.

And of course parallel universes. I'm not sure why I'm drawn to them – maybe seeing the Third Doctor take his mind-bending journey sideways in time in *Inferno* made a strong impression on my seven-year-old brain when I first discovered *Doctor Who* in 1985, but I'd always loved the idea of other worlds, exactly like our own, existing concurrently in the same space and time but just… somewhere else. In *Supergods*, Grant Morrison talks about how he used to stand between two mirrors and try to peer into the infinite, thinking perhaps the far-distant reflections of himself were in fact his alter ego from another universe, looking back. I did exactly the same thing!

I get a bit of the Morrison vibe from this (though less freaky and drugged-out). It's clear you're a comics fan. You've chosen a world with only two superheroes – surprisingly minimalist. Why only two? Why not go

hog wild and create a world with a whole pantheon and rogue's gallery to complete the deal?

Oddly, I've never thought of *Empire State* being a superhero book – it's a science fiction detective story to me, first and foremost, which just happens to have a couple of super-heroes in it. But even so, they're products of, and powered by, science and technology rather than mystical rings or the light of an alien sun. And there's certainly no spandex in sight!

The Skyguard and Science Pirate are in the story because they were the characters I needed. But you're right, I'm a big comics fan and superhero comics in particular are a real passion. I actually wrote *Empire State* after *Seven Wonders*, although the books are coming out in reverse order. *Seven Wonders* is my big fat superhero book, which most certainly does feature a pantheon of heroes and their evil opposites (and LOTS of spandex). I suspect, having written something which you might look at as a homage to the Silver and Bronze Ages of comic books, that *Empire State* was then a natural progression, focusing on just a few particular aspects of superheroism while I told a completely different kind of story.

Having said that, there's something of an unwritten history in *Empire State*. The Skyguard and Science Pirate were the protectors of New York before they turned on each other, and as Rex watches their final battle over the half-completed Empire State Building near the beginning of the book he makes reference to the "Golden Age of heroism" – clearly there was a time when superheroes were common, probably not just in New York but all over the US and even the world. Perhaps the Roaring Twenties was a decade of superheroics, before everything goes wrong with the stock market crash of 1929?

426

There's plenty of scope to explore that era – in fact, I'm hoping creators will expand on this as part of the World-Builder project.

Any chance of *Empire State* ever becoming a genuine comic book? Who would you hand-pick to be the book's artist, in a perfect world?

Hey, I'd love *Empire State* to become a comic book! Right back when the early drafts of various bits and pieces were being read by the writer's group I used to belong to, I started getting feedback that it felt like a "graphic novel in prose form", as one reader put it! Much later, when Marc *[Gascoigne, Angry Robot's publishing director]* and I were looking at the cover roughs, he said he thought the one we ultimately selected looked and felt like the kind of cover you'd have on the front of a quality indie graphic novel, which I thought was a pretty cool way of looking at it.

It would certainly be fascinating to see the transition from 120,000 words of prose into an ongoing series, although it would be a hell of a long story arc! Then again, think of the pay off for the reader when they get to the end! My dream artist would be JH Williams III, no doubt about it. His work is jaw-dropping – if you look at something like *Batwoman* it's like nothing else on Earth.

Private dick Rad Bradley was once known as "Rad Bradbury" – was this a reference to Ray Bradbury? You've got other potential allusions peppered throughout, too: Byron, Nimrod, etc. Are these on purpose? Any people might have missed?

Ah, the death of Rad Bradbury. He was the Amazon query fail – a couple of years ago, I was looking for something by

Ray Bradbury on Amazon, so I typed in my search and hit enter. I looked away for a moment, then when I looked back was confused by the lack of results. The reason was a simple typo – I'd entered "Rad" instead of "Ray". Instantly the name "Rad Bradbury" leapt off the screen – this was clearly a private detective from a 1930s pulp novel, a tough guy, not afraid to punch his way out of trouble. It had a rhythm when you said it out loud, and a weirdness about it that felt just right, if that makes any sense. For some reason, he appeared to me immediately as a large black man, bald, out of shape but who you knew was a prize fighter back in the day.

The initial draft of the book was called *Rad Bradbury versus the Empire State*, again because I was going for maximum pulp. I figured soon enough that the name would be a distraction on the cover – people would easily mistake it for Ray Bradbury, or for some pastiche – so I shortened it to just *Empire State*, but the name of the hero stuck.

Empire State took the best part of a year to write, and as with any writer I was so involved in the story and the characters that I really forgot about the origins of Rad's name. It was only when my signing to Angry Robot was announced that people started asking me whether Rad Bradbury was anything to do with Ray Bradbury. I was confused – I'd lived with him for so long that there was no connection at all for me, but I then realized it was a going to be a speed bump for readers, and why make trouble?

I chose Rad's new surname because I wanted to keep the rhythm and the Rad/Brad beat that sounded so good in my head, so he became Rad Bradley. This was a much better name as not only did it lose the Ray Bradbury thing but it became a nod to another pulp detective, the great Slam Bradley, who appeared in the pages of *Detective Comics* a full year before Batman did.

We were back to the beginning, to the 1930s, to pulp detectives and Golden Age comics. Rad Bradley was born.

The other characters are less literary, more musical – as I mentioned, Captain Carson most definitely does *not* appear in *No Lucifer* by British Sea Power, but you'll find Nimrod, Mr Jones and Mr Grieves inhabiting Pixies songs (*Nimrod's Son*, *Crackity Jones*, and *Mr Grieves*, to be precise). Music is a big influence on my writing and I like to throw in imagery and ideas from my favourite songs where appropriate. There are a couple more buried in *Empire State* – see if you can find them! In fact, there are a number of songs which have a strong connection to the book for me, not just because they influenced the story or imagery, but because during the writing or editing I found myself listening to them on high rotation. Interested readers can go check out the playlist at the end of this chat.

Byron might be named after the great poet, but he was a dog originally. Or, in the weird parallel universe where there really was a famous polar explorer called Captain Carson, he had a dog called Byron that he took everywhere, even the north pole. When Byron died, he was stuffed and now sits in Carson's library by the fire.

Hey, there are an infinite number of parallel universes. What I just said was entirely true. Somewhere.

Carson's history in the Pocket – and in the Origin, specifically his involvement with the development of the Naval robots – demanded a slightly different role for Byron, and I'm afraid a dog wasn't quite what I needed.

Every book has the DNA of its authors wound between the words and pages. Where are you in this? Not just the pop culture influences, but how is this book clearly a book that only Adam Christopher could've written?

You're enjoying asking the difficult questions, aren't you?

That's how my Angry Robot overlords programmed me. So please answer the question, and ignore the whirring photon cannon at the small of your back.

I guess when it comes down to it you're talking about voice, and voice is something that develops over time and isn't something a writer can – or should – try and influence. It's also hard for a writer to see it themselves – *Empire State* was the third novel I wrote, and right now as we speak I'm in the middle of *Night Pictures*, my sixth novel. When I compare the two I can "see" that the same person wrote both, but if you were to ask me *how* I can see this, I couldn't give you an easy answer. Is that "voice"? I don't know. I'm going to pretend I know what I'm talking about and say "yes"!

Actually, thinking about it, you've asked a devilishly difficult and also very important question. To me, you can always tell a Stephen King book is a Stephen King book. In fact, you can tell a Stephen King book is a Stephen King book so well that you can also tell that a *Richard Bachman* book is a Stephen King book! There's no way I'm going to put myself in the same sentence as King (and watch as I squirm to avoid doing just that – damn you, Wendig!), but it's a fascinating question.

Also *Empire State* is pretty far-out and weird, and I certainly don't subscribe to the theory that everything a writer writes is somehow autobiographical. I guess there's a piece of me in all the characters, but isn't that the same for every writer?

My brain hurts. Next!

The book keeps you guessing – you never know where it's going next. Further, allegiances are constantly in question and we have betrayals and double betrayals and all manner of plot tangles and plot twists. Hell,

some characters are actually multiple characters (Chairman / Missingest Man / Pastor). How did you keep track of it all? Both before you wrote and during?

I outlined the book quite heavily, although I find I work best when my outline is more like a series of linked events. When I start, I usually know the beginning, middle and end, and probably a handful of the key scenes in between. Then it's a matter of stringing them together in the right order.

I work that way because I tend to go off on tangents while I write, so a lot of time spent on a very detailed outline seems a bit of a waste when I end up ignoring probably half of it anyway.

But another important thing for me – and, dare I suggest, most writers – is that when things get going, the story starts to write itself and the characters start to develop a sort of weird independence. So while a lot of the twists and revelations in the book were there are the beginning, quite a few were surprises even to me, the writer! The scene where Carson turns traitor and pulls a gun on Rad near the end came completely out of leftfield – I remember writing it, finishing the chapter on a cliffhanger, and sitting back from the computer for a few minutes trying to work out what on Earth was going on. I think I was also grinning from ear to ear for the rest of the night!

As I'm sure you know, when that happens in the middle of a project, you know something good is going on. Originally, the Pastor, the Commissioner, and Judge Crater were all separate people – or were at various stages shifting combinations of two of the three – then suddenly their conjoined identities were revealed. It was almost as if the Pastor had walked into my office and whipped his hood off before laughing manically, like Number 1 at the end of *The Prisoner*.

The Missingest Man in New York was actually a real person who vanished – in fact, his disappearance was big news in 1930, so much so that "Judge Crater, call your office" was a popular joke on the standup comedy scene. I knew I needed someone from New York – a real historical figure – to have an equivalent, evil doppelganger in the Empire State, and for a while I tried using various Mayors of New York City, or other official figures, but nothing quite worked how I wanted it to.

Then one day I stumbled across the Wikipedia entry on Judge Crater quite by accident. It was one of those lightening-bolt moments – Shazam! I had my villain!

I find it fascinating how major events of the past can be so quickly forgotten. Poor Judge Crater, whose possibly mob-related disappearance was once such a scandal. And now he's a dimension-jumping supervillain with a few too many personalities trapped inside his skull.

It's how he would have liked to have been remembered, I'm sure.

Probably the freakiest part of this whole book for me is the nature of the Enemy. A big ol' question mark hangs over the Enemy for most of the book and even once we realize the truth it still bakes the noodle. It's great, because in a roundabout way it's saying that the Empire State is its own Enemy, and that one's greatest foe is often oneself. But where did that come from? Was it always intended to be that way? Or was that part of the story that wrote itself?

That was one of the things I'd planned, for sure. I wanted to explore what would happen if you endlessly reflected the different "states" within the story – so, New York becomes the Empire State, the Empire State becomes the Enemy, the Enemy becomes…?

432

I loved the concept of being at war with something you can't see and don't even know the name of – the fact that the Empire State turns its citizens into killing machines and sends them off into the fog, never to be seen again, is terrifying. The Empire State is locked in this kind of stasis, a never-ending nightmare. And then one robot comes back because the Chairman said it could, and up in the boardroom when he asks the machine if they can have peace the robot immediately answers back that they can, because the Chairman is really just talking to himself through the machine. It's pure horror, plain and simple. No wonder the Chairman has a breakdown when the truth finally hits him.

But, as you suggest, there is more to it than that, and that's where the various interlocking parts of the plot came together in various independent stages. "Theme" is like "voice" – I'm not sure a writer can fully control it. So, one's greatest foe is often oneself – as with the two sides of Crater, both working in opposing directions although both leading ultimately to the destruction of both the Pocket and the Origin. Kane tries to enlist Rad but is led astray and turns against him, with his own internal struggle where he has to pick his loyalties. And then there's Rad and Rex – a quite literal example, two opposing forces who are *the exact same person*.

You took a trip to New York City after *Empire State* was written, yeah? How did that feel? Was that your first time to NYC?

Actually, although I've spent quite a lot of time in the US and had spent a night in New York en route to Toronto back in 2003, my first "proper" visit to the city wasn't until September 2011! But I'd done a boatload of research and I was quietly relieved that I hadn't screwed much up!

Writing something set both in the 1930s and in a parallel dimension probably helped too, because it allowed me to bend the real geography and history a little to suit the story. But, whether I had encyclopedic, first-hand knowledge of the real New York or not, that would have happened anyway. *Empire State* is a work of fiction, and both New York City and the Empire State described within are fictitious.

One thing that did strike me on that September visit was the scale of the place. The United States is a very large country, and New York City is a very large city, but you really need to go there to understand that. I'm a city boy myself, but nothing compares to New York. It's wonderful and amazing and *gigantic*. Definitely my favourite place on Earth so far.

Did you meet your otherworldly self somewhere in Manhattan? That's actually a fine follow-up: what's the Pocket version of Adam Christopher up to?

There's definitely an alternate version of me somewhere in Manhattan, but he's always one step ahead. One day, we'll have our showdown. Maybe on top of the Empire State Building, rocket boots and powered armour and all.

Adam Christopher in the Pocket universe is a mean sumbitch, of that I have no doubt. He's cold, calculating, a total misanthrope. But not necessarily a villain. If Carson owns half a block of the Upper East Side, perhaps my alter ego has a similar complex a little further uptown, in the Pocket Harlem, which holds another set of secrets and impossibilities all of its own…

The classic question: let's say *Empire State* gets made into a television show or a film. Cast your leads!

This question makes me nervous because I immediately think of *Brown Betty*, the episode of *Fringe* set in the 1940s which is pretty much how I see *Empire State* in my own mind. I should say I didn't start watching *Fringe* until long after *Empire State* was done and dusted, but now it's about my favourite TV show. More parallel universes, see?

Chi McBride is my Rad/Rex, although with slightly less knitwear and colourful shirts than in *Pushing Daisies*. Kane Fortuna was – I tell no lie – based on a ballroom dancer, but I'd be very happy with Leonardo DiCaprio or Timothy Olyphant. Throw in Cate Blanchett as Katherine Kopek, Michael Shannon from *Boardwalk Empire* as the Pastor/Commissioner/Crater, Seamus Dever (from *Castle*) as Grieves, Joseph Lyle Taylor (from *Justified*) as Jones, and Gillian Jacobs (from *Community*) as Sam/Lisa Saturn and I'd be pretty happy. Captain Carson/Nimrod for me really is the late, great TP McKenna, who was so good in British series like *The Avengers* and *Doctor Who*, but Richard Griffiths would do nicely. The enigmatic Byron just has to be Kevin Spacey. I'm sure he wouldn't mind being stuck inside a big helmet for the whole thing.

Chi McBride. Yes. Loved him all the way back in *The Frighteners*. Though I admittedly had Rad as a Ving Rhames-ian character, but these days Ving might be getting a little long in the tooth.

Oh, Ving Rhames! He'd be great! I think he could still play it, too. See, this is the danger when you ask this kind of question. I most definitely "cast" my characters when I write, and I'm sure most readers do the same. But the beauty of fiction is that what I saw in my head while writing is completely and totally different to what you saw when reading. Every single person picking the book up will have a different experience and will conjure their own images (and cast) in their minds. But, hey, that's how it works... and it sure is fun to compare notes. If any casting director is reading this *cough*...

So. The big question. The corker. Any chance of a sequel? Might there be other Pocket cities? Care to share what you feel might've happened to Rex and Kane there in the Fissure?

Empire State has a definitive end, but that's not to say the story is over. Carson is now in charge and Rad appears to have come to terms with the rather small universe he inhabits, but how long will that last? Carson wants to explore the edges of his little world in his airship... will he be able to resist attempting a journey beyond the fog, to the lands of the Enemy? And what else is out there? Rex and Kane didn't appear back in New York, and they're not in the Empire State... so where are they? There's a story waiting to be told, I think!

The Empire State is a reflection of New York created by a very specific, single event, so I don't think there are any more discrete pocket universes. However, the Empire State is an imperfect copy, a degraded, second-generation clone of the original. Beyond the Empire State is the lands of the Enemy, which is itself an even more damaged, degenerated reflection of the Empire State. And so on, and so forth – I think there are endless further reflections, each more broken and dangerous than the last, until finally you probably get nothing but realms of white noise as the signal from the Origin – New York – is finally worn out.

But if the Enemy is out there, beyond the fog, what lies beyond the Enemy? And further, and further? How far does Carson want to take a look? And if Rex and Kane didn't make it back to either the Pocket or the Origin, did the unstable fissure throw them somewhere further away?

And if the Pocket is a protrusion of sorts of our universe into another dimension, what was there before? Is there something outside the Pocket? Maybe something that resents the intrusion...

I like the idea that the Enemy, while being this chaotic, discarnate force, itself a corrupted reflection of data from the Empire State, may develop some kind of intelligence of its own. Perhaps a distillation of the Chairman, the Pastor, the Skyguard, etc, further distorted, further *reduced* and compressed into something totally evil which leads to the birth of Enemy as a single, sentient figure. A Satanic supervillain in a Sauron-meets-Darth Vader sort of way. And what if the Enemy managed to escape and get out of the Pocket altogether, into New York?

Huh. Ask me about that sequel again...

Thanks, Adam, for submitting to this interview! You will, ahem, notice that I've holstered the photon cannon.

Always a pleasure, Chuck! Now, if you could just untie my hands, there's a good fellow...

Chuck Wendig is the author of BLACKBIRDS and its sequel MOCKINGBIRD (both upcoming from Angry Robot), as well as the "vampire-in-zombieland" book, DOUBLE DEAD, from Abaddon. You can find his thoughts on the writing life, including interviews with other writers (and another, completely different, interview with Adam Christopher!) at terribleminds.com.

THE EMPIRE STATE PLAYLIST

The following playlist is a selection of tracks that were constant companions for me during the writing and editing of *Empire State*.

1-2. HANS ZIMMER – We Built our own World/Dream is Collapsing
I suspect the *Inception* soundtrack is a popular choice for writers, as it goes so well with so many different genres. But if you need to ratchet the tension up, you can't go past the opening two tracks, which I'm going to cheat with and treat as a single piece of music.

3. THE CURE – Burn
The Cure are my favourite band and their contribution to 1996's *The Crow* soundtrack is perfect for *Empire State*. It's dark, and terribly atmospheric, and is all about standing around in the dark waiting for the world to end.

4. LADYTRON – Mirage
I had Ladytron's album *Gravity the Seducer* on almost constant loop while doing the copy edits. Like the Cure's track, *Mirage* fits perfectly, both musically and lyrically.

438

5. PIXIES – Crackity Jones
The first of three Pixies tracks. As with the Cure, I've been listening to these indie legends for more than 20 years now. One of Nimrod's agents takes his name from this song.

6. THE BRIAN JONESTOWN MASSACRE – Golden-Frost
There's an element of chaos to *Empire State*, with the corruption of data from the Origin to the Pocket, not to mention what must be going through Rad's mind as he learns about the nature of his home and of himself. *Golden-Frost* represents that well, being loose, urgent, with lyrics you can't even understand.

7. PRINCE – Electric Chair
My favourite track off the 1989 *Batman* soundtrack – how could I resist? A song about crime and punishment and internal struggle.

8. PIXIES – Mr Grieves
The second Pixies track, from which you will recognise Agent Grieves.

9. BRITISH SEA POWER – No Lucifer
Ah, the beauty of misheard lyrics. Captain Carson does not appear in this song. A Carlton Corsair bicycle does. I'll get me coat.

10. THE DANDY WARHOLS – Good Morning
Empire State happens mostly at night, in the rain – the brief moments of daylight that do appear seem to be a blessed relief for poor Rad. If the book was to be made into a film, this track from the Dandy's 1997 album *Come Down* would play over Rad climbing the hill behind Carson's house to enjoy the early morning view.

11. PIXIES – Nimrod's Son
The last Pixies song – this one has explicit lyrics, so have a care, as Captain Carson would say. Or should that be Captain Nimrod?

12. BLACK REBEL MOTORCYLE CLUB – Salvation
The Pastor of Lost Souls may be a villain, driven to insanity by… well, I'll have to make sure you've read the book before I tell you the answer to that one! But that doesn't necessarily make him *evil*. There are a lot of people in the Empire State looking for answers… perhaps they just fell in with the wrong man in their search.

You can find links to the *Empire State* soundtrack on *Spotify* and *iTunes* at *adamchristopher.co.uk*

INTRODUCING... *WORLDBUILDER*

Empire State is a story of private detectives, of superheroics, of fringe science, of Prohibition, of two worlds' fight for survival. Now you can play your part.

Are you a fan writer, a fan artist? Do you write prose, poetry, songs, plays or comic books? Do you sculpt, paint, draw, whittle or build? Do you create? We're inviting you to delve into the world of *Empire State* and create your own works to expand the universe of the book.

Welcome to *WorldBuilder*.

THE WORLDS OF EMPIRE STATE

Empire State features four separate, but connected, "realms": Prohibition-era New York around 1930; the Empire State, a twisted reflection of the same that exists within a pocket universe; New York circa 1950; and the lands beyond the fog, the domain of the Enemy.

New York, 1930
The Great Depression has hit, and Prohibition still has another three years left to run. The world is pretty much as we know it, with all the gang warfare, corruption and bootleg-

ging that existed in our own history. An age of pulp fiction, where private detectives creep the shadows in fedoras and trenchcoats. An age of jazz music and Art Deco.

Except this New York is home to two superheroes, the Skyguard and the Science Pirate. Former independent – if officially sanctioned – protectors of New York, by the beginning of the new decade they had turned on each other, abandoning their duties as they fought their own personal battle.

This is the end of the so-called "Golden Age" of superheroes, as the last two left slug it out in the skies over Manhattan. Back in the day there were many like them, working individually and in teams all over the United States. Some, like the Skyguard and Science Pirate, were powered by science and technology. Some had strange powers gifted to them by magic and the occult. Some were just born different. Some were friends… and some enemies.

The Empire State
The Empire State is a twisted, degraded copy of Manhattan, projected into a pocket dimension through a hole in our universe torn open during the final great showdown between the Skyguard and the Science Pirate. The Empire State corresponds geographically to the island of Manhattan, and is filled with the same buildings, chief of which is the Empire State Building. This is the Empire State's seat of government, where the Chairman and his City Commissioners rule the city from their boardroom on the 101st floor. The city's population is smaller than that of Manhattan, and consists of people brought into being with the city itself, or those pulled across from the Origin. The hooded Pastor of Lost Souls seeks these people out – or those who feel there is something not quite right about their world – building his own private army of brainwashed zealots.

The Empire State is surrounded by water, which is itself

bounded by thick fog banks which never clear. Sometimes people hear things, or see lights out there, beyond the water, but you don't often see these people again. The city is a totalitarian state, with a curfew, a strict Prohibition which extends beyond alcohol to include tobacco as well, and food rationing. These measures are needed because the Empire State is at war with the Enemy.

The Enemy lies beyond the fog, and the Empire State prides itself on taking the fight to them, sending great battleships called ironclads off into the fog twice a year, on Fleet Day. These are days of great celebration and tickertape parades, as the robotic crews of the ironclads march through the city to the docks, where they board their ships. And are never seen again.

The technology of the Empire State is somewhat more advanced than that of the real world. In the nineteen years that have passed since the city blinked into existence, advances in robotics and cybernetic technology have allowed the City Commissioners to use their citizenry for the war effort, taking volunteers and converting them into cyborg warriors. Captain Carson, an eccentric old man who lives in a *very* large house in the Upper East Side, may have had something to do with these advances.

New York, 1950
Just like in our history, the US of the 1950s is enjoying the post-war boom. The space race is about to begin, while the country is gripped by McCarthyism and the threat of the Red Menace. In New York, Captain Nimrod runs his own mysterious agency within the US Department of State, charged with investigating and protecting the Fissure, the portal connecting the Origin (New York) to the Pocket (the Empire State). A former explorer and scientific genius, his work with the Fissure has enabled travel

between the two dimensions via mirrors as well as via the Fissure itself, although both are expensive and the latter a little too dangerous.

The domain of the Enemy

Beyond the fog lies an unknown land, where the city of the Enemy sits on an island, a further reflection of the Empire State. As the data flows from the Origin to the Pocket, so it degrades the further out it travels and the more it is reflected through an infinite series of portals. The land of the Enemy is therefore a dark, dangerous, primal construct where the laws of physics don't always apply. The city itself is possibly self-aware in a primitive gestalt way, populated by mindless automata. As the Enemy is a twisted reflection of the Empire State, everything that happens in the latter is duplicated, but in different ways – the Enemy prepares its own fleet of ironclads, matching one-for-one the fleets sent by the Empire State. But the Enemy ironclads sail, impossibly, through the air.

The domain of the Enemy is not a place you'd want to visit, nor a place you would want to find yourself trapped in.

And if the Enemy is a reflection of the Empire State, is the Enemy itself reflected again? What horrifying realm of dust and darkness exists beyond *its* borders?

SOME BASIC RULES

You can create works set in and around any (or all) of the different realms. There is scope for almost any kind of fiction you can imagine – science and speculative fiction (but not space opera), fantasy and magic (but not swords and sorcery), even detective noir and pulpy crime.

You are welcome to use any of the characters that appear

in *Empire State* itself, but don't use them in anything set concurrently with the novel, or set afterwards. The former will tangle the narrative of the book, and for the latter, well, I might want to write a sequel one day and I want to avoid being influenced by any work set after the end of the story. You are free to use your own characters within the world of *Empire State* in any time period – before, during or after.

While the WorldBuilder is open to any kind of creative endeavour, there is one important exception: you may not create any *direct narrative adaptation* of the novel, or identifiable scenes within the novel. This means that, while you are free to create film, comics, etc, these should be *your own* stories, and not – for example – a filmed version of the book, or of scenes within the book. The same goes with audio – you can write your own stories and record them, but not simply read from the book or create an audio adaptation or performance of any part of *Empire State*.

While we are authorising fan-created content to be created under a Creative Commons Attribution-Non-Commercial-ShareAlike 3.0 Unported License, *Empire State*, the novel, is copyrighted material, not public domain nor shared under any Creative Commons license or agreement.

Have fun, and get creating!

For more information on how to join the WorldBuilder and start adding your own creations to the *Empire State* universe, visit

empirestate.cc
worldbuilderonline.com

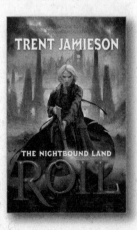
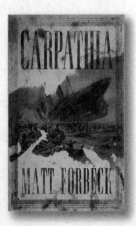

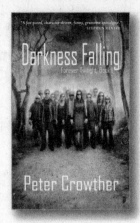

We are Angry Robot.

Twitter @angryrobotbooks

YOU THINK YOU CAN HANDLE THIS?
Track down the whole Angry Robot catalog

ANGRY ROBOT

DAN ABNETT
- [ ] Embedded
- [ ] Triumff: Her Majesty's Hero

GUY ADAMS
- [ ] The World House
- [ ] Restoration

JO ANDERTON
- [ ] Debris

LAUREN BEUKES
- [ ] Moxyland
- [ ] Zoo City

THOMAS BLACKTHORNE
(aka John Meaney)
- [ ] Edge
- [ ] Point

MAURICE BROADDUS
- [ ] King Maker
- [ ] King's Justice
- [ ] King's War

PETER CROWTHER
- [ ] Darkness Falling

ALIETTE DE BODARD
- [ ] Servant of the Underworld
- [ ] Harbinger of the Storm
- [ ] Master of the House of Darts

MATT FORBECK
- [ ] Amortals
- [ ] Vegas Knights

JUSTIN GUSTAINIS
- [ ] Hard Spell

GUY HALEY
- [ ] Reality 36

COLIN HARVEY
- [ ] Damage Time
- [ ] Winter Song

MATTHEW HUGHES
- [ ] The Damned Busters

TRENT JAMIESON
- [ ] Roil

K W JETER
- [ ] Infernal Devices
- [ ] Morlock Night

J ROBERT KING
- [ ] Angel of Death
- [ ] Death's Disciples

GARY McMAHON
- [ ] Pretty Little Dead Things
- [ ] Dead Bad Things

ANDY REMIC
- [ ] Kell's Legend
- [ ] Soul Stealers
- [ ] Vampire Warlords

CHRIS ROBERSON
- [ ] Book of Secrets

MIKE SHEVDON
- [ ] Sixty-One Nails
- [ ] The Road to Bedlam

GAV THORPE
- [ ] The Crown of the Blood
- [ ] The Crown of the Conqueror

LAVIE TIDHAR
- [ ] The Bookman
- [ ] Camera Obscura

TIM WAGGONER
- [ ] Nekropolis
- [ ] Dead Streets
- [ ] Dark War

KAARON WARREN
- [ ] Mistification
- [ ] Slights
- [ ] Walking the Tree

IAN WHATES
- [ ] City of Dreams & Nightmare
- [ ] City of Hope & Despair
- [ ] City of Light & Shadow